A
SUPREME KIND
OF LOVE

BRYN BYRNES

Published by Bryn Byrnes

Edited by A.A. Gillis

Cover Design: JS Designs Cover Art

ISBN: 9798366048552

About This Book

A Supreme Kind of Love is the debut novel by author Bryn Byrnes. A contemporary romance about lawyers falling in love and then struggling to make all work while pursuing their careers. It's steamy, sweet, heart wrenching, frustrating, and you might even find a chuckle along the way. There's nothing quite like falling in love at Christmas time, but can that love survive all the fireworks on the way to the Fourth of July?

Alexis Chambers is an enigma begging to be solved. Cooly proficient in all that she does and singularly driven to succeed. She hides behind business suits purposely designed to obscure her beauty. Ever the ice princess, she keeps everyone at arm's length. Love was no longer a consideration for Alexis Chambers, not a part of the plan. It was an inconvenience that should be avoided.

Jake Douglas is a dangerous man, dangerous for Alexis, that is. Dark, penetrating eyes that will peer into the depth of your soul if you let them. After being betrayed by his first true love, no women are part of his plan.

He is also way off limits. He's her biggest obstacle to making her way to the top of the corporate ladder and she's already engaged. He is not part of her plan.

A broken engagement. A bottle of wine. Blazing hot sexual chemistry.

Plans just might have to change.

Contents

"Love is not love until love's vulnerable."

—Theodore Roethke

Chapter 1

Alexis

Alexis stood in front of her office door. She ran the tip of her finger over the engraving of the brass nameplate affixed at eye level, Alexis Chambers, Executive Director, Women's Legal Assistance Foundation. Pushing it open, she crossed the room and, with a heavy sigh, sank into the large executive chair behind her desk. She looked up to see her assistant, Tiana, glaring at her from the doorway. Gooseflesh rose on her arms from the iciness of her stare. Alexis was not unfamiliar with disapproving looks; she had been getting them from her father for years, but his no longer had that kind of effect on her.

"Is what I just heard true?" Tiana asked coldly.

Alexis drew in a long, slow breath, forcing a smile. "Depends on what you just heard." She had dreaded this conversation more than the one she had just had with the board of directors. Tiana had been one of her first clients when she was volunteering her time at the WLAF back in law school. It took her weeks to earn Tiana's trust, but when she did, not only did she gain a client, she gained her most faithful friend. Tiana and her younger sister Carole were the two people she could always count on. They were her ride or die.

Tiana was exactly the reason the Woman's Legal Assistance Foundation existed. At twenty-one with three kids, and in a relationship that was emotionally, physically, and sexually abusive. Alexis met her during her fourth stay in a domestic abuse shelter. With the help of the WLAF she was able to escape the seemingly unescapable and start a new life.

With all the righteous indignation a second-year law student could muster, she put herself, legally speaking, between Tiana and everything that was beating her down. She bullied the district attorney until he put Tiana's abuser in jail. She managed to get Tiana full custody of her children, despite a nagging drug habit. After Tiana completed rehab, Alexis convinced her grandmother to hire Tiana as a housekeeper that she didn't need, and helped the woman stay on her feet until she could stand on her own. She was more proud the day Tiana received her paralegal certificate from Bronx Community College than she was the day she graduated from Yale Law School.

She had hired Tiana on her first day as assistant director of the Woman's Legal Assistance Foundation. Tiana still didn't know that her salary came directly from Alexis because there wasn't money in the budget for a paralegal. Most of the lawyers volunteered their time, being a non-profit sucked, and Alexis knew she couldn't do what she did without the benefit of her trust fund. But they did good work and under Alexis' leadership they had expanded services to include not just low cost/no cost legal advice and representation but social work services as well. She hoped, one day, that the WLAF could broaden its legal reach to include class action and Supreme Court appeals, maybe even lobbying state and federal lawmakers. The work and the causes made Alexis feel whole. Almost. And it was that almost that had her friend standing in her office door looking like she'd been betrayed. In some ways, that's what Alexis felt like she had selfishly done.

"Don't play cute with me, Chambers. You've never been that person. At least with me." Tiana pounded her fist into the door frame and then shook out her hand. "Did you just give your resignation to the board? Because if you did… God. I thought we were friends? You didn't even tell me first. How could you?"

Alexis had never heard her friend's voice that shrill. Tiana held her emotions in check, perhaps from years of hiding them, but regardless, she never lost control. "I'm sorry." It sounded hollow even to Alexis' ears, but she was. "I would have told you first," she continued, staring down at her lap.

"But you knew I'd be pissed, and you knew I would talk you out of whatever dumb-assed decision you were about to make." Tiana filled in before Alexis could finish. She crossed the space between them with a swagger of righteous indignation. Despite being on the receiving end, Alexis appreciated the dramatic change in her friend. Tiana never would have challenged anyone like this five years ago when they met. "Please tell me it's not that consulting firm whose brochure I saw on your desk last week. I thought that was just for opposition research."

Alexis swallowed hard and lifted her gaze to meet Tiana's. "Yes, I'm joining Dewey, Carson and Howe as a legal analyst." *And,* she thought, *someday become their president and CEO.* That was her plan. To be so successful in business, her father would have no choice but to acknowledge her achievements.

"Argh," she yelled, raising clenched fists in the air. "Alexis, how could you? Please tell me this is an April Fool's joke a week too late. That place is the temple of corporate greed and corruption. Their clients are the same thieves we face off in court with. How could you possibly go from fighting the good old boys to being their lawyer? Or was WLAF all just a game for you?"

"Tiana, you know better." Alexis' voice rose, her guilt at leaving a cause that meant so much to her tamping down what normally would be a full-scale assault on anyone challenging her integrity. But Tiana had a point, she was going to work for the enemy.

"I thought I did," she said, dropping onto the sofa across from Alexis' desk. "Girl, your gram is spinning in her grave right now."

"Don't." The memory of her grandmother was still strong and raw. She missed Ester Johnson dearly. "Gramma would understand doing what needed to be done." The woman had taught her so much. Born in a generation where women, especially aristocratic women, were seen and not heard, she had poked holes in her husband's glass floor so women of Alexis' generation could climb through their glass ceiling.

Apparently, activism was genetic because Alexis' great, great grandmother had been a Suffragette. It was that passion she felt burning in her soul and she'd already wrestled with what her grandmother would think about her going into business instead of working for a cause she believed in. She convinced herself that her grandmother would be proud to see her burst through the glass ceiling.

But her father was in her soul too. Power and status meant something to her because they meant everything to him. Somewhere in the back of her mind, she justified his constant criticism of her as his way of pushing her to succeed. Didn't fathers know the best way to motivate their children? And the best way to motivate her was to tell her she couldn't have something, or she shouldn't do something. She was stubborn, strong-willed, and determined. It's how she found the strength to walk away from a cause she'd bleed for. Her father only respected power and status and if she could become a C level executive at the most respected business consulting firm in the world maybe, just maybe, he'd finally look in her direction and not see the silly teenager who let her heart make bad decisions. Love was no longer a consideration for Alexis Chambers, not a part of the plan. If anything, it was an inconvenience that should be avoided because it would only take time and attention away from her career.

"Are you even listening to me?" Tiana's voice bringing her mind back to the conversation.

"I'm sorry."

"You already said that. Don't be sorry. Don't do it."

"I have to. You know how things are between me and my father. I just want him to appreciate me. See me as a success."

"Girl, it's only eleven o'clock in the morning. How much Chardonnay have you had? Your papa dukes ain't going to appreciate you no matter what you do. I thought you hated the dude."

"I don't hate my father." Alexis sighed, her shoulders dropping. "I don't like him much most of the time, but he's still the only father I have. Just once in my life I'd like to hear him say, 'well done'."

Tiana snorted and waved her hand at Alexis like she was batting away a fly. "How much time do I have to change your mind?"

A sad smile tugged at the corner of Alexis's mouth. "Until the end of the month. I start the first week of May. But I'm not changing my mind. Besides, I've already signed a letter of acceptance."

"Pfft, you know damn well that's not a binding contract."

Alexis rolled her eyes. She should have known better than to try to slip one by her assistant. She was more knowledgeable than half the lawyers that volunteered at the agency, she just didn't have the law degree. She'd offered to pay Tiana's tuition for law school, but she had refused every time. She said she wanted to do that on her own. When she could afford it. And if Alexis knew one thing about her friend, it was that she was every bit as stubborn and determined as she was. Tiana would be a damn fine lawyer one day and one day couldn't come soon enough as far as Alexis was concerned. "You're right. But I'm still not changing my mind. You don't have to like my decision, but I really hope you can support me."

Tiana shook her head like a mother who had just discovered her child in a lie. "I love you, and always will, but it's going to take a while for me to get past this. I'm just sayin'." Pushing herself off the sofa, she stepped behind the desk and gave Alexis a hug.

"Thanks," Alexis croaked out as Tiana turned toward the door.

"Mm," Tiana grunted, stopping to peruse the long gray gown hanging on the back of the door. "You got some shindig with T-bag tonight?"

Alexis rolled her eyes at her friend's derisive nickname for her fiancé, Trevor. "There's a charity gala for some children's hospital at the Marriott in Melville tonight. Several of the state Republican party big wigs are going to be there, so as soon as Trevor heard we had to go. He even asked my father to join us, so I'm in for a lovely evening. Cocktails and schmoozing at six followed by rubber chicken for dinner at seven."

Tiana's lips quivered as she fought back a laugh. "You deserve all the torture you get for leaving us. He must be happy you're exiting this left-wing bastion of feminism. He won't have to hide it from his fascist friends anymore."

"You really don't like him, do you?"

Fisting her hands on her hips and shifting one to the side, "Girl, that's got nothing to do with it. You deserve so much more. Someone who loves you for you, not the stuff you can give him, like one of the three wise men. Seriously, it's obvious what he's getting out of this, but what's in it for you?"

"There's plenty in it for me." *There was the friendship she and Trevor shared, and that was all she wanted in a relationship. They agree on a lot, okay, some issues. But most of all, he was what her father considered an acceptable match from an established family. He had political ambitions and that would keep her father happy and off her back about being thirty-two and single. And if it didn't make her father exactly happy, at least it would be one less thing he could criticize her about.*

"Like what? You're a damn knock out, wavy blonde hair, blue eyes, long legs that go right up there and make an ass out of themselves that would have my sister's jealous of your perfect booty, a tummy that pisses this mama right the f off and your boobs, damn girl, I bet you don't even have to wear a bra them things are so perky." She shook her head and muttered, "double D's shouldn't defy gravity like that. It ain't fair to the rest of us."

Leveling a playful, accusatory glare at Alexis, she continued, "You gotta admit your man's not much to look at and you can't even wear three inch heals and not tower over him. Unless he's packing a foot-long, I just don't get it."

"Tiana" Alexis's voice rose, and she could feel her cheeks flush. "Relationships are more than physical appearance and you should know that better than anyone." Alexis bit her lip. She regretted what she said the second it left her mouth. Tiana's abuser had been a handsome man, but that beauty barely went skin deep. "I'm sorry. I shouldn't have said that."

"Stop. That's ancient history, and honestly it makes me feel a little less stupid knowing at least he was nice to look at when my eyes weren't swollen shut. So, is he?"

Alexis admired her friend's ability to joke about something that nearly cost her life. "So, is he what?"

"Giving you twelve inches. Because if he is, I might be convinced…"

"Now you stop. Not that it's any of your business, but, if you must know, he is not well endowed," she admitted with a grin. "Sex isn't important anyway. We have friendship, even if things are a little testy right now. Mostly he doesn't complain about me being me. He didn't fight me about changing jobs and I think you might be right; he could be relieved to not have to explain his future wife's involvement in liberal causes. We make our own decisions about our own lives, and even when we disagree, we back one another. Do I like that he's presenting himself as a conservative Republican? Of course, I don't, but I still smile and nod when he needs me to. The same way he might not like that I'm going to be spending a lot of time traveling for work, but he doesn't put up a fuss because he knows it's important to me." She didn't include that most of all he's safe because she'll never have to choose between her love for him and her career. And by marrying him, her father probably wouldn't limit her access to her trust fund. Trevor might be part of the social elite, but he lacked a lot in the way of liquid assets.

Tiana shook her head and pursed her lips, letting out a slow breath. "It don't sound much like marriage material to me, but what the hell do I know? At least he ain't beatin' you."

"Don't do that. You're one of the strongest, most fearless people I know."

Tiana waved her off. "I'm still mad at you. And I've got work to do before my boss fires my ass. What time you leavin' for this fufu affair?"

"I could never fire you and I need to be on the road by four if I'm going to make cocktail hour."

"Mm hm," Tiana hummed, turning out the door. "God knows what stupid ass decision you'll make once you start drinking if you could do this stone cold sober," and before Alexis could reply, Tiana disappeared down the hall muttering.

Alexis' tires screeched as she zipped into the parking lot, pulling her Audi R8 into a spot directly across from the hotel entrance. *Praise god*, she thought, *she didn't have any time to waste circling for a parking place*. It was 6:52 PM. She made it in time for dinner with only eight minutes to spare. Something that wouldn't have happened if Tiana hadn't come raging into her office at four-thirty and pulled her physically from behind her desk.

She flipped down the visor and checked herself in the vanity mirror. "Damn it," she mumbled, "these things are useless." Flipping the visor back in place with a little more force than needed, she snatched her clutch from the seat beside her and hurried toward the entrance. She might have missed the cocktail hour, but she was there. Trevor couldn't complain about that tonight.

She ducked into the restroom and checked herself in the mirror. Her platinum blonde hair was still holding together, pulled back into a tight bun and slicked down on the side. Her make-up was good, heavier on the blush than usual, making her high cheekbones seem just on the edge of severe. Deep red lipstick completed the look. *That could use some touching up,* opening her clutch and painting on another coat. Pursing her lips together and then tilting her head, she gave herself a brief nod and slight hint of a smile, satisfied she had achieved a close enough approximation of how a respectable politician's wife should look.

Placing her hands on her sides, and traced down her gunmetal gray tapered Jovani evening gown. Tapping her tummy lightly, the corners of her mouth tugged upward. It was the same one she'd worn to the Met Gala the year before. Her return to the gym the past few weeks seemed to be working. Trevor said it made her look powerful and the stark makeup she wore completed the look.

Trevor would be eager for her arrival. The little voice in the back of her head, whispering that it wasn't her per se that he was pining for, but the visual of them together. The picture on the mantle over the fireplace type of visual. Or the campaign ad type of visual. The smiling, happy family.

Alexis' mind wandered back to another charity dinner. Back to when she was barely a teen. She had been so excited to go, dressed in an emerald satin, tea-length gown, and feeling as beautiful as a real princess. It was the first time that she had remembered feeling like she wasn't 'just a kid' anymore. Carole had stayed at home with the nanny, she was too young to go. Her mother had gone out of town to attend an artist's retreat.

She had been so excited to have time with her father. It had happened so rarely, but that night had been just them, talking like grown-ups and no lectures on how little girls should behave. How wrong she had been.

She had hoped that her father would ask her about all she had going on at school, the debate club, national honor society, student senate. Or maybe he would have shared what had been happening at his financial management firm. What they had talked about was who he had intended to introduce her to, the right families with sons who would be a good match for her. "It's never too soon to be seen as someone with suitable potential," he told her. Wealthy families with billion-dollar businesses or families with long political histories. Boys who would become the powerful men who ran the world, just like their fathers, and needed a good woman to show off beside them, just like her mother. "You should take up dance again or learn to paint like your mother. Interests that won't interfere with what your proper job will be."

"I want to be a lawyer, daddy," she remembered saying. She had been certain he would appreciate her drive and ambition. He had always talked about how important he felt those qualities were in his life.

"Hmph," he snorted. "Don't be ridiculous. You don't have to worry about business. Just be the pretty princess, have babies, and manage the house. No man wants a woman who is smarter or more successful than he is."

With a shudder, she came back to the present. One last check in the mirror and she was out the door. A short walk down the corridor, shoulders back, confident, and quick, despite the four-inch heels she sported. A deep breath in. Exhale slowly. Through the door into the main ballroom. It was show time. Time to play her part as half of the soon to be premier young power couple in New York.

She hadn't been looking forward to tonight. Her father would be there, which would mean more pressure to move up the date of their wedding, this Christmas, not next. "If Trevor was going to run for Congress, he needed a wife, not a fiancé," "visuals were important," her father kept reminding her. "Stay with that woman's thing you work for. No legitimate business is going to promote you when they know you'll just leave to start a family. At least with the woman's thing, it's not like you'd be leaving anything important."

She wasn't going to tell him she didn't have plans to start a family anytime soon. And the Woman's Legal Assistance Foundation was important, just because he didn't give a damn about domestic violence, pay equity, reproductive rights… no, that was her passion, her calling. They had gotten to Roe once, but they never would again if she had a breath in her lungs. No cadre of old men or religious zealots would dictate what she or anyone else had a right to do or not to do. That wasn't the way a democracy was supposed to work.

With a sigh, she reminded herself that she couldn't get too high and mighty. She had just resigned. She was walking away from her passion to pursue her plan. The plan to prove her father wrong. That women belonged in business. And not all men were threatened by successful women. The fact that he didn't remember the WLAF's name was all the proof she needed her present position was not the means to that end. To prove to him that a woman had value beyond her womb and the ability to look good on her husband's arm. And she *would* prove it to him. And to do it, she'd need to be a different kind of princess than he had told her she should be. She needed to be the ice princess; cold, ruthless in business and undistracted by anything as silly as love.

Walking into the ballroom, she scanned the cocktail area for Trevor. There were few things more frustrating to her than looking for him in a room full of people. At five eight, with a wispy head of thinning sandy blond hair, he didn't stand out in a crowd. He'd made her think of Niles from the TV show Frasier. She had nearly called him that a hundred times the first year they dated. Trevor was even more of a pompous ass though, but he was her pompous ass and his existence, and their plans kept her father off her back about at least one thing in her life.

She spotted him and wasted no time in gliding to his side. Deep breath, shoulders square and a polite, ever so interested in your drivel, smile. "Trevor sweetheart, don't you look handsome tonight," she did her best to project an air of a loving fiancé, placed an air kiss somewhere near his cheek and smoothed out his already perfect lapels.

"Darling, so glad you could make it and on time, at least for dinner."

She did her best to keep her pasted-on smile intact at his syrupy sweet sarcasm. What she wanted to do was turn around and walk out yelling, *I'd rather be anywhere but fucking here with you,* over her shoulder.

"Alexis, you remember Judge Silva and his wife Rhoda, don't you?"

She made a graceful quarter turn to face him and extended a weak hand to shake. "Yes, of course, Judge. How have you been? My grandfather speaks of you often." Her grandfather hated the bastard and would rather eat a shit sandwich than speak his name, but nobody expected sincerity here.

The judge cocked his head and brought his mouth only as far as a slight purse of the lips. *Perhaps I've overshot the mark a bit with that. Oh well,* she thought, *not my problem.*

Trevor continued to drone on about his plans to run for the House in two years. Pulling Alexis closer with a possessive arm around her waist that always caused an unsettled feeling in her stomach, "once we're married and on our way to a growing family," he added for effect. He gave her a gentle pat on her hip, tugging her another inch closer.

Wanting to change the topic from their impending nuptials, Alexis offered, "I'm sure the judge would be interested in hearing your plan to expand trade in southeast Asia. It is quite impressive that…"

"I'm sure," Trevor cut her off with a glare, "the judge is not interested in hearing about policy tonight."

Alexis dug her nails into her palms and fought the urge in every fiber of her body to lash out and tell him if he wanted a woman to stand silently and look pretty, she wasn't the woman for him. He could buy a mannequin for that. She forced herself to loosen her jaw and was relieved when Trevor dropped his arm from her waist. Thank God the PDA was cut short by the announcement of dinner being served.

After she agreed to marry him, Trevor changed. He sided more with her father. He didn't seem to care about her feelings or opinions. Now she was relegated to being nothing more than arm decoration. The more her father showed interest in Trevor's political ambitions, the more Trevor pressed her to become the dutiful wife her father tried to force her to be. She would finally be the senator's wife he'd dreamed she'd be. Technically, she'd be a representative's wife but, one step at a time. It never once entered her father's mind that she could be the senator.

They made their way to their assigned table at the front of the room. She saw her father already seated, but her mother's chair was noticeably empty. That was more the rule than the exception over the past few years. Her constant disagreements with her father had put her mother in the middle, desperate to keep peace in the family. She just didn't understand why her father couldn't at least try to support her, instead of doing everything he could to tear her down. Valedictorian of her high school class, Summa Cum Laude in both college and law school, were not enough to make him proud of her. Passing the Bar exam in five states, no reaction; and leading a nationally recognized legal advocacy group right out of law school didn't matter to him, either.

The only thing that seemed to placate him was the thought of her giving up everything to be a wife and mother. Her sister had always been his favorite, even though she was far more rebellious. When she got married right out of college, that was it. Alexis would never again have a chance with her father unless she won the baby race, and that was not happening. The thought of Carole wiped the fake smile from her face. They had been so close, even after she left for college, but then Carole had found Brian, made him her world, and basked in her father's approval. They had drifted apart the past few years. Now they only talked every few weeks instead of a few times a day. Alexis had lost her best friend and confidant, and her chest still tightened at the thought.

"Alexis," Gregory nodded at his daughter, taking a sip of his scotch, "so glad you could find time in your hectic schedule to support your future husband." Her stomach tightened more at the visceral emphasis on 'husband', as if to taunt her with his victory over her will. For a brief second, she felt a stinging in her eyes but pushed it back as she'd learned so well to do the past fifteen years. She was not about to shed a tear in front of her father, and even more so because of her father.

Her jaw tightened, and she could feel the pulse pounding in her neck. "I would never miss an event that was important to Trevor if I could help it. You know that, don't you darling?" the forced smile returning to her face as she looked to Trevor for support.

"Hmph," was all she received from Trevor, "Mr. Chambers, can I get you a fresh drink?" reaching for his future father-in-law's empty glass. A chill washed over her. She wondered if the AC had just kicked on.

"No thank you, son. I don't want to hear it from my wife if I walk in smelling like a distillery." He laughed, and Alexis fought the urge to roll her eyes. *What her mother said or thought had little impact on him these days,* she thought. "Did you have time to check out the home I told you about in Bay Shore? It's in the heart of the second congressional district, and the sooner you take up residency there, the better. Solidly Republican, a much better chance of getting elected if you play your hand right."

Alexis raised a questioning eyebrow, wondering what on earth he was talking about? She worked in Brooklyn, lived in Manhattan, and probably would end up transferred to another location halfway across the country in a few months; why would she consider buying a house on Long Island and especially the exclusive town of Bay Shore? Her grandfather had always told her that having money was a blessing and a responsibility. Living up to that responsibility meant not flaunting it, nor frittering it away on frivolous things. Frivolous things like choosing a home based solely on the town you lived in, screaming wealth and privilege. The blessing was spending the money on what made you happy, not on what proved to others that you had it.

"I haven't, dad." Trevor's response snapped her out of her thoughts. The sound of him referring to her father as 'dad' set her teeth on edge. Every muscle in her body tense and her head throbbed at the pressure of holding the requisite smile in place.

Trevor continued, "It's been a busy two weeks of holding the Chinese investors' hands. We should be free from their interference for a few months now, though, and I can check into it next week."

Alexis fought hard to suppress an eye-roll. Her fiancé was nothing more than a puppet. He was the Executive Vice President of his family's manufacturing company, being groomed to take it over. His great grandfather had founded the company in the late 1800s, his grandfather led it to its pinnacle in the forties and fifties and his father ran it virtually into the ground. It would be bankrupt and a distant memory today if a Chinese company hadn't bought a controlling interest to enter the market and still be able to slap on 'Made in the USA' labels. Despite herself, she let out a silent chortle. Like that sort of thing wouldn't come out in a political campaign and torpedo his chances for election. She knew that a good half of the Republican vote in the district was the white, working-class type Republicans, the America first crowd, anti-foreign everything, not the white collar, keep my taxes low, and maximize my profits Republican. If he even made it out of the primaries, any Democrat worth their salt would hammer that little factoid right down the electorate's throat. Hell, she wouldn't vote for him, but she was marrying him. It kept her father quiet.

Trevor turned to face Alexis for the first time since her arrival. "We should talk about pushing up the wedding date. I've been getting some pushback on our three-year engagement; it just doesn't look good for me. If we get married now, you could be pregnant by the time the campaign kicks into gear and that would sew up the family value vote."

Alexis could feel the heat rising in her face. She wanted to ask, "Just who is pushing?" but she didn't need to, turning pointedly toward her father. They had this conversation a hundred times if they'd had it once. She was not about to be planning a wedding and trying to start a new career in a highly competitive, male dominated, consulting firm at the same time. Not to mention the fact that she'd told him over and over she wasn't sure she ever wanted children. She'd even told him if it was that important to him, she would understand if he wanted to end the engagement. Something he was always quick to reject. "I don't think this is the place for that conversation, dear." She placed a gentle hand on his and gave it a squeeze, just a bit firmer than was comfortable.

Trevor looked her in the eyes, the corner of his mouth hooking up into a smirk, and then turned back to her father. "If that place is acceptable and we move in, I assume I can count on you to be at the rally when I announce for the House, Greg?”

“Of course, son. I wouldn’t dream of missing it.”

Alexis couldn’t help but level an icy gaze at her father. And from the smug expression on his face, she could tell that he was calling Trevor ‘son’ just to irritate her. She broadened her smile to him. “Thank you, father. You know how much it means to Trevor,” as an afterthought she added, “and me.”

“I know exactly what it means to both of you,” her father replied, and she didn’t need to hear what came next to understand exactly what he meant. “You should move up the date of the wedding, Alexis. Buying the house before the wedding is like putting the cart before the horse and just doesn’t look good. I might have to reconsider your unfettered access to the trust fund.”

Alexis tried to stifle the breath she sucked in between her teeth. While he’d hinted at this before, he’d never outright threatened to cut her off financially. She would be fine. She would make more than enough at DCH to support herself. But she relied on her trust to afford to help the WLAF. Without her contributions, Tiana would almost certainly have to be let go, along with half the paid staff. It was bad enough she was leaving, but she was doing so knowing she would provide money to help keep the non-profit afloat. She couldn’t let that happen, but she wasn’t going to give her father the satisfaction of knowing he’d hit her close to home with that threat. “What would you like to do this weekend, darling?” she asked Trevor, changing the subject though failed to be convincing in her interest in his answer to the question.

“There’s a benefit concert at the Carnegie they should see us at, other than that I’m open to suggestions.”

“I guess that means we’ll be staying in town, then?” Trevor nodded, and Alexis continued to smile. The tension in holding the smile in place causing her temples to pound, a full-blown migraine all but guaranteed by the end of the evening. Their weekend time together comprised Saturday evenings and most Sunday mornings. He had demanded some time to be a couple, and she could give him that. She preferred when they stayed at his condo on Long Island rather than her Carnegie Hill brownstone. It meant she could leave when she wanted and not have to get him out the door as soon as she could on Sunday morning.

She didn’t enjoy feeling this way. She did care for him. And there was a part of her that could understand his building frustration with her at dragging her feet on the wedding. Getting married should be something one looked forward to, was excited about, not be treated like an item on the to do list that could be delayed until it was convenient. She hoped they would at least return to the companionship they once shared as the wedding date approached. She might have even conceded to marrying him sooner if he'd agreed to have a small, family only ceremony, but he wanted the big show and the society page coverage it would get.

"Perhaps we could meet your mother for brunch on Sunday? It's been weeks since we've seen her." She sat back a bit in her chair and let out a breath she didn't realize she was holding. At least that way she could have Sunday afternoon to herself. Less of a chance for him to satisfy his 'manly needs', as he so boorishly called them. She used to thoroughly enjoy sex, and she thought she could remember enjoying it with him, too. Theirs was going to be a marriage of convenience, not a marriage of love and passion. She could deal with that. The Ice Princess was perfectly content with that kind of arrangement. She was just in no hurry to make it happen. Not until she was damn good and ready.

Chapter 2

Alexis

Alexis pulled into her grandfather's driveway just before ten on Friday night of Labor Day Weekend. She was the last to arrive. Easing in beside her sister's BMW, the crushed gravel of the stately driveway crunched under her tires. She smiled, that sound always reminded her of carefree summers, of sandcastles and salt air. Memories of being tossed into the waves by her grandfather. "She's just a little girl, George," her grandmother would scold from her chair beneath the giant striped beach umbrella. "Again Papa, again," she would plead, on the off chance this would be the time that he listened to her.

Pressing the engine stop button, she stretched her long toned legs and rolled her neck, gaining a satisfying crack, something she received more than one good scolding from her grandmother for, lord how she missed her. She could always make her feel like that happy little girl, valued, loved. Alexis felt anything but happy, valued, or loved. Seeing her grandfather this weekend might help, at least a little.

Pausing, as the hatch to her SUV slowly opened, she took in her grandfather's oceanfront summer cottage. She always felt like a fool calling it that, with twelve bedrooms, a cavernous living room, a dining room table that could comfortably seat thirty, it was larger than some hotels, let alone most people's homes. It had been built at the turn of the twentieth century by her mother's great grandfather and had remained in her family since. It kept the old charm and homey feeling despite being four stories high. She and Carole had made the most of its size with endless games of hide and seek on rainy summer days when they were here with her mother growing up.

Unlike her father, her grandfather had almost always been home. She smiled at the memory of how her grandmother would fuss and fume about him being a lazy knockabout, always underfoot, asking him when he was going to do something useful with his life. It was usually immediately after that question that her grandfather, with a mischievous sparkle in his eye, would grab a handful of her grandmother's matronly old bottom and give it a good squeeze. That leading to more fussing and fuming and not seeing them for the better part of an hour.

Shaking her head, he hoisted her weekend bag out of the back. With a huff, she tried to blow a wisp of hair away from her face. It went nowhere, stuck to the perspiration beading on her forehead. It had been a long hot drive from the city despite the AC. She wanted nothing more than to grab a large glass of chardonnay and sink into the huge claw-footed soaking tub she had loved since she summered here as a child.

She trudged her way up the walk and into the house. From the front hall, she could hear her mother and her sister, Carole, laughing. She headed out back to the patio, following the sound. It was getting late. She could get away with going to her room and that bath, but she felt obliged to be social. She left her bag in the hall and wandered to the ocean side of the house.

Her mother and sister squealed in delight as she walked through the French Doors that opened onto the patio. The breeze off the ocean was refreshing, the salt air breathed new life into her tired body.

"That must have been an awful drive, Allie." Carole said, giving her a hug. "Over four hours on the road, and with no one to keep you company. Your fiancé should have waited and come out with you." Carole shot a disapproving look over her shoulder at Trevor.

Alexis smirked and leaned in conspiratorially. "Please C, don't start anything this weekend. I just want to have a few drinks, relax, and get the metric shit ton of reading I have to do done in peace. I've been at DCH for two months and I still don't feel like I'm up to speed."

"I'm sorry, sis. I promise I'll behave." She kissed her big sister on the cheek.

Alexis noted her father was nowhere to be found, which is likely why she heard her mother enjoying herself. Her grandfather was also absent, but it was past his normal bedtime, especially since her grandmother had passed.

Trevor was sitting on a chaise, staring out at the ocean, paying no attention to anyone. She wanted to give him the benefit of the doubt that he didn't hear her arrive. Deep down, she knew that was a lie. He was becoming more and more distant from her, especially where she wouldn't budge on moving up the wedding date. He was even more perturbed at her refusal to discuss plans for children anytime in the next ten years. She had forced herself to placate him by committing to a church and reserving the reception hall, but not until next Christmas after she'd had a year and a half to establish herself in her new job.

They often skipped Saturday date nights now, and they rarely had sex. She was in the prime of her life and she wasn't missing sex a bit. Her Ice Princess persona was growing stronger and more dominant. She turned from her mother and sister and walked over and sat down beside him. "Hey you." She hoped her tone was convincing and didn't sound as disinterested as she was. "When did you get here?"

He turned slowly toward her. His face was blank. It surprised her he didn't even try to pretend to be glad to see her. He usually knew enough to feign affection in front of her family. "I got here about four. Unlike some people, I understand what a holiday weekend is, and don't stay late at the office."

She couldn't keep herself from rolling her eyes, but she kept whatever caustic remark that was bubbling up in her throat from escaping. "I'm sorry Trevor. I don't own Dewey, Carson and Howe and there are expectations I have to meet."

"Of course, there are." The venom oozing from his words sent a chill down her spine, causing goose bumps to rise on her arms. A marriage of convenience was fine with her, but she was wondering if her relationship with Trevor could even meet that low standard of compatibility again. "I'm going to bed. Please be quiet if you decide to join me. I want to actually get some sleep."

"What a shame. I was so looking forward to having sex with you tonight." The disdain for him was clear in her tone. *How have we gotten to this point? We were at least friends, not that long ago.* Her eyes burned at the tears she was holding back. She had sworn off romantic love a long time ago. She was not about to be hurt that way again. There would never be another Cody that could betray her and crush her heart.

He uttered a dismissive grunt. "As if that would ever be the case." He walked away and into the house without sparing her a glance.

She sat there staring at his vacant seat when Carole sat down in his spot, leaned over, and wrapped her arms around Alexis, squeezing her into a tight hug.

Alexis stared out to where Trevor had been looking. Flashes of lightning from a far offshore thunderstorm danced across the sky. She huffed out a laugh and leaned into her sister. "Do you remember how you always used to run into my bedroom and do this anytime there was a thunderstorm?"

"Mm-hmm." Carole hummed into her sister's neck. "Do you remember how you used to complain about it?"

"I did not," Alexis denied, turning to face her sister, eyes wide at the accusation.

Carole laughed softly. "Well, not at first, but when I refused to go back to my room once the storm was over. You used to complain cuddling with me was like hugging a campfire and in the morning, you'd be naked because you'd peel out of your pajamas in the middle of the night just to stay cool?"

Alexis snorted a laugh. "Oh, God. Yes." She'd done that a few times with guys she'd been with in college too, not that they complained, but never once with Trevor. *I must have grown out of it.* The smile she had at the childhood memory faded to a frown at the thoughts of the more recent state of her life.

"Sissy, what's going on?" her sister asked, noticing her fading smile. "You and Trevor don't seem very happy. It's like you don't even like each other anymore." Carole's husband Brian appeared holding two bottles of wine.

"I'm thinking maybe you two ladies might need these."

Carole scooted closer to Alexis and patted the seat, inviting Brian to join them. "No baby. I'm going to go read for a bit. Besides, you're long overdue for some sister time and I don't want to ruin that." He bent down and gave Alexis a kiss on the cheek and then gave Carole a good lip lock with plenty of tongue.

"Should I wake you when I come up?" Carole asked, side-eyeing her sister.

"Baby, I'll be awake. But don't rush." He gave her a quick kiss and disappeared inside.

"See what I'm talking about, Allie?"

"Carole, please. You know that has never been us. Not even in the beginning. Our marriage will be based on different things than yours and Brian's. I'm a lot different from you. I always have been."

"Allie, you're not married yet and there's nothing that says you have to go through with it if you don't love him. And I'm sorry, but I don't think you do. Sure, every marriage is different. Maybe you're not an over the moon, gaga, for someone girl, but my God Allie…"

"Please…" she took a deep breath, somewhere between exasperated and exhausted. "I know you're trying to help, but I have this. We're in a rough spot because he doesn't understand how demanding my new job is. I don't think he understands how much it means to me. My career is always going to come before my relationship. That's just the way I'm built. I'm like dad. You're like mom."

"Stop it. You're not like dad!" Carole screeched, louder than was appropriate for that hour of the evening. "You might be more like him than I am, but you're not him. There's a warm, loving person under this glacier you've built up around you. There's so much you have to give the right person if you'd just let your defenses down a bit."

Alexis stood, taking the bottle of wine over to the outdoor bar and opened it, filling her glass.

Before Alexis could argue that she would never allow herself that kind of vulnerability again, Carole continued, "You need to find a balance, sis, or you'll find yourself seventy and alone and with nothing and no one to love. For what? A nice job title and money?" She grabbed her sister's shoulders and squeezed as Alexis sat back down next to her. "Those mean nothing to you. I know they don't."

"God, Carole, don't be so morose. I'll have plenty of nieces and nephews to look after me the way you and Brian go at it. I have every intention of being the cool aunt. And when they get on my nerves, back to you, I will send them." She smiled, a genuine smile, "I'm quite content with that plan."

Alexis didn't see herself the way her sister saw her. Her career was important to her and, for the most part, Trevor, while far from supporting her, didn't oppose her. He had been better since she started making wedding plans. It might not be as soon as he wanted, but at least he knew she was serious about going through with it.

"I still don't understand why you left the WLAF. You were doing good work there, helping people, making their lives better, and you were so good at it. You left a cause you believed in for DCH, a consulting firm, big business and greed? Just the things you were fighting against. Stop trying to impress dad, Allie. Nothing and no one impresses him because he thinks that makes him be less if someone else is more. The only reason he treats me better than you is because he thinks I'm a no one, just a housewife, young, dumb and …," she waved her hand in the air and smirked. "You know the rest. He doesn't respect me. He doesn't love me. I don't think he even likes me."

"Of course, he loves you, Carole. How can you say that?"

She tilted her head, raised her eyebrows, and grinned at Alexis as if she had said the world was flat and the sun orbited the earth. "Ok, Allie. If that's what you believe. But I'm telling you, if you're doing all this just to get his approval, he'll only find something else to disapprove of."

"I guess. Maybe I'm just tired, and stressed, and feeling a little lonely because things aren't so good between Trevor and I."

Carole gave Alexis a kiss on the cheek and hugged her tight. "I love you. I just want to see you happy. Find a man you truly love. Find a job you truly love and fuck everything else. God Allie, Papa gave us a wonderful gift. With our trust funds we can do anything and still live life without a money care in the world. We can work at Walmart if we want, and nothing would change."

"It's not about money Carole and it's not about love. It's about meeting the challenge and succeeding. Moving up the corporate ladder is like winning at sports to me. Remember how competitive you were in volleyball? You practiced and practiced and then practiced some more. You did everything you could to win. I want to win. That's all. I'm competitive. It's just who I am, how I'm wired."

"Okay, Allie," she let out a deep, exasperated sigh. "I'm going to go make love to my husband, then I might fuck him after that, but think about this, please. What price are you willing to pay to win? To me, there's a point when winning isn't worth the price. I may have practiced a lot, but I never gave up who I was, what I stood for, and when something worthwhile came along, I didn't ignore it. He's upstairs right now, waiting for me to come." She gave her sister an impish wink and a wicked smile. "Use your keen lawyer, consultant brain, and do a cost benefit analysis of that." She leaned over and gave her sister one more hug. "I'll see you in the morning."

Alexis thought about telling Carole it was always worth the price to win, but didn't want to keep her from her husband. "I love you C. See you tomorrow."

Chapter 3

Jake

Jake hung up the phone and pinched his brow. If he had to tell one more marketing writer, they couldn't just put unsubstantiated claims into ad copy, like 'you'll never find another hair in your sink after just two applications of Ajax Miracle Grow Hair Elixir,' he was going to lose his mind. Not to mention the trademark issues they were going to have with a certain plant fertilizer company. He was going to crack. He would have never let Rob talk him into signing on as Legal Analyst and Associate General Counsel with Dewey, Carson, and Howe if he'd known this was what he was going to be dealing with.

Rob, his boss and best friend from college, had promised him he'd be working on multi-million-dollar international contracts. Contracts that would need his talent for constitutional and corporate law. Sure, he had a couple of those projects, but it was the rest of the kindergarten stuff that had him on edge. This firm was supposed to be filled with the best and the brightest, but every day he found Harvard MBA's recommending shit a third grader would know better than to say.

Still, he had bills to pay, and Rob had got him a more than reasonable salary. Two years clerking in the Federal Second District Court of Appeals had given him great experience, but little to show for it in the bank. He held out for as long as he could afford to for one of the Washington, DC law firms to respond to his applications, but none did. That's where he really wanted to be, somewhere close to the Supreme Court. Some guys had fantasies about a harem full of women. His was to stand in front of that panel of nine Justices and prove he knew the Constitution every bit as well, if not better, than they did.

With a sigh of, "someday," he picked up the contract on his desk and began reading. After only a few minutes, a soft rap on his open office door pulled his attention from the document. His usual congenial smile spread across his face despite the unwelcome interruption. "Come in Mary."

Mary smiled and inched her way into his office. "Here are the files you requested, Mr. Douglas."

"Thank you. You could have just put it in my mailbox and saved yourself a half-mile walk." She tucked her chin down and peered at him as she stepped closer, placing the files on the table next to his desk. "And how many times have I told you just to call me Jake?"

Her cheeks flushed, and she fluttered her long lashes. "I know, but I don't mind the walk, and you sounded like you needed them right away."

Jake had the sneaking suspicion that she had moved his request to the top of her to do list. He had overheard some women in the office assistants' pool gossiping about him a few times. More than one of them, Mary included, had suggested several carnal delights that they would be willing to explore with him. While he certainly bore no resemblance to the chiseled muscled models on front of the romance novels he saw peeking out of their totes, his broad six-foot-four frame and athletic build, helped him stand out, at least in a room full of lawyers and MBAs.

Office rumors were that he was well on his way onto Mahogany Row, the section of the fifth floor where all the C-level executives had their offices, and leading his own pod, DCH slang for business unit. The rumors likely contributed to his attractiveness as a match. He knew he had to suffer the requisite number of months in Siberia. That was another bit of DCH jargon. They referred to the remote offices in this sprawling building as Siberia. Low-level executives, or new employees like Jake, who needed a private office, mostly occupied them, not an open-air cubicle. New employees always paid their dues, no matter how much of a rising star they were. Unless, of course, your name matched those on the masthead. Hamilton Dewey III hadn't spent ten seconds anywhere but a corner office, despite his well-known incompetence.

"You know I'd get fired for calling an associate anything other than Mr. or Ms." Mary added with a smile. "Will there be anything else, Mr. Douglas?" she stammered, fiddling with her company ID hanging from a lanyard around her neck.

"I'm good. Thank you again."

He could swear he heard her mumble, "I bet you are," before she turned to leave. "My pleasure. Call me if you need anything"

Jake shook his head as Mary disappeared out his door. It flattered him, but he was uncomfortable with the attention she gave him. And she wasn't the only woman in the pool that did it. She was a very sweet young woman, quite pretty and in his age range, but… But even without the corporate policy against dating, she was one of those that would be far too devoted to him. He didn't want that type of pressure, to be that much of a focus of someone else's life. He wasn't ready for a relationship, and he had no desire for casual sex. If it was sexual release he required, there was porn and his right hand. Mary did not deserve to be a replacement for that and that was all he felt he was capable of, or willing to give, any woman.

Jake also suspected that most of the women here would lose interest the moment they saw the ten-year-old Kia SUV he drove or the studio apartment he was living in. They were looking for a man to give them the good life, luxury car, jewelry, and penthouses. He wasn't that man and didn't particularly plan to be. He was still focused on paying off his college loans and when he finished, he was content to save much more than he spent. And if there was a woman in his life, he knew from experience he'd spend too much. He had a bad habit of finding women who took too much and gave too little in return.

Rob, appearing in his doorway, snapped him out of his internal pity party regarding the state of his love life. It was time for yet another team meeting in which everyone would try to show off their brilliance to Hamilton Dewey III, his boss's boss and the nepotism poster boy, grandson of the principal partner, and only living founder of Dewey, Carson, and Howe.

They were the first to arrive at the meeting and took seats at the far end of the massive conference table. Others trickled in over the next ten minutes, including Dewey. Andre Freeman, one of Rob's peers, who settled in at the head of the table at the insistence of Mr. Dewey, much to Jake's surprise. The last to arrive was his fellow associate counsel and legal analyst, Alexis Chambers.

Alexis stormed into the conference room and dropped the half dozen files she was balancing in her arms on the table with a loud thud.

"Now that's an entrance to be proud of," Jake quipped to no one in particular. She was an enigma to him. From their first day of orientation, he noticed she kept everyone at arm's length. All the ice breaker activities designed to enable peer bonding never penetrated the wall of ice she kept around her. Perhaps most remarkably, unlike every other woman in the office, she did her best to disguise her physique instead of trying to use it to her advantage. He was desperate to know what made her tick, but he could never get her to engage in a conversation beyond the minimum of what had to be said to get a project done. At the end of the day, they were as much adversaries as co-workers. They did their best to get noticed, staying late, working weekends, not hesitating to speak at meetings. They both hoped that it would pay in the long run.

Usually, pods did not interact. They each managed their own roster of clients and prospects, but both of their pods had just been assigned new businesses in southeast Asia and certain aspects of their businesses required a unified approach. Dewey's concept was that DCH could give the appearance of being the industry trend maker if all the clients took a similar path to market.

As the meeting progressed, Jake noticed Andre's pod was setting the standards, with Rob's group having little input on the strategic direction. Though marketing and public relations were not Jake's strength, he was concerned that the best ideas were not being adopted. It struck him as odd because his pod had been assigned landing Hong Kong Diversified, an import/export giant with a rare combination of connections in mainland China, the European Union and the U.S. HKD was a whale in a sea of minnows and, in Jake's eyes, his pod should probably take the lead in developing strategy if they were to be effective in landing and maintaining the most important account.

With a nod from Dewey, Alexis stood and detailed the legal impact of new tariffs several of the firm's Asian manufacturing clients were facing. Her pod determined that the most cost-effective way for the clients to import their goods from southeast Asia was to bring product into Mexico first, make some minor assembly modifications and then ship them to the U.S. from there, effectively hiding under the NAFTA blanket, and thereby avoiding tariffs.

Jake cleared his throat and addressed the potential challenges to the tariffs. Additionally, political pressure was building in the new Administration would likely abandon NAFTA, which would render the Mexico option substantially needless and financially burdensome. Andre quickly stepped on him, dismissing his suggestion. Alexis nodded in agreement and several other members of her pod then followed suit. Dewey gave Alexis a nod, and, Jake was certain, a wink as well, and leaned back, now focusing on Jake.

Jake scanned the room and decided that he didn't want to take on the other pod or the managing partner. He waved his hand, indicating he had nothing more to add. His sense of ethics made him not want to see Alexis end up spit roasted over missing some, to him anyway, rather basic legal considerations. Con law was his thing but, in this instance, he felt it needed to be hers too. He would take her aside and bring her up to speed with the guidance he had read.

The meeting droned on for another forty-five minutes and when it finally broke up, Jake planned to hang back and walk with Alexis to their offices. This would give him the opportunity to bring her up to speed subtly and without losing face in front of the group. She, however, seemed to do everything she could to ignore him and wait him out. She won the waiting game when Rob took him by the arm and walked him out of the conference room. "Let's go for lunch," Rob said as soon as they cleared the conference room door.

"I don't know. There are a bunch of things I still need to button up and I'm not about being here tomorrow. It's supposed to be a beautiful day, and I'd like to get in one last round of golf before it snows."

"Don't sweat it. This place will function whether you get that work done today or Monday. And I specifically forbid you to set foot in this building between five PM today and nine AM Monday morning. Don't make me fire you for insubordination. Besides, you and I need to talk about HKD. If we follow what they're suggesting in our pitch, we'll get skewered."

Jake laughed. Rob was probably the least 'corporate' person he had ever met, certainly the least corporate person at DCH. It made him wonder how Rob had risen to management. His approach was unique from what Jake could see. "Fine, I am hungry, and I wasn't really looking forward to another gourmet selection from the salmonella roulette wheel in the breakroom."

Rob slapped Jake on the back. "Good call, my friend. You just have to learn to set boundaries and hold on to them."

Jake laughed again. He thought to himself that Rob had no idea how to get ahead in business. Rob had to be related to someone up the corporate food chain. There were no such things as boundaries at DCH. He would always go the extra mile to get ahead, as long as it meant not fucking someone else over.

It was almost three thirty when they returned to the office. Rob simply dropped Jake off at the door and told him to pack up and get out. It was Friday and time to start his weekend. It was apparent that was exactly what Rob intended to do. Jake wanted to get at least one thing accomplished, and quickly closed himself in his office and started typing.

Forty-five minutes later, he emerged from his hole and walked the short distance to Alexis' door and gave it a smart rap.

"It's open." Alexis yelled out.

Jake stuck his head in to find Alexis on the phone. Her head tilted and brows raised, and she held up a finger to show Jake should wait while she finished her call. "Yes Trevor, I realize that, but I just thought it might be nice to change things up. Maybe a little break from routine would do us both a little good and honestly, how often have I offered to make you dinner in the past year?" He could tell from her expression that whoever she was speaking to wasn't agreeing with her.

"Okay, well, that's fine. I've got someone waiting here. Call me later if you want." She ended the call, though it appeared to Jake the person on the other end had ended it first. "What is it, Jake?"

"Sorry to bother you, but I've pulled together a couple of notes for you to look through."

"What's this for?"

"I'm sorry," Jake said, feeling a little stupid for thinking that she would know exactly what was on his mind. "This morning, the meeting, regarding the tariffs. The Supreme Court is going to hear a challenge to them this session and I've listed a dozen cases they are likely to cite striking down the tariffs. When they do, Mexico will be a boondoggle, and I don't want you to be on the wrong side of that argument."

"Okay," she said, taking the memo from his hand. "Thank you. I'll review these when I get the chance." Alexis was looking at him with her brows furrowed, leaning forward in her chair.

"Good." His tongue felt thick under the intensity of her stare. "Well, have a good weekend."

"I'll likely be here for most of it." She said with a groan.

Jake turned and started to close her door behind him. "Hey Jake." He stopped and turned to face her. "Why would you give me this instead of sending it to Dewey and the pod leaders?"

"We're the legal team. Same project, same company. We either succeed together or fail together. You didn't seem to want to take what I had to say in the meeting without proof, so there it is."

He felt her stare as he closed the door behind him.

Chapter 4

Alexis

They were seated at an out of the way table in one of the 'in' restaurants in Greenwich Village. Trevor's brow was furrowed, and his lips were pinched together. Alexis couldn't determine whether his displeasure was because the maitre d' had given him attitude about being fifteen minutes late for their reservation, or because they weren't front and center where everybody who's anybody could see them. It was her fault entirely for being late for the reservation, getting lost in the memo Jake Douglas had handed her yesterday afternoon, causing her to stay even later at the office on a Saturday than she usually did.

Alexis had identified Jake as her greatest threat on the first day of their new hire orientation. He was dangerous. Confident and articulate in a way that put you at ease even when he was calling you to task. She had graduated first in her class at an Ivy League University and yet her legal knowledge and instincts paled compared to his, but he never came across as the least bit arrogant. It would be impossible to make him seem incompetent. If anyone would appear wanting in a comparison, it would be her.

And as if his competence wasn't enough, he might be the most naturally handsome man she had ever met. Dark, penetrating eyes that peered into the depths of your soul if you let them. A body that is the envy of every damn Greek statue in the British Museum. *I mean, how can a man look that good in an off the rack suit? He even pulled off the tightly trimmed beard.* She always hated men that weren't clean shaven but somehow on Jake Douglas, it looked good. *I bet it would even feel good rubbing in certain places.* Not that anyone had been near those certain places in years. Trevor was not fond of oral, giving, or receiving.

Combine his looks with the most impressive legal mind she has ever seen. He was dangerous. *If she was the kind of woman that went for smart and sexy or let lustful thoughts control her decisions…* She captured that thought and tossed it directly in the trash bin where it belonged. He was the competition, and she had better stay focused on that. Ice Princesses don't make friends at the office, she reminded herself. There were few opportunities to move up the ladder at DCH and from what she could tell they didn't let people stay around too long on the bottom rung so, *sorry Jake, I'll try not to step too hard on your fingers on my way up.*

Another thing that didn't sit well with her as she thought about the meeting was the amount of attention she received from the womanizing big boss, Hamilton Dewey. Half the woman in the room undid two extra buttons on their blouses just to get noticed when he was around. Alexis would do no such thing. Quite the opposite. She would never use sex to advance in business. It was going to be her knowledge and drive that got her ahead, not her ability to give head. She would never give her father the chance to claim that her body got her a promotion. She would rather die.

Bringing thoughts back to the present, she ordered her usual chardonnay, and Trevor had his champagne as they settled into their usual Saturday evening. Dinner at some expensive, trendy restaurant, stopping at several tables to make conversation, reinforce connections for his political future, before stopping for drinks at an equally trendy bar, more connections, and superficial conversations. Before heading back to one of their homes. Tonight, it would be hers.

"I spoke with your father this afternoon," Trevor said, staring at the stem of the champagne flute as he spun it between his fingers.

"Oh?" she tensed, knowing what usually came after that preamble was something she was going to be asked to do that she didn't want to or had already refused.

"Yes. I told him I withdrew our offer on the house in Bay Shore."

"You what?"

"I decided it wasn't what we wanted, and we should wait."

"I thought it was everything you wanted. Large enough for a family. In the heart of the district you want to run for Congress in."

"It is, but I have some things to sort through at the office. Now just isn't the time."

"What things?"

"Nothing for you to worry about."

Instinctually, she wanted to confront him for dismissing her concerns and making unilateral decisions about their future without consulting her, but she couldn't deny she was relieved to be off the hook for a multimillion-dollar home in a pretentious neighborhood she would have hated. She could swallow her principals and count it as a win.

Her mind meandered back to the memo and the work that was seriously overwhelming her. In her previous job, she had walked in on day one
and made a difference. She was made associate director within a month of
arriving, Executive Direct a year after that, and that was because she knew
her stuff. It was natural to her because even before she had her law degree;
she knew the law around woman's issues; she had been involved since she
was a teenager. Corporate and international law were new to her. Not the
concept, but the practice and practical application. She had a long way to
go to feel competent and yesterday's meeting and Jake Douglas's memo had
done nothing but prove to her just how far she had to go if things were
going to go as she planned. Everything he had written was spot on and,
more than that, everything he had written she should have already known.
He had saved her ass from certain failure. If he'd chosen to, he could have
made her look like a fool in that meeting, and yet he'd privately shown her
where she was missing things. It would have been so much better for his
career if he had. Jake was a different kind of man, she thought. Different
from most everyone at DCH. She appreciated it, but that wasn't going to
stop her from stepping over him when the time came.

"What do you think?" Alexis was brought back to the table by Trevor's
question.

"Hmm, what?" she answered, trying desperately to search her mind for
what he had been saying.

"It's bad enough that you spend most of your Saturday at the office,
couldn't you at least pay attention to me when I'm right here in front of
you?" Trevor's voice was cold and a little louder than she was comfortable
with in a public place.

"I'm sorry. I've got a lot on my mind right now. You know I'm under a
lot of pressure at work." Her tone was clipped and sharp, but barely above
a whisper. She would not allow herself to lose control and be the object of
public scrutiny. He could screw up his own political prospects by making a
public scene. His political failure wouldn't be on her conscience.

"I realize you have a lot of things on your mind. It would, however, be a
delightful change of pace if I were one of them."

Alexis glared at him and anyone looking at them could have seen the
shards that were stabbing at him from her icy blue eyes. She was usually
very guarded with her expressions in public, both for her own sense of
dignity and his perfect public persona. In that moment, however, she didn't
care who saw their exchange. She was nearing the end of her patience with
his playing the victim. She was tired of his constant whining about not

being first or her list of priorities. A part of her was feeling like this… like he was not worth the effort. Those feelings were reined in and shoved away as soon as they appeared. Christmas was coming. She loved Christmas, the decorations, the smells, that most people were nicer to each other. She just wanted to enjoy the season.

She took a breath and relaxed, softening her features and her tone as quickly as they had hardened before. "I am sorry. What were you saying?"

"I said that I don't feel we should bother with the time and expense of Christmas decorations at our places. Christmas Eve, we'll be at my mother's and then we're going to your grandfather's, on Christmas Day. You're never home except to sleep, so it's just a waste of time and effort."

"I don't think it's a waste of time, Trevor. I love the way a tree makes the house smell. And all the decorations make me happy."

Trevor opened his mouth to speak, but no sound came out. He let out a breath, apparently thinking better of what he was going to say, probably dig about her never being happy about anything and instead said, "I won't be putting anything up at my place and we'll end up there Christmas Eve after my mother's, in Brookville. It only makes sense not to traipse back into the city. If you feel the need to put up a tree that will never have presents under it, feel free. Just don't expect help from me."

Her shoulders sagged, and she looked down at the glass of wine in front of her. She could picture the tree in her mind. It filled her big bow window, lights twinkling, the warmth of a fire in her fireplace heating her face and causing the smell of fir to rise and swirl around the room, perhaps reaching as far as her master suite on the third floor. She could drift off to sleep, dreaming of the excitement she used to feel as a child. How she had looked forward to each day as a novel experience, a joy to behold, but now she wondered just where that joy had faded to and was this what there was to her life? A constant struggle to move ahead, find validation in achievements instead of joy in simple homey things. Of Christmas Eves to come with Trevor and whether they would just not 'bother' celebrating the holiday in their own home because they would be somewhere else, living for someone else, something else, something that they valued more than each other.

She was brought back from her thoughtful journey once more. This time by the appearance at the table of one of Trevor's many political contacts. At least she thought that was who it was. It could have been someone he knew though his family's business, but it was all the same. Time for her to snap out of it and put on the show.

Dinner came, and the conversation ended. A similar conversation followed after dinner and then a dozen more at the expensive cocktail bar they went to after. Somehow, before she realized what she was doing, she had agreed to them joining someone she didn't even know for Thanksgiving dinner for no other reason than making a show of their relationship with the right political influencers.

By the time they were walking up the steps to her brownstone, she was massaging her temple to relieve the ache that came from plastering on a smile and nodding at all the inane conversation the evening had featured. She fumbled for her keys, and she could feel, rather than see, Trevor's pursed lips and tensed jaw. They had argued countless times about him having a key. She always refused with the excuse that it wasn't even her home, it was her grandfather's, and she was just there temporarily, even though she knew it would probably be hers one day and she could give a key to whoever she wanted. It was her way of maintaining some scrap of independence. And another way of letting Trevor know she was the one in control.

Once inside, they made their way silently upstairs. There was a time that they would sit in the living room and share a glass or two of wine when they came in from an evening out. They had always been able to talk. Trevor enjoyed sharing his dreams with Alexis and she had always wanted to support his dreams. Now they existed in silence, saving conversation for when they were in public, less chance of things turning contentious that way.

Alexis pulled on her satin pajama set. She much preferred her flannel nightgown, but Trevor hated them. She could do that for him. Even though, with him lying right next to her, she still felt cold. Sliding under the duvet, she pulled it up to her chin. The chill of the late November night outside seemed to leak right into her core, and she couldn't shake it. Even when he slid in behind her, it didn't seem to matter. There was a part of her that hoped he would try something tonight if for no other reason than perhaps it would push the chill from her body. She let out an involuntary shudder as he rolled over toward her. His icy hand slid under the fabric of her top and grappled around her breast. Another shudder rolled through her body. She rolled over onto her back and gave herself to him. She was vaguely aware of lifting her hips to allow her bottoms to be removed. She could hear the tear of the foil wrapping of a condom being opened, and then his bulk was on her, his manhood invading her sex. The stubble from his beard grated against her cheek as she stared up at the gray shadows crawling across the ceiling. Robotically, she put her hands on his shoulders and sighed. She shuddered again. She was cold, very cold. There was no warmth in the room.

Chapter 5

Alexis

The first Friday in December was the date for the annual holiday party at Dewey, Carson, and Howe. As with most companies, there were standard policies and procedures, the ones found in black and white, neatly laid out in the Employee Handbook. Then were those that were not written but were every bit as, if not more, detrimental to one's career when broken or ignored. Near the top of the top ten unwritten rules at DCH was that one did not miss corporate functions, especially the company Christmas party.

Jake and Alexis left their offices in Siberia at the same time. The coincidence of their simultaneous departure forced them to make small talk as they made their way down the long corridor that led to the balcony overlooking the cavernous atrium lobby. To her, Jake seemed natural and at ease with making small talk.

She was used to small talk, too. It's what she and Trevor did; with each other and with all of Trevor's contacts, but it was always a chore for her. The further they walked, the more the tension in her shoulders eased and she could feel her face relaxing into a comfortable smile. Just before they reached the top of the stairs, a thought crossed her mind that the conversation she was having with Jake was much more enjoyable than any she had with Trevor over the past few months. "Stop it," she admonished herself.

"What was that?" Jake asked.

"Oh God," she felt the heat rising on her face, realizing she'd actually allowed her internal monolog to escape, "nothing," she stammered out. "Truthfully, I didn't realize I was speaking out loud. Too much time alone these days. I guess I've started talking to myself."

Jake smiled and placed his hand softly on her shoulder. "I think this job will do that to you. I do it all the time."

She smiled back, the flush deepening on her cheeks. She felt an odd sort of zing when he touched her. A foreign feeling yet vaguely familiar, like something from long, long ago that had been mostly forgotten.

They descended the palatial stairs to the main lobby where the festivities were already underway. Neither of them had the time to go, but rules were rules and career suicide was not in their plans.

A festive crowd of DCH associates packed the lobby. Most of them were more than taking advantage of the open bar and buffet. The air smelled of roast beef, horseradish but, mostly, of alcohol. "It appears we are arriving fashionably late," Jake added to the idle conversation they had been having. Alexis managed a polite smile and a nod, and pushed back a niggling in the back of her mind that she felt very much like a part of a couple with him. It wasn't at all an unpleasant feeling. Hopefully, his apparent understanding of her did not extend to the ability to read her mind.

At the bottom of the stairs, they offered polite wishes for a good time. That was the most amiable and extensive conversation they had managed in the past six months. As much as she wanted to view him as an adversary in a high stakes game of king, or queen, of the hill, it was hard not to like him. Having a friend at work was the thing she missed the most. She still talked to Tiana regularly, but it wasn't the same. She could talk to the woman about anything except DCH and DCH was the one thing she needed to talk about.

Alexis weaved her way through the sea of coworkers until she reached the other members of her pod. Andre was in the middle of a conversation with Dewey as she approached. Moving to avoid them, Andre stopped her, reaching out for her arm, tugging her in their direction. She was uncomfortable with the physical contact from her boss and even more disconcerted by the look she got from Dewey. A cocked eyebrow and a smirk which suggested he thought Andre was touching more than just her arm.

She cleared her throat, looking pointedly down at Andre's hand still clutching her forearm. "Is there something you need me for, Andre?" she asked with a little more attitude than was probably advisable in front of Hamilton Dewey.

Andre squeezed her arm tighter before releasing it. "Not at all. But you do need us, and I thought you would welcome the opportunity to join our conversation. Are we keeping you from something or someone else?"

"Not at all," she recovered her tone and smiled, hoping to cover the awkward exchange. "What were you discussing?"

"That we found it very interesting that you revised your position on the Mexico option for our Asia business," Dewey answered in a tone that made her think he wasn't pleased with her change of direction.

"I simply reviewed additional data that suggested Mexico would likely be an unnecessary expense for our clients affecting their bottom line."

"We also have interests in Mexico and it's also our job to see that they make money." Andre tilted his head and smiled. "See the entire picture Alexis, we can make money on both sides of that deal and that is our bottom line."

The vibration of her phone in her blazer pocket distracted her from her inclination to contradict Andre on the obvious endorsement of a strategy that was blatantly a conflict of interest.

"Do you need to get that?" Andre asked, though his tone suggested he didn't need an answer.

"It's just a text. I'm sure it can wait."

"No need," Dewey interjected. "I know how impatient you women are about texting. Go ahead and enjoy the party. We can continue this conversation another time."

She realized she was being dismissed, so she smiled and nodded. "Thank you." She turned and stepped toward a waiting tray of champagne. It wasn't her favorite, but she wanted a drink of something after that encounter, and it was close. Tipping the glass back and downing it in a single gulp, she returned the empty to the tray. Grabbing another glass, she pulled her phone from her pocket.

She hoped maybe Tiana had found a sitter after all. They were going to meet in town for drinks after Alexis was done with the party, but she hadn't been able to find anyone to watch the kids. Her brow lifted when she saw the text was from Trevor.

Her brows lifted further as she read on, eyes widening with every word. She swallowed back the second glass of champagne and reread what was on the screen in front of her.

"Mother fucker," she grumbled as she turned and paced toward the stairs up to the mezzanine level. Pressing the send icon next to Trevor's name, she gritted her teeth, and she climbed the steps waiting for his answer. Four rings and voicemail. She hung up and redialed only to get the same result.

Jake

The party was still going strong an hour later when Jake noticed Alexis walking up the stairs, talking on her phone. She dropped it from her ear, walked onto the second-floor balcony and then texted. Though she wasn't the only employee milling about on the balcony, she was conspicuous, at least to him. She wasn't wearing her usual unemotional, professional exterior; she seemed to him to be unhappy, mad, hurt or some combination of all the above.

There was something about Alexis that intrigued him, though he couldn't say what it was. It certainly wasn't because of the way she dressed. She dressed not to be noticed; always very professional, unlike some other women in the office who did their best to highlight their 'assets', she camouflaged her physique completely. The only thing he could say for certain about her was that she had long blonde hair and piercing blue eyes. Eyes that drew you into them and captured you there, holding you prisoner until they were ready to let you go.

She made another call, which was apparently not answered. He realized it could have also been conspicuous to people that controlled her future. Less than total focus to DCH 'business' while at the office was the first corporate carnal sin and her concerns appeared personal. Not his problem, probably to his benefit given the competitive nature of their relationship, but for reasons that escaped him, he was concerned.

If he was being honest with himself, he would have to admit that Alexis was interesting to him more than just professionally. More than she should be. His pod members noted he had mentally left the conversation and drew him back in. Fortunately, he thought, no one had noticed he was staring at Alexis. Office relationships were the second carnal sin at DCH.

After another forty-five minutes of mingling, idle chitchat and nursing the same glass of scotch, he figured he had made his presence sufficiently known and made his excuses. Rob tried to get him to stay longer, but Jake reminded him of the deadline he was facing and said he had a brief he'd like to finish before he left tonight. Rob relented but handed him a bottle of wine from the end of the bar to enjoy once he got home "and that's a directive from your supervisor," Rob laughed finding himself much more amusing than Jake did, but then, Jake was sober.

Sometimes Rob still acted like that popular college senior who had taken the awkward freshman that Jake was and took him under his wing. He often wondered if he would have made it through college without Rob's influence and friendship; especially after what his father had done. Refusing to go down that rabbit hole of anger and regret, Jake smiled and thanked him for the wine, put the bottle in his jacket pocket, then made his way back up the stairs to the third-floor Siberian exile that was his office.

He walked down the corridor; the party noises faded to a more distant din with each step. As he approached his office, he could see a stream of light coming from Alexis' office. When he reached her door, she had her head in her hands, face down on her desk.

He knocked on the door, but she either did not hear him or was ignoring it. Considering for a moment just walking away and giving her space, he gave in to an unexplainable urge he had to be closer to her. "Is there something wrong?"

Her head snapped up from her desk and she inhaled sharply. Recognition washing over her face, she thumbed at the corners of her eyes before exhaling and placing her hand over her chest. "What do you need?" She snapped as Jake watched her subtly try to wipe away tears.

"I'm sorry. I didn't mean to startle you. I saw you with your head down and thought maybe …," he cut himself short when he felt he was rambling. Motioning over his shoulder with his thumb, "your door was open." The emotion that radiated from her face made his stomach twist into an empathetic knowledge. She was generally, perhaps overly, professional. Cold, direct, all business, unflappable. This was the first time he had ever seen her as an emotional being. "What can I do to help?"

"Oh… no… nothing… I'm fine. I apologize. I didn't mean to snap. You surprised me. I didn't hear you come in. I thought I had closed my door."

"Hey, don't worry about it." He turned to leave, but hesitated. "Is there an emergency, something with a family member?" He guessed, but she was so composed and unemotional. Whatever it was, it must be hitting close to the heart.

"No, not really. Honestly, I'll be fine, I'm just tired I guess, but I'm sure you know that feeling," she offered with a weak smile that seemed unnaturally forced to him.

"I do." His instincts seemed to be having a tug o' war about whether to stay or go. Give the young woman her space. Tears were in her eyes and as hard as she was trying to hold them back, one or two were still running down her cheek. "I also know that talking to someone is usually the best way to get through something tough. Just the act of speaking it out loud has healing properties." He felt the need to validate that statement. It wasn't the first time he felt that way around her, and he wondered why. He didn't feel that need around anyone else; certainly not here. "I was going to be a professional counselor until I realized there was absolutely no money in it."

She smiled again, just slightly, for just a second, but this one seemed a little more natural. "Here, give me your coffee cup." Her brow creased but didn't question why, sliding it in his direction. Producing the bottle of wine from his jacket pocket, *thank God it was a screw cap. DCH would never spend money on the good stuff for its employees.* He opened it and poured some into her cup. She stared at him, raising an eyebrow. He was ready to defend his possession of wine with the truth, but opted for humor instead. "I used to be a Boy Scout. Always be prepared."

Shaking her head, her smile widened as she picked up the cup. "Thank you," tipping the cup in his direction. "It's kind of you to offer to listen, but I don't want to burden you with my life." She took a long drink from her cup.

With a shrug, he relaxed against the door frame. "I offered, so I assume full liability. And I doubt your life is any worse than mine. We're both here after eight on a Friday night and apparently with no urgent need to get anywhere else."

She took another gulp of wine. He watched as her eyes raked over his body, then held his gaze for several beats. He could see in her eyes the moment she decided to trust him and could tell it wasn't a simple choice for her. "Well, to state the facts succinctly, my fiancé just broke it off with me… by text. I have called him five times. The last three went straight to voicemail. It appears the bastard doesn't even have the balls to speak to me on the phone. Four years together and he can't manage the decency to tell me face to face."

That was not what Jake had expected. "Damn," running his hand through his hair, "I'm sorry. I mean, I think a text message break up is spineless, but four years and engaged doesn't show much character."

Her brows knit together and there was an icy coldness in the deep blue stare that met his. For a moment he thought he might have been a little too harsh, but her forehead softened, and the chill seemed to fade from her eyes. "I can't tell if I'm hurt or angry, honestly." She exhaled slowly. "He had the gall to ask for his ring back. He claims it's a family heirloom. That's the first I've heard that, and he would have made a big deal about it, especially to my father."

"Hurt and angry, seems like a pretty normal way to feel to me. Personally, I'd sell the ring, go on vacation." Jake grinned and looked over his shoulder like he could see it in his mind. "Then I'd send him pictures detailing how much fun you had without him. If I was feeling charitable, I'd give him the name of the shop I pawned it at." She gave him a wry smile, as though she was contemplating the merits of the idea. "It seems like this was a complete surprise to you."

"You could say that; last weekend we were talking about plans for Christmas. I'm not going to lie and say we haven't had our rough patches and obviously the hours I work get in the way, but he never seemed to care much."

"Not to be nosey, but did he give you a reason?"

She gave him a wave of the hand, showing that it was all fair game at this point. "He didn't. All he said is this isn't going to work. He's sorry, but he's moving on. All the best. He dropped off my stuff from his place, took his from mine and left the key under the doormat." She hesitated for a moment, took a swig of wine, poured herself some more, and continued. "I guess that's why I had to leave it there this morning. He was always pissed I wouldn't give him one of his own. He made a point of saying I shouldn't worry about getting his key to him. He changed the locks. Really? Did he think I was going to trash the place?" She drained what was left in her cup and set it down with a thud. "He's such a prick!" She grabbed the bottle and helped herself to a fill-up.

Jake rubbed his chin and then ran his fingers through his hair. "He changed the locks?" He repeated what she just told him, staring over her shoulder at the wall. "He planned this for a while." Meeting her eyes again, "he knew you had the office party today?"

"Yes, but it wouldn't really matter. We don't usually see each other Friday nights." She settled back into her chair, her shoulders loosening. Jake got the sense that the wine and conversation were helping. "You don't have to stay here and talk. I'm sure you have a significant other to get home to."

"I know I don't have to stay, but I wouldn't feel like much of a human being if I just left you here alone."

"Thanks. Guess I could use another human at this point." She laughed.

"Needing a human is funny?"

"No, I was just thinking I don't even have a damn cat to go home to."

Jake smiled. He understood the inference. "Honestly, I would say that was rather fortunate. I'm not a big fan of cats, probably because they make me sneeze."

She continued to drink and talk; he continued to sip and listen. They had been talking for just over an hour when she poured out the last of the bottle into her cup. "I'm a little embarrassed to ask, but would you mind sneaking back down to the party and swiping us another bottle?"

"I don't mind, but the party was breaking up when I came up. Every-thing is probably packed up by now."

"I guess I'll just have to hurry home. Plenty there," she smiled.

"Grab your coat and I'll drive you."

"Thanks, but I'm good."

"I'm sure you are." He smiled. "But you've had basically a full bottle of wine, plus whatever you had before leaving the party and a DUI would not make your night any better."

"It wouldn't make yours better either, and we split the bottle. You prob-ably shouldn't be driving either."

Jake shook his head, "this is the only cup I've had and there's still half left. I also had food, and you left the party before you had anything to eat."

"I call bullshit," she said loudly enough to make Jake jerk in surprise. "You've been drinking. I always make sure I'm not the only one drinking."

"On my honor. My dad is an alcoholic, and a mean one. I'm very con-scious of how much I drink." He wasn't sure why he volunteered that. "Sorry, that was probably a bit of an over-share."

She smiled. "I think that if anyone has over shared, it has been me. I apologize if I hit a nerve."

"No nerves hit. Making a drink last has helped me avoid some dumb mistakes through the years. Which is good because I've made a lot of dumb mistakes, so I just think how much worse it could be." She laughed, and it surprised him how much he enjoyed the sound of it. He couldn't remember if he'd ever heard it before in the over six months they'd worked together.

Jake raised a brow, clearly questioning if the laugh she gifted him meant she was giving in to his offer of a ride. Her gaze matched his as silence spread between them. He could almost see her mind debating whether to give in to him. "Fine. And you're right, I haven't eaten, so I'm ordering us pizza on the way."

Chapter 6

Alexis

They pulled up to her four-story brownstone on a tree-lined street in the Carnegie Hill section of the city. Jake laughed as he shut off the ignition and opened his door.

"What's so funny?" she asked, confused because the only thing they had been talking about was her giving him the directions.

"Nothing, I guess," he said with a shrug. "I was just thinking I didn't have to worry about anyone stealing my car in this neighborhood."

She turned to face him, head tilting in question. "Probably not. It's a pretty safe neighborhood."

He let out another chuckle. "I'm sure it is, but with all the Mercedes, Audis, and Jaguars," he said, jerking his thumb toward the other parked cars along the street, "no one is going to be interested in my bucket of bolts."

She began to speak, but it seemed to her that before she had the chance to utter a sound, he was out his door and holding hers open for her. Holding back her instinct to chide him for assuming she was too delicate to open her own car door, she appreciated the gesture and couldn't recall a single time that Trevor had even tried. She smiled up at him and she noticed the color rise in his cheeks as he dropped his eyes. She could feel those same eyes rake up and down her toned calves as they stretched to the sidewalk as she exited the car.

"Jake Douglas, were you just checking out my legs?" Alexis asked, mock horror in her tone.

"I would never do that," he replied, meeting her eyes and flashing her a smile that admitted to her he was, indeed, checking her out.

The flutter his smile caused in her tummy was alarming. She hadn't felt a flutter like that in a long time. Not since she was eighteen and that hadn't worked out well at all.

Reaching the top of the steps, she fished in her pocket and produced a keyring, which she promptly dropped. "Ow!" she moaned at the sharp pain in her forehead as their heads hit together as they both reached for the keys.

Jake picked up the keys. "Are you okay?" As she grunted an 'I'm fine' and rubbed her forehead where they connected, he pushed the heavy oak door open and steered them into the foyer. Tossing her keys on a table, Jake looked around. "Wow, nice place."

"Hmm? Oh, it's my grandfather's. He's letting me use it."

"That's great. Beats the hell out of my tiny apartment, that's for sure."

"Thanks," she said, slipping out of her coat and hanging it on the rack next to the door. "It always feels like home. I have a lot of fond childhood memories in this place, visiting my grandparents." She breathed out a contented sigh as she moved toward the French doors that led into the living room. She fumbled for the light switch until ultimately prevailing to reveal a large fireplace with a marble mantle that dominated the opposite wall. A large, deep red oriental rug covered a beautiful wide oak floor. To the left, arranged in the bow window, were two overstuffed armchairs in a tweed upholstery and to the right was a large sofa, solid tan, coordinating with the chairs. Further to the right of the sofa was another set of French doors that led to a formal dining room. The place oozed of refined elegance and old money.

The only thing that did not fit in the impeccably neat space was a pile of clothes and odds and ends heaped onto and in front of the chairs. On the glass topped coffee table in front of the sofa was a note.

"Mother fucker!" Alexis bellowed, irritation replacing her wistful tone of moments before. "He couldn't even have the decency to carry it upstairs to my bedroom! He just dumped it and ran." She stamped her foot in exclamation. "Coward. He's a fucking coward! You know something Jake, what you said before, me being better off without him? I was a little upset, but you are absofuckinglutely right. I am way better off without him. Oh, by the way, I was also wrong about not knowing whether I was hurt or angry… I am irate!"

Jake didn't have to look at her to tell that irate was a fitting description. Her jaw clenched, and her hands were curled up in fists so tight that she could feel her fingernails leaving marks in her palms. She turned and leveled a glare in his direction. "More. Wine. Now."

She saw his eyes widen at her tone and was glad he had the intelligence not to tell her she didn't need anything more to drink. "Perhaps you can point me in the wine's direction," he croaked, "I can grab it while you find something to hit or break that isn't me?"

The sound of his voice washed over her like a warm breeze slowing her pulse. Only her grandmother had ever had that effect on her. She was about to ask what he was waiting for until she realized the poor man had never been in her home before. "There's a wine rack on the counter between the kitchen and dining room." She motioned over his shoulder as an afterthought, realizing that he didn't know where either room was. "Red please, no sense switching horses now."

Jake turned and made his way in the direction she had pointed.

She turned and took in the pile of clothes and accessories heaped on the chairs and slumped down on the couch. Reaching up, she unpinned the customary tight bun she wore to the office, letting her flaxen locks spill over her shoulders. She combed out her hair with her fingers, feeling a little of the tightness leave her body. She shook her head at the crumpled pile of clothing and sighed. That was her life. One big mess. She felt like she had it all figured out, and in one fell swoop, it had all gone to hell.

Jake reappeared handing her a glass before opening the bottle of Cabernet and filling it halfway. After pouring his own, he sat next to her on the couch and touched his glass to hers. "To new friends."

"To friends," she answered. And they both took a good long drink.

Alexis sunk further into the cushions and leaned against him with a sigh. "This has not been the best of days." *But somehow it seems better with you here,* she thought and wondered why, when every time she'd ever faced a challenge before, she'd only wanted to be on her own.

Jake

J ake had to fight the urge to wrap his arm around her, kiss the top of her head and tell her that tomorrow would be better. Instead, he struggled to figure out what exactly to do with his arm now trapped at his side by her warm, soft body. This close, he could smell the flowery scent of her shampoo and something else he couldn't name other than to know that it was distinctly her. Despite his knowledge that anything between them was a horrible idea, his body was responding to her proximity in ways that made it quite uncomfortable for him. The doorbell rang, much to Jake's relief. Alexis tried to get to answer the door but quickly sunk back down, sloshing her wine on her white blouse as she did.

"I've got it," Jake said as he rose and walked to the door.

When he returned, she was not where he left her. "Alexis?"

"In the kitchen," she called. Scooping up his glass, he walked to the back of the house. He found her with her back to him, trying to wash the wine stain off the front of the blouse. "Crap. This will never come out." Before he could turn away, she had her top off and tossed it in the wastebasket, leaving her in nothing but a lacey bra that did little to disguise her generous form.

Despite knowing better, Jake was mesmerized by what was in front of him. He knew he shouldn't be gawking and should turn away, but he found he was physically incapable. He knew Alexis was a very attractive and shapely woman, but it was never on display at the office. One could only assume. Now, here, in the kitchen, there was no denying her assets. No denying she had what Jake was convinced were the most perfect breasts he had ever seen. That anyone had ever seen. Well, mostly seen.

Just like he always did around women, he froze. He couldn't pull his eyes away and he was locked in place. His posture wasn't the only thing rigid, and if he thought he'd been flummoxed when she had leaned against him on the couch, well, that was nothing compared to now.

"Oh. I didn't realize you followed me out here." She brought her hand up to cover her chest, but it was nowhere close to effective.

Pulling his eyes up to meet hers, "I. Um. I. Um. Sorry. You said you were in the kitchen. I thought that meant you wanted to eat out here."

"Nope" she smiled, popping the p, which prompted a giggle to slip out of her usually straitlaced lips. "Why don't you bring that back out to the living room and I'll find a dry top to put on."

"Perfect." Jake spun on his heals and left the kitchen like he was running from a pending explosion which in some respects he was. As he was setting the pizza down on the coffee table, a loud crash came from the kitchen. Before he could turn to head back, he heard a curse and an 'I'm okay' and another giggle.

Relaxed at home, Alexis was entertaining, he decided. She reappeared moments later wearing a well-worn, oversized Yale sweatshirt. "Sorry about that. I knocked over the mop and broom and maybe some other things too. I don't know why I'm so clumsy tonight."

Jake bit back hinting that maybe she'd had too much to drink, as she tipped back another big gulp of wine.

They dug into the pizza, neither of them realizing just how hungry they were until they started into it. Mostly they ate in companionable silence aside from the moans of delight Alexis uttered at the cheesy deliciousness. He could feel her glances in his direction whenever she thought he wasn't paying attention. This was not the serious, businesslike woman he knew. This Alexis sitting in front of him seemed quite different. Funny, relaxed, warm. That was it. She seemed warm, like someone that you could get close to without risking freezer burn.

They continued to talk and laugh long after the pizza was devoured. Alexis leaned forward. Jake tensed. He was sure she was about to kiss him when she reached up and undid his tie instead. "I'm sorry. This is just bothering me way too much at this point." She dropped the tie on the floor and then pushed his jacket off his shoulders. Then she unbuttoned the top two buttons on his shirt, and he wasn't sure she was going to stop there, her slender fingers lingering on the third before she pulled back her hands.

Their eyes locked, and they both inched forward. Her tongue traced her bottom lip and just before their lips met, she backed away and took a drink of her wine before topping off her glass.

On a sigh, he leaned back and stretched out his arms across the back of the couch. He noticed the graceful lines of her neck as she swallowed. He realized he had never wanted to kiss a woman as much as he had in that moment before she backed away. It would have been a colossal mistake on so many levels. Workplace romance was strictly forbidden at DCH. She was probably an emotional wreck about her engagement breaking off, even if she seemed to hide it well. She has been drinking and not in the best place to make good decisions and he shouldn't take advantage of someone. He never had and he wouldn't start now. But lord, how he wanted her. Just once. Somehow, he knew it would never stop there.

She leaned back and nestled into his side. He forced himself to relax as she settled in closer. The silence stretched on, and he couldn't help wondering what was going through her mind. Her breathing slowed, and he wasn't sure she hadn't drifted off to sleep.

"Thank you."

"You're welcome. But you picked the place. I just paid the bill."

She slapped his leg. "Not for the pizza, silly. For being here."

"It's what any friend would do." On instinct, he leaned forward and kissed the top of her head and froze there when he realized what he had done. She let out a heavy sigh that he hoped wasn't regret. "What was that for?"

She shrugged her shoulders but didn't speak right away. "I don't have many friends that would have been here for me tonight the way you have." She took a sip of her wine. "Pretty pathetic, huh?"

"If it makes you feel any better, I could say the same thing." He blew out a long, ragged breath. "It's an occupational hazard when you put in as many hours as we do. People get sick of waiting around for you to notice them. Maybe that's what happened with you and Trevor."

"Maybe. But he knew the score before we ever started dating. I'm different from you, Jake. You have no idea how different I am."

He didn't know how to respond. He knew they were different, but he didn't think they were that far apart. They both put their careers first, and they were both driven to succeed. Even if they did it in different ways, he was sure they wanted the same thing. Respect.

She had lit the fireplace when they ate, and they both got lost watching the flames. He enjoyed the silence, and he enjoyed the feel of Alexis next to him on the couch. Tonight was likely just a onetime thing. Monday things would be back to the way they had always been between them, cool, professional. It would be best to make his excuses and be on his way, but it was too hard to walk away from this. Too hard when he knew how good it felt to have her close to him.

The glass tipping in her hand told the story of her falling asleep, and he caught it just before it spilled over them both. She stirred, but quickly settled back into him after he set her glass on the coffee table. It tempted him to let her fall back to sleep. "Alexis, come on. I think it's time for you to go to bed."

"Mmm." she cooed, and she turned closer to him, resting her head on his chest.

It felt so natural. She fit him perfectly and for the flash of a moment; he allowed himself to wonder if they would fit in other ways, too. His respect for her was so strong that he'd never allowed himself to think of her in any way other than professionally, but here, after some wine and in the firelight, he couldn't help it. She just felt so right.

He let out a long, slow breath, knowing he had to do what he should and not what he wanted. Easing himself away from her, he stood and took her by the hands. "Come on, sleeping beauty. You should go up to bed and I need to get home."

She groaned as he pulled her off the couch, leaning into him so that he had to hold her upright. "Help me upstairs," she spoke into his chest softly enough that he wasn't sure he heard her correctly.

"What?"

"Help me upstairs," she repeated. This time tilting her head up and looking at him sleepily through her long lashes.

He swallowed thickly, desperately wanting every moment he could have with her, but knowing deep down the more time he spent with her, the harder it would be to go without her. Confusion flooded his mind at her request. Was she propositioning him? Was she just feeling unsteady from too much to drink? They were both a little buzzed from the wine, but she certainly didn't seem to be fall down drunk, he would have never let her reach that point. "Um, sure," he stammered out, wrapping an arm around her waist and turning toward the stairs.

Slowly, they made their way up two flights of stairs to the third-floor master suite. Stepping inside, she reached down and switched on a lamp on the nightstand next to the bed.

"So, this is my room," she explained as she slid around in front of him. Her fingers glided over the buttons on his shirt as she gazed up at him.

"It's nice," he replied, not sure what else to say at her obvious statement. "Well, I um, I should get going, I guess."

"No!"

Her sudden and emphatic response startling him. "No?" he repeated, his brows disappearing nearly underneath his disheveled hairline.

Worrying her bottom lip, she looked up at him from beneath long lashes that he had never noticed she had before. "Will you cuddle with me until I fall asleep?"

He wasn't certain that was a good idea. Here was a woman that had intrigued him from the first time they met six months ago. Someone that had been so cold, distant and totally unapproachable he hadn't even considered how deep his attraction was to her until tonight, when the wall of ice she surrounded herself with had melted away for a moment. There was no doubt in his mind he wanted to stay, but what would happen if he stayed? Selfishly, he craved the closeness she was offering. It had been months, more than a year, since he had been close to a woman. Nothing more than a cuddle could happen tonight, and would that really be so bad? Her eyes searched his for his answer with the longing that a child had for a long-wanted toy. And just like the sucker uncle he was, he couldn't tell her no. "Fine. Go change and I'll cuddle you until you fall asleep," he agreed with a heavy sigh. He truly hoped this wouldn't make things even more distant between them come Monday morning at the office.

The smile that spread across her face made his insides turn to goo. He felt like he owned the world because he had made her smile. And he realized in that moment he would probably do anything to make her smile again. Anything.

She disappeared into her bathroom and returned moments later wearing a long flannel nightgown. It wasn't what he expected to see, but it seemed to fit her perfectly now that he had a glimpse of the real Alexis who lived behind the wall of ice.

She hesitated for a moment as she stepped back into the room. Her ice-blue eyes raked over his body, deepening to the darkness of a rare sapphire as they did. He wasn't sure his affection starved brain wasn't imagining it all until, instead of crawling into her bed like he expected, she crossed the room to stand in front of him. Her flannel clad chest rising and falling hypnotically against his as she inched next to him. Warm palms seared into his chest as she placed them flat and peered up into his eyes. "Will you kiss me, Jake?" she asked in a breathy whisper.

His tentative grasp on restraint was weakening by the second. He knew he shouldn't because he doubted he'd have an ounce of control left the second he tasted her, but he bent forward anyway. His fingers snaked through her silken tresses, cupping her head as his lips met hers. Warm, soft, pliant, she was more than he dreamed she'd be. He tentatively flicked his tongue between her lips, and she answered with the same. She tasted of wine and pizza and a sweetness that was all her. The kissed deepened, and she rose more to meet him, pressing her chest against his shirt and he felt the current buzz between them. Her fingers digging into his biceps were the only thing grounding him, keeping him from losing himself completely.

With a gasp, and all the control he could muster, he pulled back from the kiss of a lifetime, wide-eyed and panting. Alexis looked back at him, lips swollen and deep pink from the impact of his mouth on hers.

"Wow."

"I'm not sure wow is enough," she said, more to herself than him. She inched back closer to him. He hesitated for a moment before stepping aside and pulling back the covers on her bed.

"Crawl in before I lose all control."

"But I want you to lose control," placing a kiss on his shoulder and wrapping an arm around his waist so that her body pressed against his again. His body went rigid at her touch, fighting every primal urge that coursed through his blood. He couldn't take advantage of anyone who was vulnerable and live with himself. Even more so if she was drunk, though she didn't seem to be.

As if she could read his thoughts, and maybe she could, he didn't know anything for certain at the moment. She let him go with a sigh. "Okay, but you might be missing your only chance." She slid under the covers and then, after he had pulled them up, she patted where his place should be in invitation.

He toed off his shoes and crawled onto the bed on top of the covers. He kissed the top of her head and opened his arms so she could snuggle into him. "You're far too special a woman to only have one night with. I'd rather have none than settle for only once."

She rubbed her hand over his chest and looked up at him. "That might be the nicest thing anyone has ever said to me."

He gave her another kiss on the top of her head and indulged himself in breathing her in one more time. If this was his only chance with her, he wanted to remember it well. "Sweet dreams, Alexis."

"Mm." Moments later, her breath slowed and evened out. Her body relaxed into a boneless slumber. He shifted to get out of bed, but she stirred, and he figured he could wait a little longer until she was sound asleep. He wasn't ready to let her out of his arms, anyway. A few minutes more would be okay. It might be his last chance to hold her, and what was the actual harm in making this last?

Chapter 7

Alexis

The dim light of early morning assaulted the slits in her sleep encrusted eyes. She forced them shut again, but there was still far too much brightness on the other side of her lids. She couldn't remember crawling into bed last night, which might explain why she had forgotten her usual routine of making sure her blackout drapes covered the windows. Her tongue stuck to the roof of her mouth, which felt like a battalion of dusty bare feet had marched through it. The dull ache in her head was all she needed to remind herself that she might have overdone it with the wine.

Rising further into the realm of consciousness, she noticed other details. First, she realized she was naked, except for a very tiny thong, and she remembered putting on a nightgown. Second, she was not alone. A large hand loosely cupped her left breast. Her eyes popped open, her heart thumped wildly inside her chest, which she tried to steady with a slow, deep breath.

Slowly, she inched out from underneath the hand in question. A deep sleepy moan answered her movement, and the large hand pulled her closer, pressing her into an even larger, solid mass of a human that was far too masculine to be Trevor. They were spooning, again, and she did not do cuddles, except that she heard her own voice asking to be cuddled until she fell asleep. Which couldn't possibly be right. But worse than that, it unnerved her how good it felt to be held against this solid body.

She was never fully functional until after her second cup of coffee and the fog lingering from last night's wine wasn't helping. She should rip herself out from the arms that held her, but that would likely wake the sleeping beast and necessitate an awkward conversation that led to him getting the hell out of her bed and out of her house as quickly as possible.

Focus, Alexis, focus. Slowly, details broke through the clouds in her hazy memory. Jake Douglas walking with her through the halls to the Christmas party. The text from Trevor ending their engagement. Being shocked, hurt, angry, and knowing the shitstorm this was going to raise with her father. Swilling wine from a coffee mug and admiring the genuine smile of the man sitting across from her with his feet up on her desk. Him driving her home and sharing maybe the most delicious pizza she ever had.

Please let him still be asleep. She tried peeking over her shoulder, but all she could see was the sleeve of his blue dress shirt. Slowly, she untangled herself from him and slid toward the edge of the bed. Her first chore was to get out of reach of Jake the mistake and any thoughts he might have about a second round. She wasn't a morning sex person, but more so when she couldn't even remember if she'd enjoyed round one. *Crap, I wasn't that drunk, was I?* Second, get dressed without waking him and third, get him out the door as quickly as possible and start pretending this never happened. She was finally rid of Trevor and despite the hassle she would face with her father; she was not about to go down the relationship road again anytime soon, which meant getting Jake out the door fast.

Carefully reaching the edge of the bed, she calculated the odds of streaking across the bedroom and into her walk-in closet without Jake getting a glimpse of her nearly naked body. Her feet reached for the floor, and she turned to see her unwanted guest.

The moment her mind registered Jake's eyes fluttering open, she squealed in horror and ripped the duvet from the bed to cover herself. The combination of being awakened by a shrieking woman and the momentum from the duvet being pulled out from under him sent Jake sprawling to the floor. He scrambled to his feet, eyes wide and hair standing up straight. "What's wrong?"

"What are you doing in my bed?"

Alexis held the duvet close to her chest, unaware that her virtually bare bottom was still visible to Jake in the reflection from the mirror over her dresser on the far wall. "You asked me to stay," Jake replied, staring over her shoulder instead of her eyes.

"I what?"

"You asked me to stay. You wanted me to cuddle you." Jake raked his hands through his hair. Alexis noticed he looked like he needed a double expresso shot as much as she did.

"I did not." Realizing that he wasn't looking at her, she looked over her shoulder. She quickly muscled the duvet to wrap around her, trying to cover her bare ass.

"You did."

"I haven't asked anyone to cuddle me since I was twelve." Her brows knit together, and she pointed an accusatory finger, but stopped as the duvet slipped down. "I was drunk, and you took advantage of me. Having sex with a drunk woman is a nasty thing to do, Jake Douglas. I didn't mark you for a scum bucket." Even as she spoke, the realization that she had, indeed, asked him to stay caused her already erratic heartbeat to quicken.

Alexis watched as the color drained from his face, a panicked expression replacing his initial confusion. "You asked to be cuddled, and that's what we did. You didn't seem drunk, buzzed yes, memory cleansing drunk no. And we most definitely didn't have sex."

"Then why am I naked?"

"Then why am I still dressed?"

Alexis opened her mouth and then shut it. She wanted to come up with a reason he was still wearing yesterday's suit pants and shirt; with the number of wrinkles there was no question had slept in them, but she couldn't. "Why am I naked?"

"I don't know. You had a red flannel nightgown on when you crawled into bed."

"I don't sleep naked. Ever," she barked, realizing there was a fluffy heap of red checked fabric underneath her feet which triggered a vague memory she quickly pushed down, not wanting to concede the high ground.

"Well, apparently you decided to at some point last night, and it would have been a shit ton more comfortable for me right now if you hadn't." She watched him begin to pace, scrubbing his hands over his closely trimmed beard. "And just for the record, Alexis, you are the one who asked to kiss me. You are the one who hinted at wanting more. This," he huffed, wildly gesturing between them, "is exactly what I did not want to happen."

"Ask to kiss you?" The shrillness of her voice breaking as bits and pieces of last night came back into focus. Jake refusing to let her drive, pizza, the fireplace, and comfortable conversation. Still, cuddling was not like adult her, but something about liking the way Jake felt seemed familiar and how could it otherwise? She remembered feeling a little buzzed and asking him to help her to her room and then, *oh my fucking God, I did ask him to kiss me. No. No. Nonono. Fuck. Yes. Like the best kiss I've ever had, yes. And I wanted more. Well, obviously at some point in the night he wanted more too because now I'm naked.* "Then why are you still here? If you're so pure in your intentions, why wouldn't you just leave once you safely got me tucked into bed?"

Jake was on his hands and knees, looking for something under her bed. He poked his head up from behind the mattress. "I think you've missed your calling, Alexis. You should have become a prosecutor."

The words he was speaking were muffled like a muted trumpet as another memory filled her head; waking in the middle of the night, feeling flushed, and pulling the nightgown off before settling back against his wonderfully solid body. *I haven't done that since I was a kid with Carole.* That detail didn't keep her from doing her best to scare him away and out the door now. "Answer the damn question." She stamped her foot in frustration squarely on the buckle from yesterday's belt. "Ow. Damn it!" she yelped and dropped the duvet in favor of grabbing of her nearly impaled foot.

Recognizing she had just provided Jake with a view of her naked body, bouncing tits and all, she grabbed the duvet back to her chest. She leveled another angry glare in his direction, hoping her laser beam like stare would force him to answer to her question.

He breathed out a heavy sigh. "I intended to leave as soon as you fell asleep, but, well," he hesitated, "you felt so good in my arms I didn't want to leave, and I guess I just fell asleep too."

She stared at him for a long moment, and her jaw flexed as she chewed the inside of her cheek. He stared back, never dropping eye contact. A warmth filled her chest, and she felt her heartbeat slow for the first time since she opened her eyes and felt him next to her. He was telling her the truth.

As much as she wanted to, she couldn't deny that she had felt damn good pressed against his chest moments ago. An unfamiliar tingling coursed through her belly, unrelated to the queasiness leftover from last night's pizza and wine. Still, DCH had a firm policy about dating and even if they didn't, whatever she felt for Jake could never go farther than right here, right now. Fuck. "If anyone saw us leaving together… This could be bad, Jake." She said with a sigh as she dropped onto the side of the bed.

"No one did. We were the last one's left in the building." He smiled at her, which drew a deeper scowl in response.

"You think this is funny? We could get fired."

"No one saw us," he sighed. "Besides, I counted at least a dozen couples," he emphasized couples with air quotes, something that usually irritated the hell out of her but this morning she felt a smile tug at the corners of her mouth, "leaving the party last night before I found you distraught in your office…"

"I was not distraught," she countered defensively.

He continued like she hadn't just corrected him, "Half of DCH would be unemployed if they fired all the office hook ups."

"You said we did not hook up," her voice raising and eyes narrowing in challenge.

He laughed, shaking his head, "The point is, that even if we did, which we didn't, it wouldn't matter."

"It would certainly matter to me. I don't want anyone to think I was sleeping with you." Her voice was laced with indignation.

"Am I that much of a troll that you'd be embarrassed to be seen with me?" There was a hint of amusement in his voice.

"God no," she gasped, fighting the unexplainable urge to close the distance between them when all she'd been doing so far was making sure they were as far apart as possible. She sighed, frustrated with the odd emotions rushing through her. "You're a handsome man, and I didn't think you'd need to fish for complements." She smiled, rolling her eyes. "What I meant was I don't want anyone thinking I'm fucking my way around the office. My reputation is very important to me, and I will not have my success marred by people thinking I got to the top by getting underneath anyone."

"I promise you that thought hasn't crossed anyone's mind at DCH."

The tone of disbelief in his voice made her feel uncharacteristically defensive. She was very purposeful about avoiding any hint of the tawdry at work, but his insinuation that she was so successful that no one would ever consider her a sexual being bothered her a little. "Are you saying that I'm a troll?"

"Now who's fishing?" he laughed. "All I'm saying is that you hold people well past arm's length. You're polite to everyone, but I can't think of anyone that I've seen you interact with that I'd say, 'oh, that's Alexis' best work buddy.'"

"Are you calling me cold, Jake? Because I swear, I just heard you say you liked the feel of me in your arms." She liked the way he seemed flustered when she pushed him. Playing games and teasing wasn't really her style, but good-humored banter with Jake was exciting in more ways than one.

A frustrated groan rumbled in the back of his throat, which he tried hiding with a cough. She thought maybe it was just her wit that had him flummoxed until she realized that the duvet she was covering herself with had slipped low enough to expose the arc of the top of her nipples. She wanted more of that feeling, even though she knew she shouldn't. "How about you get dressed and I can take you somewhere for a nice greasy breakfast? Maybe food will put you in a less combative mood," he asked with a raised brow.

Alexis didn't like the way her pulse jumped at his suggestion, and she reined it quickly under control. Well, she tried. What she needed to do is end this momentary lapse in judgement, before it snowballed into a bigger lapse in judgement, and she ended up sleeping with him because she couldn't deny the way her body liked the look of morning, rumpled Jake standing on the other side of the bed or the little voice in her head that kept whispering how much fun it would be to drop the damn covers she was white-knuckling to her chest and crawl right across that enormous bed, pull him down on top of her and kiss the hell out of him.

"First off, I am not combative," though she knew she was being this way just to get him out before she did something worse than she'd already done. "Second, I just said I don't want to date anyone I work with. And third, I will not be seen having breakfast with someone who so looks like the poster boy for the walk of shame. Those are obviously yesterday's clothes," she moaned, pointing an accusatory finger in his direction.

"Fine," he sighed, reaching for her phone on the nightstand closest to him. He tossed it in her direction. "Unlock your phone, please."

"Why?" she snapped, trapping it against her duvet covered chest.

"Just do it," he huffed in a tone that hinted at the exasperation he was feeling.

She arched her brow but did as he asked before throwing the phone on the bed in front of him.

His fingers worked across her screen before setting it back on the nightstand and picking up his own. A moment later, the alert on her phone pinged with an incoming text. "There. We have each other's numbers now."

"For what?" her annoyance was evident in her tone.

"Well, for starters, I've decided that you need a friend, and that's going to be me. Second, I can call you if I'm running late when I pick you up this evening."

Her mouth dropped open, wanting to reply but unable to in her confused state.

"I have to admit that you're right. I look like yesterday's newspaper, and I wouldn't want to embarrass you." He bent down to retrieve his suit jacket from the chest at the foot of her bed. "I'll pick you up at six for dinner. That should give you enough time to recover to a semi-human state."

She ran her hand over her face, trying to digest what he said. "Did you not hear what just left my mouth?" she gritted out between her teeth as she hoisted up the duvet wrapped around her like it was the train on an elegant gown and crossed in his direction. "I will not compound last night's mistake by making an even bigger one by going out on a date with you. Christ, twenty-four hours ago I was engaged. I'm not going to start dating again. Even if I didn't work with you."

A smirk filled his face, and she could see the mischief dancing in his eyes, which only stoked up the voice in her head that urged her on to do what he was suggesting. She had just brought it to heal, too. He strode around to meet her, wrapping her in a hug and kissing her cheek. "Thanks for letting me help last night." He pulled back, grasping her shoulders, and her body reeled from the embrace and kissed her forehead before turning toward the door. "See you at six and dress casual. I'm not into fancy places, just good food, and I have the perfect place in mind."

He was out her bedroom door before the shock wore off and she scurried after him as fast as her decency would allow. "I told you I'm not going on a date with you, Jake Douglas," she yelled after him, catching sight of him already halfway down the stairs.

He stopped and looked back up at her, dimples that were just too lickable under the scruff of his morning beard. "Then don't think of it as a date. We need to talk this out or it's going to be an obviously awkward Monday at the office. You don't want rumors circulating, so we'll just hash this out over an enjoyable meal." Without looking back, he bounced down the stairs and out of sight.

"Jake," she yelled after him, but all she heard in reply was the front door closing behind him. "God," she groaned, turning back toward her room, dropping the comforter from her body and trailing it behind her. "I am so not going anywhere with that man," she muttered to herself, hurling the duvet back onto the bed with a huff and padding into the master bath.

She stood in front of the mirrored wall and splashed water on her face, clearing some cobwebs from her mind. She dried her face and took in the rat's nest of blonde locks tangled around her face and chuckled, noting to herself that Jake had not pointed out her hypocrisy when she noted his appearance. Trevor would have never let a comment like that slide.

She shuddered at the memory of what now felt like four years of her life wasted. They had an agreement, one which she had always felt had benefited him much more than her. She'd always known he wasn't the sharpest tool in the shed, but if he didn't want all that she and her family brought to the table, then that was more than fine with her. She could deal with her father. Losing her trust fund is something she could deal with. She could not deal with accepting a relationship for the sake of peace in the family. No, not again. Not now. Not ever.

She crossed to the large, glassed-in marble shower, turning the nobs and sending a stream of hot water falling from the double waterfall heads. Allowing the water to flow and steam to engulf that bathroom, she slipped into the adjacent walk-in and pulled out fresh underwear, leggings, and a hoodie from the drawers. An early winter chill was in the air, and she was looking forward to napping off this fuzziness, wrapped up in comfy blankets on the couch in front of the fireplace. She might even indulge herself and binge watching one of the hundred series she had been meaning to get around to but been too caught up and work and maintaining the sham of a relationship that she and Trevor had become.

Her eyes caught the row of dresses and, without thinking, her hand reached up, pulling out her favorite forest green jersey wrap. It was her go to dress for a casual evening out and when she thought about it, she hadn't worn it in a very long time. Trevor didn't do casual, always wanting to be seen at the most upscale, trendy restaurants and bars. Their evenings out were all about show and nothing to do with comfort. She held the dress in front of her, looking into the three-way dressing mirror at the end of the closet, loving the feel of the fabric against her bare skin. The cut was just low enough and the hem just high enough to be flirty without being obvious. It would be perfect for tonight and with the right accent, she could definitely pull off a holiday look.

Huffing, she shoved the dress back onto its rack. There wasn't going to be a 'tonight' to wear it for. Once she had showered and poured some coffee down her gullet, she was going to call Jake and tell his arrogant ass just where he could shove his dinner and they would be fine at the office Monday morning because they were both going to act like last night never happen. Nothing happened to pretend it didn't, anyway. And that was just fine with her because nothing ever could. Nothing would for a long time, anyway. Not until she was well and truly established in her career, and certainly not with anyone she worked with, especially with Jake Douglas.

She turned and stomped toward the shower, sliding the door shut behind her with enough determination to shake the glass walls. The water poured over her naked body, and she felt just a little human again. She squeezed too much body wash onto her loofah which she decided was just fine because she was going to scrub whatever dangerous pheromones Jake had rubbed onto her, off, so that she could get all these confusing thoughts out of her mind and focus back on what really mattered and not how sexy she'd feel wearing that dress and how nice it would be to see those twin dimples peering across the table at her on the date she was definitely not going to go on tonight.

No way. No how. Jake could pretend they were just talking and working through things to make it less awkward Monday, but she knew a date when she saw it and going to dinner with Jake would definitely, positively, be a date. And a date with Jake Douglas would definitely, positively, be the biggest mistake of her life.

Chapter 8

Alexis

Alexis hopped on one foot, leaning against the closet door jamb, as she slipped on the satin pump that matched the forest green dress she was wearing. She had purchased these shoes to go with this dress but only wore them once as their four-inch heels made her tower over Trevor. That was something he had always hated, and she had decided it just wasn't worth the aggravation, even if she enjoyed wearing heels.

Worrying about how tall she was in heels was the least of her concerns this evening, and she cursed herself for not finding the courage to call the whole thing off like she had planned. Apparently, regardless of how hard she had scrubbed herself in the shower this morning, whatever it was about Jake Douglas that had her making bad decisions hadn't completely washed off. Despite picking up her phone a dozen times to cancel, she put it down every time with the excuse that she didn't know what to say. Hadn't she already told him no multiple times before he walked out the door? She had, but somehow, she was still getting ready to go out on a non-date with him. And she had not spent extra time making sure her make-up and hair were just so and scoured the back of her closet for the long-lost pair of pumps that perfectly matched that dress. No, of course she hadn't. She didn't agonize over just the right scarf to accent the dress but still leave enough of a peek of cleavage to make it tempting. Nope, not her. She was not a girl that made an extra effort for a guy and certainly not for a non-date with a coworker that could only be described as her greatest rival and biggest barrier to promotion.

She wasn't going to double check her make-up in the mirror either, causing her to gasp in frustration when the doorbell sounded. She looked at her bedside clock, confirming that it said 5:59. "Gah," she fumed. Jake had to be one of those annoying people that were always on time.

She hesitated in front of the mirror, letting out a deep breath and smoothing down the front of her dress. There was a thrum of anticipation coursing under her skin, and she had to admit the face staring back at her in the mirror held little of the irritation it usually did on a Saturday night when she was going out with Trevor. Maybe Jake was right. This wasn't a big deal, and they could just have a nice evening out as friends. It wasn't like she'd be inviting him to share her bed again. There was no way she was going to do that. No way.

She made her way down the two flights of stairs to the foyer and pulled open the heavy oak door. Her breath caught as she took in Jake standing there. His hands tucked casually in his jean pockets. Jeans which hugged his muscular thighs nearly to the point of bursting at the seams. Her eyes trailed up over his broad chest, which stretched the sweater he was wearing nearly as much as his thighs did his jeans. He was wearing a leather bomber jacket and a smile spread across his face, showing off those damn dimples. "Wow," she hummed on a sigh.

"Wow, yourself." His smile widening as if it was humanly possible, and she cringed when she realized that the 'wow' wasn't in her head as she had thought. "I said casual, but you look stunning."

"Um," she hesitated, biting her lower lip coyly, a very un-Alexis thing to do, "thanks, but you've certainly seen me in a dress before."

"Not like this. You're always neat and proper in a business suit, but …"

"But what?" she asked when he went silent, looking her up and down, which normally would have raised her feminist hackles, but instead raised other things she didn't want raised by anyone, but especially him.

"Nothing. Sorry. You look great, and I feel like I should go home and change."

She smiled and stepped aside, realizing she hadn't invited him in. "Would you like a glass of wine before we go?"

"Thanks, maybe after, but we have a table waiting."

She started to correct him and say that there would be no version of this evening's events, which would result in inviting him in afterward for a drink or anything else. The bullet she dodged last night was far too close to risk another shot. No. Nope. Nada. She smiled and shrugged on her coat.

The shiver that ran down her spine as she walked down the front steps to his car had nothing to do with the press of his hand on the small of her back. No. It must have been the gust of raw wind off the Hudson.

When Jake had explained on their way there that it was just a basic little Italian place, Alexis was expecting the usual pizza joint. What she discovered was that Jake had quite undersold his favorite place. It was a cute little restaurant tucked down a narrow side street, not much more than an alley-way. The type of place that you couldn't find unless you knew it was there.

The second the tinkle of the bells on the door announced their arrival, the smell of deliciousness that assaulted her made her mouth water. The first floor had a couple of tables stuck to the side, which made it appear mostly like a takeout joint. The row of paper bags next to the cash register left little doubt that takeout was a big part of their business but the stair-case along the right-hand wall led up to two additional floors, both with six cozy booths, three down each wall and two tables in the middle for larger parties. It was quaint. It was romantic. She fell in love with the place in-stantly. And it was the antithesis of the haughty, over-priced places she was used to on date night.

It was clear their waiter knew Jake and he greeted her with a smile that made her feel like an old friend, too. A bottle of red wine appeared with-out being ordered and a matronly woman with salt and pepper hair pulled back in a tight bun, nearly as wide as she was tall, provided them with fresh, warm bread and a large antipasto. If she hadn't known better, she would have sworn the woman was Jake's mother, and he introduced her as Mama Santori. Which she quickly corrected him to say that friends called her Mama S and Alexis should, too. This was not the simple pizza and a beer joint he had made the evening out to be.

There was no doubt in Alexis' mind that Mama S owned the place even if the 'Santori's on the menu hadn't given it away, and she orchestrated the help around the tiny space like she'd been doing this her entire life. The surrounding tables filled up quickly with other patrons and the sounds of conversation and laughter surrounded her like a warm, fluffy blanket. She could almost hear Trevor's complaint about the noise and lack of class it showed; he preferred the sterile murmur of the chic uptown eateries. This place felt like being home.

The service was excellent, and she couldn't ever remember having a better meal. When she pushed herself away from the table against the back of the booth, she felt like she was ready to burst, fat and happy. She barely suppressed an unladylike belch, much to Jake's amusement, when Mama S appeared frowning. "You no like Mama's food, darling?"

"What? Oh no," Alexis stammered. "I think it might have been the best meal I've ever had, but I'm so stuffed if I eat another bight I might ex-plode."

"You need to feed her more, Jakey. She eats a like a bird," the woman chided him, pinching him on the cheek. Alexis stifled a giggle behind her napkin as the color in his cheeks rose to the hue of the Bolognese sauce on his plate.

Mama S returned moments later with a cappuccino, tiramisu, and her leftovers packaged to go. Alexis didn't know where she was going to put the delicious-looking dessert, but offered a silent thank you to the gods for the wrap dress she was wearing being a little less confining than her designer clothing.

She found enough room to finish the sweet treat and savored the rich goodness of the coffee. She really wished she could curl up in the booth and drift off into the happy little food coma she had started. A laugh escaped her as she took in the large brown bag on the edge of the table containing her leftovers.

"What's so funny?" Jake asked.

Alexis sighed. "I don't ever remember bringing home leftovers before."

"Seriously?"

She nodded. "Trevor was one for those places that don't give portions that sate your hunger, let alone have anything to spare."

"Well, if you don't want it, I'll bring it home." The sincerity of his tone took her by surprise. And when he continued, "it will hurt Mama S if you leave it behind." His concern for someone else's feelings had her wanting to wrap him in her arms and not let go.

A warm smile spread across her face. "Are you kidding? There is no way I'm leaving this here. It's coming home with me, bucko; just keep your hands off it. I plan on enjoying every bite."

Jake chuckled as a waiter came by and dropped the check on the table. Jake snatched the black folder off the table and put it on the seat next to him so fast it was like he was stealing something.

"I'm fine with you paying if that's what you're worried about." Alexis laughed.

Jake gave her a confused look for a moment until realization spread across his handsome face. "As you might have noticed, Mama S has a certain fondness for me," he said with a chuckle. "After the first five or six times I came in here, which may or may not have been over the course of about two weeks because, one, it's close to home, and two, it's the best damn food I've ever had, anyway, she stopped letting me pay and adopted me as one of her own. Whenever I argued with her about it, she shut me down and if you hadn't already guessed, you're never going to win an argument with her."

"I can see that being a thing." Alexis laughed and felt her cheeks heat.

"So now, one of the waiters will slip me my check if they know she won't see them. If not, I just leave a big tip in the jar next to the register on my way out."

As if on cue, Mama S appeared next to Jake as he slid out of the booth and bear hugged him around the shoulders. "Where have you been a hiding this lovely creature?" she asked, patting Alexis affectionately on the cheek.

The color in Jake's cheeks rose again and Alexis noticed those little tingles in her stomach getting stronger. She hoped she wasn't getting sick. "Nowhere Mama," he smiled. "This is our first date, so of course I had to bring her here."

The woman's expression deepened as she looked into Jake's eyes. "Una cosa così bella da dire," she crooned, covering her heart with her hands over her ample chest. "Such a lovely thing to say. Now you treat her like a lady and don't let her go," her finger wagging under his nose.

Alexis was nearly in tears, trying to contain her laughter at what was playing out between the two people in front of her. Whatever she was expecting this meal to be with Jake this evening, Mama S had been the furthest thing from her mind. She was just about to thank her for the lovely dinner and couldn't wait to tease Jake about what she had just seen when Mama S turned to her, and she realized she was about to be on the receiving end of some motherly advice.

"My Jakey's a good boy, one of the few. Don't you dare hurt him." Alexis was not one to be easily intimidated, she'd been standing up to her father for years, but this woman scared the crap out of her and while she didn't spell it out specifically, she was certain that if Mama S found out she had done her 'Jakey' wrong she might just end up being fish food on the bottom of the East River.

"I'll certainly do my best not to Mama S." Her expression morphed from menacing to motherly love in the blink of an eye as she pulled them both into her hug.

"Now you two go have some fun." She smiled, patting them both on the cheek. "And bring her back soon. We need to fatten her up. Too skinny. Too skinny," she hummed as she disappeared into the kitchen.

They both smiled as they watched her go. It had been a wonderful meal, melt in your mouth, orgasmically wonderful Alexis thought, and she wasn't ready for the evening to end even though she knew it should.

As they walked down the street toward where Jake had parked his car, the silence was heavy around them. It wasn't the awkward silence of two people that had run out of things to say to each other, showing it was time to move on. It was the silence of comfort and the absence of a need to fill that space with useless chatter. Before she realized she was doing it, Alexis brushed his hand and then interlaced her fingers with his. He squeezed her hand tightly without a word, and they walked that way until they reached his car.

The ride back to her brownstone was quiet, too, each lost in their own thoughts. He found a place to park and stepped around to open her door before she had a chance to tell him she was fine walking on her own. She had the sense he would have insisted on walking her to her door, anyway. He seemed like he was one of those old-fashioned guys, courteous without all the machismo bullshit.

As they reached the top of her stairs, she was about to thank him for a wonderful dinner and say good night. She should thank him for a wonderful dinner and say good night. "Would you like to come in for a bit?"

He hesitated for a moment, searching her eyes. She was certain he was going to refuse, which would have been an enormous relief because she didn't know why she'd just invited him in when she meant to say good night. "Sure," he smiled and there were those damn dimples again. "For a bit."

Chapter 9

For the past six months, they had been on parallel hamster wheels, running like mad at the prize of a permanent place on one of the management consulting pods for DCH. There were dozens of pods in their office alone and ten times more worldwide, so it wasn't like there was a shortage of positions to be filled. The challenge was that DCH, like most other consultants, only wanted the most aggressive, motivated players. Being good at your job wasn't enough. The willingness to crush others on the way was the key to success there.

Beneath that veil, it was unclear to them how this new friendship fit. Alexis knew she wouldn't think twice about advancing her own cause at Jake's expense. The Ice Princess didn't lose. But she knew it would bother her now, and she didn't like that feeling at all.

After an hour of conversation where they agreed they would do their best to maintain the status quo at work, Alexis put on a Christmas rom-com that Jake admitted he would normally not have watched. She sunk into his body while they watched and the warmth of him holding her made her forget all about the subject of the movie.

As the end credits rolled and Alexis emptied the last of the third bottle of wine into his glass, he looked around her spacious living room, the crease on his forehead making her suspect something seemed off to him. After a moment or two, he let her in on his thoughts. "You don't have a Christmas tree. What's up with that?"

Her brow furrowed she released a heavy sigh. "I guess I can blame that on Trevor. He said it was a waste of time and money for us to decorate here. I mean, I understood what he was thinking, we had no plans to spend much time here, but he gave no thought to whether I might enjoy it on my own, everything revolved around him or us," she used air quotes, "but now, it's so close to Christmas, even if I had time, all I'll be able to get is a Charlie Brown tree... next year I guess."

"But you're saying you'd like one?"

She hesitated, sucking in her bottom lip, "I guess, but it's late and I don't even own lights or ornaments…" She sighed again and waved her hand like she was swatting away a pesky fly. "I'll live. One more thing I can add to good reasons for being eternally glad he's gone."

Jake breathed out a laugh. "I think you should have a tree if you want one. Who cares if no one else gets to see it? You get to see it every night when you get home from work and before you leave in the morning." They were silent for a few minutes and returned their attention to the movie when Jake sat up straight and turned to face Alexis. "Don't make plans for Tuesday night… we will decorate your tree."

"No, really Jake, it's okay. I don't want you to feel like," she turned to him, resting her palms on his chest and she was very conscious of how close they were and the intensity of his eyes as they met hers.

"Stop. If you're saying no because you really don't want one or because you don't want me involved, I will respect your decision, but otherwise, I insist."

She looked into his face, searching his expression. "You're serious? You'd really like to do that for me…, with me?" A voice in the back of her head chastised her for sounding so much like a needy little child, but she couldn't seem to tamp down the excitement she felt at someone, no, at Jake wanting to do something like that with her. She was more than used to guys interested in what she could do for them, physically and otherwise, but Jake wanted to do something just for her.

"I am. I'm a real Christmas geek and it's been a long time since I've had someone to share it with. I'd love to do that with you. It would be nice to decorate a tree with someone." He opened his mouth to continue, but stopped himself.

Alexis tugged at her bottom lip, she should shut this down. Jake was a nice guy. Despite the rivalry, she didn't dislike him, and she could certainly use a friend. The few she had other than her sister and Tiana were people she knew through Trevor, and even if that didn't mean they were off the table now, she didn't like any of them well enough to reach out to them. She had always been a Christmas person too, before Trevor anyway. With him, it just always seemed like one more obligation to fulfill, another appearance that needed to be made for appearance's sake.

Here was this guy she barely knew offering to do something just for her, with her. Something that deep down meant a lot to her and even had the bonus of giving Trevor the silent middle finger. He was history, and she could do any damn impulsive thing she wanted. She had plenty of money and she could waste it on whatever she wanted to. She'd certainly wasted enough of her time and money on him over the past four years.

With a deep breath of resolve, she smiled. "I would love to do that with you." Her eyes stung, and she felt her throat close. She wasn't used to struggling to keep her composure. If she continued to say what was in her heart, she would fail. She tried anyway, "This means a lot to me…" she had to stop looking at him, she was about to lose control, "this is the first time that I can think of that anyone has ever stopped to look long enough at me to realize I wanted something without me having to ask for it. How did you do that?"

"I don't know," he shrugged. "I don't think it was terribly hard to figure out. You have decorations up around the house, you're watching sappy Christmas movies, it just didn't fit that you didn't have a tree. I mean, even a fake one would have been understandable despite their moral inferiority." A mischievous twinkle flourished in his eyes.

She rolled her eyes and swatted his shoulder playfully, letting her guard down more than she intended. "I have seen some perfectly lovely artificial trees. I'm particularly fond of the silver ones with blue balls," she offered, struggling to keep a straight face.

Jake snorted and bit his lip.

"What?" she asked, batting her lashes up at him.

"Nothing," he grunted, holding back a laugh.

"Out with it."

"Nothing really. It just my natural male aversion to blue balls, I guess."

"Jake," she moaned, placing a hand on her chest in mock horror. It surprised her to see extra color in his cheeks, like the joke he had just made embarrassed him. She was more surprised by how they made her belly flutter and the heat rise in her own cheeks. "I'm sure you don't have to worry about that. I've seen the way the admin assistants fawn over you." As soon as the words were out of her mouth, she chided herself for going there. It surprised her she did, and she was even more surprised how badly she wanted to hear a denial from him.

She immediately regretted going there, and the lightness in his eyes disappeared instantly, and his brow creased. He took a steadying breath before he answered in a low, almost growl. "I'm not that kind of man."

Alexis swallowed, feeling flushed with embarrassment. She'd hit a nerve that she hadn't meant to. She could tell there was a story behind his reaction, but she could also tell now was not the time to ask. "I'm sorry. I don't think you are. I was just teasing."

He released a heavy sigh and looked up at the ceiling before looking back into her eye. "No, I'm sorry. I know you were teasing. It just that," he worked his mouth as he stopped and started to say something and sighed again. "I would never want to be seen as abusing my power like that. I just wouldn't go there."

Before she knew what she was doing, she leaned up and kissed his cheek, easing back after just enough to focus on his face. "I know you wouldn't Jake. I can tell you're an honorable man."

The hint of a smile tugged at his lips as he returned her gaze. "Thanks," he croaked, clearing his throat. Their eyes locked, and they were so close they were sharing the same air, which suddenly seemed almost too hot to breathe. Her tongue swiped over her lips as his parted. He inched closer, holding her gaze. Her head tilted slightly as she eased closer to meet him, lips parting in anticipation for what she knew would be a life-changing moment.

With a sharp intake of breath, Jake leaned away, straightening himself. "Um, I should, ah…, I should go. I didn't realize it was getting so late."

Alexis straightened in surprise, her head shaking, trying to grasp what had changed. They were going to kiss; she was certain of it. She might not be the world's most experienced dater, but she knew when a guy wanted to kiss her and there was no doubt Jake had wanted to kiss her every bit as much as she had wanted to be kissed. She was also sure she wasn't sending mixed signals. She was right there, ready and willing. And what the hell? She was sure that he'd been wooing her all night. That was some dinner they had shared, the hand holding, cuddling on the couch. Really, what the actual hell?

Jake pulled himself up from the couch and had to reach a hand onto the arm of the sofa to steady himself.

Alexis didn't miss his stumble and got up, taking hold of his very solid biceps. "Oh, no you don't Mr. Douglas. You wouldn't let me drive last night, so I'm returning the favor tonight. And as I'm sober enough to know I'm too buzzed to drive, you are staying right here."

"Alexis, I …"

"No, you are not fine," she cut him off before he could finish the excuse. "And I will not take no for an answer."

He hesitated for a moment. "Fine. Thank you."

Her mouth opened like she expected to have to argue further, then snapped it shut and smiled. "Good. Cuz I would have hated to have to had resorted to physical force," she said with a wink. The smile he gave her in return had her stomach fluttering again, which must have been all that wine sloshing around down there and not something like giddiness. Alexis Chambers did not do giddy, schoolgirl, doe eyes sort of dreamy man shit. No, she most certainly did. NOT.

She picked up her wineglass from the table and drained the last of it just for something to do that wouldn't betray her excitement about Jake agreeing to stay. It was totally all about his safety, anyway. Right? She grabbed his glass and headed toward the kitchen. When she came back into the living room, she found him pulling a throw off the back of the sofa and he'd shifted the pillows to one end. "What are you doing?" she asked, knowing but having to ask despite herself.

"Trying to get comfortable? Or have you changed you mind about me staying?"

"That is the worst couch in the world for sleeping on." She said, thrusting her hips out and placing her hands on them in frustration. "Any time I've conked out, I've woken up with pain in muscles I didn't know I had."

"Then where am I supposed to sleep?"

"You slept with me last night and survived. What's wrong with my bed?" She almost gasped in surprise at her own words. Of course, she knew that there were no other options available once she nixed the couch, but she hadn't consciously thought the rest of it through. Apparently, she'd done it unconsciously because here she was telling him he had to sleep with her again after she'd already decided before they went out for dinner that it would never happen again.

"Um, that wasn't really on purpose, and I slept on top of the covers."

"Are you going to force yourself on me?" she couldn't help but smile at the way he was trying to do the gentlemanly thing. It had her heart thumping hard against her ribs and she wasn't sure if it was out of fear or anticipation of feeling his solid body next to hers again. Maybe a little of both.

"No." He narrowed his gaze at her in consternation.

"Of course not, and I'm not going to molest you," probably, "so let's just be the big grown-up adults we are and share what I'm sure you agree is a very large and comfortable bed and not be silly about it."

"That's probably not the best…"

"Seriously? If the guest rooms were made up, you could certainly sleep there, but they're closed up with the furniture in storage. So let's just share the bed I have and not make a big deal about it."

Before he could argue more, she grabbed his hand and tugged him hard toward the stairs. Alexis was not petite by any standard, but she was still considerably smaller than Jake's six-four solid frame. She knew he allowed himself to be led up two flights of stairs. She hoped that in the morning neither of them would regret this because if they did, then a tense office environment just got a lot worse.

Chapter 10

Alexis

Alexis felt her body shake as the substantial torso behind her jostled her out of a sound sleep. The sound of his deep baritone rumbling a scratchy, sleepy, "no. Sorry. You must be looking for Alexis." Pulled her further into consciousness.

Nudging her, he reached around handing her the phone. "Sorry. I answered your phone by mistake."

She stretched and brushed tangles of long blonde hair away from her face. "Who is it?"

Jake shrugged, "I didn't ask, but she thought maybe I was Trevor," he whispered.

She scowled, still trying to shake off the fog of sleep. "Hello?" she croaked, her voice still thick with sleep and not sounding the least bit pleased about being woken.

"What's going on?" Alexis winced and held the phone from her ear, trying to escape the shriek coming from the phone. "Who is that in bed with you, Allie? Is he the reason you broke it off with Trevor? Dad's fucking furious you didn't tell him yourself."

"God, Carole." She groaned. "Could you drop the volume by maybe a hundred? We're on the phone. I don't need to hear you all the way from the Hamptons without it."

"I've been worried sick about you! Why didn't you answer your phone?"

"Why would you be worried about me? I'm sorry I've been busy." Sneaking a side look at Jake and mouthing, *my sister*, to him in answer to his questioning brow. "My phone was on vibrate and didn't hear it. What time is it, anyway?" She grabbed Jake's arm, keeping him from sliding out of the bed and pulling him back against her the way he'd been before the phone interrupted her contented cocoon.

"Why didn't you tell me about Trevor? What happened?" Carole went on, ignoring her question. "What happened to the perfect power couple?"

"What do you mean? Why didn't I tell you? Did he call you and tell you to check up on me today because he had some delusions about me being distraught?"

"No, he didn't call me today or any day. You know we didn't like each other very much. It's obvious you broke it off with him a while ago. You should know you couldn't keep up the charade all the way through Christmas. Skipping Thanksgiving was one thing, but you knew you'd both be expected at Papa's Christmas day. Allie, I know we don't talk as much as we used to, but you're still my best friend. You can tell me anything and I'll support you. We've stood up to dad plenty of times and you know you're Papa's favorite. He may bark and spout off, but really whose house are you in rent free? You know he'll support you, too."

"Carole, I don't know what you're talking about. I haven't kept anything from you. Trevor broke it off with me. This Friday night, as a matter of fact, and the son of a bitch did it by text. While I was at the company Christmas party."

There was absolute silence at the other end of the phone. "He broke it off with you two days ago?"

"Yes, that's what I said. You know I haven't been happy lately, but Dad liked him, and I was tired of fighting over the need to get married." Finally, she had shifted her focus enough from how much she enjoyed having Jake in her bed to really absorb what Carole wasn't saying. "Carole, why are you surprised that he broke it off with me? And more to the point, why do you think we broke it off before? Beyond that, how do you know we broke it off in the first place?"

There was absolute silence a second time. "Um, I don't know Allie…"

"Carole, you do know why you thought that. You obviously felt you had enough evidence to think I was hiding it from you, so out with it."

"Shit, Allie…, Damn it. I'm sorry. It hurt me you didn't trust me anymore."

"Carole, I will love you forever, but stop." She trailed off, watching Jake cross the floor toward the bathroom wearing nothing but his boxer briefs.

"Allie? Are you still there?"

Her tongue stuck to the roof of her mouth for a moment until he disappeared and shut the door behind him.

"Um, yeah, sorry. Just tell me what you think you know."

"So, Brian is in Florida with friends playing golf this weekend and I woke up this morning and got on social media for like the first time in a month."

"So, what… Trevor changed his status to single? I always told him I thought that status stuff made him seem like a high school kid."

"Well, not exactly. He changed his relationship status to 'in a relationship with', I can't even remember her name, and there's a post this morning with the two of them looking like the happy couple. She's so mousy looking, seriously Allie, she can't hold a candle to you, but I was like, what the fuck and dug around. She's one of those that's like too stupid to know they should hide their stuff from public view so not everybody can see it, which I guess worked out okay for us because I trolled her profile and there are pictures of them together for the past six months. Allie, I'm sorry, you must be devastated. I'll be there in forty-five minutes; we can drink wine and order pizza and think of a hundred ways to get revenge on his cheating ass," she ended, inhaling loudly as she had completed the litany without a single breath.

Oddly enough, Alexis wasn't shocked, a little angry at herself for missing the signs that he was cheating, but it didn't hurt her. She was confident she was not in denial about it, either. "I'm sorry. I'm sorry you're the one that had to dig all this up. I love you with all my heart, you're the best sister anyone could ask for. And thank you for offering to come all the way into the city in a snowstorm. That means the world to me…"

Carole cut her off, "You mean the world to me too, and that's while I'll be there as soon as I can." Jake returned to the room and this time she was at least able to continue to focus on the conversation as she watched him all the way until he tucked back into bed behind her.

"Carole, hold on, let me finish."

"I'm sorry, go ahead, but I'm coming. I don't care what you say. You shouldn't be alone right now."

"As I was trying to say, I really am okay. I was upset at first but then with the help of a really caring coworker," she flashed a quick glance toward Jake, "I figured out that I was honestly just pissed off. Pissed off at him and pissed off at myself for letting it go on as long as I did. He never showed me respect, and that's even more evident now. Carole, I never really loved him, I just said yes because of Dad. I was tired of hearing his bullshit. It's a blessing, honestly C, I'm good."

"I still don't think you should be alone, and I wouldn't mind some time with my sister. It's been too long, Allie."

"It has been too long, but, well, this morning, I think I've got other plans, you know?"

"What?! Allie, no! don't make a dumb mistake just because you're hurting and mad at Trevor. Are you trying to say mister deep voice isn't already dressed and out the door?"

"Nope, still lying right next to me," she glanced over to Jake with a coy smile and placed a hand on his thigh, which she decided was even harder than his biceps.

"Okay, so, me coming there would make it a little awkward. I really wanted to see you, though."

"Aw, me too, but I'll see you Christmas Day at Papa's. And I promise I'll call you later, but right now I have other things to do."

"I guess there's nothing wrong with getting over Trevor by getting under someone else and if he looks half as sexy as his half-awake voice sounds…"

"Time to say goodbye," she half shouted, cutting Carole off. "I love you."

"Bye, love you too."

Alexis hung up and gave an enormous sigh. "I love her, but ever since she got married, it's like she's the older sister." She reached over and cupped his cheek, brushing her thumb over his whiskers. The tickling sensation on the pad of her thumb flowed through every nerve in her body, right to her toes. Her lips met his in a featherlight kiss without her consciously intending to. Pulling back, she offered him a shy smile before sighing. *What on earth am I doing? I must be crazy.*

Jake cleared his throat and smiled. "So, I couldn't help hearing some of that. Trevor was cheating on you?"

Oh good, change the subject. Perfect. "That's what Carole thinks."

"I'm sorry, that really sucks, even if you say you didn't love him, still…"

"Oh, I'm plenty pissed at the little fucker, trust me." She sat up and leaned back against the headboard with a huff. "He can come beg me for the ring for all the good it will do him. There's a sewer drain right across the street; I could hold it out in my hand and just before he took it, throw it over his head and down the drain. He'd have a stroke, right there on the steps. You could watch from the window; it would be hilarious."

"Note to self: never cross Alexis."

"You better believe it, buster," she laughed, puffing out her chest in his direction. Jake's gaze dropped to her chest as she thrust her shoulders back. She looked down, realizing that the thin fabric of the t-shirt she wore to bed stretched tightly across her chest, highlighting her hardened nipples. *Why do I keep flashing him?* She lifted her arms higher, covering the offending appendages.

"You kissed me," he mused, "and you haven't been drinking."

Her eyes dropped to study the bed covers before she slowly lifted her gaze, meeting his through her long lashes. "I did. You kissed me back."

She watched his throat intently while his muscles contracted around a nervous swallow. "I did." He held his hand out and slowly she raised hers, twining her finger through his. "I'd like to do it again."

Her tongue traced her lips. "I think I'd like that too."

And before the sound of the last word left her mouth, he pulled her toward him, and their lips crashed together. Her free hand snaking into his wavy hair, urging him closer. His hand finding the small of her back and pressing her soft curves against his hard chest. A whimper of desire escaping her, begging for more of this, whatever this was. Their kiss deepening and becoming more desperate with each second.

Alexis let go of his hand and began mapping the ridges of his muscular chest, down, down, down until her delicate fingers reached the waist of his boxer briefs.

Suddenly Jake pulled back with a gasp, creases forming between his eyes. "Are you sure you're okay with this? Once we take this next step, I'm not sure I'll be able to stop."

She pulled him back closer. Her lips pressed against his. "I feel something for the first time in I don't know how long. I don't care if we shouldn't be doing this. I don't care if the timing sucks. I want to feel again." Her hand dipped inside his briefs and wrapped around his thickening cock, stroking its silky, steely girth. "I want to feel you. All of you."

His lips crashed into hers as he pressed her backwards onto the bed. Her hand gripped tighter around his shaft and slowly pulled up, drawing a guttural moan from deep in his chest. He tore the t-shirt she wore over her head, tossing it to the floor and cupped her breasts in his hands. "Fuck," he groaned, breaking their kiss to look down at them, his thumbs flicking at her pebbled nipples. "You're even more beautiful than I dreamed of."

Her cheeks pinked, and a smile tugged at the corners of her mouth. "You've been dreaming of me?" she teased before pressing her lips back to his, not waiting for or even wanting an answer.

He trailed kisses from the corner of her mouth, along her jawline, to that sensitive region behind her ear before dropping down her neck and across her collarbone to his ultimate destination. His mouth found the puckered berries, dark pink, and pulled it into his mouth. She hissed as he drew it between his teeth, walking the exquisite tightrope between pleasure and pain. She lost her hold on him and he slid down her body, instead threading her fingers through his hair and holding his head against her body.

Fire was burning beneath her skin. Her desire was hot and needy for his touch. His kisses were so gentle, and she needed more. Arching her back off the mattress, she pressed her core against his side. Her desire seeping through the thin sleep shorts she wore, and he growled. She knew he felt the same need she did.

His fingers looped under the elastic and pulled the satiny fabric from her hips, peeling them the length of her long, toned legs before wedging his shoulder between them, spreading her wide. Slowly, he kissed his way up the delicate skin on the inside of her thighs. "I need you Jake," she moaned on a sigh.

"Patience," he breathed. His breath heating the already warm skin near her apex.

"The next time," she huffed. "I need you so bad and I need you now," she demanded, tightening her grip on his hair so much that he winced at her firm insistence.

He moved to grab his wallet off the nightstand, but she pulled him back toward her, leaning up to capture his mouth with hers. "I'm clean and I'm on the pill, if you don't mind. I don't want anything between us."

For a moment, he hesitated. He was safe too; he'd been nearly celibate since Stephanie, twelve years…

With a nod, he situated himself back between her legs and fisted his throbbing cock. Slowly he drew the head the length of her folds, coating himself with her arousal. Notching himself at her entrance, he held her gaze and eased inside her inch by delectable inch. Her mouth formed a perfect O, matching the throaty sound escaping it. "God…, Jake," she mewled as he stretched and filled her like no one had ever done before.

She was so turned on. So wet for him. She worried he might not get the friction he needed, but when she looked at his face, it was looking at pure bliss. And when she looked into his eyes, it was almost as if she could see into his soul. The connection she felt with him was unlike anything she had ever come close to experiencing.

Their hips rocked in unison, and she trailed her hands down, flattening them on his hips and pulling him closer, forcing him as deep as he could inside her. She spread her legs wide and hooked her feet behind him, driving him even deeper. "Don't hold back. You won't break me. I need all of you. Now." She urged him on and whatever was holding him back snapped, thrusting hard into her and teasing out a scream of ecstasy. The harder and faster he pounded into her, the greater the pleasure in her cries and the sharper her nails dug into his flesh.

"Yes. Yes. Yes," she moaned, marking each time their bodies slammed together until her head tilted back and her body went stiff. Her vision narrowed so that all she could see was Jake's face and the way he looked at her like she was the only thing in the world. Her release washed over her like a tidal wave.

Jake's body tensed in response to hers. She could feel his cock swell and throb as he emptied himself into her. Their cries of fulfillment blending as one.

Her entire body quivered as her orgasm rolled through her from her toes to the tips of her fingers and after what seemed like both an eternity and an instant, she melted back down onto the bed with a contented sigh.

Jake collapsed on top of her, trying to brace himself so that his bulk didn't crush her. She held him tighter in her arms, forcing him closer. As her brain cleared away the post-orgasm haze, Jake pulled back and rolled to his side. She could feel the proof of their lovemaking flowing from her, and it sent another shiver of pleasure through her body.

She giggled, following him to her side and running her finger along his chiseled jaw, rough with morning stubble. "Thank you." She dropped her eyes to his chest to avoid his heated gaze, but the sight of his muscles had her thinking about the naughty desires of wanting to start all over again.

His finger gently hooked her chin up to meet his gaze again, and he leaned in, placing the whisper of a kiss on her lips. Then he brushed a wayward strand of her hair behind her ear. "You are so damned beautiful."

The sincerity of his voice sent a wave of warmth through her body, and she placed a kiss on his lips before turning and allowing her body to mold into his. "Hold me just a little longer?" she sighed in a long slow breath. "I'm not ready for this to end yet."

His arm wrapped around her midsection, just grazing the underside of her breasts. "It doesn't have to end at all if you don't want it to."

She placed her hand over his and gave it a squeeze before closing her eyes and enjoying how well their bodies fit together. *I wish that were true. I really do,* she thought, and she gave it to the temptation and drifted off to sleep.

Chapter 11

Jake

They woke to find a covering of white, fluffy snow, enough to give the city the appearance of a snow globe, freshly shaken and settled. Jake peered out the bow window at the street. Pinholes of sunshine punctured the grayness and illuminated the frozen crystals that were the last to arrive but were still eager to meet their fellows below. The beauty and serenity of the scene stirred his long dormant romantic heart.

He could feel Alexis moving to stand behind him. Her arms enveloped his chest, and the heat of her body easily penetrated the thin cotton fabric of the shirt she'd thrown on, sending a shiver up his spine. "It looks like a Christmas card out there." He could feel her smile as she kissed his bare shoulder.

"It does." His eyes scanned the sky, estimating the amount of daylight left. "You know what would make it even better?"

"Mm, what?"

"Us walking down the street with your tree."

Alexis squeezed her way around him, wedging herself between his solid frame and the window. "I thought you wanted to do that on your own."

"I said I wanted to do that for you. That doesn't mean I wouldn't like you to be with me when I do." His finger tucked under her chin, lifting her face to meet his. He could see the emotion welling in her eyes. "Would you like that? It could be the start of a wonderful tradition."

Jake watched as she looked at the ceiling and inhaled. She was hesitating, and he wasn't sure why. Breathing out, she tiptoed up and kissed his cheek. "I'd love to go get a tree with you."

The first two tree lots they had visited offered nothing more than Charlie Brown specials. Jake thought maybe they had wasted what little daylight they had left on a hopeless mission, and it would force them to walk back to her home empty-handed. They could drive out to The Island, but he was leery that suggesting that would break the moment and bring Alexis back to the doubts he had seen her wrestle with before agreeing to this adventure.

They rounded the corner and spied a sign for trees halfway down the block. The tree that was being hoisted on top of the SUV double parked in front of the lot contained more branches and needles that all the trees they had seen in the previous two places combined. Alexis picked up her pace. Shaking his head with a chuckle, he lengthened his strides to keep up. Her excited pace made him think of a kid whose parents had told them to walk, but they were so excited they could barely manage it.

When they reached the front of the lot, he took in dozens of beautiful Frasier firs. The sparkle in her eyes warmed him as she surveyed the rows of choices before her.

After what he was sure had been at least forty-five minutes of pulling trees off the racks while she strolled around them, she had still not decided on a tree. He could tell by the faraway look in her eyes that she was trying to picture each one in her living room. This woman did not resemble the cold, calculating Alexis Chambers he knew over the previous six months. The woman that easily owned every conference room she walked into. Whose no-nonsense, icy exterior gave no hint of the warm heart and childlike enthusiasm underneath. This was the warm, loving woman that somehow, despite her purposely cold exterior, he had sensed was there. He would gladly stand and hold every tree in Manhattan just to see her happy.

A smile filled Jake's face when he noticed the subtle relaxation on her forehead. "This is the one?" he asked.

Her brows lifted slightly. "How did you know?" He could hear a concern in her tone, which she tried to cover with a joking, "or are you just done with holding trees while I make up my mind?"

His gut was telling him she wasn't sure how to feel about him being able to read her emotions and was tempted to play along with her joke. Still, the idea that he could keep her off balance was too strong to ignore. "I'll do this for as long as you need, but I could see it in your eyes. This is the one you've been looking for."

Her eyes widened and her brows disappeared under the brim of the white wool hat she wore against the cold. She opened and closed her mouth several times before managing to say, "I guess it is," her tone still with more than a hint of surprise. "Let's go see how much this beast is going to set me back."

"It will not set you back a dime because I said I was doing this for you."

"I can't let you do that. Christmas trees in the city are ridiculously expensive."

"I'm well aware, but I said I was going to do this for you. Please don't argue with me about it." That had come out harsher than he intended and ran his hand through his hair in frustration. He had to stop being so sensitive about money. It was doubtful she was insinuating he couldn't afford it, or worse, that she was far more able to afford it, even if that was true. He was from nothing, a drunk father who, even though he owned a successful construction company, never seemed to make ends meet. A father who wouldn't bat an eye at spending the week's grocery money at the bar or a 'sure' bet. The only sure bet was that he would explode in a rage if anyone questioned where the money went.

When he saw the scowl on her face, he felt worse than before. "Okay," she drew out cautiously.

Fuck "Look. I'm sorry." He looked down and spread the slushy snow back and forth with the toe of his shoe. "I didn't mean to sound so…"

She stepped forward and kissed him softly, surprising him into silence before he finished his apology. "I'm the one who should be sorry. Carole is always telling me I don't know how to let anyone do anything for me." She laughed, but there was no humor behind it. "She says I'm too hell bent on being independent. I have to do everything for myself." The shrug she gave told him she agreed with her sister.

Jake nodded and reached lower on the trunk for better leverage, hoisting it to his shoulder with a grunt. "Let's get this beauty home and see how nice it will look in the bow window." He set the tree down in front of the lot's attendant with a nod and reached for his wallet. The attendant was a man of moderate stature but with substantial girth. His balding bowling ball of a head topped with a pilling, knitted hat and his smudged red chamois shirt and dark work pants, along with a week's worth of black stubble and well chewed cigar stub made them think the lot might be a fundraising front for the Bowery Boys.

"Six-hundred" he said with a crooked smile that was more of a sneer, making Jake consider the possibility of criminal intent even more.

Alexis inhaled audibly and her eyes widened. As Jake turned to look at her, she opened her mouth to speak. He narrowed his gaze at her. She closed her mouth, saying nothing. Instead, she looked to the sky and pursed her lips together in a failed attempt to whistle. He couldn't help but laugh at her feigned nonchalance. Pulling out his wallet, he paid for the tree without complaint.

"We've got time invested in this tree and we both agreed it's perfect."

Jake was not about to let usury stand in the way of his romantic gesture, but muttered to himself about heading out to the Island to get a tree next year. That thought followed quickly by a mental self-admonition that he was way ahead of himself. He was nothing more than a rebound for her. When she was ready to move on, he'd be nothing more than a memory. He could never consider that a woman like Alexis would ever be interested in him. He might know that this six-hundred-dollar tree would have him eating boxed mac and cheese for a month, but she didn't need to know that, and he could live with that deception for now. She wouldn't be around long enough to know the truth, anyway.

Alexis

Alexis snuck glances, as he labored to move the furniture around as she directed. He never once questioned her when she pointed one way and then decided on the other. She couldn't help but think Trevor would have never even offered to lift a finger to help her. He would have sat there and watched her struggle if he'd bothered to stick around at all. More than likely, he would have found an excuse to leave, telling her she should just hire someone to do it. *"People like us don't bother with things so mundane."* An icy chill raced up her spine like he was standing there right behind her.

Deciding she needed to shake off the frigid darkness that was seeping into her thoughts, she asked, "Do you like hot chocolate?" Jake looked up from the chair he was trying to shove into place with an expression she couldn't read. "It just feels like we should have some, and I am a little chilly from our tree hunting adventure."

"That sounds perfect, thank you." He smiled and whatever displeasure she thought she saw in his expression had disappeared; if it was ever there to begin with. Jake is not Trevor, her conscience reminded her. It was difficult for her to let her defenses down enough to resist the habit of the constantly needing to defend herself, to fight for what she wanted.

Alexis walked to the kitchen and put on the electric kettle. She was trying to reach the box of instant cocoa, which was just out of her reach, even on tiptoes, when a solid male form pressed against her back. He put one arm around her in a hug. And with the other arm reached above her to grab the box. He set it on the counter as she turned to face him. She cupped his face in her hands and guided it toward her waiting lips. Her mouth pressed lightly against his until he welcomed her in. Deepening the kiss, she thrust her tongue into his mouth and claimed him.

His hand traveled down her back, and squeezing her ass tightly, and hoisted her onto the counter. She spread her legs to accommodate his wide body. She could feel every inch of his hard length press against her core as they pulled each other closer. His hand slipped under her sweater, fingertips trailing softly up her side until he cupped her breasts in his hands, squeezing her peaked nipples between his thumb and forefinger, causing a whimper to escape her mouth through their kiss.

The kettle released a shrill whistle, snapping them out of the moment.

"You have some kind of power over me, Mr. Douglas," she sighed, pushing herself off the counter and then flushed scarlet when she realized she had spoken that aloud.

Jake smirked as he grabbed two mugs from the counter. He scooped the mix into the mugs, and she poured the water. He grabbed some half and half from the fridge and added a little into each mug. She gave him a questioning look to which he responded, "keeps it from tasting too watery and cools it just enough so you won't burn your tongue. We wouldn't want injured tongues, now would we?"

The suggestion in those words had her squeezing her thighs together to find some relief from what she was craving. No man had ever had this effect on her before and she wasn't sure what to make of it, but until she was sure, she decided she might as well enjoy it. Smiling, she gave him back as sultry an answer as she could manage. "We most certainly wouldn't want that." Twining her fingers in his, she led him back to the living room. They toasted each other with the cocoa and then set about hauling the tree into place.

They sat down on the couch and admired the tree, sipping their cocoa. Jake questioned her about what she liked on the tree; white lights or colored, did she like all the ornaments to be the same or was an eclectic, sentimental mix, more her thing, tinsel, garland, both… it had been a long time since she felt like someone was listening to her. While it might be something as insignificant in the grand scheme of things as Christmas decorations, it was nice. It felt good to be heard.

"Thank you so much for doing this with me." She leaned up and kissed his cheek before settling with her head on his shoulder. "This has turned into the best weekend I've had in a long, long time."

His fingers traced lazy circles on her arm as he held her. "I'm glad because I was just thinking the same thing." She was relaxed and content and felt like her body melted into his. It was as if they were made for each other, two pieces in the same puzzle. They sat quietly, lost in their thoughts.

After a few minutes, or maybe twenty, her mind returned to what it usually focused on: work. "So," she paused, taking a deep breath, "not to risk killing the mood, but we probably should get around to talking about how we're going to manage things tomorrow."

"I've been thinking about that, too."

"You're certainly going to have to control yourself better. I can't even make cocoa without you copping a feel." The girlish giggle that escaped her surprised her, and from the expression on Jake's face, he wasn't expecting it either.

"Ah yes, but you were braless, and I just couldn't help myself. I'm guessing that won't be an issue tomorrow," he said with a wink.

She laughed, "That's a safe bet, but I'll remember that weakness and use it against you in the future." She ran a finger along the sharp line of his jaw. "What other weaknesses do you have?"

He smiled at her and the look of mischief in his eyes had her clenching her thighs tight again. *Gah, how can he do that with just his eyes? I must be losing my mind. This is so not the Ice Princess I need to be.*

He snort laughed as his eyes widened. "I would probably black out if I knew you weren't wearing panties under those conservative suits of yours. Probably any time, honestly."

She could feel her cheeks flush as she laughed so hard tears ran down her face. "Do you have some kind of phobia about woman's underwear?" The heat in his molten chocolate eyes had her soaked, and she pinched her thighs together hoping to feel some must need pressure.

"Fear is not the emotion that comes to mind, no." He paused for effect before he continued. "Seriously, Alexis, I don't believe we'll have a problem. You're the most competent, professional person I know. If there's anyone who can keep their feelings out of the way of business, it's you. And I've been attracted to you since the first day of orientation. I've been able to keep it professional." He swallowed hard. "Well, until Friday night anyway," he laughed nervously.

"Thanks. That's means a lot that you see me…" slowly his words sunk in, her eyes widened and her jaw gaped before she snapped it shut, swallowing the lump of realization in lodged in her throat. "You've been… For six months? Not a word?"

He looked down at his hands, twisting his thumbs back and forth. He nodded.

Alexis pulled back from him and his head dipped lower. She thought he was about to push himself off the couch when she slid her fingers through the hair above his ear. She moved closer and brushed a kiss on his cheek before settling back next to him.

"It really is a perfect tree." She sighed and smiled.

"It is."

"How about Chinese for dinner? They're fast and they deliver."

"Perfect," he sighed, letting out a long breath.

Fifteen minutes later, the doorbell rang. "Wow, that's fast, even for them." Alexis mused, heading out of the living room to answer the door. She looked through the peephole and froze. She took two steps back and caught Jake's eye, "It's Carole," she whisper-yelled with an urgency normally reserved for teenagers being caught doing something that their parents wouldn't approve of.

"Is this unusual?" he asked, smiling like he thought this predicament was funny.

"Very. Guess you get to meet my family more quickly than you expected," she mused in a tone that conveyed both agreement to the inevitable and amusement.

"I can hide if you want?"

The impish smile on his face doing things to her lady bits that she'd rather it didn't with her sister just on the other side of the door. "Don't be silly." She continued in a hushed tone, "I just figured we'd have a little more time before my family had the chance to send you running." She brought her hands up to cover her face, not wanting him to see how embarrassed she was at letting that slip. With a heavy sigh, she turned back toward the door. "At least you get the easy one first."

"I know you're in there," came the muffled yell from the other side of the door. "Hurry up Sissy, I'm freezing my tits off out here."

Alexis rolled her eyes at her sister's plea and heaved the door open with a sigh. "Hey little sister, this is a surprise."

"Hey Allie." She pushed through the door, wrapping Alexis in a hug. "I have more info about Tea Bag, and I figured I'd better deliver this nugget in person." With a flurry, she slid out of her coat, draping it over an empty hook. Alexis watched Carole's eye open wider as she turned and caught sight of Jake walking toward them. "Oh… um… I'm sorry," Carole's eyes darted back and forth between her and Jake before landing back on her, "I figured you'd be alone by now."

Alexis ignored the inference that this was uncommon behavior for her. It was, but that wasn't relevant. "Carole, this is Jake, Jake my sister Carole."

He smiled at her. "It's a pleasure to meet you."

She forced an awkward smile. "It is nice to put a face with the voice. I am sorry for interrupting your plans for the evening."

"You're not interrupting at all," he said politely. "We've just finished putting up the tree and Chinese is on the way. I'm sure there'll be enough for all of us."

"Oh, Ali, I really am sorry. I'll just go." She whispered now, rather pointlessly, with Jake standing three feet away. "I didn't think I'd be cock blocking you on a work night."

Alexis felt the heat rise on her cheeks. Carole had that effect on her. Her little sister had no filter and gave zero fucks with who or where she was. What was on her mind was coming out of her mouth. She envied Carole because of that. Somehow, she'd escaped the scrutiny and expectations of their father. Comments like that from her would have always received a harsh rebuke about how a lady of breeding and wealth should behave. "You're not cock blocking me. Yet," she said with a wink at her sister.

Carole's jaw dropped and Jake's brows lifted so high they disappeared under his hairline. Composing herself, Carole turned to face Jake. "I'm not exactly sure what you've done to my sister, but keep it up. I quite like the sassy version of Alexis."

Alexis wrapped her sister in a hug and kissed her cheek. "I'm sure you do." Guiding her toward the living room, she asked, "would you like a drink?"

She nodded, falling in step next to her sister. "Wine, please."

"I suppose we could do that for you." Alexis replied, stepping toward the kitchen.

Jake raised a hand, waving her off. "You two relax. I know where the wine is. Carole, do you prefer white or red?"

"Chardonnay please. I assume, unless the world has gone to hell more than I know it already has, she'll have at least a bottle or two of that in the fridge."

Alexis laughed, "No, that part of the world is safe from chaos. Honey, there is some in the fridge and please bring me a glass too."

"Honey?" she mouthed at Alexis, her eyes widening. Regaining control of her expression, she dropped into a chair, exhaling. "Mom wanted to come with me. I'm glad I could talk her out of it, or this really would have been awkward."

"Dear God Carole, what's the big deal? I honestly don't care what Trevor has done or what he's doing. He's a chicken shit little weasel and frankly, I'm glad to be rid of him." Dropping her voice and leaning toward Carole as she sat on the edge of the couch, "I doubt I ever would have found Jake if all this shit with Trevor didn't go down the way it did. And I kinda like him, C."

Carole's eyes were back to Anime size and her mouth formed an O that any self-respecting goldfish would envy. Gathering her wits, she exclaimed, "Really?!" that was much closer to a shout than a whisper and if looks could kill Alexis would have offed her sister, then and there.

"Really what?" Jake returned, handing Carole a full glass of golden liquid. He turned and plopped down on the couch, pressing up against Alexis, handing her a matching tumbler, and placed a possessive arm around her shoulder.

"Nothing," she said, scrunching her brow and giving her sister her best glare. "Carole doesn't believe I'm not feeling some kind of way about Trevor cheating on me." She snuggled in closer to Jake, instinctively feeling protected. "We talked about this. I'm pissed, but mostly at myself for missing the signs."

Carole's eye shifted between her and Jake, and a smile slowly formed on Carole's face. "You know, you guys look like you've been together for years." Alexis choked on the denial she was trying to spit out, and her sister continued. "Seriously, it's like you fit together or something. Kinda cool, really. I am happy for you Allie. Honestly, I am."

"Well, I know you didn't come into the city to tell me that, so out with it. What is this major intelligence briefing you're dying to give? And why did you involve mom? I know she didn't stumble upon it on social media on her own."

"No, she didn't. I told mom because I needed her opinion on something."

"Oh?" Alexis's voice tipping up a half octave, wondering what conspiratorial thought or intent caused her sister to consult with the family queen of reconciliation and accommodation. She knew Carole wouldn't be here to advocate for Trevor and couldn't imagine what it could be.

"Yes, so after we hung up yesterday, I went back and went through the bimbo's profile again, paying more attention to the dates she posted the pictures. I figured you might want to let him know you knew he was a fucking cheater if you ever talked to him again and for how long. I also knew you wouldn't waste time trying to figure it out, so I hired myself as your research team." The sound of satisfaction in her voice made both Jake and Alexis smile.

Carole continued, "Do you remember I told you I thought she was rather mousy?" Alexis nodded she did and took a sip of her wine. "Well, I still do, she's like five-foot nothing and maybe a hundred and five pounds, another reason to hate her," tapping herself on the thighs showing that she, like her sister was more of a full-figured sort of girl. "But, anyway, so I scrolled all the way back and the first picture she posted of him was at this company picnic type thing in early August. There were like four more on Labor Day, but that must have been from before because we were all at Papa's that weekend."

"Nope," Alexis interrupted, "he left Sunday night, remember? It pissed him off we wore thong bikinis on a 'public' beach. We had a fight, and he accused Brian of being a cuckold because he let you do that."

"That's right, Brian was fucking ready to take a swing at him, and would have, if dad wasn't there. Anyway, that's not the point, so I'm going through these photos and it's like the only thing she posts other than memes, but starting in the middle of October it's different, only head shots, no full body shots until Thanksgiving. There was like a family photo or something and it's all head to toe. You know what, sis? She'd put on some weight. Her face wasn't so boney. I'd guess maybe fifteen to twenty pounds. Funny thing though, it's all in one place: her abdomen. That's when I had to go see mom. She says one hundred percent, I'm like ninety/ninety-five." Carole raised her eyebrows and lifted her chin like she was waiting for her to catch onto something that Alexis should find obvious. When she didn't respond, Carole sighed and hunched her shoulders. "She's pregnant Allie. That's why all this was so sudden. He knocked up the mistress and she must be putting the screws on him to make it legit."

Alexis looked straight at her, almost glaring, and then burst out laughing hysterically. When she finally got control of herself, "Oh my God. That is just perfect Carole. He's been on me for two years to commit to a timeline to start a family. Told him I wasn't even going to think about it. Pissed him off to no end. He never did figure out I was just being difficult because I hate being pressured. Now that you described her a second time, I think I know who she is. You said a company picnic? I bet she's the admin assistant I met in his office when I stopped by at lunch one day. She couldn't look me in the eye, didn't speak in more than a whisper. Any chance you could bring your account up on my laptop? I'm dying to know for sure now."

"Really?" Carole glanced over at Jake. "I guess I could."

Alexis caught Carole's side glance toward Jake, and it occurred to her he might be less than interested in the drama around her now ex-fiancé. "Do you mind? I'm sorry vindictiveness isn't my most flattering quality."

Jake laughed, "Well, it is a side of you I haven't seen, but honestly, I'd probably be a lot more pissed than you have been under the circumstances. Figure out if it's who you think it is. I might have an idea for you to get your revenge."

"What?"

"Nope, not until you're sure you're right."

"Now you have to do it sis, I want to hear Jake's plan, don't you?"

"I do," Carole smirked, "I'm really beginning to like you."

They all went upstairs to the office and Carole logged on to her account. In a minute she had the pics up on the screen and Alexis wore a smile of satisfaction. "That's exactly who I thought it was and I would guess that this has been going on for a while. I met her before I started at DCH, March maybe?" Turning to face Jake and crossing her arms, she asked, "now what is this plan you have?"

"Well, you said he was asking for his ring back, right? So, give it to him." Alexis narrowed her gaze at him and pursed her lips, she wasn't so sure she wanted to hear the plan if it involved giving Trevor what he wanted, she was much more inclined to make him suffer and go without, at least for a good long while. "I think you should dress up to the nines. I mean, you can't help but look good, but be a little more on the sultry side. You know damn well you can turn every head in the room any time you want to." She blushed at that and squeezed his arm; she was guessing where this was going. "Drop by his office unannounced and instead of bringing the ring to him, walk right up to that secretary's desk and hand it to her. Say something like, 'I know Trevor wanted to give this to you, but I couldn't resist meeting the woman who was fucking my fiancé. Oh, and wait to have it sized until after the baby is born, swollen fingers and such, you wouldn't want to lose it, you might need to pawn it to pay the bills once he moves on to his next new toy.' Then just turn around and walk out without another word."

Alexis stared at him with an evil grin. Carole turned around in the chair and stared at him. "I absolutely love it. He would die a thousand deaths because everyone there who's important, and more important above him, knows who you are, sis. A scene like that would go around the office grape vine like wildfire. He'd be ruined politically, and if there was ever an over-proud, self-important little fuck, it is Trevor. Oh God please sis, let me at least stand in the door and watch you do it."

Alexis gave him a huge kiss. "That is exactly what I am going to do. I know right where her desk is, zero privacy and in plain view of the conference room. Management meeting is every Wednesday at ten. I will tell Andre I've got a doctor's appointment and will be in late. Remind me to never piss you off, okay?"

Jake smiled, "I'm thinking we're both better served staying in each other's good graces."

Chapter 12

Jake arrived at her front door just after eight Tuesday evening, arms full of bags containing everything they needed to decorate the tree. It took him three trips to bring all he had purchased, and it took all the restraint she could muster not to question how many trees he thought they were going to trim. She couldn't deny the pleasant flutter in her belly that his enthusiasm gave her. The urge to drag him on top of her on the couch and forget about the tree was almost too strong to resist.

They set about decorating the tree with a combination of playful banter and companionable silence. They shared smiles and laughs, gentle touches and soft kisses and a lengthy assessment about the precise placement of the lights.

Alexis alternated between contented bliss and feeling like her skin couldn't contain the swell of emotions that were roiling inside of her. She was uncomfortable in a satisfying way, but not in a way that she was accustomed to. She was uncomfortable in a way that she hadn't been since her very first love, her only love, her only heart break because it was the only time she had ever allowed herself to be vulnerable, and follow her heart.

She didn't date in high school, not what she'd call dating, anyway. Her father arranged introductions to young men from the proper families, families with wealth and power. He'd even arranged her prom date. A boy from a good family who had been plucked away from his prep school in northeast Connecticut to be her escort for the evening. She'd only met him once before and he was an insufferable snob, making disparaging comments about her friends' lack of sophistication all evening.

She attended public schools at her mother's insistence, and she was sure that her grandfather had been the driving force behind it. Her mother had never once stood up to her father over anything consequential. Her date had been more than happy to have his driver drop her off at the after-party on the beach. It was about the only thing they'd agreed on all night.

Her dating life was about the only thing she ever felt like she did that satisfied her father, and that was because she allowed him complete control. Except for that one time in the summer, she was eighteen, just before she left for school. The look of disdain in his eyes when he discovered her disobedience hurt, but not nearly as much as the damage to her heart that happened when she tried to make her own choices. She was strong and independent and had no problem blazing her own trail, but with relationships, she was safer allowing her father that one piece of control. Staying removed kept her heart safe and it least it was one thing she didn't have to fight him on.

Jake would never get her father's approval. He was everything that her father warned her against. He hadn't gone to an elite prep school or an Ivy League University. From what little Jake had shared about his family, she knew he didn't come from money. But Jake made her feel things she hadn't felt in a long time. With him, she didn't have to be anything other than herself. He had no expectations for her behavior other than to make her happy just the way he was doing tonight. He had certainly more than made her happy in bed, and that had never happened before. She could enjoy this time with Jake for as long as it lasted. And why not? She deserved a little fun, didn't she? Just as long as she didn't allow her heart to take over.

As Jake tucked the end of the garland strand around a bow at the back of the tree and crawled out from underneath the stalwart fir to survey the finished work, Alexis searched through the chaotic pile of bags and boxes on the sofa. "What are you looking for?" he asked, stepping back, looking over their Christmas tree masterpiece.

"Tinsel. I want to finish this off so we can move on to even more enjoyable things." Her smile was wide, and there was a lecherous twinkle in her eyes.

"You said you didn't like tinsel; why would I get you something I knew you didn't like?"

"But you like tinsel; you told me you did. I want this to be our tree, not mine."

"It is our tree. I bought decorations based on your suggestions. These ornaments all mean something to me, mostly because I got them for you, but some, like this one, pointing to a Red Sox ornament. That's me, right? Can't be many of those in this city."

She crossed the room and wrapped her arms around his neck, planting a firm, wet kiss squarely on his cheek. "You are a unique man, Jake Douglas.

And only because of that, will I forget you snuck a Red Sox ornament onto my tree." She giggled and turned from him, facing the tree. She held his hand to her chest, enjoying the safe, content feeling she had with his broad chest pressed to her back. It was a beautiful tree, the most beautiful tree she could ever remember having, but she suspected that much of its beauty came from the man that made it a reality for her, rather than the true esthetic value of the tree itself.

There was a large part of her that wanted him badly at that moment. To feel him inside her and to be as close as they could humanly be. There was an equally large part of her that wanted to do nothing at all to break the aura of that moment, the warmth of their embrace, the room lit only by the tree and what washed in through the windows from the street, the homey sound of the Christmas music playing in the background, being alone together in their thoughts.

Finally, one of those thoughts that went running through her mind manifested itself into spoken words. "I know we made plans for Christmas Eve, but what are your plans for Christmas Day?"

"I don't have any."

"What about your family?" She realized in all their conversations he had never said a word about them other than that he had a brother and sister.

"My sister, Amber, asked me to dinner, but my father will be there. My brother has his family in Maine and that's a bit too far for a day trip. So, my apartment is where I shall be. Don't worry, I'll have my roast beef and holiday pudding and watch a marathon of movies."

"Is your father's drinking so bad that you can't even stand to be near him on Christmas day?" She hoped she'd managed not to make that sound like an accusation. The curiosity was killing her, but she didn't want to force Jake to share if he wasn't ready. There just felt like there was more to the story than she knew.

"His drinking is bad, but there are other reasons." He stepped away from their embrace to adjust an ornament that didn't need adjusting. "I'd rather not ruin everyone's Christmas. He'll do a fine job on his own."

She wanted to ask more, but sensed that he didn't really want to talk about it. She had a feeling he would when he was ready, so no reason to push it now. She took a deep breath and blurted out the question that had been weighing on her mind before she had the chance to second guess herself. "Would you like to join me at my grandfather's? I can't promise it will be peaceful and argument free, but maybe you would enjoy my company enough to make it worth your while?"

"Don't you think my presence alone would cause a bit of an issue? Wasn't your father rather fond of Trevor?"

"Fond is not an emotion my father is familiar with. He approved of Trevor because they shared a 'traditional view of the woman's role in the family'. He's from a reputable family, blah, blah, blah." She twirled her hand in the air, demonstrating her lack of empathy with the sentiments. "I will have an issue with my father. It might be about Trevor, or whatever else he can think of that I disappoint him for, whether or not you're there. I could use all the moral support I can get. Regardless, I would like you to meet my mom and grandfather. Carole will have told them both about you by now and at least if you're with me in the flesh, my mother will know that you're real."

"Why would she think I wasn't?" Jake asked with a chuckle.

Alexis peered up at him from under her thick lashes. "Maybe Carole and I have concocted fictional boyfriends in the past?" Jake cocked a brow and smirked, leaving no doubt he expected her to continue. "When my father wasn't trying to marry us off to the right family. My mom was always one to suggest we should meet one of her friend's sons when we reached dating age. More than once I came home from college for the weekend only to find a strange boy sipping tea with my mother. Fortunately, she would never do that if we were dating someone, so Carole and I had a string of fictional boyfriends. She didn't catch on until Carole was a junior in college." Laughter was building as she told the story, and she finally had to stop and breathe because she could no longer get the words out. Wiping the tears from her eyes she took a breath, "one day mom finally called our bluff and asked someone over for Carole to meet. It was the weekend she brought Brian home to meet my parents. Mom was mortified, Carole was furious, and the poor guy didn't know what to do or say."

"I arrived about a half hour before this whole thing went down, so I swooped in and took the guy out for pity drinks. Turns out he got over his embarrassment quickly and tried to get pity sex to go along with the fifty-dollar glass of scotch he ordered."

Alexis looked up when she heard what she thought was a growl escape from Jake's throat and saw his jaw flex and fists clenched at his side. This reignited her laughter. "Easy there, slugger. I put him in his place. The only fucking he gave me was that bar tab and mom hasn't tried her hand at matchmaking since."

"But you think she'd do it on Christmas day?"

"Um, not really, but she might," she said with a sigh. "I love my mother dearly, but she's a peacekeeper. She doesn't see my father for the controlling asshole he is and tries to keep the two of us from arguing. She might think that having someone there will keep dad from being an ass. So, yeah, I think she just might invite someone to join us for dinner."

"Is that why you want me there, Lex?" he asked, his voice low. There was a darkness in his gaze that differed from what she had seen before from him.

"No," she said, grasping his arm and cupping his jaw with her other hand. She grazed his cheek with the pad of her thumb. "I want you there because I want to spend time with you. And I want you there because I can't bear the thought of you spending Christmas alone."

She smiled up at him, her sapphire eyes sparkling so brightly he felt his heart pounding out an erratic beat. "I know you'll like Brian." She sighed, realizing that she was sounding like an excited kid trying to talk her parents into a trip to Disney. "Papa's harsh on the outside, but he's all bark and my mother will like you for no other reason than I like you. Not bragging, but I am Papa's favorite and once he sees how good you treat me and how happy I am, well, you'll have an ally for life, lest of course you hurt me, then you're screwed."

Her smile dimmed, and shoulders sagged. "It's a lot to ask of you. If you're not ready for that sort of 'couple type thing' I understand, really, I do. I know we're going fast here…"

He stopped her mid-sentence with a kiss. "I've noticed something."

"What?" she asked, thoroughly confused.

"When you're nervous, you talk very fast and breathe very little."

"I do not," only half-feigning offense.

"Okay, you don't…," his warm smile wrapping right around her heart and the playful glint in his eyes sending an electric charge straight to her core, "but you do." He waited a moment before replying, which had her heart racing in anticipation, which she figured was why he did it. "I would be glad to go with you. I can't think of any reason I could have for not spending the most amount of time I can with you. Just as long as you're sure I won't be in the way or cause problems. I don't want them to think we were together before Trevor pulled his shit, giving your father an excuse to blame you. As Carole pointed out, we are very comfortable together for a couple that has just started dating."

A breath caught in her throat at the word dating, but she pushed past it, not ready to think too hard about it. "You think people would think that? I mean, I do feel that comfortable with you, but there's still so much I need to learn about you."

"I do. I've never once felt comfortable spending a holiday with someone I was seeing and her family. To me, it's something you do when you're serious about someone, not 'dating'. Does that make sense?"

"It does. I feel the same way honestly. The only other person who has ever been to Christmas at Papa's is Trevor. The jerk just assumed an invitation the first year. Probably should have told him no and saved myself over three years of my life." She drifted back off into fascination with the tree, but moments later his statement that he was serious about her, about them, finally sunk in. Her body twisted to face him and tipped up on her toes, pressing her lips to his. "Do you really mean it?" she said breathlessly as she pulled back from the kiss.

Still trying to regain his bearings after the kiss, he wasn't sure what he was supposed to have meant. "Mean what? Yes, I'll go with you on Christmas day."

"No, do you mean you're serious about me?"

"That's not obvious?"

"A girl likes to know for sure."

"Yes, Alexis. I am very serious about you."

Her brain was screaming for her to pump the brakes. *Run woman, run! You just escaped one mistake, do not jump into another. Your career is your priority and anything, and anyone who complicates things needs to go. Jake is a MAJOR complication.* Her brain was right. She knew that and while Jake might be fun, serious should not be a consideration. *Let him know now you may have today, but long-term was not a possibility.* But her heart and other body parts further south were of a completely different opinion. Seriously, it was the music they needed to hear, and the dance party was on. The pounding in her chest made it impossible to pay attention to anything her head was trying to say. She knew she'd never felt this way about anyone before. Maybe, just maybe, this was what love felt like, and that was serious as a heart attack, something she felt she might actually have based on the erratic way it was slamming inside her chest.

Chapter 13

Alexis

The clack, clack, clack of her heals echoed off the tile floor and her long, purposeful strides carried her, taking a sharp left into Jake's office with no hesitation. She didn't even check to see if anyone was looking in her direction. She didn't care, there was still far too much adrenaline coursing through her veins. She had to get it off her chest, or she felt like she would explode.

She closed the door behind her with a sharp click and locked it. Jake looked up from his reading and cocked an eyebrow when she locked the door. Without saying a word, she walked over to him, sat down in his lap, cupped his face in her hands and crashed her lips hard against his, forcing her tongue inside and claiming him.

"Oh my God, Jake! That worked out even better than we imagined! I walked in, and I was afraid that she wouldn't be at her desk, but she was. I walked up to her. She didn't see me coming. I stood in front of her desk, she has that little counter thing, like a reception desk, and she looked up with a smile and started to ask if she could help me and stopped mid-sentence. She went from cute little rosy cheeks to ashen with a hint of green. I thought for a second she might vomit all over her desk."

"I said just about exactly what you suggested. You should have seen her! I don't think she could have spoken if she tried. I put the ring on her desk. Gave her the once over, she is most definitely pregnant, and then just turned and walked back toward the door. As I was turning, I noticed the other people just gawking at us. Honestly, I was so jacked up, it was the first time I realized anyone else was there, you know what I mean? And then I noticed Trevor flying out of the conference room, a look of sheer terror on his face. I didn't acknowledge I even saw him. I just kept walking. Just before I got to the door, he caught up and grabbed me by the arm. I didn't know what I was going to say to him. We hadn't rehearsed that part, but when he grabbed my arm, it just set me off."

"He. Fucking. Grabbed. You?" Jake gritted out. She could feel his body go rigid with tension beneath her.

"Easy there, alpha boy," she said, smiling. "Let me finish. I told him he'd better take his hands off me or I'd press charges for assault and battery and, as an officer of the court, he should know I would do it. He immediately dropped his hand. He asked me what the fuck I was doing there, grave mistake on his part because, first he yelled it, bringing everybody's attention to him, and second because I told him exactly why I was there, loud enough for everybody to hear."

"I told him I was returning the engagement ring he asked me to return, and I gave it to the secretary he'd been fucking for the last nine months, and I pointed in her direction, just in case anybody was confused, but of course they weren't. I told him I figured I'd save him the embarrassment of having to come and beg me for it. I congratulated him on his impending fatherhood and said it quite surprised me he could knock somebody up with the pathetic little worm he called a penis."

"All he could manage in reply is something like jealousy being unbecoming. I just laughed in his face and told him I was many things, but jealous wasn't one of them. I told him I was relieved to be rid of him. I told him I was pissed because I wasted four years on him. I told him I was grateful because I was with a wonderful, real man now." She was stroking Jake's chest through his shirt and wishing that she could do more. "I told him I've had more and better sex in the past week than in the four years we were together." The enthusiasm for her on Jake's face filled her with such a feeling of being loved and appreciated she felt like she would explode with happiness. She knew it was impossible, but she wanted to be with him in that moment more than she had ever wanted sex in her life. There was a need for him in her very core she couldn't begin to describe. "I said I was happy for the first time in nearly four years and thanked him, because now I was with a man who I loved, who loved me back and respected me as a person, not treated me like property, or only valued me for what doors I could open for him or the money in my bank account."

"I noticed one of his closest friends at work was standing with his arms folded and a smirk on his face about ten feet away as I turned to walk out the door. I gave his friend a wink and then walked out."

"It sounds like it went even better than you hoped for."

"It did." She sighed, the tension leaving her shoulders and her heart rate slowing slightly. "I might have looked like the crazy ex, but everyone knows what he did, and with miss thing great with child, it's going to be hard for him to deny, redirect and obfuscate. Anyway, I'm sorry. I know I shouldn't be in here, but I just couldn't wait to tell you." She gave him a kiss and got off his lap. "God, I love you. You will come over tonight, right?" That was more a directive than a question.

"If you'd like me to." His smile dimmed and his brow tightened like he was trying to figure out a riddle. "I'll be late, though, and I'll have to stop at my apartment and grab some clothes."

She sensed that something was troubling him and hoped he wasn't feeling like he was invading her space. "Of course I want you to. Why don't you grab clothes enough for a few days, so you don't have to keep stopping at your place? Only if you want to, though, no pressure," she quickly added, taking two steps toward the door before stopping. It might be impossible for her to make love to him right now, but she could certainly mess with him a little. She reached up under her skirt and pulled off her panties, putting them in his hand and closing his fingers around them. Leaning in, she whispered in his ear, "let's see if you really pass out knowing I'm wearing nothing under this skirt."

She gasped as he grabbed her and pulled her down into a fierce kiss. "Damn if I don't love you too," he growled against her lips before releasing her with a firm pat on her bottom.

She turned with a wink, opened his door, and walked out. "Let me know if you have questions about that. I'll email you the doc. Thanks!" She called over her shoulder, heading quickly to her office.

Her body was buzzing. The force of his kiss when she handed him her panties curled her toes, and she almost came on the spot. She knew anyone that looked at her would know her mind was on anything but business. *Best to get inside my office and calm the hell down.* Before her carefully curated Ice Princess persona got ruined. She grasped the handle to her office door and froze. *Ho. Lee. Fuck. He just said he loved me. No, he just told me he loved me, too. I told him I loved him first. I told him more than once.*

Releasing the door handle and pivoting gracefully on her four-inch heals she inched her way back toward Jake's office. Reaching out to the handle on his office door like it might be connected to high-voltage wires, she twisted it slowly and inched it open, slipping inside.

Her heart was pounding like a timpani in her chest and the elated feeling she had just seconds ago was replaced by a sense that she was about to be attacked violently by wild animals. In seconds, she realized that her world had completely imploded. What used to be down was now decidedly up.

Easing the door closed behind her, she stood there in silence for a moment before meeting his gaze. She swallowed. "Did you just say you loved me?"

Jake nodded. He met her eyes with a blank stare.

"Did *I* say that *I* loved you?"

Jake nodded again.

"Oh." She opened her mouth again, then closed it. She repeated this process several times before uttering a nearly inaudible, "okay," and turning back out the door, closing it behind her.

Walking slowly through a fog, she made her way back to her office, shut her door behind her, and collapsed into her chair.

How could I possibly have let this happen? I can't be in love. I don't do love.

Another voice, the Ice Princess, chimed in, *Well, you've certainly fucked this up. Because you most definitely are in love and unless you want to ruin your plans, you better un-fuck it up and fast.*

Looking up slowly from her unfocused stare, her eyes met Jake's as he appeared inside her office. He silently walked to her, leaned over, and kissed her. "I meant it. I love you. I know it's quick, but I do. And I hope you meant it too." He didn't wait for her reply. He simply turned and walked back out of her office.

This was going to get harder and harder to hide; and harder and harder to stick to her plan.

Chapter 14

Alexis, the Summer she was Eighteen

Cody was every girl's dream. Sandy blonde hair, always just a hint of mess, tanned with the perfect number of freckles dotting his face. Bright, bright blue eyes and dimples that made you want to do all sorts of naughty things. And sweet lord above the body. A chiseled Adonis with sun kissed bronze flesh instead of marble. He was sex on two sticks, two muscular, toned, tanned sticks with a smattering of sun-bleached blonde hair disappearing below the waist of his board shorts.

Not only did he look good, but he was the kindest boy Alexis had ever met. The only son of one of Hollywood's A list couples, well, they weren't a couple anymore, but his mother had bought the 'cottage' three lots down from her grandfather's the winter before. He was with his mother for the summer before heading to his freshman year at an Ivy League University, the same one that she had been accepted to in their pre-law program. They could find an apartment together off campus. They had it all planned. Well, she did anyway, and he hadn't told her not to.

When she met him walking on the beach Memorial Day Weekend, he had looked like a lost little boy. She smiled at him, and he smiled back. That was all it took for her newly eighteen-year-old self to fall for him. She didn't have any idea who he was, but figured he must be from a 'good' home. Few locals walked this stretch of beach, just people from other 'cottages' like her grandfather's twelve-bedroom estate. They quickly became inseparable and then they became a 'thing'. Alexis had never felt this way before. It was like she loved him so much that her chest was too small to contain it. She couldn't wait to kiss him. Anytime she was with him, her body felt like it was humming.

Late at night, when she couldn't fall asleep because her mind kept re-living the days that they spent together, she would touch herself. She had been on a date or two and even experienced an awkward kiss, letting one date get as far as second base after a football game. But her focus was on school and not boys. This sexual awareness was all something new to her.

After three weeks together, his mother left for a movie shoot, leaving him in the care of a nanny. A nanny, that at eighteen he didn't feel he needed, and a nanny that didn't much care what he did as long as she had some basic idea of where he was doing it.

Carole had turned fifteen at the end of April and was well on her way to being the typical teenage terror to her mother. Too busy trying to control the tempestuous Carole, Alexis flew under the radar and scrutiny of her mother. So long as she checked in regularly, she got the same type of freedom Cody did, the only exception being she had a curfew. A loosely enforced curfew.

The week before the fourth of July, as the rest of the summer people had taken up residence, they left a crowded bonfire and went back to Cody's. He led her through the house and straight up to his room. They passed his nanny on the way and she simply smiled and winked at Alexis, making her cheeks burn in embarrassment. Alexis knew what the wink was for, Cody was a hunk and oozed sex but she'd never… the most they'd ever done was kiss and the furthest she'd ever allowed a boy to go was second base and that was over her shirt and bra for all of fifteen seconds before she pushed him away.

Alexis knew Cody had experience, and she desperately didn't want to disappoint him. But she wasn't going to be forced into something she wasn't ready for. Laying on his bed feeling his hands and mouth all over her body, she decided she was as ready as she'd ever be until he couldn't produce a condom. One thing she knew she wasn't ready for was a kid or a disease. She stopped him there and the fact that he didn't complain in the slightest only firmed her resolve that Cody would be her first, just not tonight.

Two nights later they made the same journey, but when they got to his room, she found a serving bowl full of condoms on the nightstand next to his bed. He smiled at her, and she nodded. She was ready.

The first time was often awkward, often painful, but for Alexis, it was anything but. A moment of discomfort and then more pleasure than she could have ever imagined. There was no doubt in her mind that Cody had plenty of experience. That caused her a pang of jealousy that she cast aside for no other reason than her body was so on fire she couldn't spare the band width to focus on it. As they lay in his bed, basking in the afterglow, the emotions that had been boiling up in her chest finally burst forth and came out in the simplest of phrases, "Cody, I love you so much." Tears were pooling in her eyes as she cupped his face and kissed him softly.

"Me too babe, me too," was his reply.

She walked home that night and she felt like her feet never hit the sand. She swirled into her grandfather's and knew she must have somehow looked different. Both her mother and grandmother looked up from their reading with raised eyebrows as she passed through the living room toward the stairs up to her room. She could see them exchanged a look but never said a word more than good night. She certainly felt different, and she couldn't wait to feel it again and again.

Over the next four weeks, they spent more time in his room than they did anywhere else. By the end of July, the serving bowl needed a refill. Alexis would have done anything for Cody. She was in love, and she knew he was her forever love.

The first two weeks of August were very hard for her, as Cody had to go to Los Angeles to be with his father. Cody would often take hours to reply to her texts and wouldn't always return her calls until the next day, sometimes two. But he always apologized, and she believed his excuses. He seemed so sincere, and she loved him. He was her forever love.

The week he returned, she felt something had changed between them, but she couldn't put her finger on it. He was still more than affectionate. They still spent most of their waking hours together. He still always replied with a megawatt smile and a 'me too' when she said she loved him. It was their thing. But there was just something different about him.

The Wednesday before Labor Day Weekend, she went into the city with her mother and sister to do some school shopping. It was nearly nine by the time they got back, and her mother had wanted to stay in the city for the night, but Alexis had pleaded, Cody would be back in school in a week. She didn't want to be away from him. Her mother had conceded, with a sigh and a comment about young love. She was out of the car and running for Cody's practically before the car had fully come to a stop.

She had texted him when they were about a half hour away, but he hadn't replied. Maybe he was taking a nap, she thought, or on the beach at a bonfire and didn't hear his phone. When she looked up to his room, she noticed the lights were out, but there was a dim, flickering light. He had put on candles for her. There was that swelling in her chest again. How did he do that to her?

She was relieved to find his door unlocked and ran up the stairs, taking two at a time. She stopped for a second outside his door to catch her breath and then opened the door. "Surpri…." She stopped, the word dying in her throat, hand on the doorknob. Cody raised his head from between the legs of a woman who had another girl sitting on her face.

Alexis was right. There were candles lit in the room and a very heavy cloud of pot smoke. He had promised her he wouldn't smoke around her, but obviously that was the least of the disappointment she was feeling in the moment.

"Hey babe, get that dress off and join us." Cody slurred in a raspy voice. He sounded drunk and high.

"Join you!" Alexis screamed. "What the fuck, Cody? How could you do this to me? I love you. You said you loved me." Tears were streaming down her face, and she felt like her head was going to burst. The room was spinning, and her vision was closing in, dark at the edges. She felt as though it was a struggle to keep Cody in focus.

"Aw, come on. Don't be such a prude. I wanna see you make out with another girl while I fuck you. That would be so hot, babe." He slid off the bed and she could she his face glistening with the other girl's arousal. She felt the bile rise in her throat and fought with all her strength to keep it down.

The touch of his hand on her shoulder pulling down the strap to her sundress snapped Alexis back to the present. She slapped it away, stepping back from him and hitting her back against the edge of the door. "Don't touch me! This isn't what you do to someone you love."

"I never told you I loved you, Alexis. You just assumed it. You're fun to hang out with, but you're just a fuck." He shrugged, showing a toothy smile. "A really fun fuck but that's all,"

A part of her wanted to bring her knee up and crush his balls so he could never fuck anyone again. But she thought if she felt his touch, she would burst into flames. She wanted to argue and say that he had told her he loved her, but she realized he was right. He never had. All he had ever said was, "me too". She had filled in the words he refused to say. She wanted to say something that would hurt him the way he had hurt her. But she knew there was nothing left to say. She turned, slamming the door behind her, and ran from the house as fast as her legs could carry her.

She walked back toward her grandfathers in a daze. She turned to walk up through the dunes but couldn't bear the thought of facing anyone. Tears still streamed down her face, though she was too distraught to make a sound. She walked further, eventually reaching the public area of the beach. She climbed up on an empty lifeguard chair and stared out at the Atlantic, keenly aware that the swelling in her chest was no longer there. Nothing was there. She felt empty inside except for the excruciating pain left from where her heart had been torn so callously from inside of her.

She didn't know how long she sat there but was aware that one by one the fires on the beach were going out and the night breeze was chilly against her bare skin. Trudging her way back to her grandfather's she waded through the icy Atlantic water numbing her legs to the knees, but not as numb as she felt in her chest.

It was well after curfew as she crept into the house, hoping everyone was asleep. Instead, her father was waiting for her in the living room. Her eyes were red and swollen and her hair a tangled mess from the ocean breeze and nervously raking her hands through it, trying to make sense of how she could have been so naïve. She knew she looked like shit, and she knew she had broken curfew, but she was glad to see her father. She could use a kind word right now. Sure, they hadn't exactly seen eye to eye when she hit her teenage years, but she could remember him kissing away the pain of her skinned knees and her heart was more than skinned right now.

Their eyes met, and she froze in place. He finished whatever amber alcohol he had in his glass and set it on the end table, slowly rising from his chair. He took a step toward her, and she raised her arms to accept his hug when he spoke.

"I hope you're very proud of yourself Alexis," his visceral tone causing the hair on her arms to rise.

"I'm sorry?" her voice was shaky and confused. Her arms dropping back to her side.

"I've tried to tell you, but you're too damn stubborn and think you're so smart." His eyes narrowed and cold as he stood inches from her face. She could nearly taste the alcohol from his breath. "Love is for the stupid and the weak. You marry into the right family and advance your position. Power and money, Alexis, that's all that matters." His gaze raked over her body as he shook his head. "Otherwise, you end up just like you are now; a hurt, weak, little slut who's ruled by nothing more than that stink between your legs."

Her jaw dropped, and saliva filled her mouth. She was sure she was going to vomit as everything inside her chest twisted into a painful knot. Her father perused her again before turning and walking away, leaving her alone in her shame.

Alexis spent the next two days in bed, only coming out for meals. Her mother had tried to talk to her, but she'd just waved her away. Cramps, she had said. Her mother knew better, but also knew not to push her. She had waited for Cody to text her; to at least feign an apology. She had hoped her father would knock on her door and do the same, but neither of the men who had hurt her so deeply cared enough to say they were sorry or admit they were wrong. Slowly, she built up walls around her. She built herself an icy castle and locked her feelings deep inside. She emerged from her exile around noon on Saturday as if nothing had ever happened.

Saturday night, she forced herself to head to the beach for the usual Labor Day bonfire the kids from the cottages always had. They all stood around drinking the booze they had stolen from their parent's bars, getting drunk and smoking cigarettes and weed. Alexis saw Cody arrive with a girl that had been in his bed that night. He glanced her way, but she turned, pretending she was paying attention to the group she was with. The pain had dulled in her chest and her grandfather's scotch was helping to numb what was left behind. All she felt now was empty and cold.

Brandon, a boy that she had known since she was six or seven and who her mother had always said had had a crush on her, was in her group and flirting with her like he usually did. She always laughed him off and did her best to make it clear she wasn't interested. Tonight, she flirted back. Each time he moved closer, she stepped closer to him. Every casual touch he gave to her, she responded with one slightly more intimate of her own, until he finally worked up the courage to kiss her. She kissed him back with a side eye to make certain Cody could see. And when she knew Cody was watching the show, she upped the ante and caressed Brandon's crotch.

Moments later, she walked away from the fire, hand in hand with Brandon. But she felt nothing, nothing but empty inside. And empty inside and feeling nothing was all she was ever going to allow herself to feel. She would never be hurt like that again. Little girls got hurt. Ice Princesses knew better. She knew better.

Chapter 15

Alexis

Alexis glanced toward the passenger seat at Jake. His expression was unclear in the fading light of the early winter's late afternoon. Few of the homes they passed showed any sign of life. Christmas day was not high season for the wealthy families that summered here. They would be home in their Park Avenue penthouses or off in Aspen at their ski lodges. She placed her hand on his thigh as she turned down the long, hedge-lined lane that spilled directly into her grandfather's oceanfront home.

Was this really fair to him? Her conscience asked as she looped around the circular drive and came to a stop. *It's a little late now*, another part of her brain replied, and that was true. Deciding to ask him to join her at her family's Christmas dinner was a steep ask given the contentious nature of the relationship with her father, but she really felt like she couldn't avoid it. They were spending most nights together and Jake would sit alone in his apartment if she hadn't.

And the truth was, she enjoyed his company and wanted to spend time with him. Selfishly, she also hoped that his presence would keep her father in line, though she wasn't entirely sure about that. More and more through the years, her father seemed to take pride in embarrassing her. He might even take some sort of satisfaction out of scaring Jake away. She'd seen Jake in the boardroom and doubted he'd spook that easily, but who knows, at least the boardroom was neutral territory. Here, he was completely out of his element.

Jake put his hand over hers as she gave his thigh an affectionate squeeze. "How are you doing?" he asked, surprising her.

"I think I'm the one who's supposed to be asking you that," she chuckled, though with little amusement behind it. "You're the one walking into unknown territory."

Turning, she opened her door and slid out of the car. "Let's get this shit show over with," she muttered under her breath. Catching sight of Jake's raised brow over the roof of the car, she shrugged her shoulders. "It's true. This probably isn't fair to you, but I'll be honest, I'm really glad you're here."

"I'm glad I am too. At least you can count on one person to have your back, no matter what."

They cut their conversation short as the entry door swung open just as they hit the top step.

"Merry Christmas, Allie girl." The elderly man shouted who could only be Alexis' grandfather. Despite barely being taller than his granddaughter and slightly built, the man had a commanding presence. He would undoubtedly take control of any room he was in.

"Merry Christmas, Papa." She leaned into his hug and a purposely sloppy kiss on the cheek

Jake extended his hand. "It is a pleasure to meet you, Mr. Johnson."

"Jake," he shook his hand and looking him straight in the eye, "It didn't take you long to swoop in and scoop up my granddaughter. I heard about you almost before I heard her engagement was off."

Alexis recognized the boardroom version of the polite smile Jake forced for her grandfather. "No sir, I don't believe in hesitating when something this special is available. I don't want to give the competition a chance."

"You don't think it would be more gentlemanly to perhaps give her a chance to get her bearings?" George asked with a bit of an edge to his voice.

"Papa." Alexis broke in. "At least give him a drink before you start the interrogation."

"It's okay. I expected at least one person to question my intentions today." Jake turned and kissed her cheek before turning back to face George. "In the time that I've known Alexis, I don't believe I have ever seen her not in control of her environment. As a gentleman, I would never take advantage of her, but Alexis is a very special woman, and I was not about to risk someone else coming along while I sat and waited."

George looked Jake over from head to toe and back again before meeting his gaze. The silence between them as they stared each other down had Alexis shifting from foot to foot and wondering if she should grab Jake and make a run for it before the rest of the family arrived. She hadn't expected trouble from her biggest ally and if he had it in for Jake, things were going to be a disaster.

"Good for you," George smiled, and both men looked at Alexis. The breath she released sounded like the ocean wind during a Nor'easter. "I like a man who goes after what he wants," George continued, "And I don't remember seeing my Allie girl looking this happy in a long, long time. I assume that's your fault." Jake's shoulders relaxed and the tenseness of his smile melted away. "Now, what would you like to drink while we wait for the others to arrive?"

"Well, sir…" Jake began.

"Please call me George."

"Thank you, I may be jumping the gun giving gifts, but Alexis told me you were a fan of single malt whiskey, so I brought you a bottle of my favorite. Perhaps we can share a glass of that?"

"Wonderful." George's eyes twinkled with excitement. He peeked into the gift bag eagerly. "What have you brought me?" he asked, pulling out the bottle.

Alexis smiled with relief. Her grandfather would be there for her, for Jake too, if she needed him.

George discovered a bottle of Mortlach, Distiller's Dram, sixteen-year-old single malt scotch whiskey. "My mother claimed my family has distilled whiskey for hundreds of years. She was proud of our Scottish heritage." Jake explained as George inspected the bottle.

George nodded. "Thank you very much. This is very thoughtful of you." He gave Jake a wink. "My granddaughter knows bribing me with good scotch is a sure way to my good graces. It's a shame my son-in-law won't be so easy on you. Don't worry, I've got your back son, and if this," holding up the bottle, "is as good as I hear it is, I might just cover your left flank as well." He let out a little chuckle, laughing at his own joke.

They walked into the large living room. There was a huge fieldstone fireplace that dominated the far wall. In front of them was a wall of glass that looked directly out onto the Atlantic Ocean. Several sectionals were arranged throughout the room, forming small conversation areas. The end opposite the fireplace opened into a formal dining area, the table already grandly set for Christmas dinner. Just to the left of the entrance hallway they had just come through was a full bar with six stools.

George stepped behind the bar and poured Alexis a glass of red wine before opening the bottle of scotch and pouring a dram for Jake and himself. He passed out the drinks and toasted them. "To Christmas and love," winking at his granddaughter. "Cheers."

They touched glasses and Alexis added, "cheers."

Jake toasted with the Scots, "Slainte Mhath!"

George smiled with a twinkle in his eyes, "Slainte Mhath"

Alexis looked at them, questioning just what they were up to. George stepped in. "It means 'good health' in Gaelic."

Alexis turned to Jake with a hint of surprise in her voice. "You know Gaelic?"

Jake smiled. "No, just a few words and phrases my grandmother taught me when I was a boy."

George gasped a satisfied "Ah," as the amber liquid warmed his throat on the way down. "It seems, young man, that your taste in whiskey is every bit as good as your taste in women."

A short while later, the doorbell rang. "I'm getting too old to keep walking back and forth. And too kind to make my housekeeper work on Christmas Day." George waved his hand in the air, directing Alexis to get the door. They laughed, and she went to let in the next members of her family.

George smiled as he looked up to see Carole and Brian walk in. "Look what the cat dragged in." He said, laughing and spreading his arms wide, inviting a hug. He leaned over the bar to get a kiss on the cheek from Carole and shook Brian's hand. "Carole, I hear you have already met Alexis' new beau, Brian. This is Jake."

Carole and Brian had barely received their drinks when the doorbell rang again. "Damn," Carole said, "I had hoped we'd get a few minutes to catch up before they got here."

"We just saw each other ten days ago." Alexis laughed, slapping her sister playfully on the shoulder.

"I know, but that was before you returned the ring. You haven't said a word about how that went."

"I texted you it went even better than we planned, not much more to say and that's already more than I want to talk about him today. I'm going to get the door."

Alexis led her parents into the room and sidled next to Jake. He stepped away from his conversation with Brian to greet them.

"Mom, dad, this is Jake Douglas." Placing her hand on the small of Jake's back, she wasn't sure if it was a show of support for him or to help her ground herself and relieve the twisted feeling in her gut. She worried her bottom lip as Jake extended his hand toward her father.

"Mr. Chambers, it's a pleasure to meet you." Her father nodded with a humph as Jake turned to her mother quickly. "Mrs. Chambers, Alexis tells me you're a talented artist."

"Really?" The surprise in her mother's voice came nowhere close to the surprise she felt herself at hearing those words come from Jake's mouth. Her mother was a talented artist, but she didn't remember ever sharing that bit of trivia with him and wondered where he had learned that.

"Yes. I must agree if you're the same Lois Chambers who painted the seascape over the fireplace in Alexis' living room."

The forced smile on her face relaxed into a natural one, and her heart skipped a beat with excitement. Her mother's painting had hung there for as long as she could remember. She hadn't even thought to mention it to Jake because it was just part of the room, but somehow Jake had noticed it and intentionally mentioned it to make her mother, and her, feel noticed.

"You're too kind, Jake, but thank you. I actually painted that while I was pregnant with Alexis."

"I didn't know that." Alexis tilted her head and placed her hands on her hips like a child who had been left out of a favorite game.

"Of course, you did dear, you've just forgotten is all because we never talk about my art in front of your father anymore."

Alexis ground her teeth together and was about to launch into how her father was just a selfish jerk who couldn't stand anyone's success but his own, but reined it back. She inhaled deeply before slowly exhaling through her mouth. "He still hasn't accepted that you've become popular since you started painting again after Carole and I went to college? Why does he always have to cast shade on everyone else's joy?"

Her mother shrugged her shoulders as if it was just the way things were. "At least you shouldn't have to worry about your father today, dear. I gave him a stern talking to, and he is very aware now what Trevor was up to for the last nine months. That took him down a few pegs in his eyes, but he's not convinced the two of you have been together for just three weeks. That's mostly Carole's fault, because she was gushing at how happy the two of you looked together. He's convinced no one gets that attached this soon. He forgets how we were," she said with a dry chuckle. "He forgets a lot of things from when he was young." She added half under her breath, as they all turned and joined the others at the bar.

"Alexis tells me that your true love is constitutional law. Why did you go after a position like DCH." George asked, meeting Jake's eyes from his position behind the bar. "You've got to be a damn good lawyer to get that gig, so I'd think the DC firms would have been falling all over you."

Alexis squeezed Jake's arm in support. She knew DCH wasn't Jake's first choice, and it discouraged him he hadn't had interest from any of the prestigious Washington law firms.

"That's a question I've asked myself more than once. Honestly, DCH came in with a very lucrative offer and was first in line. I got offers from a couple of lesser firms in DC, but they were less money and there's law school to pay for. I'm closer to my brother and sister here in New York. I like what I do well enough for now."

"If you ever want to make a switch, please let me know. I have some connections in Senator Pace's office and a couple of firms in town. They'll see you if I ask. The rest will be up to you."

"Thank you. I appreciate that."

Alexis leaned over the bar and gave her grandfather a kiss on the cheek. "Thank you, Papa, I love you." He then took her hand and slipped something into it. She smiled and gave him another kiss on the cheek.

"You knew I would, right?" George asked her.

She nodded and smiled wider. "I'll be right back," she whispered in Jake's ear, and headed down the hall. Looking over her shoulder, she could see Brian leading Jake away from the bar. She let out a sigh of relief as she closed the bathroom door behind her. At least she didn't have to worry about her father cornering Jake without her there to defend him if he was talking with Brian.

Alexis walked back into the room and couldn't resist a little eavesdropping as both men had their back to her.

"You certainly made an impression on Carole. She couldn't stop talking about you when I got home on Monday. Alexis seems happy, and I can't say I've ever seen her that way in the five years I've known her. I've seen her kiss you more in the fifteen minutes we've been here than I've ever seen her kiss Trevor." Brian cut himself off, shaking his head. "Sorry, you're probably sick of hearing about Trevor."

"To an extent, I guess." Jake forced a polite smile, "but so far I've been coming out on the plus side of the comparison, so I won't complain."

"Man, you would have to be a pretty puckered up asshat to lose a comparison with him. Carole and I couldn't stand him. Honestly, I think the only person in this family who cared for him at all was Greg and that's because, I think he thought maybe Trevor could convince Allie to give up on her career. Greg just doesn't want her to succeed. It's more than outdated social norms, nobody can quite put their fingers on it."

"Unfortunately, he will not care much for me at all then, because I want her to succeed and would do just about anything to support her."

"I definitely feel supported and appreciated." Alexis reappeared at Jake's side, deciding she had heard enough. Kissing him on the cheek, she shoved her panties into his pants pocket.

He arched his brow at her in a silent question and she simply batted her lashes and smiled. The heat rose on her cheeks as he reached into his pocket, and she couldn't suppress the giggle that escaped as she watched the realization of what was in his pocket wash across his face.

"What's going on?" Brian asked.

"Oh nothing," she sing-songed, tipping up and down on her toes and loving that Jake had reacted just as she had hoped.

"I should have never admitted to that."

Brian laughed and shook his head. "I don't really want to know, do I?"

"Nope," she and Jake answered in unison.

George cleared his throat loudly enough to get everyone's attention and pointed toward the large Christmas tree next to the fireplace. They all made their way in that direction to exchange their gifts.

Once they exchanged gifts and cleaned everything up, they moved to the dining room. Things had been tense, but cordial, with Greg and, given what Alexis had prepared for, things were going better than expected. Until they weren't.

Greg looked the length of the table at her and opened his mouth as if he was about to speak. Instead, he cleared his throat and took a sip of his wine. As he set the glass down, he shook his head and glared at her. "Honestly Alexis, I don't understand how you can act this way. It's no wonder Trevor ended it with you."

"I'm not *acting* any way dad." The happiness that had been on Alexis' face seemed to fade quicker than the air out of a punctured balloon. "You'd prefer me to be miserable?"

"I'd prefer you to be married to Trevor. Your word obviously means nothing, and that is an embarrassment to this family. You have put an indelible stain on our reputation. Four years is too long to make any man wait. No wonder he found someone else. He certainly wasn't a priority for you."

Alexis watched as her mother's face grew a deeper shade of scarlet with each passing second, the veins bulging on her forehead as she leered at her husband. Carole and Brian looked at each other open-mouthed before turning to look across the table at Alexis. Her jaw clenched tightly. The veins on her forehead were likely just as pronounced as her mother's. They certainly felt that way.

Out of the corner of her eye she could see her grandfather, napkin pressed to his mouth, seemingly as a muzzle to hold back whatever imprudent immediate response had been trying to escape. He cleared his throat with a rough growl.

Whatever George was going to say was interrupted by the scrape of the chair across the floor as Alexis rose to her feet. Her usual vibrant blue eyes burned with the dark gray of an angry winter ocean. "You are blaming me because he cheated!" Her shout masked the brittle hurting tremor in her voice she felt was just below the surface.

"He was a fine man, Alexis, and would have been a good husband, a strong provider…"

"Don't you dare say another word!" Lois bellowed, cutting off his words. Her thrown napkin sailing over his shoulder. "I warned you about this. I told you not to ruin our Christmas with your narrow-minded selfishness! You've always been jealous of Allie's success. Just because she could achieve what you never did. You would defend a misogynistic, egocentric, pathetic weasel of a man who disrespected our daughter by being unfaithful, even before marriage. He was so ignorant and careless he impregnated his affair partner, and you blame her for it happening! Did you not see how happy she was until you opened your damned mouth! That is the first time I have seen her look that way since she was a teenager. Does that not matter at all to you? Honestly, I don't know who you've become."

Alexis looked on as her father clenched and unclench his jaw. His right eye was twitching, a tell she had long ago learned to mean something truly vile was about to spew out of his mouth. "Yes, I noticed how happy she was. Far too happy for a relationship that only supposedly began a few weeks ago. I don't think for one moment that Trevor was the only one straying from that relationship. It wouldn't be the first time you've played the whore."

Jake

Jake spent the evening quietly watching the interactions between Alexis' family. In a lot of ways, it was the same as his own. Everyone enjoying each other's company and their time together but was ever conscious of her father. Waiting. Watching. Wondering when the calm would be interrupted by a storm. Not sure when, but certain the thunder would come at some point.

He promised himself that he wouldn't lose control of his temper and ruin this family's Christmas. It wasn't his place to interfere with her family drama, and he wanted to make a good impression. It was important to him, but more importantly, he knew Alexis wanted that, too. He could do this for her. He would do this for her.

The moment Trevor's name left Greg's mouth, he felt his body coil, ready to pounce. All he could see and hear was his own father. Insulting his mother, threatening his brother and him. A man only concerned with himself and pouring hate onto those he was supposed to love. His heart pounded in his chest, his jaw clenched tight, and he fisted his pant legs doing his best to let Alexis handle this herself.

His tension eased as her mother confronted her father. But he should have known better. Men like that don't back down, they double down. He held back from lashing out at the man who reminded him so much of his father even as Alexis stood beside him, but as "whore" registered in his brain he could take no more. "Perhaps it would be best if you and I finished this discussion outside," Jake growled as he rose to his feet. "Your family shouldn't have to listen to this, especially on Christmas day." He felt Alexis squeeze his biceps, though he wasn't sure if it was to calm him or encourage him.

Greg's nostrils flared, his eyes narrowing to nothing more than snake-like slits. "Are you calling me outside to a fistfight?" his voice raging so loudly Jake notice Carole wincing out of the corner of his vision. "You have one hell of a nerve butting into this family's business. I don't know what kind of gold you are trying to dig but I can…"

Jake cut him off, all pretense of respect gone from his tone. "Are you so cognitively impaired you can't comprehend that I said if you wish to continue this discussion, we should do so away from…"

"Jake please," Lois interrupted, narrowing her eyes at him the way only mothers do to show total submission is required. "The only one who will step outside is Greg. It's time for you to go home. I warned you. You need to leave. Now. You've cast a pall over every holiday and family gathering for fifteen years. I. Am. Done. I will not put up with it any longer. Do you hear me?" She took a deep breath and leveled her tone, but still maintained the glare she was leveling in her husband's direction. "Carole will give me a ride home; if I decide to come home." She brought her wineglass to her lips and took a long sip. "You'd best be in the guest bedroom either way. You're going to stay there until you get to a point where you can legitimately see you're wrong and make the appropriate apologies to everyone."

"I am not apologizing to a single soul, not as long as I'm the head of this family."

From the opposite end of the table, a fist slammed down, shaking every piece of China and silverware and startling everyone except Lois. "I am the head of this family. This is my house and my daughter just told you to leave it, Gregory. I suggest you do so. Right. Now." The silence in the room was thick. Jake found Alexis' hand on his arm and placed his hand over it.

Greg glared at the end of the table. He was beet red and looked like a boiler ready to explode. Jake was the only one at the table that he didn't look at. He looked as though he expected support from Carole and Brian, but their expressions were equally full of disdain for him. Pushing his chair slowly back from the table, he walked out without another word. The front door slamming so hard it shook the house.

A tense silence filled the room.

"Please forgive me for not defending you sooner, Lois," George said softly, giving her a sad half-smile. "Jake has only been with Alexis for a few weeks, and he had the character to stand up for her. The rest of us have put up with his temper tantrums and arrogance for far too long."

Alexis' hand was still on Jake's arm, and he noticed it was shaking. He turned to her and saw that she was valiantly trying to hold back tears. He drew her into his chest and stroked her hair. She broke down in deep, sorrowful sobs.

"I am so sorry, Alexis. I should have held my tongue. I've made a terrible mess of things."

"It's not you." She croaked through her sobs. "I can't believe he hates me just because I want to do something with my life." Jake wrapped his arms around her as her body heaved against his chest. Her mother and Carole came around and tried to comfort her as well.

Brian and George sat there in silence for a few more minutes until George got up and poured Alexis another glass of wine. "Here sweetheart, have a few sips of wine and then come sit by the bar. I think we could all use a few drops to calm our nerves." A glass of scotch appeared in front of

Jake. He offered Brian a silent nod of thanks.

He continued to hold Alexis as she continued her muted sobs as the rest of the room stood in silence. George cleared his throat, breaking the stunned stillness. "I am sorry Lois. I should have stepped in years ago."

"You have nothing to be sorry for, dad. Greg has always resented that your money kept us afloat for years until he finally succeeded at something. He could never admit he wasn't able to do it on his own. It would have ruined his little fantasy image of himself as the 'provider'. God forbid he would let me help."

Alexis pulled her head up from his chest and spoke in an unsteady voice. "Does he really hate me just because I succeeded in things?"

"He doesn't hate you, honey. In his own way, he loves you. It's just hidden underneath a lot of self-loathing that he hides with anger. He's angry because you got into Yale, but he didn't. He's angry because you went to grad school and became a lawyer. He wanted to, but couldn't get into the right law school, so he just gave up. He is jealous of you, and he is rather Neanderthal in his views about what women should and shouldn't do. You don't have any desire to be barefoot, pregnant and in the kitchen and he doesn't quite understand why you wouldn't want that. In a distorted sort of way, he's probably upset at you because you won't let him protect you like he thinks he's supposed to."

"God, wow mom, how have you done it?" Carole interjected.

"Because he was a good, kind man. At least he was when we met. He just doesn't quite fit in anymore and it's been dragging him down for years now. He won't go to counseling because he thinks that would be a sign of weakness."

Alexis looked up at Jake and smiled. She leaned up and kissed him and then nestled back into his chest.

"What?" Jake asked, thoroughly confused by her expression.

"I am very lucky to have found you, that's all. I came very close to marrying an inferior version of my father. You stood up for me today. No one had done that for me before, no one that's not in this room, anyway."

George looked at Jake, smiled and tipped his glass in his direction, "You've got some pretty big brass balls, young man." He laughed as he took another drink. "You can certainly make a first impression."

It already mortified Jake, thinking back at the confrontation. "I want to apologize to all of you. I'm afraid I stepped way out of line today and only made matters worse. Too much bad family history of my own." He shook his head and looked down at his feet.

"I think what you did was very honorable and brave. You continue to get top honors from me for what it's worth." Carole smiled and toasted him with her wineglass.

Brian added, "You just got a full immersion course of a Chambers' family Christmas. It truly isn't Christmas day until someone makes someone cry."

Chapter 16

Jake

The crunch of the gravel drive under the tires turned into the thump of side streets, then turned into the hum of the pavement on the state highway. Jake stared out at the passing buildings, some adorned with holiday lights, many businesses closed so employees could enjoy the day with their families. Hopefully, more festive than where they just came from or the shitshow that was certainly taking place around his sister's table. He hated that Alexis had her own family drama to deal with. That was his excuse for not sharing his own story with her. *She has enough crap to deal with; she doesn't need mine as well,* but there was a part of him that didn't want to expose his darker side; have her shut him out like Stephanie. He didn't want to be the one that wasn't quite good enough for a change. The younger brother who wasn't manly enough to work with his hands. The one who was always dreaming about the future instead of working for the present.

"You're awfully quiet. Planning your exit strategy?" Alexis said with a laugh that sounded anything but genuine.

He could sense the uncertainty in her voice and hated it. "No one is ever going to scare me away from you, Lex." The deep sigh she breathed out made him think she didn't agree. "How are you doing?" he asked, sensing she was holding back.

"I'm fine." She smiled and reaching across the console, placed a gentle hand on his leg, giving it a playful squeeze. "I'm sorry you had to see that side of my family. Honestly, I'm used to it at this point. Dad has been a miserable, narrow-minded asshole for years now. I was in middle school the last time I remember us not having an argument when we all get together. We all just expect it now. Today was just a little nastier than normal." She leaned over and kissed him on the cheek.

"What was that for?"

"That was to say thank you. You were so wonderful today, really you

were, and my family thinks so too." Her broad smile easing the tension
in his shoulders, "you may not believe it, but you made one hell of a first
impression."

He couldn't hold back the laugh that burst out, "Oh, I know I made an
impression. I was just hoping it would have been a positive one."

"It was positive, sweetheart. It was."

Maybe that's true, he thought, *but that certainly wasn't the case with his own family.* Both his brother and sister blamed him for not letting go of the past. 'It
was time to move on,' they'd tell him. 'He's the only father we'll ever have.
You can't be mad at him forever. Stephanie was just as much to blame as he
was,' her sister kept reminding him. And maybe that was true for part of it,
but he was still the reason his mother died and he couldn't forgive him for
that. Neither his brother nor sister seemed to agree. So now it was best if
he just stayed away because, unlike when he was young, he didn't hold his
tongue anymore.

They were now on the expressway. It was nearly vacant this late on
Christmas night, so at least they would make good time getting back into
the city. A companionable silence fell between them as they drove, under-
scored by a Christmas playlist playing softly through the car's speakers.

Jake's mind drifted back to his own family and how fucked up everything
had become. It had all started much like it had with the gathering they had
just come from, only for his family it had been at a backyard barbeque on
summer Sunday and not a formal dining room at Christmas dinner.

His parents had separated when he was a senior in high school, though
it had been a long time coming. His father was an alcoholic, and it had cost
him job after job until he finally went into business for himself. Somehow,
he'd managed not only to hold his construction business together, but to
be profitable. Which only meant his father always had money to drink, not
that the family's bills were finally being paid on time.

Jake also suspected that his father had been unfaithful, multiple times,
but no one ever said a word about that. His family was adept at keeping
stuff unsaid. The problem with stuff unsaid is that it always seemed to
come out, eventually. For reasons he didn't understand, neither of his
parents seemed in any hurry to divorce and they had even tried to reconcile several times in the two years they were apart. His father was a mean,
selfish son of a bitch who would never change and he desperately wanted
his mother to be happy and the sooner his father was out of the picture,
the sooner she could start on that journey.

He had been looking forward to this weekend for many reasons. He missed his family and though he was enjoying the independence he had by staying upstate at school for the summer, it meant even more time away from Stephanie, his first love. And the one who he thought would be his last. They had met when they were kids in grade school and were inseparable from the start. By the time they were twelve, they finished each other's sentences, and no one ever doubted they were each other's forever.

His first year at college had been a strain on the relationship, though. Stephanie had planned to attend the same university, but the week before freshman orientation, her parents had told her they just couldn't afford to send her, and it was too late to explore other options. She forced Jake to go anyway, with a promise to join him next year. They hadn't talked about it much since, but that didn't mean it was far from his mind. He'd stayed on campus for the summer because he'd gotten a good job working for a law firm and he made enough to afford his own apartment. One that was big enough for the two of them which meant all she had to do was come up with tuition and between scholarships and loans he knew she could do that, and he would be there, with a lawyer's salary to pay for it all once they could start their forever.

He had gotten Stephanie her own key to the apartment and was planning on making a big show of giving it to her after the barbeque before everyone went home. Even his brother, Teddy, was there for the party. He had disappeared to college in Maine, and this was his first time home, other than Christmas, in five years. Jake couldn't wait. He was as nervous as if he was going to propose, though that would come soon enough. He wouldn't mind moving up the wedding. They didn't have to wait for graduation like they'd planned. Especially if they were already living together like they would be now.

Mom had insisted on hosting the barbeque, which he took to mean she and his father were making another attempt to fix their marriage. He had never hated his father, but he certainly didn't like him much. His father was like Jekyll and Hyde when he drank; at the beginning he was the happy-go-lucky life of the party but somewhere into his cups he became a mean, ornery bastard and if you confronted him in that state, you didn't know whether he would lash out with his tongue or his fists but whatever it was it always hurt. His words leaving the deepest scars, though the memory of the bruises on his mother's beautiful face still hurt him the most.

Stephanie had arrived two hours late for the party, only just in time to eat, and his father was already well on his way to drunk and obnoxious. More than once, Jake had caught him out of the corner of his eyes flirting with her. He really would chase anything in a skirt when he got this way, and he knew he should confront him. He regretted getting her a job in the office at his father's company. God knows what the hell he's done to her there, but she's said nothing to him about his father, so maybe it's not so bad. He's probably not that drunk at the office. Stephanie deserved his protection, but he also knew it would ruin the mood for the surprise he had for her, so he hoped things wouldn't get any worse before he could make the presentation and announce the start of their future together.

He would have already done it, but there was something off with her today. Maybe it was his father's inappropriate behavior or maybe whatever made her late had her worried, but whatever it was she wasn't sharing with him. All he got were those two dangerous words 'I'm fine' which only meant she was anything but.

He decided that if he waited any longer, his father would likely ruin the whole surprise, so he nodded to his sister, Amber, to put their plan in motion. Stephanie loved games and he and his sister had put together a scavenger hunt that would give Stephanie clues to lead her back to Jake, who would sit at the picnic table with a wrapped present holding the key to their apartment. Amber hurried off inside to get the clues for the game and as soon as she was back, he would start it all in motion. Looking around the yard, he spotted Stephanie leaning down and whispering something in his father's ear. He smiled and laughed and patted her ass in a way that was far too familiar to be appropriate.

That was the last straw and if he'd gotten one trait from his father, it was his father's nasty temper. "What the actual fuck, dad?" he yelled. "How about you keep your hands off my girlfriend's butt?"

Everyone had turned in his direction, but he only had eyes on the two of them. Stephanie's face was scarlet, and it made him wince to think that he'd embarrassed her in an attempt to defend her. The smile had disappeared from his father's face and was replaced by a sneer which Jake knew preceded whatever depraved thing was about to come out of his mouth.

"Watch your mouth boy," he growled like the beast that he was when he was drunk. "Or I'll knock some respect into you right quick and don't think just because you're some hot shot college punk, I won't. I'm still your father."

Jake had reached his limit. He had kowtowed to his father to keep the peace all his life. Never once had he had the courage to stand up to the man when he beat his mother, but that cowardice would stop today. He was just as big as his father now and he was sober. It wouldn't be a fair fight, but he didn't care. Today would be the day things changed. "No father of mine would treat a woman that way, especially not his son's girlfriend."

A laugh escaped his father that he'd never heard before. It was laced with evil and venom towards him that made Jake wonder it really was his father staring back at him. "You stupid little shit," his father spit. "She's not your girlfriend anymore. She found out what a real man was when she came to work for me. I've been fucking her for months and you were too caught up in your books to know or care. In fact, little boy, as soon as the divorce is final from that cow you call your mother, we're going to get married. She's already carrying my baby."

Everything came apart at once. Jake noticed at the last second his brother's clenched fists before they crashed into his father's face, sprawling him backwards in his chair, landing with a thud on the ground. Stephanie frantically fawning over his fallen father only confirming his father's words and the clatter of breaking glass behind him drew his attention to see his mother standing with her mouth open, all color gone from her face before she melted to the ground with the bowl of fruit salad that had crashed at her feet seconds before.

His sister came out of the house and screamed, which startled him into action. He wanted to join his brother in beating his father senseless, but his concern for his mother, who had already endured so much at that monster's hand, had him moving in her direction.

He didn't remember much of the rest of the day. He didn't know when his father left, and he hadn't spoken to him since that day. Amber told him months later that Stephanie had tried to apologize before she left without his father, but he had no recollection of speaking to her. Or what he might have said in return. He remembered a dozen calls he'd ignored until she finally stopped calling. He really didn't care what she had to say. Hers was an even greater betrayal than his father's as far as he was concerned, because his father had never once claimed to love him.

The final wound that killed his soul was the divorce papers being served the following morning. Ellen Douglas had endured years of abuse in order to protect her children, but Jake could see the relief in her eyes behind her unemotional exterior. The stoic way his mother had taken them from the marshal that delivered them. Jake could see the pain in his face when he had her sign the receipt. It's why he was focusing on constitutional and not family law. Much less personal, the last thing he ever wanted was to have a grieving wife crying about an unfaithful husband in his office. Or worse, having to work for a client like his father, he'd give up law before stooping that low.

It was that fear of witnessing pain that had him driving back to school later that day. He had offered to stay with his mother, but she had insisted she'd be fine, and his sister was home for the summer if she needed someone to talk to. She had errands to run anyway, including a meeting with her lawyer so that she "could bleed that bastard dry for both of them," she'd said, though the tears in her eyes betrayed the hurt she was trying to mask with anger.

That was the last conversation he'd had with his mother. No final I love you. No words of appreciation for all she'd done to make his life happy and normal. Just a few words of shared disdain for a man she'd once loved, the same man who had never seemed to love his youngest son at all.

He'd been doing the best he could at refocusing his thoughts toward his upcoming second year of a dual major in psychology and pre-law when his phone rang with his sister's ring tone. Two hours into his drive back to Buffalo, it tempted him to just ignore it. He'd be fine with time, and he didn't need his big sister asking stupid questions about how he was doing. Things sucked right now, but he'd get through it. He'd call her back when he got there and let her know he was home safe. She'd make him do that anyway and then ask the same damn questions again. But when she called back immediately after he sent her to voicemail, he knew something was wrong. He should take the call.

He didn't know how long he'd been on the side of the highway when the NY state trooper pulled up behind him. All he knew was that he didn't think he'd ever be fine again. The trooper had been very understanding when he'd explained that his mother had been killed in a car accident. She died on impact when a truck stuck her driver's side door. She'd apparently failed to stop for a red light.

She must have been upset. He should have stayed an extra day. He should have been the one driving. She always held it together in front of him and his brother and sister, but he'd heard her crying dozens of times when she thought no one could hear. She must have broken down when she got in the car, safe from disturbing his sister and him. She didn't see the stop light through the tears that his father had caused her. He might not have been driving that car, but his father was guilty of killing his mother just as much as if he had been. He would make his father pay someday.

"Jake… Jake," Alexis' voice cut through the fog of the painful memory.

He blinked his eyes, trying to focus on her pretty face, and the world came back into focus around him. They were parked outside her brownstone, and he'd been lost in painful memories for nearly an hour. "Is everything okay, sweetheart? You haven't said a word, and it's like you didn't even hear me talking to you."

"I'm sorry, babe. Lost in thought, I guess."

"Well, from your expression, they weren't very happy thoughts, having second thoughts about getting involved with me and my dysfunctional family?" she asked, worrying her bottom lip with her teeth. It was a tell he recognized meant she wasn't as confident as the rest of her body language suggested.

"Oh, God. I'm sorry," he said, leaning across the console to cup her cheek tenderly in his hand. "No, babe, not at all. I was just remembering my family drama. Please don't think that."

"Do you want to talk about it?"

He shook his head and got out of the car. She grabbed the canvas tote with their gifts in it from the backseat. Once inside, she emptied the bag, placing the gifts under the tree, and produced a single unopened package from the bottom of the bag.

"I have one last gift for you." She announced with the enthusiasm of a child and pride in keeping the secret the entire day.

"You do?" Jake said, completely surprised. "You've already done too much."

"This is kind of a gift for both of us, but it's for me to give, I suppose."

A vee formed between Jake's eyes as he unwrapped the gift. He didn't know what she could give him that would fit in a box that small. A smile ticked at the corner of his mouth because the only thing that came to mind was a ring. The thought would have scared the hell out of him if he hadn't thought of how ridiculous that would be. It was far too soon, and that was his job. Though he wouldn't put it past Alexis, to break with tradition.

Inside there was a picture of a highboy dresser that matched her bedroom set and as he took it out of the box to ask her what it meant, underneath there was a single key.

He looked at her for confirmation, explanation. "I bought you a dresser so that you can keep your clothes somewhere and not have to go back and forth in a duffle bag. And that is a key to here, your key. I went to get a copy made a few days ago, but found out it had to be specially made by a locksmith, and only Papa could authorize it. That's what he handed to me today when you asked what we were doing. Anyway, his condition was that he had to meet you first and approve before he would let me have it. Just thought you'd appreciate knowing you passed the test with flying colors."

Jake swallowed; the emotion was still thick with the memory of another key that was meant for a gift. A gift that was supposed to start a forever. Forever was something that he hadn't allowed himself to think of since that day. "Thank you," he said, sounding forced rather than the genuine way he meant it to his ear. "This is so kind of you, yet another thing you've done for me you can't fully know how much I appreciate."

Alexis took a deep breath. "I would really like you to be here full time. Make this your home, too." Jake watched as she shifted her weight from leg to leg. "If that's not what you want," she hesitated, "the key is still yours, so you can come and go as you please."

He could tell she was nervous, her teeth pressing into her bottom lip so hard they might draw blood. If he was being totally honest, the thought of moving in did scare him a little, giving up his freedom, but he knew he was at her place practically every night as it was. It was worth trying. It was time to start feeling again. His hand cupped her cheek just before his lips pressed against hers. With a sigh, she parted her lips in response and he wasted no time slashing his tongue between them and claiming her mouth, claiming her.

He broke the kiss, causing her to gasp, bringing a satisfied smile to his face. "Thank you, Alexis. This means so much more to me than you can ever know." Knowing he should say more, but not wanting to break the moment, his eyes dropped before rising to meet her gaze again. "Someday I'll share the memory I was lost in, but not today."

Her fingers pressed against his lips before he could say any more. "I'm here whenever you're ready to share." She kissed his cheek and then tried to remove the lipstick smudge she'd left behind with her thumb. "Come on. Let's grab a bottle of wine and soak in the tub. I think we could both use a little relaxation."

A smile filled his face, and he took her hand. Leading her toward the stairs, he whispered in her ear, "the tub sounds wonderful but with you naked I'm not at all sure it's going to be relaxing."

She squealed as his large hand squeezed her ass and she ran ahead of him up the stairs. "You'll have to catch me first!"

Chapter 17

Jake

Alexis had dropped Jake off driving his piece of crap SUV for the one AM flight to Seoul just before ten. She had insisted on driving him there but hadn't wanted to drive her own car in case someone had recognized it. He and his five-person team would be all on the same flight and no one in the office could ever know about their relationship, though with every passing day, he knew they would one day be discovered. Eventually, someone would see them at a restaurant or start asking questions because they were not acting the same, as hard as they tried to, at the office.

He knew how he felt when she was near. There was just no way to disguise it completely, and the slightest of blush had replaced her normal stoic appearance more than once in a meeting. Their secret was on borrowed time, and he just wished she was a little more ready for that day to come.

He couldn't deny that she had taken a bold step toward commitment when she'd given him a key to her home and asked him to make it his. And there had been that one day in the office after she'd returned Trevor's ring, but she'd done nothing close to that since then. She barely acknowledged he existed; she was even more distant than before they became a couple.

The way she was outside the threshold of her townhouse caused far too many flashbacks to the signs that Stephanie had given him. Scanning the restaurants they were in, before she would take his hand, looking over her shoulder when she didn't think he noticed as they walked down the street and always staggering their arrival time at the office. They could never arrive or leave at the same time. It was exhausting him to keep everything straight, and he knew it was taking its toll on her as well.

Jake was relieved when he settled into his first-class compartment, noting the sliding doors which would allow him to avoid his team during the fourteen-hour flight. He'd been on enough of these trips to know that conversations about the presentations always devolved into company gossip and he didn't want to have to keep his guard up for that long. This way, he could close everyone out and focus on the last-minute review of his portion of the work and then sleep. Jetlag, on a trip halfway around the world, was real. They lost a day on the way there and then arrived home at exactly the same time they took off after a fourteen-hour flight on the way back, something that still baffled his mind.

Despite all the angst around keeping their relationship secret, he'd never been happier. Certainly, a level of happiness he'd never expected to find again, nor a level of trust. When Alexis gave him that key, it was all the proof he needed to know that Alexis trusted him implicitly, which meant he could do the same for her. She told him she'd never even considered giving Trevor a key, and maybe it was petty, but that tidbit had him soaring. He could trust her to have his back, and that was a level of trust he didn't think he'd ever find after Stephanie's betrayal.

The first few days of the trip were uneventful, consisting of lower tier meetings with Korean clients. Rob had charmed them with his usual casual flair. Jake had seen it dozens of times, but worried that Rob's act wouldn't play as well in a more traditional Asian culture. The Koreans were, if not westernized themselves, at least used to the American culture to the extent that it didn't cause friction, but he was worried that his boss's casual attitude and lack of formality would not be well received by the Hong Kong delegation which was the primary reason for their trip. Failure to impress the C suite executives they were meeting with from HKD would cause the loss of millions of dollars for DCH and Jake knew that would cost all of his team dearly career-wise, most likely their jobs.

Jake's worst fears were realized when casual Rob appeared for their first meeting Monday afternoon directly from the eighteenth green, khaki slacks and a FootJoy shirt did not impress the suits sitting across from them at the Park Hyatt conference room table. He wasn't entirely sure they weren't going to walk out of the first meeting before it was halfway through. He wouldn't be surprised if they were all on a flight home by tomorrow and looking for a new job the day after.

During the first break, Jake pulled aside An Yang, the COO of HKD. With a great deal of effort, he got the man to share his vision for the partnership and agreed to dinner that evening, just the two of them, before joining Rob and the others at some club.

Dinner had gone well, and Jake felt a bit more confident in the likelihood that they'd be able to close the deal. He and An had bonded over a common vision, one that he'd tried very hard but without success to get

Rob to adopt. Hopefully, he could get Rob alone before tomorrow's session and find out what the hell Rob was thinking. He was his friend besides being his boss and this does not give a shit attitude was odd, even for him. Rob was keeping something from him, and they had very few secrets. The only one he could think of was Alexis, and that was one he had no intention of sharing.

An had been quite vocal about the lack of proper respect he felt toward not only his company, but personally. While Rob was a VP, An felt it would only have been fitting to have a C level executive from DCH in the room. Jake had smoothed that over, but just. Another misstep by Rob and it would likely be the last of that deal. Much to Jake's horror, the Octagon Club where he and An were meeting the others was a hip, twenty something hang out and while it may have been the best, most exclusive club in Seoul, it was too young and too techno for him let alone the fifty-something executives they were supposed to be entertaining. An never made it into the building, politely excusing himself with a bow and walking away.

The disinterest from the executives of HKD in the meeting the next morning was obvious to everyone in the room but Rob. When the meeting broke up just before noon, Jake knew they were going home without the HKD contract signed and he would need to be looking for a new position soon. He wanted badly to call Alexis but couldn't put her in the position of having to hold back this type of information from her boss, and he didn't know what she'd think of him after such a colossal failure. The unacknowledged doubt that he wasn't good enough for her had never been so close to the surface of his conscience before. She was way out of his league, and he didn't know how he'd ever be able to support her in the lifestyle that she was accustomed to.

Much to his surprise, An and his associates finished their scheduled meetings even though they were obviously less than impressed with what Rob and his coworkers were presenting. The only time they were engaged at all was during the segments that he spoke about tariffs and legal hurdles they would face importing their goods directly to the U.S. When the final meeting was over, An pulled him aside. "Mr. Douglas, I thank you for your honesty and thorough knowledge of our business. Please to forgive my forwardness, your talents are being wasted here. I sincerely hope that our paths will cross again under more favorable circumstances." He gave him a solemn bow.

His words had taken Jake off guard and the best he could manage was to return the bow and mutter something to the effect that the pleasure was all his.

The next day at noon, when they boarded their flight home, it was only the knowledge that in just a little over twelve hours, he would be back in Alexis' arms. It was the only thing holding off the impending sense of doom. His days at DCH were numbered, if not already gone, and he didn't know what that meant for his relationship.

He had made it through ten hours of the flight when his luck at avoiding everyone he worked with ran out. Rob's head appeared over his compartment wall, and the level of mirth in his friend's face surprised him. Surely, he must know that coming home without a signed contract would not be well received at the office. They might have the weekend, but shit was going to hit the proverbial fan first thing Monday morning. Jake raked his hand through his already disheveled hair. "Rob, what the hell is going on? You look like you've just won the lottery. We'll all be lucky to still have jobs by Monday afternoon."

Rob laughed and nodded toward the front of the cabin. Too curious to finally get an answer, Jake pulled himself up from his seat and followed.

Stepping up behind him and nodding toward the seated flight attendant a few feet away. "Seriously Rob, those meetings were a fucking abortion, and you look like you don't have a care in the world!" he uttered in a hushed voice, though his anger made it so his words were far from private.

"Relax, my friend," Rob smiled. "I was going to talk to you last night, but you disappeared and didn't answer your phone."

"Yah, well, the knowledge that I'll soon be unemployed had me feeling less than social. So just tell me now."

Rob's carefree attitude usually helped to calm Jake, but right now, it was just pissing him off even more. He was tempted to give him a good shove or sucker punch him, but he was pretty certain it was some kind of federal offence and getting dragged out of first-class in handcuffs by JFK security didn't seem like an improvement on his already fucked up situation.

"I really don't give a damn about HKD because I'm leaving DCH to start my own firm. Those three Korean companies we met with are all coming with me, and that's about a hundred million in billables over the first two years. So yes, my friend, I'm smiling, and you should be too, because I have every intention of taking you with me."

His mouth moved, but he couldn't utter an intelligible sound. He slumped back against the bulkhead wall, which was the only thing keeping him from falling over. He knew the contracts of the companies Rob was talking about and there was no way DCH would let them go without a fight. The hundred million in revenue and then some would disappear in legal fees. His friend had obviously not thought this through. But worse than that, he had just assumed that he would go willingly with him. Even without Alexis to think about he would never take a risk like that. DCH was his way to bank enough money that he could afford to do something meaningful with his life. Use his law degree for good and not profit, but first he had bills to pay, six figures worth of student loans.

"Don't you think you should have asked me if I was interested before destroying my career for me? I'm not leaving DCH for a start-up. I don't want to leave DCH period."

"Oh, come on Jake, you don't want to work for DCH. You never did."

"You're right, I don't. I don't want to do consulting, but I need the paycheck for now and not one that's risky at best." He hated throwing cold water on his friend's dream, but he was smarter than this. At least Jake thought he was, but then he'd never thought Rob was selfish and he'd obviously not considered or cared about the impact of trashing an account would have on the people he worked with. "Besides, I know those contracts inside and out and you're going to lose your shirt trying to get around the non-compete."

"See, Jake, that's where you've underestimated me. I never once signed a non-compete with DCH. And I also know that you haven't signed one either. So, both of us have nothing to worry about and can easily take them to the cleaners for suing us when they know they have no chance to prevail. Nuisance suits can be costly, and I know you know that. So, what do you say? Be my lawyer?"

Jake let out a heavy sigh. He could see the hopefulness in Rob's eyes. Rob had a zest for life and a carefree attitude that Jake wished he could have half of. It's one thing that he admired most about his friend. But the last thing he wanted was to dive deeper down the hole of consultancies and, even more important than that, was his relationship with Alexis. Taking the job with Rob would mean half his life spent in the Pacific Rim, thanks, but no. Long-distance relationships were not something he would willingly do again.

"I'm sorry, Rob. I'm not interested. That's not what I want long term and you deserve someone committed to more than a couple of years."

"Are you sure, buddy? It would certainly make your relationship with Alexis a hell of a lot easier to manage."

"What are you talking about?" the knots in Jake's stomach tightened at his friend's words and he knew his feigned ignorance was as believable as a forged check in crayon.

"Just how long have you been plowing that grade A pussy? Two, maybe three months?" Jake threw his shoulders back and pressed his chest into Rob's with a growl. No one talked about her like that in front of him and while this wasn't the place to throw down, he certainly wasn't going to let Rob get away with it. Rob took a cautious step back and raised his hands in surrender. "Sorry, man. I was just a joke, but seriously, you won't be able to hide that forever, and at least one of you will get the ax when it comes out. And it will probably be her. You know how sexist Dewey is."

As pissed as he was at him, Jake knew he was right. "How long have you known?"

"Known?" Rob said with a chuckle. "About ten seconds since you confirmed it, but I've suspected it since just before Christmas. You guys were wonderful at hiding it. I never would have known if I hadn't seen you with Stephanie back in college. There was just a way you looked at her that told me there was something going on there."

Jake raked his hands through his hair and turned away. "Fuck."

Rob put his hand on Jake's shoulder and gave him a squeeze. "Seriously dude, don't sweat it. No one else even suspects anything."

"Yah, well, you can't be sure and you're right, they'll fucking fire her without a second thought."

"She's a bright girl. It wouldn't take her a week to find a better job."

"I know, but for some fucked up reason, she's stuck on making the C suite at DCH and I won't be the reason she doesn't make it." Jake noticed the question in Rob's eyes and answered before he could ask. "Family drama, but not mine to tell."

"Well, you've got plenty of your own, that's for sure."

Before Jake could reply, the seatbelt sign lit, and they announced the plane was making it's decent toward JFK. They were nearly an hour early, and he couldn't wait to see Alexis. This had turned into a shit show of a week, and there was a lot he had to talk to her about. But more important than that, he needed her; needed to get lost in her more than he had ever needed anything in his life.

As he went to turn, he saw Rob check his phone and roll his eyes. Rob shook off his questioning look and took a couple of steps toward the flight attendant, bending down to speak to her. Jake settled back into his seat, pulling his things together, preparing to land.

Sitting back, he was met with a glass of scotch extended from Rob's hand. "You're going to need this. My phone's blown up with messages from Dewey. We can have lunch on Monday and talk everything through."

"Thanks," Jake said, taking the amber liquid. There wasn't much to talk through. His career was about to go into a death spiral, and he was going to have to let down the one friend he had since freshman year in college. The guy who had opened a very hard door for him at DCH and even somehow brought him onto his team. And there was a good chance that Alexis would want nothing to do with him after all this went down, but hey, maybe it was all for the best. Maybe his father was right all along, and he was just a worthless fuckup who thought he was better than everyone else.

Chapter 18

Alexis

The first couple of days of Jake's trip went by in a flash. There was so much to do at the office. She was there past ten every night and in by eight the next day. The time difference made it difficult to stay in touch, but they'd texted, which was enough to take the edge off, they had been together every day since before Christmas and she was surprised by how much she enjoyed being together, never the dread of waiting for their time together to be up like it was with Trevor. Maybe it wasn't her after all.

The weekend was a little harder, but Carole came into the city on Saturday, and they'd spent the day together for the first time since she couldn't remember when. By Wednesday afternoon of the second week, Alexis was feeling good. She wasn't missing him too badly and the heavy workload she was facing helped. He would be home Saturday around noon. She was going to do something special for his return. She just hadn't decided what it would be yet.

Shortly after two, her phone rang. It was Andre, her pod leader, calling her to join a meeting he was sitting in on. When she walked into the room, Andre was seated in the middle of the conference table, not his customary position at the head. Instead, Hamilton Dewey III sat there, the managing partner. There were others in the room that she recognized but didn't know by name. Andre motioned for her to sit next to him.

Ham, as he was known around the office, primarily to distinguish him from his father, who was CEO and co-founder of the firm, nodded at her and continued speaking. "Alexis, let me bring you quickly up to speed. I received a call about two hours ago from the COO of HKD. To put it mildly, he was not impressed with what he had heard from Rob's team regarding strategic vision and marketing plans. It took me the better part of forty-five minutes to bring him back from the ledge and dropping us all together."

Alexis' heart rose to her throat. She knew what this meant without having to hear anything else. Jake's pod was about to be fired. Even if he didn't get fired, it would not be good for his future with the firm. She knew how much it meant for him to succeed here, just as much as it meant to her. Alexis nodded to show that she understood. She could not speak.

Dewey continued, now addressing the entire room. "The only aspect of the presentation that he felt was worth our fee was the legal assessment." Alexis exhaled loudly, feeling a sense of relief. She quickly glanced around, realizing her mistake, but no one seemed to look in her direction. She couldn't afford to be making errors in judgement like that. Maybe Jake wouldn't lose his job after all. "The new kid especially impressed him." He looked toward Andre, looking for a name.

"Jake Douglas is who you're referring to, I believe sir." Andre interjected.

"Right," Dewey resumed, barely registering the name. "Unfortunately, that means we need to make some moves. Frankly, I've never been happy with the way Rob manages his team. I should have acted before now. I will meet him here Saturday when he gets off the plane." Alexis knew what that meant, and so did everyone else in the room.

"Andre, I'm adding HKD to your portfolio. Rebecca and Jane will be let go on Monday. I've had IT open access to their files to you. Roger, Maggie, glean what you can from their notes and see if any of their work is salvageable. Just make sure if you use it, you wrap it in some fresh paper, so HKD doesn't recognize it. I will find a place to move Victor. He's done decent work, but Andre, you don't need another lawyer on your team long term. Which leaves us with Jake…" Dewey tapped his fingers on the table and stared above everyone as if what he was looking for was written on the wall. "As I said before HDK seemed to like him and I don't want to rock a boat that's already taking on water." He looked over at Alexis. She couldn't remember feeling more uncomfortable. She felt naked and didn't like it a bit.

"Alexis, I need you to work with him on this project. Unpack everything he has done, get him to fully explain all his work and then make it yours. As far as he is going to know, you're collaborating with him on this project. We've got three weeks before we have to go back and present an alternative strategy and it better be good or DCH will lose over fifty million in billables over the next six months. Do this well, Alexis, and you'll get your own pod to lead. Do you understand?"

"Yes, sir." The certainty she in had in her voice surprised her. Her emotions were tearing her apart inside. "Out of curiosity, where will Jake end up?"

Dewey's expression was not one Alexis could easily read beyond knowing he did not expect to be questioned, certainly not by her. "Frankly, do you job right, and he'll be gone as soon as you're ready to step in. Don't and it's your ass on the sidewalk. Clear enough for you? I've got too damn many lawyers already." With that, his attention was back on Andre and the other details.

There was absolutely no empathy in his words. He was 'matter of fact' and didn't give a damn how she felt about it. Years of dealing with her father's lack of empathy and outright attacks against her made it easier for her to remain composed. She supposed she should be thankful to him for that. Hamilton Dewey III could not make her flinch, no matter what he did to her. What had her stomach feeling like it was about to hurdle out her throat was what this meant for her and Jake.

Why Jake? Anybody, anybody else in the company, damn anybody else in the world, she knew she wouldn't think twice about taking down. Business was survival of the fittest and DCH was the fucking major leagues. She knew she was good at it and had long since rationalized her way around many less than savory business decisions. Now, though, how was she going to do this?

She knew very well she could never keep this from Jake, but if anyone found out… they'd both lose their jobs and then where would they be? Maybe he'd figure it out on his own; of course, he would. A person with half his business and legal acumen would see the writing on the wall. If that's the case, then she didn't have to tell him, but then he'd also know that she knew and was keeping it from him. It would be the end of their relationship, even if he forgave her, it would break their trust, and damage like that… He'd shared a little about what had him so distracted on the ride home Christmas day and the way his father and that little bitch had betrayed him. There was no way she could keep this to herself and keep Jake, too. She had to tell him what was happening. A couple of months ago, this would have sucked but just been another day in the life. Today, the man she loved more than she ever thought she could love anyone; they had ordered her to screw with his pants on and her only other choice was to commit career suicide.

The meeting ended, and she hadn't really heard another word. She hoped she hadn't missed anything crucial. It seemed like a ten-mile walk back to her office. She was so lost in her mind that she practically ran over Mary, one of the administrative assistants, walking out her office door.

Steadying herself, Mary grinned at her, "someone must really have a thing for you!"

Alexis cocked her head questioning as the woman walked past her and back to the cubicle down the hall. She walked into her office to find a vase of two dozen long stem roses on her desk. Perhaps the most perfect roses she had ever seen, each one of the red, yellow, pink and white blooms perfectly poised, just spreading their petals.

Alexis didn't have to read the card to know who had sent them. Jake could be the only one and he could not understand how terribly heart wrenching this was for her at this moment. She closed her door behind her and inched her way to her desk. Picking the card out of the bouquet, it felt like a bomb ready to explode. She wished it was. It would save her from having to face the next three weeks of her life. Tears spilled down her face as she read the words Jake had written.

Let these roses express just a few of the wonderful new emotions I have found in you. Red for the love and passion I have for you and for your courage and beauty. Pink for the admiration I have for you, for the joy I feel with you in my life, and for the sweetness of your heart. Yellow for the delight I have in our friendship and the new beginning we have found together. Finally, white for the purity of our love for each other but also for the silence and secrecy that we must maintain… for now.

With all my undying love—You know who.

She wanted to throw them at the wall and hold them in her arms all at the same time. She was thankful he wasn't in the office next to her, but half a world away. She wanted to hold him so badly, to crawl into bed and get lost in his love and never get out, and she never wanted to see him again. She ached for him, but she was so mad at him for scaling her defenses, weakening her hard resolve and unfeeling focus on getting the prize that she desired. *Fucking Trevor, if he'd just kept his dick in his pants… this was all his fault.* She never would have had that moment of weakness. She could have continued to be the Ice Princess, and everything would be a lot easier right now. *Damn him, Damn him to hell!*

She sat in her chair staring at the roses, silently crying for the rest of the afternoon. She knew she should text Jake and thank him. She just didn't have the words to say. At around seven, she decided it was likely safe enough to leave the office without being seen. She didn't have to look in a mirror to know that her mascara was smudged, giving her a serious case of racoon eyes. Her crying, at work no less, this shit just had to stop. Tomorrow she would decide what to do with the flowers. One thing for sure is they couldn't stay on her desk and taunt her. She closed the door and walked to her car. The Ice Princess had better be back on the job tomorrow, but how?

Chapter 19

Alexis

Alexis pushed opened the door to her brownstone, bending to scoop up the mail on the floor. The click of her heals on the marble entryway echoed off the walls, making her feel an emptiness she'd never felt there before. How was it that Jake's absence was so palpable after only a few days? She'd always prized her solitude and yet now she felt hollow inside, like an important part of her was missing. She shivered, trying to shake the chill of loneliness aside.

She walked to the kitchen, grabbed a bottle of wine, and headed upstairs to her room. She instinctively turned on the TV for background noise and found it immediately irritating. She turned the TV off and hurled the remote at the wall. It shattered into a dozen pieces. She stepped toward the mess to clean it up, turned back and sat cross-legged on the bed, staring across the room at her reflection in the mirror.

It had been too long since the flowers had arrived at the office. She had to text him. This wasn't his fault, and she couldn't take it out on him. The man was about to lose his job after that prick Dewey had even remarked that Jake was the only reason the firm still had a chance at salvaging the account. Still, how could she pretend everything was fine? Silence was safer than having to lie to him. She couldn't text him, 'hi hope you're having fun, thanks for the flowers and oh by the way you're getting canned in three weeks after I steal all your work.' She stared at the phone a long time, then finally typed, "They are so beautiful! I love you too." She just prayed he wouldn't reply and try to start any kind of conversation. She pressed send.

Alexis took a long drink of the wine and refilled her glass. She returned to analyzing the reflection of the woman staring back at her from the mirror. She didn't seem familiar to her anymore. The Ice Princess wasn't the one looking back, even though she'd be praying for her return. She saw a woman that didn't know what her next move was. And that hadn't happened in…, well, a very long time.

The thought crossed her mind that she could walk in tomorrow and hand in her resignation. She had plenty of money in the bank, monthly income from the trust her grandfather had set up, and no rent to pay. She couldn't do that though and live with herself. It would give her father the chance to say I told you so and she would never, never allow that to happen. Not even if it meant losing Jake. Had she turned into one of those weak women that would sacrifice what she wanted in life just for a man? *Like hell she was!* Resignation was not an option. Jake was just the unfortunate victim in this, but she could not allow her emotions to interfere with her plans.

She could call her grandfather and ask him for help. He had offered to help Jake on Christmas Day. It was Jake's decision to ask for help, not hers. She would be upset if Jake had taken it upon himself to make career decisions for her, she knew she would. Alexis stared at the mirror a while longer, and then a while more. Still unsure if it was her place to do it, she picked up the phone and called her grandfather. She gave him a synopsis of what had happened and the position she was in. He had taken a liking to Jake; family takes care of family he said. After a half hour on the phone with him, she felt a little better and a little worse.

What made the call less than desirable was her grandfather's near insistence on making introductions for her, too. He felt she wasn't seeing the complete picture, either from Jake's perspective or the likelihood that she would become cannon fodder herself, especially if the account wasn't saved. He also warned her that Jake might not want his help; he might want to use his own connections to 'earn' a position rather than 'owe' one to someone else. That concept she fully understood. It's what made her circumstances so difficult. This was 'her' position, and no one was going to take it from her.

It tempted her to call Carole just to vent. She needed someone that wasn't as businesslike as her grandfather but resisted making the call. Somehow, she felt if she told Carole before even letting Jake know, he would feel like she was telling everyone about his business. She would feel that way if it was the other way around.

Tired of looking at the unfamiliar reflection in the mirror, she instead began contemplating the wineglass in her hand. This worked for less than an hour until the wine was gone. Perhaps it was that the wine was impeding her ability to focus, or that her brain could not handle any more pondering of the impossible to reconcile, but she could no longer brood on this. She felt she would go insane. It was time to go to bed.

Reaching for her nightgown after finishing her nightly routine, she saw his shirt hanging next to it. She stood there naked, just looking at it, and took it off the hook and breathed in his scent. God, she missed him, and, in that moment, she hated herself for that weakness. Returning it to the hook, she pulled her nightgown over her head and crawled into bed.

Her mind continued to mull over all that she had been thinking, over and over again. Ten, twenty minutes, an hour passed, and still she laid there, no closer to sleep. Rolling herself out of bed, she trudged to the bathroom and on the way back out stopped in front of the hook with his shirt. After staring at it, for how long she didn't know, she removed her nightgown and pulled the shirt over her shoulders, returning to bed. She held the fabric close to her face. He was with her and sleep finally came.

Chapter 20

Alexis

Alexis was thankful that Jake was not a prolific texter. It made it possible to not have to evade questions about what was going on at the office, what she was working on. Their communication was mostly around when she could expect him home and the normal, 'miss you', 'love you' texts that simply said they were in each other's thoughts.

She made it through the last two days of the week with reasonably good focus and could be moderately productive. There were two additional calls with her grandfather, and he had helped her to work through some, if not most, of her conflicts. He had guided her to the conclusion that honesty was the right policy and that if she truly loved Jake and thought they had the chance of a life together that they could overcome anything but if they could not trust each other, that would be very hard to fix. There was the risk that with the knowledge of what was about to happen, Jake could blow up and take a scorched earth approach at work, but neither she nor her grandfather felt he would allow temper to control him that way. That scenario was the only one that concerned Alexis about her future at DCH; that was her priority.

The one thing left for her to figure out was just how to bring the subject up. If she hadn't had all this weighing on her mind, she would be over the moon to see him today and would probably have jumped him the second he walked through the door. She had the suspicion he might be of the same mind. She honestly didn't know if she could really get into it knowing the impending conversation they would have to have and somehow the thought of saying, 'oh by the way dear before you stick that in me you should probably know that DCH has ordered me to stick it in you.' That would be a boner breaker if ever there was one.

She was still carrying on the active debate with herself Saturday just before noon when he walked through the door and dropped his bags in the foyer. She was in the kitchen, poured a cup of coffee for him, took a deep breath, and managed a genuine smile and walked out to great him. He looked exhausted, obviously after a fourteen-hour flight, but also wore an expression of deep concern. His face lightened some at the sight of her and gave her a full and deep kiss. Despite her angst, she could feel the tingle inside. It was reassuring.

"Thank you," he said as she handed him the coffee. "I have never been so happy to see someone in my life. I think somehow you've become even more radiant since I've been away." And he kissed her again, spilling coffee down his leg.

"Why thank you. I believe the concept is absence makes the heart grow fonder. I am very glad to see you too, though you look a bit more jet lagged than radiant," she giggled. His brows furrowed at her before the tugging at the corners of his lips won out and he smiled. "I'm sorry, is that too honest?"

"Ah well, all that time in a tin can at 600 miles per hour will do it to you. That and there's something going on at the office. Robs phone blew up as soon as we landed. There were like six messages from Dewey for him to go directly to the office as soon as he was through customs. He wasn't sure if we all had to go, but said he'd let us know if they expected us to join him."

Alexis swallowed hard. That solved the problem of how to broach the subject. "Well, I had hoped for a little more of a happy reunion before I told you, but yes, there is a lot going on. Go in and sit down and I'll get my coffee and bring you up to speed."

He gave the cocked eyebrow, but didn't question her, giving her another moment or two to collect her thoughts.

Jake

He parked himself on the couch and was glad to be home. She came in and joined him, coffee cupped in both hands. As she took the deep breath before she started it confirmed his fears.

"Crap, well, where to start…," Alexis hesitated, "if misery loves company, then understand the last two and a half days have been hell for me." Jake's eyebrow cocked again, not sure what was happening, just that it wasn't going to be good. "My understanding is that HKD called Dewey sometime on Tuesday pretty upset about the presentation, primarily the marketing strategy. As a result, Andre, myself, a couple others in my pod and two partners who I don't know were called into a meeting. The long and short of it, Jake, is that Robs getting fired even as we speak, Andre will take over the lead on the account and present a revised plan to them in three weeks. Rebecca and Jane are getting let go on Monday as soon as they walk through the door. Victor is being reassigned somewhere. And the very best part of this is that I've been assigned to get as much understanding as I can from you on your legal strategy in the next three weeks because, God bless you, you were the only bright and shining light for HKD in the whole damn presentation. Then they're going to let you go, too. Welcome home honey, how was your trip?" Somehow, the sarcasm in her tone made it a little easier to swallow for him.

"Fuck" Jake just sat for a moment and let it all digest. "I knew Rob did a shit job on this. Jack ass! Fuck!" He scraped his fingers through his tousled hair before leaning back onto the couch and tipping his head to stare at the ceiling. "So, the best part of this is that you've been told to debrief me so they can let me go and not lose the account, that's right?"

"That pretty much sums it up. I'm not supposed to say a word that would give you the sense you're about to be let go. You're just joining our pod as far as you're supposed to know."

"Hmm, okay. What are you going to do?"

"What do you mean, what am I going to do? I'm going to learn as much as I can from you. Obviously, you know what the hell you're doing."

His head snapped forward, staring at her for a long while, pondering what to say and how to say it. "Um, you're telling me that even though they're going to fire me, despite doing a decent job, you are planning on helping them be able to fire me at no cost to them?"

"Do you expect me to quit because you're getting fucked?" Her tone clearly told him she thought he was being more than a bit dim-witted. Which he knew he was the moment that last question has left his lips. But, still, he didn't like being called out on it.

"No but," he hesitated, running his hand through his hair, then rubbed his jetlagged face and looked at the ceiling again. "Well, maybe… yes. I mean no, it just seems like you're perfectly fine with me getting the ax as long as I get you the information you need to look good and succeed." He felt his temper boiling, despite already knowing what she was telling him. And what she was telling him was exactly what he had been prepared to tell her to do. He hadn't considered that she'd be the one that would replace him and somehow this all felt like she was betraying him, even though he knew very well that she had no choice if she wanted to keep her job. A job that he had been more than blunt about telling Rob just a couple hours ago, she was determined to keep. He knew this wasn't her fault, but something broken inside of him was telling him it was, and he believed that voice even though he knew he shouldn't.

"Jake, that's not fair at all! I'm not fine with it, perfectly or otherwise, but just what am I supposed to do? Am I supposed to tell them no, I won't do it, because while I'd screw anyone else in the company at the drop of the hat, Jake is my boyfriend, and I will only screw him literally and not figuratively? I'll have you know I left that meeting at two-thirty to discover your flowers being delivered, as if I needed anything more to make me feel like a Judas. I spent the rest of the afternoon crying, sending my calls to voicemail, and only snuck out of my office at seven when I didn't think anyone could see my red eyes and streaks of mascara trailing down my face. This has been literally ripping me apart for two days. I love you with all my heart. This. Sucks. But I don't think me quitting is going to serve any purpose at all, other than to give my father an opportunity to laugh at me and tell me I told you so. Women can't handle being in business."

Her words hit home with Jake. He could rationalize that she was in a no-win situation. The trouble was that he was still far too emotional to allow that to seep through into his consciousness and acknowledge they were equally metaphorically fucked. All he could manage was a very self-serving "I'm sorry if I didn't get your troubles, I'm more focused on the fact that I'm going to be out of a job I busted my ass for, after doing what sounds like a rather impressive work. I've got people to prove wrong, too. Guess I lose." He put the coffee cup down on the table and stood up. "I think I need to take a walk. Maybe the cold fresh air will help clear my head." He turned and walked toward the door.

"Wait a minute Jake, I'll come with you."

"No," he said that more sharply than he meant, but didn't bother to correct it. "I want some time by myself." He could hear her continuing to plead with him as he slammed the door and rushed out into the frigid January afternoon. He obviously couldn't think clearly while she was around, and he needed to get his head straight and fast.

Chapter 21

Alexis

Her eyes stung as she fought to hold on to her precious composure. Her heart was pounding in her chest and had a bitter taste in her mouth. The only other time she'd ever felt this way, she was standing in a bedroom doorway realizing she'd believed in a lie. She couldn't be making the same mistake twice; she wouldn't allow it. "Please Jake," her voice sounding desperate, "I won't say a word. Please. Let me walk with you."

Silence was her only answer as he grabbed his coat off the rack. The thud of the door slamming shut behind him made her jump and lose the last bit of control she was holding onto. Wiping the traitorous tears from her eyes, she sat hard on the chair, fully intending to pull on her boots and follow him. She was a fighter. She didn't give in, *but he needs time to think,* a small voice in her head broke through over the staccato thump of her heart.

With a sigh, she set her boots back on the mat and leaned against the wall. Her eyes searched the ceiling for answers that weren't there. Tears trailed down her face, causing a shiver as they cooled, spilling down her neck. She could taste the bitter fear she felt at the possibility it was over and wondered how she hadn't noticed how much she wanted him here. Sure, she enjoyed his company, and the sex was like nothing she'd ever experienced before, but that was nothing. She never needed it before. It was nice to have, but she could certainly live without it. She had for half her life. This time, though, she felt like something vital to her survival was being ripped out from inside her.

"Oh, Jake, I'm not ready for this to be over," dropping her head to her hands and fighting the sickening feeling in her stomach. "Please choose me. Just this once choose me," her muffled cry echoed off the high walls and marble floor accompanied by the soft sobs shaking her body.

It had been nearly two hours when Jake walked back through the door. His cheeks were red and raw, his eyes glistening not only from the effect of the icy January wind that whipped through the city but from the hurt that still shone through his dark brown eyes.

Alexis peered out at him from her spot on the sofa. Wrapped tightly in a throw so that only her eyes peered out from beneath the hem of the blanket and prayed a silent prayer that he would say something to her, anything, as long as it wasn't goodbye. His gaze met hers but revealed nothing that showed what he was thinking behind his hollow eyes. Slowly, he slid out of his coat, hanging it on the rack.

Alexis released half the breath she was holding in. At least he wasn't planning on leaving immediately.

Bringing his hands to his mouth, he blew on them, rubbing out the cold before scrubbing them over his face and through his tousled hair. She had never seen him look so tired and flustered. In her mind he looked like a man searching for answers with no idea where to find them, so unlike the boardroom Jake, that was always in control, prepared.

Taking a deep breath, he closed the distance between them with long but cautious strides. "Can I join you?" he asked, nodding toward the sofa. With all her heart, she wanted to open the blanket and invite him in, but knew if he rejected her, it would break what little composure she was holding onto. Too unsure of her voice, she nodded, and he settled down next to her, just close enough for her toes to touch his thigh.

"I…" words caught in his throat. His nose was dripping from the cold, and he wiped it clean with his sleeve. It was an instinctive mannerism that had Alexis fighting back a smile despite the tension in her body. She glimpsed the uncertain boy he once was, and it made her want to hold him even more. Clearing his throat, he began again, "I'm sorry. This must have been very difficult for you. I'm exhausted and, well, just a little frustrated at doing my best and not failing, but failing anyway. I didn't mean to take it out on you. I shouldn't have taken it out on you. Can you forgive me?"

Tears that she didn't think she had left in her escaped the corner of her eyes as the tension in her muscles uncoiled. A smile spread across her face so wide that she could taste her tears. Opening her arms, she wrapped the blanket around him and pulled him into her body. She shivered not just from the cold that still clung to him but from the relief at having her prayer answered.

She took his face in her hands, snot and all, and kissed him, forcing her tongue into his mouth. He surrendered himself to her, and she captured him before he could change his mind. "I have nothing to forgive you for."

She forced out through the emotion in her throat. "I would have reacted a hundred times worse."

"Are you going to want an unemployed failure in your life?"

She was stunned at the seriousness of his tone. Her grandfather warned her to watch for the hurt, and she chided herself for not expecting it. She kissed him again. "You are not a failure, Jake Douglas, and you will not be unemployed an hour longer than you want to be."

Jake leaned back, brows arched, "I doubt it's going to be as easy as that." She worried her bottom lip, questioning again if she should have approached her grandfather before asking Jake if he wanted her help. But it was too late, and she wouldn't lie to him. She also knew she would have done it even if Jake had told her not to. He deserved these opportunities, even if he was too stubborn and prideful to ask for help. Besides, she needed it, too. It was the only way she could think to relieve the guilt she felt at whatever her part was in his undoing at DCH.

"I didn't get a chance to tell you before you went for your walk," she said cautiously, not wanting to reignite the trouble they had just avoided. "I told my grandfather what was going down after I found out. He has made some inquiries for you, and he wants you to call him when you were ready." Alexis studied the war of emotions coursing across Jake's handsome face. Guessing that confusion was safer than outright anger, she continued, "he said you would first have to get past the jet lag. He said it usually took him three or four days to feel human again. And then you would need to get past the sting of being, his words, 'Rogered but good with your trousers on'. He said he's happy to sit down with you over a single malt and he'd walk you through the choices."

"Choices?" he croaked, his voice breaking like a hormonal teenage boy.

Alexis nodded quickly and smiled, sensing Jake's nervous curiosity. "He didn't give me all the details, even though I gave him my best pout, but he said something about the Department of Justice and the Southern District of New York. He mentioned Rock and Wagner in Manhattan. They do constitutional law, right? There were a couple of others, but I was so excited I pretty much just heard buzzing after the first two."

Jake sat silently and Alexis held her breath while she waited for him to say something, anything at all. The silence went on long enough that she thought she'd be okay if he yelled at her as long as he gave her some kind of reaction. She could tell he was digesting what she had just told him, but couldn't stand the waiting any longer. "I'm sorry if you're mad at me, sweetheart," using the term of endearment to hopefully temper his reaction. "I just wanted to help."

Jake's gaze focused back on hers, and a smile tugged at the corner of his mouth. He brought her palm to his lips and gently kissed the underside of her wrist. "Thank you." Turning her hand over, he kissed her knuckles one at a time. "There was a time when I would have been furious that you didn't let me take care of this myself. But if there is one thing I've learned in my time at DCH, it is that deals are made by relationships. Success because of those relationships doesn't lessen the value of the accomplishment. Thank you for opening these doors for me. Now it's up to me to take advantage of it and not waste the opportunity you've given me."

"Well, it's all Papa's connections; I just made the call." Palming his face and brushing her thumb over the ridge of his chiseled cheek, "he must really like you, Jake. I asked him to help my best friend from college find an internship and all he did was tell her to use his name when she called a firm. I don't think she ever got high enough up the food chain for his name to mean anything to who she was talking to, and he wouldn't give me the name of his contact. From what he insinuated the last time we talked; these firms are ready to schedule interviews whenever you are."

"Really?" he commented with a bemused laugh, "Rock and Wagner were my dream firm down in DC, I couldn't get so much as a confirmation from them they even received my resume." He shook his head, the smile slowly fading from his face. "You didn't answer my question, though. Would you still want me if I was an unemployed failure?"

"Jake, I want you in my life. I don't for a minute think you would ever allow yourself to be a failure or be unemployed. You could be a dishwasher and I would still love you and if you couldn't find work, then I've got more than enough resources for both of us. I only want you, no one else, no matter what your status is. How about we grab some hot cocoa and find our way upstairs to bed? It's been over a week since I've felt your body next to mine and I want you, soon to be unemployed, or not."

Jake smiled a very weary smile. "That might be one of the best offers I have ever received." He stood from the couch and pulled her up with him. "I will do everything I can to make sure you are successful with HKD. It will take some late nights to get it all done in three weeks, but we will." He kissed her forehead and pulled back, and gave her a mischievous grin. "It will involve some risk for you, though."

A vee formed between her eyes, "why would I have any risk?"

"Because I'm getting fired anyway and if I'm working late with you, then we are going to fuck in every possible position and place in that office before I walk out the door. We might even break into Dewey's office and leave a big ole stain right in the middle of his fucking desk."

She wanted to protest and remind him she was not getting fired and preferred not to risk it, but she had to admit just the thought of what he was suggesting, and the tone of his voice had just soaked her panties straight through. All she did was smile and give him an exaggerated eye roll. He would know she was on board.

"The flowers were beautiful. Thank you. They're still in my office. But the card is being framed and it will be on my nightstand, next to our bed, until the day I die. Those were the most beautiful words I have ever read."

Chapter 22

Jake

Jake arrived a half hour ahead of Alexis at the office Monday morning, early even for him. He wanted to be in his office before as many people as possible. He knew it wouldn't take long for the rumors to fly, and curious glances would be cast in his direction wherever he went. There would also be more than enough well-meaning coworkers giving lip service to support him. They might be honest, but they certainly wouldn't be there when the tide turned on him. They could too easily be stuck in the undertow surrounding him. Getting too close to him could sink their careers, and no one would risk that. He didn't blame them, but he didn't have to associate with them either.

What was surprising was that there was no formal announcement of the personnel moves. He'd expected an email, but he saw nothing, which was only going to make the rumor mill a hundred times worse. Rob had been let go. He'd received a cryptic text from him Saturday evening saying the deed was done and he'd been given more than ample severance to tide him through the start-up phase and would Jake please reconsider joining him.

Rob had been a good friend to him since college. Rob was the only one who knew the complete story about Stephanie, but Rob hadn't changed much in ten years. He was still more frat boy than businessman and Jake's priorities had changed. He didn't think of happily ever after anymore, but he knew he wanted some kind of tomorrow with Alexis. When he told her he loved her, he meant it. He just didn't know what love meant. Not beyond doing whatever he could to help her meet her goals as best he could.

It had surprised George when he'd called him yesterday afternoon. Alexis had told him that her grandfather expected that he'd need a few days to get past the jetlag and the whiplash of impending unemployment. But Jake had been adamant about not wasting time and, at the end of a two-hour conversation, he decided to pursue a position with Rock and Wagner. He'd sensed that Alexis had opinions, but she kept them to herself, and he wasn't about to ask. It was his decision to make, anyway. The entire premise of their relationship was that it was based on personal freedom and not having to make sacrifices just to maintain a relationship. If they stayed together while they pursued their careers, that was great, but if their paths diverged, then they would go their separate ways, grateful for what they had while they had it. He told himself he was fine with that, even if the twisting in his stomach told him something different.

Jake was still mulling what the uneasy feeling in his stomach meant when he stealthily eased out of the office at lunch. Employees leaving for lunch was nothing out of the ordinary except that it was something that he had never done. Under the circumstances, he was concerned someone might question it or, more likely, invite themselves along. He had a call to make, and he didn't want any prying ears nearby to overhear his conversation.

When he returned, he quickly stepped into Alexis' office and let her know about the positive call and that she would be on her own for dinner tomorrow. She smiled and congratulated him, saying she would just grab some pizza on the way home if he promised to be her snack before bed. They both smiled and returned to their all-business mode.

The meeting was much as he expected, with Dewey leading the way and deriding the incompetence of Jake's old team. It sorely tempted Jake to point out the load of misinformation he was giving Andre's pod, but opted for a more prudent approach. He didn't have an offer yet. As the meeting was breaking up, Dewey called Jake back to speak privately once everyone else had left. "Douglas, I want you to know something. Freeman," it took Jake a moment to register that he was referring to Andre, "is dead set on keeping Chambers on once this transition is complete, which is going to frankly, boot you out on your ass. I'm of a mind to stop that. HKD was damned impressed with your work and what the client wants is what they get in my book. Watch your back with that little vixen. She'll knock anyone over who gets in her way, just like her father. Do a solid job through this and you'll stay, and she'll go. Just remember that, but fuck up, and I'll have no choice. I just think a man should know what's on the line."

"Thank you, Mr. Dewey. I appreciate your candor," told him, though it was a bold-faced lie. There was nothing about Dewey he appreciated.

"Good, now get back to work." Jake nodded as Dewey clapped him on the shoulder like he was some kind of father figure. Dewey didn't notice him rolling his eyes in disgust as he walked out of the office.

Fuck, fuck, fuck. So this is what it's come down to. There was no doubt in his mind that he would step aside for Alexis. No job was worth losing her. Alexis needed to know that she wasn't on firm ground, either. *Perhaps they could both make a change together? Would Dewey just slide Victor back into the account for the sake of some consistency once he had turned in his notice, leaving her out of the position, anyway?* His mind was buzzing with 'what ifs' and 'could be's'. He would be very glad when all of this crap was done. Worst of all, this meant a damn awkward conversation with Alexis tonight. There was no doubt she needed to know just as soon as possible what she was up against.

Jake walked back to his office slowly, hoping that Alexis would have other things to do before wanting to jump in and learn all she could about HKD. He really didn't want to have to play dumb with her until they got home. She'd likely see through him, and it wasn't a conversation to have with others around who could overhear them. Andre was in her office when he walked by, and Jake quickly closed the door behind him when he went into his office. It would at least offer a slight barrier against non-urgent interruptions. He wanted a few minutes to sort all of this out.

As luck would have it, Alexis didn't try to get together with him that afternoon. Just before five, he sent her a text stating he was on his way home and would have dinner ready for her when she got there. She replied with a string of heart emojis and a promise to text when she was on her way. She followed with a quick note that it wouldn't be later than eight. He rolled his eyes. Always the company woman.

Chapter 23

Jake

When she walked through the door at seven-forty-five, he was just taking the filets from the broiler. The table was set, and she looked truly pleased to have dinner waiting for her. Even more impressed when she realized that he had prepared one of her favorites, bleu cheese encrusted filet mignon, roasted new potatoes and asparagus. He handed her a glass of red wine and gave her a warm, wet kiss that sent tingles down her spine. If this was all a ploy to get her into bed early, not that it was necessary, it was certainly going to work perfectly.

"To what do I owe this special treatment?"

"Nothing more than the very obvious fact that I love you very much, Miss Chambers."

"Really? That's all? How nice."

"It's more than enough. I didn't enjoy being away from you for a week and want to show you just how much I appreciate you."

She blushed and gave him a kiss. Then took a sip of her wine. "Mm, that hits the spot. Both the kiss and the wine. I think today was an eternal day for both of us."

"It was. I don't imagine the next couple of weeks are going to be any easier."

"No, they won't. So…, I've been dying to know, what did Dewey want with you after the meeting?"

Damn, no sliding into this conversation, he thought. "That's part of why I wanted to do something special for you." Her expression changed to instant worry. "He told me that Andre was adamant about keeping you, but he wasn't so sure because I had made a positive impression at HKD. He told me to watch my back with you and if I could hold my own, you'd be gone and not me."

"He really said that?" She wasn't so much questioning the accuracy of Jake's reporting, more the fact someone in a management position with purposely throw something like that out on the table–her versus him. She noticed Jake wasn't certain she wasn't challenging him. "Christ, he is such a tool. What the fuck are we going to do?"

"Well, obviously you're staying because I'm going. There is no way in hell I'm going to compete with you. I love you, and what we have here is far more valuable to me than anything. But in the long term, I really think you should make a change. This won't be the last time something like this comes up and we won't be able to have each other's back then."

"I guess I should at least think about it, but all I can hear is my father and his fucking 'I told you so'."

"I know, but finding a better job, more money, that wouldn't shut that crap down a bit?"

"Maybe, but he'd just try to spin it so it sounded like I was running away from DCH and not toward a better job. That's the way he is, Jake. He hates me and the jealousy he had for any achievement I have would allow him to think positively."

"Funny, does Dewey know your father?"

"Yes, I think so. I'm not sure how, but dad mentioned him specifically when I told him I was taking this job. Why?"

"Because he said you reminded him of your father. It wasn't terribly complementary to be honest."

"Christ Jake, what did he say about me?"

"Don't bother, it doesn't matter."

"It matters to me. What did he say?" She was getting upset and Jake couldn't think of any good way around it. He was kicking himself for even asking if they knew one another.

"Basically, he said to watch my back, you were one that would try to win at all costs. I wanted to beat him down, let him know it wasn't true, and I certainly had no cause for concern. Didn't though, don't worry."

"I wish you had, but honestly, I know you couldn't. Wouldn't have done either of us any good. Definitely not the time to seek a moral victory."

They sat in silence. Jake ate, Alexis pushed her food around on the plate, barely eating half the filet. That was definitely not her usual attack on a marvelous piece of meat. She spoke several times but stopping herself and going back to her thoughts. Jake let her talk when she was ready, rather than pushing the issue.

"I'm sorry Jake, you went to so much trouble. It's delicious. I just don't have much of an appetite." She forced a smile.

"It's okay. I certainly understand." Jake got up and cleared their plates and loaded the dishwasher. Alexis grabbed the bottle of wine and plodded to the living room. Jake followed behind shortly and gave her a kiss on the top of the head before sitting across from her in one of the overstuffed armchairs.

Alexis sat there for a long time, staring out the window and sipping her wine. She would occasionally glance over at Jake and he would look up and give her a smile, then look back down at his knees. "What are we going to do?" She broke the silence. "Are you going to help me get up to speed on HKD or attempt to fight it out?"

Her expression was steely. It took him by surprise. He didn't ever remember being on the other end of that look. He'd seen it in meetings before, but not toward him, and certainly not in the last several weeks. The question offended him, and that tone came out in his reply. "I believe I have already given you the answer to that question."

"You said you were leaving, but you don't have a job yet. What if you don't get offered a position at Rock and Wagner? You won't change your mind? That's a pretty hard thing to do Jake, just fall on your sword for the sake of love." There was a powerful undercurrent of disbelief in her words and the acid way she emphasized love had a sour taste rising in the back of his throat.

He certainly did not like the inference that he was being less than genuine with her. He had many flaws, but his word was his word. It might be the only thing that his father had done for him. "I meant what I said, Alexis. What have I ever done to make you believe I would not be completely honest with you? Either at work before we were together or especially since. Have I gone back on my word once? Have I lied to you?"

"Not that I know of." She replied flatly.

Jake clenched his jaw so tight he was surprised he didn't break a tooth. "Not that you know of! What the hell kind of answer is that?" he shouted. His eyes flared. He caught himself before he spoke again and took a deep breath, stood up and walked over to the bow windows. He looked at all the million-dollar brown stones on the street, the BMWs, Audis and Mercedes, and thought about the home he was standing in right now. For the first time since the night of the office Christmas party, he felt like he didn't belong here, and he wanted out. He felt like the lower middle-class kid who went to a state school, and even that was more than he could afford. He knew he could never be cold and calculating and take what he wanted at any cost. Worst of all, he knew Alexis was someone who could be that way. Someone who would stick a sword in his back if she had to, to get ahead, to get what she wanted and not put love first. He didn't doubt she loved him. Assumed that he might be the first man she ever loved. But he thought she would walk away from that love if it stood in the way of her other goals. Had he really allowed himself to fall in love with the wrong person again?

Alexis

His reaction had startled her, even had her a little scared. She watched him standing at the window and wondered what was going through his mind. She didn't completely understand why he was so upset. She was only clarifying his intentions. It was a basic rule of questioning. Ask the same question in slightly different ways to see if there was any difference in the answer, to look for inconsistencies, to be sure she had the truth and was protected. She hated the silence; it made her stomach feel like a twisted ball of twine.

Jake turned around and stared at Alexis, and she stared back at him. He spoke in a very soft, calm voice, not soft enough to mask his hurt. "I told you I would do everything I could to get you up to speed on the account. I told you I could never fight you for the position because our relationship was more important to me than any job could ever be. I meant it then, and I will keep my word. I will fall on my sword for you, Alexis. If you feel the need to run me through with one of your own for good measure to prove your worth to a company that has proven it doesn't value either of us, then feel free. It will not change my decision. If you would like me to, I will go upstairs and get some clothes to stay at my place for a while, just say so now. Otherwise, I am going to go up to bed. I'm tired and I don't believe talking further is really going to be very productive for either of us."

Alexis looked at him blankly, holding her wineglass to her mouth without drinking. She didn't know what to say or to think at that moment. Her stomach knotted more tightly than ever. She felt a vast hole inside, but couldn't tell exactly what was missing.

He looked at her for a moment or two more and she said nothing. He looked down at his shoes and then walked to the stairs. Once she heard his footsteps reach the third floor, the tears rolled down her face, no sobs, just silent tears.

How was she ever going to do enough to keep her job and keep him, too? Was it that important to prove her father wrong? She couldn't face Jake tonight, but she couldn't bear to ask him to leave.

Pulling a fleece blanket over her, she sat her wineglass on the sofa table. She stared out the windows for a long time before sleep took her away.

Alexis woke at six the next morning to her watch alarm just in time to see Jake go out the front door, gym bag in hand. Without saying goodbye. Her body ached from a restless night on the couch. Her head hurt from too much wine, but that was nothing compared to the ache she felt in her chest, right where her heart lived.

She managed to pull herself together and get ready for work. She got into the office just after eight to find Jake's door already closed. She wanted desperately to knock, but resisted the urge. She went to her own office and tried to get her bearings. All she could think about was Jake, four feet away on the other side of the wall. She could hear the click clack of the keyboard as he was typing and the occasional muffled sound of a phone conversation. She pulled herself together just before a call from Andre, summoning her to a meeting on the second floor. As soon as she hung up, she could hear Jake's extension ring. They would have to find a way to work through this.

Chapter 24

Jake

Their demeanor in the meeting was exactly as it had been since the day they started; professional, courteous, and to the point. No one in the room would suspect a thing. It was just as it should be. Except for Jake and Alexis, it was not as it should be at all. For nearly two months now, when they had shared a space in the office, there was an unspoken connection between them. They thrived on each other's energy, today that connection was nothing but tension. Not in the good, sexual tension, sort of way, but in a cable pulled too tight, ready to snap and whip back and castrate you sort of way.

Jake knew they could not continue like this. They were going to have to talk it out and talk it out tonight. The trouble was, he couldn't afford to have his mind on her while he needed to focus on his interview. He had to get through what had to be done today and then get his head into what was now the most important interview he was ever going to have. He had to have this job. Even if Alexis abandoned him in favor of her job, he would not go back on his word to her. He didn't have enough set aside to survive much more than two or three months, and even that would mean a diet of Ramen Noodles and store brand white bread.

Just before five, Alexis opened Jake's door and walked in, locking the door behind her. She sat down in the chair in front of his desk. He stopped his typing and looked up at her, giving her a hint of a smile. More than either of them had given each other all day.

"I just wanted to wish you good luck tonight and I'm sorry for last night. I hope we're able to do a better job of talking things through tonight when you get home." She exhaled as though she was just able to unburden herself from a very heavy load.

"Thank you. I'm sorry for what happened last night, too. I wasn't certain you wanted me back there tonight."

"Of course, I do. It's our home." Moisture pooled at the corner of her eyes, and he watched as her grip tightened on the arms of the chair.

He smiled a sad smile. It wasn't his home. It was her home. He was a long-term guest. "Thank you for that. This has been the worst day I've had in a very, very long time."

"Me too." She sighed. "Anyway, get your head in the game and knock it out of the park tonight. I know you can." Her mood seemed to lighten just slightly as she got up to walk out. She stopped after one step toward the door and walked back to his desk and leaned over and gave him a very gentle kiss on the lips. "I love you, Jake Douglas. No matter what dumb ass thing I say or do, don't you ever dare forget it." She turned and walked out the door without looking back.

Jake sat for a moment, looking at the empty door. He let out a deep breath that felt like he had been holding in for months. He picked up his phone and texted her, "I love you too. Ditto. Ditto. Ditto." He went back to his typing.

Another hour passed and Jake sat back in his chair. He proofed through the words staring back at him on the screen. Highlighted text and replaced it with words he felt were better. Proofed it a second time and nodded, satisfied that it was as good as it was going to get. He pressed print. Pulling up a second document on the screen, he sent that to the printer as well. Inhaling deeply and letting it out slowly, he walked down the hall to the high-volume printer. He stood there for five minutes while sheet after sheet poured out of the machine.

Grabbing the single sheet in the top feed, he gave it another read. He felt better proofing something on paper versus the screen. With a wry smirk, he placed the paper on top of the copier and signed his name. He folded it neatly, placed it in the envelope and sealed it, tucking it into his breast pocket with a tap. Moments later, the machine stopped it humming and whirring and the out-feed trays shifted and stopped in place. Making his way back down the office hall, he opened Alexis' door and neatly placed the stacks of documents on the center of her desk and pulled a flash drive from his pocket, setting it on top of the pile. An odd urge overtook him. He placed his index and middle finger to his lips, kissed them and then transferred it to the stack of papers.

Closing her door behind him, he walked out of Alexis' office and up to the fifth-floor executive suites. Down the hall to the reception desk in front of a door labeled Hamilton Dewey III, Sr. Managing Partner. Pulled the letter from his breast pocket and placed it on top of his inbox. He walked back down to his office. His mouse hovered over the curser above the message box:

Shredding the disk will remove all data permanently. Are you sure you wish to proceed?

He hesitated just a moment. He clicked Yes, turned, removed the canvas carry bag that was neatly folded in his briefcase, placed the few personal items on his desk into it, removed his law degree from the wall, shoved it in the bag with the rest. Took one last look around the office and placed his office keys and company ID on the desk.

One more deep breath and it was time to leave for his interview.

In the morning Hamilton Dewey III would read:

Dear Mr. Dewey,

It is with deep regret that I submit my resignation, effective immediately. I have passed along all relevant papers and information for all accounts presently under my purvey to appropriate personnel. I have provided Miss Chambers with all documentation and notes regarding the HKD account.

I sincerely appreciate the opportunities that have been given to me during my short tenure with Dewey, Carson, and Howe. However, I find I can no longer continue in any capacity where such blatant disregard for honesty and integrity toward clients and employees alike flows from the top down.

Further communication should be directed to my personal counsel, Sullivan and Tate, LLP.

Regretfully yours,

Jacob L Douglas, Esq.

Chapter 25

Jake

Jake was five minutes early for the interview and proceeded directly to the maitre de station. The man behind looked up with a seriousness and air that set him back slightly. Jake abhorred pompousness, and this man exuded it out of every pore in his body. "I am with Mr. John Rock." Jake said curtly, returning pompousness with formality in the extreme.

Expressionless, the maitre de nodded, "This way sir, Mr. Rock is already seated."

John Rock was an impressive man, despite his ivy league professorish demeanor. A full head of snow-white hair, impeccably cut, horn-rimmed glasses, set on a large, bulbous nose. Steel-blue eyes peered out from behind the glasses that were topped with white caterpillar brows, reminding him of Mark Twain or Albert Einstein. Age had drawn extensive maps on his face, but he looked very fit, particularly for a man who was nearly eighty. He stood to greet Jake with a firm handshake and a sincere smile.

Whatever nerves Jake was feeling, and there were plenty, they dissipated at the handshake. They sat in unison and Jake noticed a drink already waiting for him. Rock noticed Jake's eyes catch the glass and offered a knowing smile. "George might have mentioned your shared affinity with us for fine single malt. I trust you don't mind I took the liberty of ordering my favorite for you?"

"Thank you, sir. That was kind of you." Jake lifted his glass in acknowledgement.

"Remember, it's John, please." Jake nodded apologetically. "I retrieved your resume from our system. I'll also let you know I gave the clown that summarily tossed it in the reject pile before even giving it the courtesy of a once over a written performance warning."

Jake nodded an acknowledgement, but sensed John didn't expect a com-

ment from him about it as he never hesitated before continuing. "It is a
very impressive resume and a 4.0 is no easy get at any university. Your bar
results are just as impressive." Surprised, Jake cocked his head in a silent
question, which John answered with a half-smile. "Yes, I have connections
that can get me sealed information. I have done my homework on you,
Jake. I know you expected as much and have done yours on me as well."

Jake nodded, "I have."

"Good. The purpose of this dinner, for me, is twofold. First, I want to
take some time to get to know you, hobbies, interests, just what makes your
motor run. I do my best to know all my employees. Unfortunately, we're a
very large firm now, so it's impossible, but I certainly know my senior people. So, tonight will be just the start of that, assuming you come on board.
Second, and I expect what you're most interested in, is to present you with
two opportunities I believe have the potential to be a good fit for us both."

Jake was taken aback. He was prepared for a tough interview with
uncomfortable questions about why he was leaving an industry leading
employer after less than a year. Prepared to dance around his relationship
with Alexis and why he was willing to put that before his career. Prepared
to have his constitutional law knowledge tested extensively. He was not
prepared to hear that he was going to be offered not one but two positions
to choose from before he even said or did a damn thing. "Thank you," he
swallowed, quickly gaining his footing, "John. Where would you like me to
begin?"

"Let's get the business part out of the way first so we can enjoy our meal
here over lighter conversation. The food here is truly worth every nickel
of the extravagance." He continued to outline the opportunities in significant enough detail that Jake had to ask only a few clarifying questions. The
first and one both of them saw as the premier career opportunity was to
join the team of lawyers specifically dedicated to the Supreme Court. They
would also work on certain federal appeals but only those likely to continue
on to the high court. He would have a significant role in the group, in no
way the back bench, lackey position he had just left behind at DCH. The
second was slightly more modest and based in New York.

John added to the end of his description of the second position a qual-
ification, "I sincerely apologize for any intrusion into your personal life,
Jake. But I want you to know that the position here in New York is strictly
offered in deference to George. He shared that you and his granddaughter
have recently started a relationship. And if he's intervening on your behalf, I assume it isn't just some casual fling. George is quite protective of

his family, and I doubt he would have called me for this if he didn't think you'd be a part of it someday. "

"Consider your options carefully. Finding a good woman to have by my side is, without question, the single most impactful thing I ever did for my career. My wife and I have been together for over fifty years. She has been there in good times and bad, even when I was an unholy asshole toward her." John chuckled, making Jake think he must be remembering at least one specific incident. "It's your decision, and only you know your true feelings for her. Perform half as well as I believe you can, and a DC opportunity will come up again, so don't feel you're possibly losing your only chance at the prestige of the Supreme Court and judicial and political connections that come with it."

"Thank you, sir… John," he corrected himself, "I appreciate your candor; I don't find it intrusive at all. I am very fond of Alexis, and she will certainly figure into my decision."

"Good. I know George will appreciate that. I probably shouldn't share this, but he expressed great affection and respect for you. Trust me, that speaks volumes for a man with his reputation for being cold and calculating. He is not prone to allow any emotion to interfere with a business decision. I would have more expected encouragement from him to ship you to a Siberian office if I had one to send you to." John laughed.

Jake smiled and took a sip of his truly remarkable glass of whiskey. "I don't know him well, but that would be my guess, too." Dinner arrived as if to place a period on the business-related portion of their meeting. They continued with small talk, Jake revealing interests and plans. Some of what drives him toward success and John sharing some war stories and revealing a bit of himself as well. Jake had made a point of asking him about his success in maintaining a healthy marriage despite what was obviously a demanding and successful career.

The dinner ended as it began with a smile and a handshake. Jake agreed to consider both options carefully and he would make his choice by Monday. John offered more time if he felt he would need it, but Jake politely refused saying he would, "carefully consider yes, ruminate excessively, no." John nodded, and they parted with Jake feeling an immense relief knowing that not only was he landing on his feet but exactly where he wanted to be. Where he belonged. He also had the sense that he had just met an old friend, or maybe a grandfather he never knew he had.

Chapter 26

Jake

Jake walked through the door at the brownstone shortly before ten-thirty. He half expected Alexis to be waiting on the couch, eager for news that he had found a suitable position and that hers was safe at DCH. He had stepped out in faith that his seemingly reckless resignation would result in assuaging her fears. It was an act of his faith on many levels. He also had to admit to himself that it also felt damn good to extend both middle fingers toward a man and his company that obviously had little regard for him. Only his commitment to make Alexis successful would prevent him from truly fucking them in their collective corporate asses.

The downstairs was dark except for the light left on for him in the foyer. There was a brief handwritten note from Alexis beneath the lamp.

Please hurry, I'm waiting eagerly for the bedtime snack you promised me.
Love, A.

Jake smiled and turned off the lamp. He took two stairs at a time to their bedroom, stopping only briefly to catch his breath before entering. He walked into a room glowing with candles, casting a soft warm aura over Alexis. She was lying on the bed, wearing a royal blue corset that fit snugly into her trim waist. The shelf style bra pushed her breasts up and out but left them fully exposed. She wore white thigh-high stockings attached to the garter snaps that fell from the corset. Her long blonde hair fell over her shoulders and spilled out to the side of her full, round breasts. She looked every bit as ravishing as he dreamed she would when they had picked out the outfit together. Despite the wonderful picture of seduction that lay before him, his gaze went straight to the lustful smile on her face. It was only when she bit her bottom lip that he realized she was also slowly moving one of the several toys they had purchased in and out of her obviously soaked pussy.

"Do you like what you see?" she asked, knowing the answer from his expression.

"I fucking love what I see. Are you enjoying your new toys?"

"You can tell that I am, can't you?" She purred, her voice low and throaty. "I thought perhaps that you might enjoy a bedtime snack as well. I want to hear all about your evening, but maybe we should snack first and talk later?"

"Sounds like a perfectly wonderful idea to me."

"Good, perhaps I can watch you while you get more comfortable, Mr. Douglas. You have far too many clothes on, in my opinion."

Jake simply smiled and slowly and seductively removed his suit. Alexis put on a show of her own, turning on the rabbit she had been playing with, which had obviously pleasurable effects on her expression. He was down to just his boxer briefs and was just about to remove them when she asked him to stop.

She removed the toy and set it down. She gracefully slid off the bed and kneeled in front of him. The sight of her kneeling, dressed as she was, caused his already growing cock to spring to full attention. She softly trailed kisses along the length of his shaft through the fabric of his briefs. He could feel her hot, moist breath on him almost as keenly as if it were skin to skin. His cock twitched and jumped at her touch and when she nipped him gently with her teeth, he thought he might explode then and there.

She curled her thumbs under the waistband and dragged down his briefs, his steely rod standing straight up and pointing to the ceiling. Her mouth closed around the tip, then steadily took him deeper, inch by splendid inch. A groan reverberated deep in his throat, losing himself in the sensation of her warm, wet mouth. Softly, he ran his fingers through her hair, following the up and down motion of her head.

She moved her mouth off his cock and traced her tongue along the length of his shaft, then gently kissing and licking his balls while she stroked him, her thumb expertly applying just the right amount of pressure under the tip of the head. She continued bringing him right to the edge of climax before he reached down and pulled her up off her knees.

He kissed her long and full, pressing up against her, the head of his cock rubbing against the stitched satin fabric of the corset. In one motion, he broke off the kiss and turned her, bending her forward so that she was face down on the bed. He dropped to his knees and buried his face between her legs, laving her wetness from top to bottom. His tongue darted in and out of her opening and she was so hot and wet he wondered how long she had been toying herself, waiting for him to arrive. He reached between her legs and found her swollen, sensitive clit and worked circles around it with his thumb. He could clearly hear her moans even as she was face down into the comforter. After a moment or two, his tongue ventured north to minister to her forbidden entrance. She tensed at first and then relaxed and gave in to his mouth. Fingers joined his thumb, venturing inside her pussy and finding her perfect pleasure spot with ease.

The intensity of her moans increased with the speed and pressure of his fingers, and he could feel her pussy tighten around his fingers just before she released into her first orgasm. Her legs were shaking, and he leaned into her to hold her weight. She fisted the bed covers tightly as she moaned something unintelligible into them.

As the last waves subsided, Jake stood up behind her and thrust himself into her without warning. A guttural moan burst out of her as his solid length filled her completely. Looking back over her shoulder, she met his eyes and shared a lustful gaze. She reached back and spread her ass wide for him, "fuck me Jake, fuck me so hard you make me scream."

His primal grunt filled the air as he pistoned into her, rippling the soft flesh of her perfectly full, round ass. She arched her back and pushed into him, taking him as deep as she could. As she had just barely come down from orgasm when he entered her, she quickly responded as his hard, fast thrusts targeted that special spot inside her relentlessly.

"Yes. Fuck yes. God, I love that cock. Fuuuuccccccccccck." She spasmed, her excitement spilling out of her, covering his cock and stomach, soaking the carpet below.

Her body was still pulsing with the last waves of her second release when he gripped her hips, turning her onto her back and hefting her onto the bed. He buried himself deep with a single hard thrust. Hooking her legs over his shoulders, causing her to exhale a rasping whimper of pleasure. Their eyes connected as he continued to thrust hard, fast, and deep inside of her. His balls slapping against her, her thighs and ass soaked with her own juices. She grabbed her flailing tits, pinching her peaked nipples. Jake looked into her hooded eyes and then watched as her fingers toyed with herself. "Oh god, I'm going to cum baby."

She moved as fast as a cat on a mouse. Pushing off the bed and dropping to her knees in front of him, tilting her head back, opening her mouth and sticking out her tongue as if she was a porn star who had been doing this for years. "Yes, Jake, yes, give me your cum. I want your hot sticky goo all over my face." If Jake had been even slightly less possessed by lust for her, the sheer porn quality of those words might have seemed a totally comical mood killer but in his present state of mind he saw red and jerked himself hard, quickly painting her pretty face with streams of cum spraying into her eyes and hair, dripping the last few drops onto her tongue before she greedily took his softening cock into her mouth milking out the last drops of his release.

He drew her up from her knees again and kissed her. Her hands found his deflating cock and played with it unconsciously. They both came, but there was a part of him that still wanted more. Perhaps to avoid the looming conversation, perhaps for more obviously carnal reasons. He kissed her full and deep.

She leaned back to look at him and kissed him again, harder and deeper than the first. He was tempted to give in to her carnal thoughts, join her in her continued lust but his sensible side knew that if they continued, they would collapse together and drift off to sleep leaving an important conversation to be rushed in the morning before she had to go out the door.

He walked into the bathroom, grabbed a damp washcloth and towel for her face. She giggled a bit when he returned and cleaned her face. "Don't you think I'm sexy like this?" she teased.

"I think you're very sexy like that, which is exactly why I needed to clean you up before I give you my update. I could never concentrate knowing how much I wanted to add even more to your collection." He gave her an impish grin, followed by one more deep kiss.

He had wished he had the forethought to bring a bottle of wine up with him. They both would likely need a sip or two to wash down the conversation to come. She excused herself to the bathroom and returned wearing a flannel nightgown and threw him his pajama bottoms. "I think we'll both be able to focus better clothed."

"I can't deny you have a point" as he snaked a hand under the hem of the gown and up between her thighs.

"That's defeating the purpose, isn't it?"

"I suppose, but you know how hot I think you look in flannel."

"I do. It's a rather uncommon fetish, isn't it?" She giggled some more. He smiled and removed his hand.

"So, how did it go? Do you have a second interview set?"

"I'm not getting a second interview." He said, doing his best to stay dead pan.

The smile disappeared from her face, and she put her hand softly on his leg, "Jake, I'm so sorry …"

He stopped her, pressing a finger to her lips. "I didn't expect to, given that John Rock was my first interview."

She nodded, concern still obvious in her expression. "Did he at least give you a time frame of when he might decide about making an offer?"

"He did." Jake was struggling to maintain a straight face, fighting back the smile tugging at his lips. He managed a second or two more for dramatic effect, but couldn't hold it any longer. "Actually, there is no need for a second interview because he gave me two offers before we even ate dinner."

"You're kidding Jake, really!" Her voice rose higher than he'd ever heard from her before, and she leaned forward and hugged him tight to her chest. "Oh, Jake, thank God." She fell back against the headboard. He could see the tension leave her body like one of those blow up Christmas figures after you unplug the fan. "I just couldn't take another day like today."

"I don't think I could either, or another night like last night." She hung her head. "Before I tell you about the offers, because we will need to decide about these together." She gave him a quizzical look, but didn't interrupt. "After you left my office this afternoon, I made a decision." Her eyebrows raised. "Today was my last day at DCH. All my documents for HKD are on your desk, along with a flash drive with all my files. They're for your eyes only. My letter of resignation is in Dewey's inbox, and I cleaned my office out. I erased my hard drive. You have the only copies of my work, so they can't do a damn thing with Hong Kong without you."

He could see his words registering in her eyes. "You didn't think to talk to me about this first?" she said, pulling herself up again. "Don't you think maybe I could have used you around to help me out a little with the transition instead of just bolting out the door and leaving me hanging? What the fuck Jake?"

"Honey, I'm not leaving you hanging. I'm right here and I'm not going anywhere. You can call me anytime from the office with questions. I'd do anything for you," he said, grabbing her shoulders and looking into her eyes. "You know that. How could you ever think I would leave you hanging?" He put his hand gently on her cheek.

Turning away from his touch like it was a hot iron, she sprang from the bed and paced. "Because you did. What happens in a meeting when I don't have the answer to a question? Oh, hold on a sec while I ring up my boyfriend and see what he says. Shit, Jake."

"Alexis, seriously. You already know ninety percent of my work; it's not rocket science. Everything I've done is right there in black in white on your desk." He labored to keep the frustration out of his voice. He didn't understand where her insecurity was coming from. "This was the only thing I saw to do to guarantee you to win in this race neither of us deserves to be forced into."

"I had to swallow the poison pill. What happens if I give two weeks and they make me a counteroffer? What if Dewey decides tomorrow, he's sticking with me and you're out the door? Jesus Lex, haven't you seen enough to realize that very little of the political play is in our hands? I walk out the door without notice, flipping off the ivory tower. They're totally over me and it's your best shot at hanging on. I went way out on a limb with this, and I did it for you. I didn't wait until after my interview tonight. I did it before I knew just what I was walking into. I fully expected to have to jump through some hoops for Rock. Sure, I was confident I'd have a job, but cutting the cord before I even talked to the man, don't you think I was sacrificing just a little?"

She turned to face him, and raised a pointed finger at his face, opening her mouth on an inhale of breath, then after a beat, letting out a long exhale. "Of course you were, and I appreciate it. I do. There's just so much I'm nervous about and you're my security blanket. I have to be honest with you. I don't like that feeling much. I've never needed someone before and don't know why I should need someone now. On top of which this was a big decision to make all on your own. You really should have talked to me about it first."

Jake swallowed hard. "You're right. I should have talked to you first. I'm a hypocrite. We should make decisions like this together. I'm sorry, I was trying to do what I thought was best for you, for us. I guess I thought I was covered when I told you I would do whatever it took to keep you in that position you want so badly. You walked into my office this afternoon and told me you loved me. That made my final decision. I didn't want any more angst caused by DCH to come between us. I did this for you. I did this for us."

She looked at him for a long time. Thought things over a bit more and then leaned in to give him a very soft gentle kiss on the lips. "I do love you, I must. I act like a total slut around you and am glad of it." She laughed at that. "Please promise me something, though."

"Of course."

"No more unilateral decisions like this. We talked in vague terms about you falling on your sword. I just really would like to know just when and how you're planning on doing it. Not find out after the fact."

"That's fair and, of course, I promise. I admit I was wrong despite the right intentions."

She smiled and then out of the blue swung a pillow at him, whacking him in the face.

"Hey what was that for?"

"Because you promised we'd fuck in our offices before you left–all that fun is gone now."

He laughed and took it as a sign that he may just be forgiven. "I am very sorry about that, but better missing out on that fucking, then to end up you getting fucked in the boardroom by me or anyone else. On the bright side, I'll have a new office soon. We can fuck in all we want. Well, at least you can visit out in the open. I'm afraid I won't be welcome to violate you at DCH."

"I'm guessing you're going to be persona non grata by five past nine tomorrow morning," she said with a chuckle. "Now tell me about Rock and Wagner. He gave you two offers? I've never heard of anything like that."

Jake talked Alexis through his meeting with John Rock and gave her the details of the two offers he got. He gave special attention to the NYC offer and the conversation he had with John around his relationship with Alexis, what it could mean long term. He finished by saying that he was leaning heavily toward the NYC offer.

"How can you possibly be thinking about New York when Washington is clearly a higher rung on the ladder? Jesus Jake, to argue in front of the supreme fucking court! That's your dream, isn't it? Think of where that position could lead; the connections you could make. You could find a gig with a PAC or as a lobbyist. You would have so many options, politics, a seat in the federal courts, who knows, it could lead to actually fucking sitting on The Court someday. Associate Justice Jacob Douglas, wouldn't that be a kick in the shorts?"

"Slow down there, girl." Jake shook his head and laughed. "I'm not the one in this relationship with the Ivy League law degree. Those are grand dreams, but they're not my dreams."

"What do you mean they're not your dreams?" she asked, the smile fading from her face. "You told me your love was constitutional law. You told me that becoming a judge would make you happy someday. How is the Supreme Court not the apex of those two things?"

He realized she hadn't been listening to him and if she was, then she was purposely ignoring the fact he was trying to make a decision that focused on their relationship more than his career. His words came out more angrily than he intended, the combination of hurt and frustration with her showing through in his tone. "Do you really care so little about me?"

"What on earth are you talking about?" She snapped back. "I'm really excited for you. I just don't understand why you'd give the New York job a second thought when DC is everything you've told me you're interested in and it's more money."

"I told you why. Because the DC job would be a significant hindrance to our relationship. I really don't want anything to do with a long-distance relationship." *Again*, he added silently to himself. "You know what our lives are like, working most weekends, late nights, constant travel. Here, at least, we get to regularly be together, even if ninety percent of it is while we're asleep. I thought I made it clear that I don't see any job as more important than you."

"Jake, I love you, but this is an incredible opportunity that may never come again…"

"Alexis, I told you that John was very clear that it would come again. No guarantee on when, but he specifically said I could count on another chance at Washington down the road. It seemed to me like he was encouraging me to choose to work on our relationship first, if you were truly what I wanted in a partner, if I believed we had a chance at long-term success."

"Think of the time you'll lose, though. It could be years before it comes along again. Suddenly, you're forty and trying to lay a foundation when there's an entire crop of people our age now that are younger and hungrier than you. Jake, you have to strike while the iron is hot. If we're meant to be, we'll make it work. If we don't, so what? You've got the job you've always dreamed of."

"If we don't so what?!" His voice rose so high every dog in a three-block radius barked. "Really? That's how you feel? Oh, it's nice and all. He's a great guy. We have common interests. The fucking is divine, but so what… other fish in the sea? I'll tell you something. That is not the way I feel about you. I don't see you as so easily disposable. I don't see love as disposable."

"Don't put words in my mouth! You know that's not what I said. I'm really trying to be supportive of you. I'm thinking about you, what's best for you. Don't make it sound like I don't care because I do."

"And I'm not saying you're not being supportive of me, not at all. I appreciate your excitement for me. But you don't seem to share a concern for what it could mean for us. What I don't think you are is concerned about us and the relationship we have but, more importantly, could have. When you asked me to move in here, I know it was quick, maybe too quick, but I thought we were one of those rare couples that just caught lightning in a bottle. I guess I was thinking I saw what I wanted, but never thought I could have. Maybe you just don't have a view of a future for us. Honestly, it's okay if you don't, just tell me. I guess I just assumed you did."

"Jake, oh Jake," she sighed a heavy breath. "I have no idea at all what's going to happen to us down the road, and neither do you. I can't see making all these plans for what ifs when you have a real honest to God perfect opportunity for what is. Six months down the road we have a blowout about the toast being too dark and split up and now you're pissed at me because I cost you this big chance and you sacrificed, yada, yada, yada. I start to feel guilty because you lost out on this gig. Honestly, don't expect me to refuse a big promotion just because we have this relationship. If I walked in tomorrow and they tell me I've been assigned to lead my own pod in Los Angeles, I'm on the next fucking plane, I promise you that. I love you. I don't want anyone else, ever. I'm just not going to make career decisions based on us. I don't think you should, either."

Jake inhaled sharply and opened his mouth. He was about to point out the hypocrisy in her words. Of how she was telling him she would do exactly what had started this whole argument. Deciding without consulting the other when he realized to her it wasn't the same. To her, he hadn't made a career decision without her, but an 'us' decision. There was no place in 'us' for career decisions. He closed his mouth.

"What?" she asked, shoulders back like she was ready for another point to debate.

Shaking his head with a sigh, "nothing. Maybe we should just go to bed and talk about it some more once we've had time to think it over. John said he would email the formal offer sheets in the morning. I need to look at the details."

Her eyes dropped and her shoulders sagged as she nodded. "Okay."

Leaning over, he kissed her forehead, then pulled her closer and wrapped her in her arms. Slowly, her body relaxed, and she melted into his embrace. "I guess we just had our first fight."

"Mm," she snorted into his chest. "I didn't like it at all, Jake Douglas. Not at all."

His hand combed through her long blond hair and then down her back. Despite the war of emotions raging in his chest, he smiled. "Neither did I."

Her hand raked through the hair on his chest, and she traced the outline of his nipple with her fingernail, with a touch as light as a feather causing him to intake a sharp breath. "Jake?" she mewled as her fingers works slowly down his chest and over his belly.

"Mm?"

"You know what I think I would like?"

"Mm-hmm. I think I would like that too."

Chapter 27

Jake

Jake had been half aware of Alexis leaving in that nether land between consciousness and dreams. He pulled himself out of bed, unwilling to give into the temptation to laze the day away. He had decisions to make, and he knew they would have to talk again tonight. There was just no way to ignore the white elephant in the room. He tossed on a sweatshirt and padded his way down the two flights of stairs, down the hall, and into the kitchen to make his morning coffee.

He had just settled onto the couch, mug in hand, to enjoy the luxury of watching the morning news shows when the phone rang. It was the DCH main number, and he knew Alexis would call on her cell if she needed him. He wasn't surprised to hear Hamilton Dewey's bellowing voice on the line when he answered and was glad that he chose **record call** before answering.

"Disregard for honesty and integrity! I'm suing you for liable, you arrogant little fuck." Dewey's voice boomed through his earpiece. "If you think I'm going to come crawling to you and beg you to stay just to salvage an account, you're a bigger jackass than I thought."

A smirk tipped at the corner of Jake's mouth, and he switched the phone to speaker, settling back on the couch. He felt a perverse sort of satisfaction knowing his resignation had gotten such a rise out of the middle-aged asshole. Bringing the mug of steaming liquid to his lips, he took a long sip, creating a silence that had the desired effect of setting Dewey on edge.

"Don't ignore me, Douglas. What is it you expect to get out of this little stunt?"

"First, be aware that this conversation is being recorded."

"Ha! I thought you were a half decent lawyer. You just gave away your advantage. New York is a single party notification state. Now you can't try

to trap me into saying something that could work to your advantage when I
haul your ass into court for breach of contract."

Jake couldn't hold back the chuckle that slipped out. "Oh, I'm sure you'll
say something actionable; you already have by contacting me directly instead of through my counsel as I directed. But, given your personal lack of
integrity, I notified you because now you can't claim to be somewhere like
Florida, where both parties need to be aware of recording. Second, is there
a purpose to this call other than to spew empty threats?"

"I don't make empty threats. I've already directed the legal department
to take action on breach. You've also erased the files on your computer.
Those were company property, Mr. Douglas. You have one hour to be in
my office and rectify this situation. If you're lucky, I won't pursue further
action against you after you serve out your two-week notice. If not, I will
have you disbarred, and you'll never work anywhere again. You have no
concept of the power I wield in this city."

He knew he should just end the phone call; the threats of retribution
were more than enough for Jake to sue Dewey personally and the firm,
but that would be far more aggravation than it would be worth. It would
also prevent him from throwing all Dewey's crap right back into his face.
"I shouldn't be surprised that you are as ignorant about your own company's policies as you are arrogant. I did not complete a full year of service
at DCH and was therefore not under contract. First year employees are 'at
will' and contracts are only given after a year's probation. It is no longer
my 'will' to be in your employ and I am under no legal obligation to give
you notice and I provided a letter of resignation which more than meets
any assumed duty of notification. All the work I have produced on behalf
of DCH is saved, per company policy, on the network servers or other
digital media. I have provided Miss Chambers with hard and digital copies of my briefs, presentations, notes, and research for the HKD project
to make her transition to that account as seamless as possible. This also
exceeds expectations, real or assumed. As for your tirade about my future
ability to provide for myself, I am going to ignore your obvious threat, as
I am well aware of its emptiness. I already have an offer from a firm and
know for a fact that any attempt to besmirch my reputation would not only
be dismissed as pure fabrication based on your reputation alone but also
as slander and liable toward their reputation, given my association to their
firm. I hear you have a lovely villa in the Cayman Islands. If you wish to
continue to maintain the deed to it, I strongly suggest you heed my instruc-
tions and contact me through my counsel should you find the need in the

future. Good day Mr. Dewey."

He leaned forward to disconnect the call, but not before he could hear Dewey scream in rage. The second half of the reply to Dewey's threats had been a bold face bluff, but one he was confident would work because of the accuracy of the beginning of the conversation. If Dewey had actually contacted human resources and the legal department to sue him for breach, then he pitied the poor bastard that had to tell the idiot he didn't have a leg to stand on. As for Rock and Wagner's desire to pursue legal action on his behalf, that was all bluff, and if he didn't decide soon about which offer to take, he might lose both. Especially if he became too hot to handle. No one wanted to bring on a new employee embroiled in a legal battle with a former employer. He certainly wouldn't. Once he was under contract, that would be a different story and he would make certain it was iron clad so that if he was dismissed, he would have a of golden parachute.

Pushing himself off the sofa, he padded his way back to the kitchen and refilled his coffee. His hand raked over his morning stubble, and he let out a long, slow breath. He knew he had five days before he had to give John his answer, but with Dewey on the warpath, it wasn't worth risking it. John had more than insinuated his lack of respect for DCH as an organization, so Jake doubted Dewey posed an actual threat, but then again, he couldn't be certain.

Alexis had been more than clear that she thought he should take the offer that put him in the Washington office, but his gut was telling him that was a mistake. Not only was their foundation not strong enough after being together for only a few weeks, but his history with long-distance relationships had been catastrophic. Regardless of how new their relationship was, he'd known nothing more certainly than that he wanted Alexis in his life, long term. She had a point, though; he knew that if she ended the relationship to advance with DCH, he would be resentful of passing on the DC job. He settled back onto the sofa, drinking his coffee and staring at the wall.

After over an hour of contemplation and failing to find anything magically appearing on the walls, he made his way up the stairs and into the shower. He was not about to waste his day lost in thought. He needed a fresh perspective. He thought about calling his brother, Teddy, but he'd likely be in the middle of his workday and if he bothered to answer the phone, he'd never get his full attention despite his brother's best intentions. His sister was not an option. All she ever did was twist their conversations around to him forgiving his father. Today was not the day to open that can of worms. No day would ever be that day for him.

The only other neutral party he could think of was Rob. Who knows if he's even in the same time zone, but it was worth a shot. It would mean hearing Rob berate him for putting Alexis first. Making the same mistakes he had with Stephanie, but he knew that wasn't entirely true. Still, he did need to talk to Rob to make sure he didn't say anything about his relationship with Alexis to anyone Rob might still be in touch with at the office. It couldn't hurt him, but he was pretty sure nothing good would come of it for Alexis.

Once out of the shower and dressed, he picked up his phone and called his best friend.

Rob picked up after the second ring. "Jake. When are you starting?"

"Hello is the normally expected greeting, jackass," Jake laughed. "And what do you mean, when am I starting? Where?"

"With me, of course." He laughed, "I know you're out at DCH and you weren't yesterday, so unemployed Jake must be freaking the fuck out. I was going to give you until tomorrow morning to douse the flames that must be consuming your hair right now."

His hair hadn't been on fire per se, but the knowledge that Rob already knew about him being gone from DCH changed things. Rubbing his temple with his fingers, he groaned, "how did you know I was out so fast? It's only been a few hours"

"Oh, I still have my sources. But you've got to tell me what really happened. I've heard everything from you being escorted out by security to breaking Dewey's nose in a conference room brawl." Rob chuckled. "I'll be honest. I'm really hoping the last one is true, but I guess they're not mutually exclusive."

Jake pinched the bridge of his nose and winced, thinking of what Alexis was having to endure in the middle of it all, if Rob had heard this much from a distance. She would not be in a great mood when she got home, so he'd better plan something nice for her to appease the beast. They still had decisions to make and best to make them in a positive frame of mind. "Sorry to disappoint, but neither is true. Though the way Dewey sounded on the phone this morning, I bet he wishes he could have taken a swing at me."

Rob snorted, "Really? So that leads me to believe you resigned without notice."

"Yup. Left a letter on his desk last night."

"Well, you should be happy to know that your departure has created quite a stir and no end to the crazy rumors. I even heard one that had you canned because you asked Chambers out and she filed a complaint with HR. Don't worry, I didn't tell anyone about your dirty little secret. It wouldn't hurt you any now, but I know you care about her and she wouldn't escape some form of punishment, even with you gone."

"Thanks, man. I was a little worried about that."

"Seriously, dude?" There was an awkward silence for a moment and Jake was just about to apologize when Rob spoke again. "So, are you going to tell me what actually happened? When we talked a few days ago, you were all about making DCH work until you could do something… real was the word I think you used?"

"I left so Alexis and I wouldn't end up being pitted against each other, because that was what Dewey was doing. He flat out told me it was going to be me or her once the HKD deal got done."

"Fuck. Dude, seriously?"

"Yup, told her before we even got back from Asia that she was to get close to me to learn all she could about the HKD account, and once she did, they'd let me go. Then the slimy fat slug pulled me aside after a meeting the other day and told me keeping her was all Andre's idea, and if it was up to him, and it was, I would be kept on, if I could land the account."

"So, Jacob Douglas, the honorable man that he is, swallowed the proverbial poison pill for his beloved. Not only wouldn't she do it for you, it wouldn't even cross her mind."

Jake felt his jaw clench, and he fisted a throw pillow, ready to hurl it across the room. He didn't like his friend's opinion of Alexis and he liked it even less that even he had to admit there was truth in Rob's words. "I should have known better than to try to talk to you about this. I know you don't like her. I'll talk to you later…"

"Jake, I'm sorry," Rob cut him off. "You're right. You're a grown assed man. I should just keep my opinions to myself. Let's not let this get in the way of a good thing. I'll have to start you at the same rate as you were at with DCH but as soon as the first client payments come in, I'll double your salary and make it retroactive to your start date which should give you a nice lump sum check in about two months. I'd start now at the higher rate, but you know how many expenses hit with a start-up."

"Rob, I told you, I'm not coming to work for you."

Jake could hear Rob's heavy exhale. "Look, I said I'm sorry. I'm sure once I get to know her, I'll see things differently. I could really use you here, man. We've always made a great team; don't change your mind just because of my jackass mouth. It's never gotten in our way before."

"Rob, I'm not changing my mind. I told you on the plane I wasn't going with you."

"Then why the call the day after you quit?"

"I was going to ask your opinion on a couple of offers I have, but after what you said about Alexis, I already know what you're going to say, so never mind."

"Seriously, Jake, I'm sorry. You know I'm here for you, just like you've always been for me." Rob paused but continued when Jake didn't respond. "Who do you have offers from? I'm guessing you're not looking for another business consulting gig. As you know, working for me would be the best in that department."

Jake shook his head, not having any intention of raining on Rob's parade. "Definitely not consulting. I'm never going down that road again."

"So, where then?"

"Rock and Wagner..."

"Dude, why is there even a second option?" Rob cut him off. "We talked about them when you were still in law school. That should be a simple choice for you, even if the second offer is more money."

"Both offers are from R&W."

"Wait, what?" Rob's voice crackled. "How do you have two offers from the same firm?"

"Long story." Jake answered with resignation in his voice. Sinking back onto the sofa, he explained his options to Rob.

After he finished, there was a long pause as he waited for Rob's reply. "You still there?" he asked, wondering if he had given up during his long-winded description of both of his offers.

"Sorry. I'm just trying to figure out what questions you have that don't make this an obvious choice. The Washington gig is everything you've always wanted. Sure, moving is a pain in the ass, but I'm sure you can get them to cover expenses, at least some of them. And if this is about Alexis..."

"Don't go there again, Rob," Jake's tone left little doubt in the warning it contained.

"I'm not, Jake. I trust your judgement. And who you're involved with is none of my business, anyway. What I was going to say is that I'm sure you could work a long-distance relationship. New York to DC isn't that far. You could drive it if you wanted to."

"You're forgetting that my record with long-distance relationships sucks."

"Oh, Christ on a cracker, Jake. Please tell me this nonsense isn't all about you and Stephanie. She was just a stupid cunt and didn't deserve you. She got what she deserved in the end, didn't she?" Not waiting for Jake to answer, he continued, "you're older and wiser now and if you and Alexis are the real thing, then it will last. If not, I promise you there will be a large crop of beautiful women just begging for a chance to woo an eligible, good-looking lawyer."

"I'm not interested in being wooed. I never have been," Jake grunted.

"Fine. No wooing. But if you walk around fearing getting betrayed by a woman and not willing to stray too far away, I promise you that you'll end up lonely because no woman worthwhile is going to put up with being on a leash just because you've got trust issues."

"I don't have trust issues,"

"Whatever." Rob dismissed the argument. "Fear of abandonment. I don't care what you call it, I'm not the one who wasted his entire fresh-man year as a psych major. But you're asking me to tell you to take a job that isn't perfect just so you can stay close to someone who might leave you for their own career and I won't do it. If you want June Cleaver to be waiting for you in the kitchen every night and follow you wherever you go, I promise you, Alexis Chambers is not the woman you want. Maybe my impression of her wasn't totally accurate, and she has some wonderfully redeeming qualities, but submitting to you as her lord and master is not one of them. At least we can agree on that."

"Okay, you have a point," Jake admitted with a sigh.

"I have a lot of valid points and another one is that you're far too tal-ented to give up your goals and follow her around wherever she goes. So, if you're going to succeed, either she has to leave DCH or you're going to have to learn to have a long-distance relationship. One way or another, you're going to end up there because she'll leave you behind in New York. You know she will, and then what?"

Jake leaned forward with his elbows on his knees and his head in his hands. He knew what Rob was telling him was the truth, even if he didn't much like hearing it. It's what Alexis had said she would do more than once. He knew he should be feeling happy about the Washington job and not the tight feeling in his stomach, like his breakfast was coming back up for a repeat appearance. "Thanks. I appreciate your honesty."

"Pft," Rob hissed, "I've always got your back, man."

"I know," he agreed with a heavy sigh. "I'll talk to you later."

"You better. And we'll have drinks the next time I'm in DC."

"Drinks, absolutely. Where? I'll let you know when I do."

"DC, man. No other choice. Oh, and seriously, good luck with Alexis. She's a beautiful woman and I imagine she's a good one when you don't stand between her and whatever she has her sights on."

"Ha," Jake laughed, unable to disagree, "that she is. I'll catch you later." Hanging up the phone with a stretch, he strode toward the hall, pocketed his keys and wallet before throwing on his coat and heading down the street. Rob and Alexis had both told him to follow his dream job to DC, but he couldn't escape the feeling that to do so would ultimately end his relationship with Alexis. Hoping the cold, fresh air would clear some cobwebs from his mind, he ambled down the streets before finding a bakery drawing him in. Coffee and a pastry for lunch were something he hadn't done since college. Figuring he could grab some fresh bread for dinner, he headed inside and allowed the aroma of deliciousness to calm his frazzled nerves.

Alexis walked through the door just before eight, giving him a big smile and a kiss. "God, what is that sumptuous aroma?" she moaned, shrugging off her coat and hanging it on the rack near the door.

A smile spread across Jake's face, and he shrugged, "might be home-made beef stew."

"You cooked us a homemade dinner?" she asked rhetorically, sliding into his arms and kissing his neck. "I could get used to you being unemployed."

Stepping back from the hug, he looked down with his brow raised.

"Oh, stop," she pushed his shoulder, stepping past him and heading for the kitchen. "I was just teasing you. But it is nice to come home to dinner waiting instead of sorting through takeout menus."

"It is." He followed her back to the kitchen. "I went out for a walk at lunch and was lured into that bakery a couple blocks down." Shaking his head laughing, "I shouldn't have done it on an empty stomach because I ended up with four loaves of bread and then had to go to the market and get something to go with them."

Lifting the lid covering the pot of simmering stew, she let out another pleasurable moan. "Feel free to go out on an empty stomach every day if this is the result. This smells amazing and I'm famished. I never got lunch today."

"How bad was it? I talked to Rob just before noon and he had already heard the rumors about my departure."

Alexis shrugged, reaching up into the cabinet and pulling down the soup crocks. "Other than Dewey storming into my office about ten and demanding to see what you had given me; it was pretty much a normal day. I spent most of it reviewing your notes." She exhaled, dropping her shoulders. "I'm sorry I was so pissy last night. You were right. You gave me everything I needed, and I really didn't doubt you." She looked up at him through her long lashes. "I was really just doubting myself."

Jake ladled out the stew into the bowls, then kissed the top of her head. "We both could have managed things better, but I knew you'd do just fine."

Silently, she moved the bowls to the counter and set out silverware before sitting up on the high-top chair. Jake edged onto the chair next to hers and took a spoonful of stew to his mouth. "Ah," he gasped, grabbing the wine she had poured for him and took a swig. "Cat tongue, damn it."

She laughed, "you didn't know it was hot?" He narrowed his gaze at her, trying to look angry but fell short of the mark. Feeling like there would never be a better time to ask, she directly addressed the pink elephant in the room. "Have you made a decision?"

Jake set the spoon down in his bowl of stew and leaned back, hissing a slow breath between his pursed lips. He had been hoping the meal he made would be enough of a distraction to delay this conversation, but pink elephants are hard to ignore. His stomach churned, and it had nothing to do with hunger. All his father's words about him thinking he was more than he was. That he thought he was better than the rest of his family. Too good to show up for family events.

Then there were the words her father had said at Christmas. Greg might be an insufferable bastard, but Jake imagined that the rest of her family wondered if his interest in Alexis wasn't, at least in part, what she could give him in the way of increased status and opportunity. And hadn't he already taken advantage of that increased opportunity? He wouldn't have a decision to make about his dream job if not for Alexis and her grandfather. John Rock never would have given him a second thought. He certainly hadn't when Jake reached out before Alexis.

You quit DCH before you even had an offer. You did that because you loved her, the voice in the back of his head countered. *But would you have done it without the virtually guaranteed job she had set up for you? Would you really have done that without a safety net?* Deep down, he knew Alexis was too good for him, but he couldn't help but want her. But why would she ever want him long term? Was he really any different from Trevor?

She raised a brow as she drew a spoonful of soup to her full, red lips.

The debate raging in his mind could go to hell. There was only one thing that really mattered to him. "I've been trying to sort it out all day. It comes down to one very critical piece of information, really. One thing I need to know beyond a shadow of a doubt."

Alexis met his stare with a knowing gaze. "You want to know what my intentions for us are, don't you?" she sighed

Jake nodded. "That's one way to phrase it, yes." After everything that happened with Stephanie, would Alexis do the same thing? Would she find something she thought was better than him? "I'm not naïve enough to believe we're ready for marriage, but we're living together and that means we're committed to a long-term relationship as far as I'm concerned."

"I love you with all my heart. I love you more than I thought was possible this soon in a relationship. I love you more than I have loved anyone, more than I thought I could love anyone."

He stopped, looking for the words to frame the question the right way. The best he could do was the cliché. "Do you see me as maybe being Mr. Right or am I just Mr. Right Now?" He paused and just stared into her eyes, hoping he'd find the answer there, but her expression was blank.

He looked down at the rapidly congealing bowl of stew. Picking up the spoon, he toyed with it absentmindedly. "Maybe I only read the signs I wanted to read; heard you say what I wanted you to say, but I believed you felt about me how I felt about you. When you asked me to move in with you after only three weeks. How you said you hated not having me here beside you. I felt that way too, you've never once made me feel like anything less than someone you loved more than… God I don't know, you made me feel like I was someone special, someone you cared for more than you cared for anyone else before."

He couldn't hide the anguish on his face. "You are all that, Jake. You have it right. I've never once been close to loving anyone the way I love you."

The smile tugging at the corner of his mouth couldn't break through the despair he felt inside. "That's why I want to take the New York job. Washington might be my dream job, but I have other dreams that are way more important to me. From the moment I saw you in your office, saw the real you. You're the dream I most want to chase. I know there's no guarantee, but there's no guarantee I'll ever come close to all those possibilities you listed off last night. Not one of those wouldn't be a thousand times sweeter than having them with you by my side."

Tears began to trail down her face. "Jake, you are Mr. Right. In just a few weeks, you have shown me more that I've seen in my life. You've shown me love and integrity I didn't believe were even possible to see in a man."

She thumbed the tears from her cheeks. "But I still don't see anything beyond right now. My dream was, and still is, my career. I need to prove to everyone that I am good enough to be there. Showing my father that I am worth so much more than pumping out babies and volunteering for whatever the charity de jour is. I have to prove to myself that I'm right. I doubt I could forgive myself if I didn't give it everything I have."

It was the response he was preparing himself for. She had said it before, perhaps he held some small hope that when confronted with a choice between him and the absolute of ambition, she would seek at least a small compromise, but she held true to herself and in an ironic sort of way Jake was glad of it. She was who she said she was. She knew who she was and would not change that on a whim. He wished he had that kind of cold resolve, the ability to deny your heart.

"I want you in my life, Jake. I adore you, but I will choose to climb up that next rung when the opportunity presents itself. You can't allow me to be your dream. That's not fair to either of us. Honestly, I don't truly know why you can't just be happy in what we have right now and not be so consumed by what the potential is for our future."

"I am happy with what we have if it means we are trying to work toward a future. What I can't be happy with is living under the cloud that someday you're going to come home and say see yah, I'm off to my next big thing and, well, it just doesn't make sense to string you along anymore."

"Christ, what do you want me to do, fly to Vegas with you and elope? Would that prove my undying love? The foundation of love is trust, isn't it? I trust you to love me even though we're apart sometimes. Won't you give me the same trust? Take the job in Washington. Pursue your dream. Trust in your dream and trust in me." She pushed her bowl away with a heavy exhale. "Shit. I'm the one who just got cheated on and I can trust you enough to encourage you to take a job in another city and believe that our relationship will survive. Why can't you do the same for me?"

He wanted to scream at her he'd been cheated on, too. Cheated on not only by his first love but betrayed by his father. All of it made possible by him pursuing his dream of becoming a lawyer. By trying to have a long-distance relationship just like what she was pushing him toward now. She was right, though; he wasn't trusting her, and she didn't deserve to pay for other's transgressions. "I'm sorry. You're right. I trust you completely, but I'm not treating you like I do." The words tasted bitter on his tongue as he spoke. He was never one of those that couldn't admit his mistakes. Not trusting her was a mistake but, at the same time, he could see a path that would make this the most regrettable mistake of his life.

Moving alone to Washington was like paving the way to their end, but staying in New York would likely be only a temporary extension. She wouldn't hesitate to take the next step in her plan for success, so why should he? "If I go to Washington, we'll spend every weekend together?"

Alexis dropped her eyes to her lap and nodded.

"I need to hear you say it, Alexis."

Looking up at him from beneath her long, graceful lashes, "Every weekend that we can. You know I'm off to Hong Kong in a week. I can't control having to be away on weekends sometimes."

Running his hands through his already tangled hair, he breathed out a heavy sigh. "You know what I mean. When we're home and if I choose to fly to where you are. I don't want to hear complaints because I choose to fly to Chicago just so we can have dinner on a Saturday night."

"As long as I don't hear complaints about spending all Saturday afternoon in a hotel room alone because I'm working." There was a little snark in her tone, but he noticed a smile tugging at the corner of her mouth, despite her attempt to hide it from him.

"What about this is amusing you?" If she said something about him caving into her will, he was going to lose his mind. He hated smug winners.

"Nothing," she said, pursing her lips together, fighting harder to conceal the smile.

"Well, something has you fighting back a grin like the cat who got the cream."

"Fine," she huffed, rolling her eyes and letting the grin escape. "While I hate being pressured and, even worse, feeling like I'm forced to make a choice I'm not ready for, it felt really nice to hear you threaten me with flying somewhere just so you could have dinner with me. No one has ever offered that kind of devotion to me before. It feels nice." She brushed her thumb up and down his five o'clock shadow before leaning over and kissing his forehead. "I know it's going to take work."

"More work than relationships already do, which is why I think a long-distance relationship is a dangerous plan. But you're worth the effort to make it work, so I'm willing to try if you are."

She slipped off her stool, so that she was wedged between his legs.

Pressing her palms against his face, she pulled him to her lips. Tasting of red wine, stew and a flavor that was all her, he lost himself in their kiss. His hand enveloped that back of her head as he deepened it and she melted further into him. Pulling back from the kiss and tracing her finger over his lips, she asked, "is that answer enough, or do you need to hear me say that I'll do more than try?"

Chapter 28

Alexis

Alexis settled behind her desk the next morning, looking at the pile of documents Jake had left behind for her. Running her fingers over the stack, she smiled. While he might have been ethically obligated to preserve the work, he'd done this as an extra step she knew he'd taken just for her. Once she'd gotten over the shock of his seemingly rash decision, she also realized that he'd made it solely with her in mind. He'd done all this, putting her first before himself, not asking a single thing in return.

She'd never experienced that kind of love before. Even her mother, who'd always been there for her, sometimes did things she felt were more for herself than for her. It both awed her and scared the hell out of her. *Could I ever do the same thing if faced with a similar choice?*

There was a part of her that was profoundly relieved that Jake had decided to go to Washington. It absolved her of the guilt of standing in the way of his life plan. Still, she wondered if by pushing him to make that decision she hadn't pushed him over the top of a precipice that would eventually lead him away from her for good. Had she just signed the death warrant of the best thing that had ever happened to her in her life? She didn't for a minute believe in soul mates or having one true love but in her early thirties she knew that a love like they had for each other was uncommonly rare and to find it at all, let alone more than once, was unlikely.

A rap on her door brought her back to the moment. Andre poked his head through and told her to join him in Dewey's office. Whatever this summons was, she doubted she was going to like it. Every day seemed to bring more drama and conflict and as much as she knew this was part of reaching the next step in her life plan, she missed just being able to do her job as a lawyer and avoid all the palace intrigue.

You could have knocked her over with a feather as she walked out of Dewey's office after the meeting. Perhaps all the palace intrigue was worth it after all. She now had her own pod to lead and while it would mean splitting time between New York and Denver until the HKD account was solidified, she had just taken a giant step ahead in her plan and well ahead of what she expected.

Alexis: Are you home?
Jake: At the market right now, but I can be home in fifteen. What do you need me to bring you?
Alexis: Nothing. I'm on my way. Big news. Tell you when I get there.
Jake: :-)

Gathering a few folders from her desk and stuffing them into her folio, she turned to find Hamilton Dewey standing in her doorway. "Oh!" she pressed her hand to her chest. "You startled me. I didn't hear you knock."

"I didn't knock. It's my damn building."

Alexis stiffened her back, squaring her shoulders at the terseness of his words. "What can I do for you, sir?"

Dewey's jaw clenched for a moment in reaction to her clipped words before he smirked. "I neglected to tell you that there's a distinct possibility we will relocate your pod to this office eventually, so don't plan any move yet. We're still reviewing the fate of the Denver office. It's been underperforming for quite a while, and we may decide to close it and integrate what little is good about it to other locations."

"Thank you," Alexis nodded, not knowing what else he expected her to say.

Dewey turned away but stopped and met her gaze. His eyes narrowed into dark, menacing slits. "I was going to give this assignment to Douglas before he lost his balls at a little competition between the two of you. Obviously, it would have been a colossal mistake on my part to give a pussy like that his own work group to manage. But it got me wondering just what your motivation is, Alexis. I can't imagine your darling daddy letting you work your way up the corporate ladder. Doesn't he expect you to marry and start popping out babies? I don't want to be left high and dry when you do your daughterly duty."

Her hands balled into fists at her side, nails digging deeply into her palms. "My father plays no role in my decisions," she gritted out between her clenched teeth.

"Hmph," he snorted. "Too bad I didn't know you and daddy weren't that tight sooner."

"I didn't know you knew my father, let alone why our relationship is any of your concern."

"Every relationship my employees have effects their performance and their performance is most definitely my concern, don't you think Alexis?" The smile on his face conveyed anything but happiness. He paused for a moment, almost seeming to want her to take the bait. When she stood stone still, never blinking, he coughed a humorless laugh. "You should know I never would have hired you. Your father was a ruthless, back-stabbing bastard and the apple never falls far from the tree. But you had already signed the employment agreement, and the lawyers told me I'd be vulnerable to a suit if I tried to void it. Knowing your father as I do, I didn't doubt it."

Alexis felt blindsided by this conversation and couldn't decide how to act. "Then why did you just give me a promotion, if you feel so strongly that I'm the same as my father?"

"Because you're capable Ms. Chambers and because the more I talk to you, the more I realize the further you advance the more pissed off your father is going to be." Before she could reply, he turned and walked briskly down the hall. "Good luck in Denver. You're going to need it."

His parting words echoed around her office as she sank back into her chair. *What the actual fuck just happened?*

Sighing, Alexis folded her laptop closed and tucked it into her folio. She had been staring at the screen for the past hour since the plane had reached cruising altitude. When she'd told Jake about all that had happened and how she had to be on this plane to Denver, he'd said very little. He hadn't congratulated her on the promotion. He hadn't told her to be cautious around Dewey and watch her back. He hadn't said much of anything at all. He simply nodded from behind, his hands that were steepled in front of his face. When she tried to meet his gaze, he didn't even appear to be looking at her, but looking through her.

She felt like he was walling himself off. She'd even suggested a quickie to tide them over until she got back, but he'd refused, without offering an excuse. Perhaps pushing him to stick to his plans and finding out she was moving forward with hers had been too much. What she did know was that she didn't like the distance between them at all and it had her feeling more alone than she had in a long time. Solitude was something she'd always longed for, yet today, alone, was the last thing she wanted to be.

Her driver had barely pulled away from the curb at Denver International when her phone rang. Digging through her purse, she fished out her phone, hoping it was Jake and at least they could have a conversation about what was going on. Anything would be better than the silence she had from him before she left for LaGuardia. Her shoulders sank for a moment when she saw the caller ID but at least this call wouldn't involve an argument and a call with Jake didn't have the same assurance.

"Hi Papa, this is a nice surprise."

"How are you, Allie girl? How are you and your fine young man getting on?"

God, she thought, *that's a really good question that she wished she had the answer to.* "Not all that good, Papa. I think I might have fucked it up."

"Oh child, what would make you think that? He didn't grab the job with John and break it off with you because if he did, I'll make his life a living hell. He won't be able to get a job at a fast-food joint when I'm done with him."

Her grandfather's protective streak made her feel warm and, despite the tension still raging in her body, she smiled and the tightness between her shoulders lessened. "No. Not at all. He would never do anything like that. Not in a million years."

"What is it then? I don't think I've ever heard you so discouraged. Not even after that Hollywood prick broke your heart."

With a heavy sigh, she shared the past forty-eight hours with her grandfather, not bothering to sugarcoat anything because she knew the wily old man would see right through her bullshit. When she finished, there was a moment of silence and then an exhale that sounded like a gust of hurricane force wind on the other end of the line.

"Why would you push him to take a job that he clearly didn't mind passing on? I've known John for years and if he told Jake he'd have another opportunity down the road, he'll have another opportunity down the road. Jake was willing to wait, willing to wait for you. Clearly you love him. Why did you push him away?"

"I wasn't pushing him away, Papa," she argued, but even she didn't believe what she'd just said.

"Alexis Anne Chambers," the sound of her grandfather using her full name sent shivers down her spine, even from two-thousand miles away, "I don't like you lying to me but what's worse, you're lying to yourself."

Damn it. Why does he always see through me? She didn't enjoy being on this side of his scrutiny. This was usually Carole's role. "Fine," she groaned, sounding like a petulant child even to herself. "Because he's brilliant Papa, he has no idea just how gifted he is. I'm a damn good lawyer, at least I think I am, but when I read his work… It's precise. It's thorough. It's irrefutable. He didn't plod through case law and pull-out ideas. His margin notes Papa, I don't know how to explain it, really. I can't hold a candle to the instinct he has. He deserves this chance, and I can't take that from him. There's no doubt in my mind if he makes the right contacts, he'll be sitting on The Supreme Court someday, he will. I can't be the reason he loses that."

"Sweetheart, I truly doubt he feels the same way. I know you didn't grow up in a very loving home, at least during the years you could remember it, but you saw a lot of your grandmother and me. I promise you we both sacrificed for each other, and I would do it all over again in a heartbeat."

He paused and let his words wash over her. The more she thought about them, the greater the tightness in her stomach became. Blinking rapidly to fight back the stinging building behind her eyes, she raised her hand, squeezing her temple. "There's more to it than standing in the way of his success, isn't there, dear?" George's voice was soft and deep and wrapped around her tight, comforting her even as they forced the unsavory truth she'd been trying to deny from her lips.

"Yes."

Silence hung awkwardly before he pressed her. "What is it? I think you need to say it out loud."

She shook her head, but relented. "If he takes this, then I won't have to consider sacrificing for him when the time comes."

Another moment of silence passed between them as her admission settled around her. "Mm," his deep baritone finally agreed. "Alexis, you're thirty-two. Maybe it's time to reevaluate the plans you've been making since you were eighteen. Things have changed. You have changed. And I'm sorry that the two of you have made things more difficult for each other, but that doesn't mean you can't work your way through it if you do it as a team. You just have to decide what you're willing to sacrifice and what is worth sacrificing for."

His words were kind and understanding, and she didn't like them one damn bit. In her heart, she knew he was right, but she also knew what her priorities were. "I know you're right, Papa, but it's too late. He accepted the job today. It's too late."

"It might be too late to keep him from going to Washington, but it's not too late for everything else."

Maybe he was right, but she didn't see how they could both get what they needed and remain together in the long run. She'd just have to be grateful for whatever time they could have together in the meantime. "I've got to go. I'm at the hotel. Thanks Papa, and thank you for all you've done for him."

"Don't mention it dear, He did it himself; I just helped to open a door. Bye dear."

"Bye Papa."

She looked at her phone before tucking it back in her purse and taking her suitcase from the driver. Wheeling it behind her into the lobby, she threw her shoulders back and drew on her inner Ice Princess. She had work to do here and whatever needed to be worked out between her and Jake would just have to wait until she got home. This was her first test on her next step up the ladder, and nothing or no one would stand in her way.

Chapter 29

Alexis

Alexis opened the front door to the brownstone just after six Saturday morning, setting off the alarm, forgetting that there was no delay when the alarm was set to home. She had hoped to silently sneak into bed next to Jake and grab a couple of hours of sleep before having to face him. The redeye flight home had been one of the bumpiest that she'd ever been on, so she had, at most, a ninety-minute nap.

Any hope that she had about him sleeping through the alarm, in the five seconds it took her to disable it, was dashed by the pounding she heard as he rushed down the stairs. He hit the second-floor landing with a thud and stopped dead when he saw her standing in the foyer. "Oh. It's you."

Her heart squeezed in her chest at the emptiness behind his words. It's not that she was expecting a marching band to welcome her home, but she had hoped that he'd at least be happy to see her. "Wow, how to make a girl feel welcome in her own home."

His hand rapidly scratched through his tussocky tangle of bedhead. "I'm sorry," he spoke through a forced smile that had her feeling even less welcome. "The adrenaline is still pumping pretty good. The alarm scared the shit out of me."

"Yah, well, I forgot about that too. It kind of ruined my plans to wake you up with a good morning blow job." The breath that escaped her at the smile that tugged at the corner of his mouth surprised her. Her heartbeat slowed in relief. The thought hadn't crossed her mind, but at least now she knew he still had feelings for her instead of the blank expressions from the day she left and the handful of matter-of-fact type texts they'd exchanged since she'd been gone.

Jake walked down the stairs and grabbed her suitcase after planting a soft kiss on her cheek. "Come crawl into bed. You look exhausted."

Maybe the kiss on the cheek was him being self-conscious about morning breath, but it had never once bothered them before. He'd completely reformed her on the beauty of morning sex and never once shied away from tonsil hockey before brushing their teeth. And telling her she looked exhausted might have been honest, she was sure she did, but it was completely unlike the Jake she knew. He would have been more focused on being happy she was home than how she looked.

Following him up the stairs, she tried to shrug off her concerns about his behavior. She knew she was probably reading too much into it. If she had been woken from a sound sleep to the alarm and fearing an intruder, she probably wouldn't have been all sunshine and rainbows, either.

Settling down into her own bed and getting wrapped up in Jake's muscular arms helped to assuage her angst and exhaustion overtook her, dropping her into a deep sleep. It was nearly noon when she woke alone in her bed. There was a cold cup of coffee on her nightstand with a note telling her he had errands to run and would be home before dinner.

After jumping in the shower, bringing her slightly closer to feeling human and a little less jetlagged, she holed herself in her office and set to sorting out the mess she found in Denver. The grunt she got from him in the way of acknowledgement that he was home only reinforced her sense that something was bothering him. The exhaustion she felt deep in her bones was the excuse she gave herself for not asking the questions she needed to ask.

In the two months they had been together, they had only gone out to eat three times, and each time it was to Mama C's, a place that she found as comfortable as home. When he suggested they go out for dinner, she agreed only because she figured Mama C would sense whatever was eating at him and give him a good whack in the head. When he took her to some chic place in Greenwich Village, she had an uncomfortable flashback to her life with Trevor. The only thing missing was Trevor's need to be seen and the incessant interruptions, as he made sure to speak to precisely the right people. To be honest, she would have preferred it to the silence that hung between them.

When she tucked her panties in his pocket as they left the restaurant, she was sure that would snap him out of whatever funk he'd been in, but he barely raised an eyebrow. By the time they got home and were undressing for bed in total silence, she couldn't take it anymore. She didn't give a damn if they had a knock down drag out before bed. At least she'd be feeling something. "What is wrong?"

He turned to face her as he was sitting on the side of the bed and pulling off his shoes. Meeting her eyes for a moment, he turned back to focus on his shoes. "Nothing."

"Don't you dare 'nothing' me, Jacob Douglas. We may only have been together for a couple months, but you're acting like I pissed on your Cheerios and you're just too much of a gentleman to yell about it."

"My Cheerios are just fine."

"Argh," she huffed, picking up a pillow and whipping it at his head, landing a direct hit.

"What the hell? Everything is fine. I'm tired and I'm stressed. We both have a lot going on. You're not exactly miss affectionate either."

"I've never been miss affectionate," she grumbled, grabbing her pillow back and pulling it to her chest. "You're the one that has pried that side of me out into the open. I want that. I need that from you. I need my Jake."

"I thought what you needed was what you just got in Denver. To make that next big step up the corporate ladder. I figured you'd come home revved up and ready to go."

"I am happy about that, but I'm also damned nervous. But I need you to be happy. To be happy for me. And to be my safe place where I can leave all that stress behind. I didn't know I needed that before I met you. But now that I do…, I'm scared. It feels like you're pulling away. This will never work if you pull away."

Their gaze met, and she hated the sting of the liquid pooling at the corner of her eyes. She had never been this tearful in her life. Where was the Ice Princess when she needed her? Jake breathed out a heavy sigh before reaching across the bed and pulling her into his arms. "I'm nervous too, Alexis. I don't do well with change and we're going through a big one. I'm not pulling back. I'm just trying to adjust to the new us."

Her body softened into his embrace, and she sighed when he kissed the top of her head. "I don't like that we're going to be apart either, but that doesn't mean there will be a new us, just one that sleeps apart more than we'd like. But let's not let that get in the way of when we are together."

In the back of her mind, the Ice Princess she carefully crafted her entire adult life was screaming like the Wicked Witch of the West after a bath. *You need me now more than ever. You'll never make it to the top without me. Now is not the time to listen to your heart.*

Chapter 30

Alexis

They left the brownstone on Monday morning, heading in different directions. Alexis headed to Newark and a flight west, Jake to LaGuardia and south to begin his life in Washington.

After three days in Denver, Alexis flew back to New York to prepare for the Hong Kong trip. Her home felt eerily empty when she walked through the door late Wednesday evening. A shiver ran down her spine that she blamed on the January wind but felt more like loneliness that she had never felt before in her place. The bed seemed far too large without Jake beside her, and she struggled to sleep even though she was exhausted. They'd only spoken once since Monday morning and had only found the time to text a handful of times. She needed to hear his voice, and she hated that need. Glancing at the clock and seeing it was already after midnight, she pushed away the temptation to call him. Tomorrow, she'd do it for certain.

Fumbling her way into the conference room, she dropped the files she was carrying onto the table with a thud. Her mind flashed back to a few months earlier when she had made a similar entrance and caught Jake's teasing remark from across the room. She winced as the memory pinched at the hole in her chest that had been there for a week. And chided herself for feeling that way. He wasn't gone. They were still together, and in just a little over twenty-four hours, everything would be just fine. He'd be back in her bed.

Because of Jake's preparation and the client's desire to keep the legal work the same, most of her responsibilities were minimal at the meeting. In fact, it seemed to her that her sole role was to defend Jake's work and keep the rest of the team from messing things up by making changes. Four times already she had been forced to challenge Andre on his recommendations that went against the recommendations held within the tomes sitting in front of her. She was being forced to think about Jake and she hated she felt his absence so keenly. She'd needed no one before, and she'd be damned if she'd let him infiltrate and interfere in her career.

In the middle of the meeting, when she received a string of texts asking her opinion on places to live, she fired back an angry reply.

Alexis: In the middle of a meeting. Just pick a damn place. It's not like I'm going to live there.
Jake: Really?

When she saw his reply, she huffed and tossed down her phone.

"Something we need to be concerned with?" Andre asked from the other side of the conference table.

Alexis looked up from her seat and realized the question was for her. She could feel the heat burning her face. "No. Nothing. It's personal," she snapped, burying her embarrassment and frustration behind an angry tone.

Cocking his brow, Andre tapped his pen on the pad in front of him. "Then let's keep the personal drama out of this business meeting, shall we?"

Alexis set her jaw and bit back the sarcastic reply that hung on her tongue. She might have just been given her own pod, but getting into it with Dewey's golden boy could ruin that in a heartbeat. He had always been supportive of her, but she didn't deceive herself into thinking that she'd win out if he turned against her. And she knew him well enough to know his only loyalty was to himself and he'd be happy to crush her if she challenged him. She also knew Jake was the source of her frustration. Andre was just the one sitting in front of her.

Andre continued the meeting, not waiting for her reply, and she was thankful when it came to a close soon thereafter. She made her way back to her office, setting her things down on the side of her desk and sinking back into her chair. Looking up, she saw Andre standing at her door. Not waiting for her invitation, he stepped inside and pulled the door closed behind him.

"Is there something I can help you with?" she asked, her tone showing that helping him was about the last thing she wanted to do. She was tired and pissed and if it was just the two of them, he was much less likely to take offence. At least, that's what she told herself.

"I don't know what's crawled up your ass, but you'd better find a way to cleanse it, and fast."

"I beg your pardon," she gritted out, glad at the chance to have a tangible target in front of it instead of hundreds of miles south.

"You can beg all you want. But if you think for one minute if this HKD deal goes sour, you'll still have that pod in Denver to call your own, think again."

"Is that a threat? Because I'm already well aware of what's riding on this trip."

"I hope you are. Your boyfriend royally fucked us, and I will not let either him or you put a stain on my career."

"Boyfriend?" her voice cracked, and she hated hearing it climb so high it was nearly inaudible to the human ear. Her heart was pounding furiously against her ribs and feeling like it was trying to climb right out her throat at the same time.

The corner of Andre's mouth hooked up, and he rested his hip against her desk. He dropped his voice so low she could barely hear him, even though the door was closed. "Don't play dumb with me, Alexis. You're way too smart for that shit. And I'm way too smart not to notice an office fling when I see one. Funny, I never would have thought you'd let anything or especially anyone get in your way to the top. What I'm most surprised about is that you actually have feelings for him. I just figured it was some kind of fucked up play to get around your biggest obstacle. I've been here fifteen years, sweetie, and I thought I'd seen it all." Shaking his head, he spit out a derisive chuckle. "But I've never seen a guy give up a promising career for a piece of ass. You must have some kind of magic cunt."

Alexis opened her mouth to refute the truth or scream at his vile words. She wasn't sure which, but closed it without uttering a sound. Thoughts were racing so fast in her head that she couldn't sort them. Jake may be gone, but he could still say something to Dewey and ruin her. Her stomach churned and she could taste the bile rise at the thought of being at a disadvantage to Andre. She was furious at herself for misjudging him so completely.

The other corner of his mouth turned up, completing the sneer. She knew Andre could read her discomfort. He pushed himself off her desk and walked toward her door. Turning, he stopped and waited for her to meet his glare. "Do your job and land me this HKD account and you'll never have a thing to worry about. You'll have your pod in Denver and can pick whoever you think you need to fuck to climb the next rung. That incompetent douche canoe, Dewey, will be none the wiser."

The door closed behind him, leaving Alexis in stunned silence. But mostly furious at the truth that lay behind Andre's words. She was letting her feelings for Jake interfere with her work, and mess with the carefully scripted plan she had to make it to the top. And she'd better get her priorities straight or everything she'd worked and sacrificed for would fall to pieces.

Chapter 31

Jake

Jake spent the week looking for a place to live. There would be certain expectations for him. He couldn't find the cheapest rent and damn the neighborhood. That was not the life he could choose anymore. He looked in Georgetown and Alexandria, further out of the city to Annapolis, and while the rents were not quite what was being asked in Manhattan, it was a minimum of three times more than what he was currently paying. It was not the type of money he was accustomed to parting with. The thought that kept creeping into his mind was that Alexis would be so much better at this than he was. He needed her to help navigate this world, but she'd been clear about having more important things to be concerned with.

Letting out a deep cleansing breath, Jake tried to rid himself of the pall that had hung over him since yesterday afternoon's reply from Alexis. He'd tried to insulate himself from her relegating their relationship to secondary status by distancing himself from her, but when she'd pushed herself into his arms Saturday morning, he'd foolishly hoped he'd been wrong. But after telling him outright that she never intended to have anything to do with 'their' home in DC he resigned himself to the ultimate demise of their relationship. He needed no more confirmation of that than the fact that she hadn't bothered to call or text since summarily blowing him off, saying she was busy in a meeting. Even the longest of business meetings don't last overnight and into the next morning.

Not that he was ever the type to be glued to his phone, needing constant affirmation of any woman's affection but she knew his reservations about long-distance relationships and her actions, save for when she returned from Denver Saturday morning have done nothing but reinforce his belief that their relationship was on borrowed time. Her drift away from him was well underway.

He took another deep breath before exiting the elevator into the posh, tenth floor offices of Rock and Wagner at the corner of 17th and I Street. A brunette, who reminded him unnervingly of Mary from DCH greeted him with a smile that was just slightly too inviting to be professional. "Right this way, Mr. Douglas. Mr. Rock is waiting for you," she purred, sliding from behind the reception desk before motioning him to follow her as she sashayed down the corridor to the executive boardroom. He made a mental note to avoid that sexual harassment suit waiting to happen. Even if he believed that his relationship with Alexis was heading south fast, his position on dating from the secretarial pool remained firm. No way.

John greeted him with the same warm handshake and smile he had at their first meeting in New York two weeks before. "Welcome Jake. I must admit, I was nearly certain we'd be doing this in New York when I gave you the choice between the two. Just be clear, once the ink is dry on this contract, you're locked in here for two years."

"Thank you, John." Jake returned his smile and handshake. He found it impossible not to have a certain fondness for the man, even if he was a shrewd lawyer and ruthless businessman. "I would have agreed with you that night; seems I was wrong." Jake tried to force a neutral expression to cover the raw feeling in the pit of his stomach. There was understanding in John's expression that told him he hadn't been successful. He exhaled slowly before continuing, "That said, I'm truly looking forward to this opportunity and have no regrets about the choice I have made. New position, new life to start in a new city."

John nodded and smiled. "I trust you have thoroughly reviewed the contract. What questions can I answer?"

Jake smiled, "I honestly haven't seen the contract yet. I caught the next flight down here after our conversation Monday to look for a place to live and start learning my way around the town. If you sent a review copy over to my apartment, I imagine it's waiting in the mailbox for me. I apologize."

John laughed. "Well, I appreciate your eagerness. Let me walk you through some of the major points and then you can take some time to review it thoroughly. I'm free again after lunch and would be happy to answer questions then."

Jake walked out of the meeting and found a coffee shop across the street where he could review the full text of the contract before meeting John again after lunch. If he'd read the contract in advance, it would have saved him a fair amount of the anguish that had been churning in his stomach since his arrival. He was being given a signing bonus that would more than cover any upfront costs of moving and the buyout of the remaining five months of his lease in New York. If he met even half of his performance incentives, he would make five times more than his salary at DCH, a number that already made his head swim. He realized that this contract had a significant penalty in the non-compete clause, but felt he could negotiate some restrictions away. Beyond that, there was nothing at all he found objectionable. Two years, with a two-way option for two more. Even if it did not turn out to be half what he thought it would, two years would pass soon enough, and he could move on providing he did not practice within New York or DC and did not attempt contact with clients on record with the firm post departure for two years.

After lunch all the "I's" were dotted and all the "T's" were crossed, Jake signed his name, and John Rock handed his newest attorney a very large check to help him on his way to his new home, well as close as it could be to a home without Alexis. He had a powerful urge to call her and bring her up to date with his good fortune, but she'd made it quite clear she didn't want to be bothered at work. He held out a faint hope that she might show a little excitement for him when he got to her place later tonight. He should probably stay in DC and continue house hunting over the weekend, but knew that would just speed along the end of their relationship and he wasn't ready for that yet.

After a brief meeting with the team of paralegals and interns that would report to him and choosing the way his office would be decorated with the in-house designer, he said his goodbyes and made his way to the parking garage. He had just begun the internal debate on what to do with the several hours he had before his flight home when a text dinged on his phone.

The seed of hope that had sprouted in his heart at the sound was quickly trampled when he saw it was from a realtor he had contacted. A property had just come on the market that he thought would be perfect for Jake and hoped that he had time this afternoon to see it, as the realtor was sure it would be off the market by Monday.

Jake rolled his eyes, feeling the unnecessary urgency in the realtor's text, but decided it was as good a way as any to spend his afternoon, and the location was conveniently close to the airport.

The minute he walked through the door of the property, he knew it was the one. It was a row house on the edge of Daingerfield Park, and he'd pay in a month what his first job as a teenager had paid him in a year. The location was perfect except perhaps for a bit of noise from Regan

National Airport, depending on how the wind was blowing, but no place was perfect. And despite being more than a hundred years newer than the brownstone, the layout and the feel of the place seemed very familiar. The temptation to have Alexis see it before he signed the lease was strong, but then he remembered her words, "I'm never going to live there."

Dropping the pen on the newly signed lease, the realtor reached over and shook his hand before handing him the keys.

"Thank you, but isn't this a little premature? The lease doesn't go into effect until February first."

"It's only a few days, and the owner is more than happy to have someone in the building sooner rather than later."

Jake nodded and walked around the home one more time before closing the door behind him. He sat in the drive looking up at his new home and then scanned the neighborhood. It lacked all the historic charm that the brownstone had, but the wealthy feel of the neighborhood was the same. Shaking his head at the strain of his engine turning over as he turned the ignition, he sighed. He really had to get a new car, too. He hated the idea of keeping up with the Jones' but there were expectations he was supposed to meet. His new salary and bonus check didn't seem quite so excessive after all.

Chapter 32

Alexis

Mercifully avoiding weather delays and uncharacteristically light traffic, Jake made it to the brownstone just before eight-thirty on Friday evening to find Alexis on the couch underneath a sea of paper. She lifted her gaze from the document she was reviewing to meet his as he stood in the foyer looking at her.

"How was your flight?" she asked, returning her attention to her work.

"Fine," he sighed, walking into the living room. "I was hoping we'd at least be able to have dinner together," he said, motioning to the half-empty takeout containers strewn across the coffee table in front of her. The frustration in his tone mirrored her own.

"Maybe tomorrow night," she replied, not looking up. "I wouldn't bank on it, though. I've got a lot to get through before I head for Hong Kong on Sunday."

Jake opened his mouth. Then closed it, grabbing a container holding General Tsao's chicken and sank into the armchair. "I'm happy to help you if you want."

Blowing out a breath that did nothing to move the strand of her blonde hair it was meant to get rid of, she glared at him. "I'll deal with it myself. I've already been more than reminded that there's already too much of you in these documents. I don't need to defend you any more than I already have."

"Defend me? What the hell is that supposed to mean? Why have you felt the need to defend me to anyone?" he barked, tossing the container back on the coffee table.

"Because this is all your work, and you just walked away, leaving me to figure it all out. And because when I do, I realize there is no way I can improve upon it and when the idiots I work with try to ruin it, I have to tell them they're wrong even though I don't know how to explain it. And when one of them is my boss, and he gets pissy and tells me he'll ruin me if I don't stop making him look bad with my boyfriend's work, it bothers me. Okay?"

Jake's jaw dropped, and his eyes widened at her words. Seeing the realization wash over his face at the words she had just thrown at him made her gut clench, and she sank back into the couch. "That's right Jake. Andre somehow figured out we're fucking and was quite blunt about the fact that he has no problem using that little tidbit of information against me if anything goes badly with this trip to Hong Kong."

Leaning forward with his elbows on his knees, he sighed, "I'm so sorry."

"Yah, well, sorry doesn't change a fucking thing," she snarled before tossing the file she was holding onto the table and sending two containers of Chinese to the floor, spilling out over the expensive oriental rug beneath. "Fuck," she muttered, seeing the mess. "Just leave me alone and let me work so maybe later…," she stopped, cutting herself off before saying we could spend some time together because in that moment, she just wanted to be by herself and not feel the longing in her chest that was always there when Jake was in front of her.

"Maybe later what?" he asked, kneeling down and trying to clean up the mess of food.

"Nothing," she huffed. "Leave it," pointing her chin at the mess that was now mostly picked up. "And leave me so I can get this done." Picking up the bottle of wine on the table, she tipped it up, trying to refill her glass before realizing the bottle was empty. With a huff, she pushed herself off the couch and stomped toward the kitchen to get another. When she returned to the living room, there was no sign of Jake until she heard the front door close behind him.

It was nearly midnight when she pulled herself out of her work long enough to realize that Jake hadn't returned. She knew him well enough that when he was upset; he liked to walk, but the longest he'd ever been gone before was a couple of hours. If she was being honest with herself, she knew she was completely to blame for their disagreement. She'd taken out all of her frustration from the week on him virtually as soon as he walked through the door. She was mad at him, well, more because of him, but none of it was really his fault. And now that she'd finished going through everything for the umpteenth time, and not feeling like doing it again would make a bit of difference, she realized she missed him. Truly missed him.

Searching the coffee table amidst the sea of paper for her phone, she finally dug it out and found no missed texts or calls. She hadn't bothered to take it off of do not disturb since Thursday. A knot formed in her stomach. She lived in a very safe neighborhood, but he'd been gone for three hours. He could have walked anywhere and run into some thug looking for an easy mark. Or he could have slipped on a patch of ice, hitting his head, breaking a leg, a dozen scenarios, each more dire than the last flew through her head. Her fingers flew across the phone.

Alexis: Where are you? You've been gone for hours.

A wave of relief coursed through her as she saw the three little dots float on the screen, showing he was typing a reply.

Jake: You told me to leave you alone. That's what I did.

She sighed, knowing he was right but feeling frustration with him all the same. She didn't need him acting like a rejected high school kid.

Alexis: Just come home and let's go to bed. I'm sorry if I hurt your feelings.

Jake: You didn't hurt my feelings and I'm already home.

Alexis headed for the stairs, shaking her head at being so enrapt with her work that she'd missed him come through the front door. She hoped she hadn't missed him speak to her when he came in or she'd have even more to apologize for. But as she reached the top of the stairs, her brow knit together in confusion, and she tilted her head, peering into the darkness in her room. "Jake?" she asked, wondering why she couldn't at least see the glow from his phone. It had only taken her a few seconds to climb the stairs. Flicking on the light, she found the bed just as she had made it this morning before she left for work.

Alexis: What do you mean, you're home? I'm standing here looking at an empty bed.

Jake: My home Alexis. Not yours.

She sank down on to the bed and put her head in her hands. Her throat ached when she tried to swallow down the baseball sized lump that had formed there and she found it impossible to see the keyboard to type a reply before she rubbed the moisture from her eyes.

Alexis: Your home is with me. Please come back. I miss you.

She hated sounding needy or desperate, but she was tired, and she was desperate with the need to have him hold her. She had no choice but to admit it, at least to herself.

Jake: I miss you too. It's late and my car is parked at the airport in Washington. I'll see you tomorrow. Maybe then we can both try to be in the right frame of mind to figure things out.

Thumbing the tears away that were rolling down her face, the Ice Princess inside her was indignant, but her heart pushed her back with unusual force. *This is all your fault, you bitch. You're ruining something good.* Not prepared to be silenced, the ice princess countered, *the only thing getting ruined is the career you fought so hard to build up. For what? Love? I thought you were a smart girl and learned that lesson when you were eighteen.* The argument between her heart and the Ice Princess raged on until well after two, when sleep finally had the last word.

Chapter 33

Jake

Jake's first two weeks on the job were a blur. Long hours in the office and reading every night at the hotel pushed his brain to the limit of what it could effectively retain. He honestly believed his efforts were paying off as he was contributing to the workload of his team. They immediately assigned him to put together the draft version of a Writ of Certiorari for a case the Illinois Attorney General was petitioning the Supreme Court to hear. It would be a long time, if ever, before he would stand before the court in person, but he was confident his work would be there soon. It was a heady feeling that he never thought he would ever have and couldn't quite wrap his mind around.

Despite all the work and planning to move, there was rarely an hour that passed that she didn't cross his mind. He'd picture her in her office or sitting with her legs tucked underneath her reading on the couch at night. He'd still wake up in the middle of the night not knowing where he was or why she wasn't cuddled in next to him. He was waiting, praying for the new reality of their time together being sparse to settle in.

Alexis had shown up at his apartment at ten that Saturday morning with coffee and a dozen bagels in the way of a peace offering. She'd asked for forgiveness with a promise to be a much better girlfriend when the whole mess with the HKD account was behind her. She'd even promised to go to Washington as soon as she returned from Asia and help him pick out furnishings for his new home. He'd accepted her offer even though he didn't intend to spend money on furniture he'd likely not have any use for. He didn't need to furnish fourteen rooms when all he would use were four. *Who needs a family room if you don't have a family, right?*

When she had to rush to Denver to deal with her new pod and backed out of going to Washington, he wasn't surprised and only slightly disappointed. Their relationship quickly became brief phone calls every few days and sporadic text messages.

His third week on the job began with a last-minute trip to Springfield to meet with the state Attorney General Edward Young. It was just him and the managing partner of R&W's Washington office, Richard Williams. Richard explained he was going with him for two reasons. The first was that he could provide a safety net for him if Young was less than pleased with the tact they were taking. He was not about to throw a new attorney that had only been with the firm for two weeks under the bus. Young was a powerful, well-connected politician and knew it. And second, the firm wanted to convey to Young that he was an important client. Richard made clear it was Jake's work, and he would lead the discussion. He wasn't to rely on help or defer to the senior man.

Jake would have been a fool not to have a butterfly or two, but he let no one see them. He handled some aggressive questioning and defended his choice of precedents to emphasize impeccably. At the end of the meeting, Young was fully on board and green lighted the work to prepare for the final brief.

Jake was feeling good about things during the flight home. Richard gave him some well-deserved encouragement and as they were leaving Reagan National and calling it a night, he told Jake that the final draft was all his. The catch was it had to be on his desk by Friday when he went home. Jake swallowed hard. That was a big ask, but in his mind, he had no choice but to deliver.

It was just after eleven pm Friday night when Jake set the final draft on Richard's desk. Several of the interns and younger attorneys had told him to meet them at a local bar when he was done for a celebratory cocktail. At that hour, he didn't expect to find them still there, but decided he could use a drink and didn't really want to drink alone in his hotel room. He could use with just a little human contact. Soon, he could sleep. He was meeting his brother at LaGuardia for the trip down in the U-Haul tomorrow evening. Alexis had encouraged him to hire a moving company saying that he should get used to using his time more wisely but when he said he couldn't justify spending money to move his meager possessions, she hadn't argued and simply decided to stay in Denver for the weekend and stay out of his way.

Somewhere in the back of his mind, he knew she was relieved to have an excuse to stay and work and not feel like she was abandoning him when she did. More and more each day, he felt like their relationship was more of a chore to her than a choice. He couldn't help but wonder if this was how things felt the way they did with her and Trevor. One thing he knew for sure was that regardless of how things ended up between them, he would never be unfaithful like Trevor. He would go, milk a scotch for an hour and enjoy watching all the drunk college kids make fools of themselves.

It surprised him to find half of the group from R and W still in session at the bar. On top of which, to replace those that had left, one intern had gathered some of her fellow grad students at the table. At first, Jake didn't mind the scenery or the company, but as more than one of the grad students began to flirt and flirt hard with him, he knew it was time to make his excuses and head back to the hotel.

The boldest and likely the most attractive of the grad students, Linda, followed him out of the bar and caught up to him on the street. "Hey Jake," she called to him as she ran along in her five-inch platform heels. "I thought maybe we could find somewhere quieter and continue our conversation and maybe get to know each other a little better."

Jake gave her a pleasant smile but knew the game and had no interest or intent at swinging at the pitch. "I'm sorry, Linda, is it?" she nodded and could see her wince when he asked for confirmation of her name. It bothered him to do that to her when his memory for names was impeccable, but he needed her to believe without question he didn't care enough to be interested in her. "I have a flight to catch tomorrow, and it's been a very long week. I need to call it a night."

Her shoulders slumped, and a hint of irritation crossed her brow. Clearly, she wasn't used to being the one rejected. "Oh sure, I understand. Maybe another time?"

"Thanks," Jake said, maintaining what he hoped was a pleasant but uninterested tone. And he turned, walked away and wondered when the hell he had changed that much. Linda was very attractive, and he wouldn't have had a snowball's chance with her when he was in college. He shuddered at the realization that for a moment he'd considered her offer. Had his bond with Alexis shifted so far from what it had been that he no longer thought of himself as being in a committed relationship?

Jake flew back to New York the next afternoon and was met by Teddy at the airport as planned. They had his small apartment loaded into the U-Haul in just over an hour and were on their way by nine. They rolled into DC about three in the morning and crashed on the floor of his new place.

Teddy spared no time in getting on Jake about the opulence of the townhouse and how his possessions were sadly lacking both in quality and quantity. Teddy had always been the pragmatic of the three siblings and his teasing of Jake should keep Jake from getting too full of himself. Teddy was convinced Jake was trying to show off a bit by renting a house quite so hoity toity.

Jake had some thoughts on that himself, a little buyer's remorse after he signed the lease, but who else did he have to spend it on and why should he deny himself just a little evidence of some hard-earned success?

Mid-afternoon found the truck unloaded and returned. And Jake spent some time showing his brother around the city and his office. He picked up some papers while he was there. He would take Monday at home to get settled at his boss's insistence, but he'd still be working. That's what he did now, work. He had plenty to do, but it was also a good excuse not to think about her. Well, try not to. He didn't usually succeed for long.

Jake hadn't realized his phone had died until much later Sunday evening and decided to just charge it and worry about missing messages later. He hadn't had a good talk with his brother in years. He was too busy, and his brother was focused on his own wife and kids, so their brotherly chat was a welcome treat for them both. They sat on his ratty couch in the middle of his not ratty living room and reminisced. They looked toward the future and Jake's prospects after R&W. Teddy tried a couple of times to lead Jake into talking about what kept Alexis away from his migration to the nation's capital for a new and exciting job. He even teased him that she was just a fictional figment of his imagination, as Teddy had yet to meet her. Jake avoided, obfuscated, and flat out ignored Teddy's questions. "She had to work. Can we please just leave it at that?" The tone in his voice gave Teddy notice it was not a topic for conversation, even more forbidden that his relationship with his father.

Jake brought his brother to the airport early Monday morning and thanked him for the help, then took the short drive back to his new home. He knew it would take him little time to unpack his belongings and there were two things on his agenda for the rest of the day. A new living room set, one that looked like it belonged in his house and to check out of the hotel that he had spent his first two and a half weeks in. As he rounded the corner and started down the street, he added a third task to his list. A new car, just as it had in Alexis's neighborhood, his Kia stood out like a sore thumb here. Teddy would kid him about trying to keep up with the Joneses, but he was fine with that.

He took care of the low hanging fruit first. Hotel was wrapped up and on to the living room set. Jake knew he had no flair for decorating, but how hard could it be to find something he liked? He discovered he had to visit four showrooms before finding something he liked that didn't require a three month wait for customization. His new living room furniture would be delivered on Thursday afternoon.

Two of three off the list, he set about the most challenging for him, a new car. He had never been one to care about or even place the least bit of value in having a luxury vehicle. An engine that ran and wheels that turned had always been his maximum requirement in transportation. He stopped at all the usual dealers: Lexus, BMW, Mercedes and Audi, but despite his ability to pay, he couldn't justify that kind of money for an engine and wheels. He decided he wouldn't be able to reach a decision that day and re-solved to head back to his house and figure it all out. As luck would have it, he turned down a street with a used car dealership specializing in used lux-ury vehicles. He left the lot an hour later with a six-year-old pristine looking Land Rover, problem solved for tens of thousands less. He hadn't gone around the conspicuous consumption bend after all, at least completely.

Jake drove into his driveway with his new, to him, Rover and quickly went about setting up his apartment. He finally turned his phone back on to order Chinese for dinner and tossed it to the counter. He sat in his soon to be well-furnished living room eating his dinner and relaxing with noth-ing to do for the first time in what felt like weeks. Clicking on the TV he settled back into his sofa with a sense of relief. Not having a dozen to do items jamming his mind made him realize just how much he missed Alexis. He realized that not only had he not told her about his new car, he hadn't even mentioned that he was thinking about buying one.

The surge of a memory flashed through his mind. An ugly argument between his mother and father. Him standing in the driveway with a shiny new Mercedes. Her with tears streaming down her face asking how he could do such a selfish thing when the Chevy they had ran just fine and them behind on almost every bill. He'd even used the grocery money for the week as part of the down payment. The one time he hadn't drank it away, Jake remembered thinking. Four months later, he watched it being towed from the yard. His father had never made a single payment. He'd been fired for being drunk on the job site only three weeks after he bought the damn car. While he certainly would never be fired for being drunk and he could more than afford the payments on his Rover, that he didn't even consult with Alexis had him feeling queasy and far too much like his father. Couples should talk about these things; his mother had told him years later. Though he and Alexis weren't married, he somehow felt he had betrayed her by buying the car.

Grabbing his phone from the cushion next to him, he called her. His heart sank when it went directly to voice mail and with a sigh, he left what had become his standard message. "Hi it's me. Just checking in. Call me when you can. Love yah, bye."

When she finally called back, he was already in bed and almost asleep. She apologized, laughing at herself for not remembering there was a time difference. With a promise to make time at a reasonable hour tomorrow, she hung up, and he drifted off to sleep.

Chapter 34

Jake

Jake closed the door behind him and shrugged out of his coat before hanging it on the coat rack. Picking up his messenger bag, that was stuffed to overflowing with notes and case files requiring his review, he slogged into the living room and tossed it on the couch. He sighed as he scanned the space that used to feel so much like home. Now there was an awkward little niggle in his gut that made him feel like he was trespassing.

Doing his best to shove the uncomfortable feeling to the back of his mind, he set a fire in the hearth and hoped to chase off both the early February chill and the coldness he felt in his heart.

Alexis was due back from Denver in a couple of hours, and he hoped to make a dent in his work before she arrived so that they might get some uninterrupted time as a couple this weekend. Her work and his move had dominated the past few days, and he hated the feeling that his worst fears about embarking on a multi-city relationship were being realized.

When Alexis dragged through the door, pulling her suitcase behind her, he looked up to see a familiar smile fill her face. The knot in his stomach slowly loosened as she quickly closed the space between them and straddled him.

"Hi," he smiled up at her as she wiggled her hips, working herself onto his lap.

"Hi, yourself," she mewled, brushing her lips against his with a feather's touch.

He shivered both at the sensation and at the chill she'd brought in with her from the cold winter's night. "You seem pretty happy to see me, Miss Chambers."

"I am," she grinned, with a mischievous twinkle in her eyes that he hadn't seen in weeks. She shifted her hips back and forth, pressing her core against him, bringing his cock instantly to life and straining against his pants. "Mm, it feels like maybe you're happy to see me too, Mr. Douglas."

"I'm very happy to see you, especially like this." He brushed his thumb over her lips before kissing them. "I take it you've had a good week."

Her smile broadened, and she nodded. "I signed two new clients today, probably saving the Denver office from being shut down. There have been several account losses there and I know Dewey was close to moving my pod here to New York and letting everyone else go. Now that I've added about fifty million in billables over the next two years, it might actually be enough to keep the place afloat while they rebuild their portfolio."

Jake did his best to push the pride he felt for Alexis forward and dampen the fear that it would mean her moving halfway across the country. "I always knew you were a rock star. And it's nice to see you happy. We've had a rough few weeks."

Her smiled dimmed, but only slightly. Resting her head against his forehead, she kissed his nose. "I'm sorry. I've been so tough to live with. But can we not focus on that? It made my heart so happy to come home and see you sitting on the couch with a fire in the fireplace. It's nice to feel like I'm home instead of just at some place I live. Does that make sense?"

Cupping the back of her head, he pulled her close, pressing his lips against hers and swiping his tongue between them as she melted into him. Moaning, she wrapped her arms around his neck and pressed her body against his, surrendering to his strength.

He pushed his bag and papers to the floor before turning and laying her down. Her flowing skirt hitched up her legs as he wedged his body between them. His stiff cock evident as he ground their bodies together between layers of slacks and thick tights. She exhaled with a shuddering sigh, pulling him back into a lip bruising kiss.

"What was that sigh for?" he asked, pulling back and gently cupping her cheek.

Slowly, she pulled her gaze up to meet his beneath her long lashes. "I was afraid that after how crabby I've been for the last couple of weeks that maybe you wouldn't feel the same about me. That maybe you'd realize I wasn't worth all the headaches."

Brushing a stray strand of her soft blonde hair from her face, he placed a soft kiss on her forehead. "I've told you before that you're worth everything to me, headaches and all. The only thing I ask is to be a priority in your life. We have to try harder, babe, if we're going to make this long-distance relationship work. We're missing too much. I didn't even know you were pitching new accounts. And I know there are things in my life you don't know about either. It's neither of our faults and we're both to blame. I miss you, babe."

"Oh, honey, I miss you too. I promise to try harder. I do." She wrapped her legs around his hips and arched her back into another kiss. "Take me to bed, Jake. Let's spend the weekend entirely under the covers."

"I like the sounds of that very much," he smiled, rocking back on his knees before standing and offering her a hand. Grasping his hand, she pulled herself off the couch and into his arms. Raising up on her toes, she kissed his cheek, then trailed her lips over the powerful line of his jaw before taking control of his mouth. Swallowing a moan, she eased away from him and smiled.

Raking his hand through her long silky locks, his dark gaze nearly took her breath away with its intensity. "Go ahead up. I'll bank the fire and bring up your suitcase."

A soft smile filled her lips, and she traced her fingertips over his cheek before turning and heading for the stairs.

Silently, she went about her bedtime routine before crawling naked under the covers. She had never slept naked before Jake and now it felt foreign not to, even when they weren't together. It seemed like a wasted effort to get dressed, only to get undressed again. A thought passed through her mind that she would be perfectly fine not to get dressed again until Monday morning before she left for the airport again.

Before she got any further with that line of thinking, Jake entered and placed her suitcase at the foot of the bed. She peered down at him from under the luxurious comforter, all but her nose and eyes hidden from view. "I've missed you leering at me getting undressed every night."

She laughed, "I don't leer." Trying hard to sound indignant, she failed because, well, he was well aware she totally leered.

He moved around the room, lighting dozens of candles, before turning off the lights, leaving the room lit in the soft flickering glow. Stepping to the side of the bed, he slowly unbuttoned his French blue dress shirt, letting her drink in his chiseled torso beneath. Watching as her tongue snaked out and traced her lips, he reveled in her obviously growing desire. Her nipples peaking against the crisp cotton sheets and flush spreading up her body, confirming that suspicion.

Her hand trailed down her body, over the peaks of her breasts, tracing a line over her stomach, then below her navel. Slipping out of his shirt, he tossed it onto the chest at the foot of her bed. His hands deftly unbuckled his belt before undoing his trousers and letting them fall to the floor. A sharp hiss of breath escaped her mouth as the outline of the hard, thick length of his cock became visible against the tight fabric of his boxer briefs. Her fingers drew along the damp folds of her sex as he hooked his thumbs under the elastic of his briefs before pulling them down over the taut muscles in his legs.

His cock sprung out from its prison and stood straight and firm against his abdomen. He fisted the base before stroking it from base to tip twice. "Fuck," she moaned. "How do you make me want you so bad by just getting undressed? You haven't done more than kiss me and I feel like I'm ready to explode."

With a grunt of amusement, he crossed the bed to her on his hands and knees. Caging her beneath him. He leaned down and rained soft kisses from her shoulder up her neck. "Trust me babe, I'm going to do a lot more than kiss you," he breathed into her ear before nipping it with his teeth.

"Gah," she gasped as he pulled the covers down, revealing her naked body.

A smile spread across his face, and his eyes darkened more with each inch of her body that fell under his gaze. "You are so fucking perfect." His voice was a low, throaty rumble. Shifting his body without taking his gaze away from her, he wedged his legs between hers. She tipped her knees wider, opening herself to him. Offering him all that he wanted.

Hooking her thighs over his shoulders, his tongue laved a path along her center, stopping at the apex of her thighs and flicking over her sensitive bundle of nerves. Up and down, up and down, then swirling around her clit with his tongue. Each time changing the pressure, softer, harder, she raised her hips, pressing her core to his mouth. His arm, softly but firmly, rested across her waist, pushing her against that mattress and letting her know he intended to be in control tonight.

A whine of protest escaped her lips just before he slipped two thick fingers inside, filling her, her eyes rolled back on a moan. "Yes," she hissed as he began to slowly thrust them in and out of her while continuing to circle her clit with his tongue. With a twist of his hand, he hooked his fingers, hitting her special spot, causing another ecstatic gasp. "Fuck, Jake. Yes. Just like that."

Before the echo of her words had left the air, He quickened his pace, and she exploded into her release. His face was soaked with her arousal, and her legs shook with the tremors of each aftershock that coursed through her body.

Gripping his shoulders, she guided him up her body even as the last shudders of her orgasm faded. She shifted and bucked her hips against his, letting him know she was still wanting more.

"God," she moaned, "I need you inside me." Surprising him, she pushed him to his back. Swinging her leg over him, she grasped his thick cock and pressed the tip against her entrance. "Fuck," she keened, as she lowered herself down, inch by perfect inch. Once he was fully seated in her silky tightness, she rocked her hips, grinding her clit against him. Rolling her pelvis back and forth, her eyes fluttered closed, head lolling back on a sigh of ecstasy.

"That's it, babe. Take everything you need." Her nails dug into his chest, where she balanced herself against him, causing a hiss of pain to pass his lips. She locked her eyes with his and they peered into each other's souls.

Jake's fingers dug into the soft flesh of her hips, helping her maintain her pace. He could see her fight to keep eye contact as passion overtook her body. With each thrust into her depths, her breath stuttered, and he could tell she was close.

The tingle at the base of his spine and the tightening of his balls signaled he was even closer, but he had to hold out for her. He had to bring her over the top first. Harder and faster, he drove into her until a flood of arousal flowed out of her, and her pussy pulsed, clenching like a vise around his cock.

Falling forward on top of him, her body spasmed erratically. Unable to hold back any longer, Jake let go and throbbed his release into her on a grunt of utter relief. The pain from where her nails dug into his shoulders only intensifying the bliss of his climax. He would gladly carry the red crescent scars as a reminder of this moment of pure perfection.

She nuzzled her chin into the crook of his shoulder with a contented sigh. His hands rubbing gentle circles on her back before he wrestled the comforter from beneath them and wrapped it over her in a warm, safe cocoon. "Don't you dare move another inch," she cooed. "I want you inside of me. Forever."

Chapter 35

Jake

Their Monday predawn commute to the airport was considerably more content than it had been before. What they had started Friday night continued for the entire weekend. They had only ventured out of the bedroom for two hours Saturday evening for dinner at Mama C's. The weight that Jake had felt like he was carrying around seemed lighter.

Alexis promised to fly to Washington on Friday so that they could be together on Valentine's Day, and she could see their new home. After a tearful apology for being 'such a selfish bitch', which he corrected her, saying she'd just been under a lot of stress, she had started calling his place theirs. She insisted he let her buy the dining room set so that she could put her touch on the home. They both knew she wouldn't spend a great deal of time there, but she wanted to be a part of his day-to-day, even when they were hundreds of miles apart.

Their weeks passed quickly, and they spoke every night. Neither of them minded their conversations lasted only a few minutes and there was rarely a text during the day. They weren't kids who needed constant contact to feel connected. They were adults with careers that required a lot of time and attention.

Jake was every bit as consumed with his work as she was. He spent his days and most evenings preparing a host of documentation for his writ for Illinois. He'd never felt more pressure in his life, and, for the first time, he almost wished that people had a little less confidence in his legal abilities. It seemed like he'd gone straight from Little League to the majors overnight. Fuck up on a case that went before the Supreme Court, and you made it to the nightly news. Nothing like the thought of ten million people hearing about your incompetence to make a guy humble and triple check his work.

Alexis arrived as promised just after one on Friday afternoon, though her flight was into Dulles and not Regan, he wouldn't complain a bit. No one batted an eye when he left for the afternoon, but then he'd been in the office past ten every night that week, so he didn't feel too guilty about an early departure. He already knew that Alexis would have work to do over the weekend and he saw them sitting companionably on his new sectional in front of the fire, slaving away together. He had open authorization to subscribe to any online law library he chose so he could truly work from anywhere there was Wi-Fi.

He spotted her just as she came out of the United arrivals door at the far end of the terminal. Honking the horn twice, he saw her scan the cars along the curb, looking right past him. Putting the phone to her ear, he assumed a call from work distracted her. Seconds later, he was startled by a call ringing through his Bluetooth. "Hey, I'm right by the curb."

"I'm looking," she huffed out of breath from struggling through the gauntlet that is air travel today, "but I don't see you."

He laughed, putting the car into park and opening his door. "You're looking right at me." She still kept searching until she finally spotted him standing by his car and waving. Her mouth opened, then closed as she tucked her phone back into her pocket and walked in his direction just as a uniformed TSA agent barked at him to get moving. He had the strongest urge to flip him the bird and tell him to suck… lemons, but decided it might be detrimental to his career.

"You didn't tell me the Kia was in the shop," she laughed, tossing her bag into the back seat. Jake tilted his head and raised a brow in her direction as she settled into the seat beside him. "Not that I'm complaining," she said with a contented sigh. "I do so love the heated seats this time of year."

He laughed and shook his head, realizing that he had never told her he had a new car. How had they ever become that disconnected? At least things were a little better now. Maybe they could make this work after all. "I've had this a couple of weeks. And I have to agree the heated seats are nice, but the heated steering wheel is my favorite."

"Good point, but why didn't you say something? Did you think I'd tease you about coming over to the dark side?"

He shrugged his shoulders before making a turn onto the highway on-ramp. "I think we were struggling with communication at that point, and it didn't really feel like you cared what was going on with me."

Having to concentrate on traffic, he couldn't see, but felt her shrink a little into her seat. Reaching across the console, he found her hand and gave it a gentle squeeze. "We're doing better now. And that's what matters."

Bringing her hand to his lips, he kissed each knuckle before letting it go. "So, you approve of my new ride?" he asked, trying to lighten the mood.

"I do. And I can't wait to see the new place. From the way you describe it, it's a modern version of home."

He laughed, "Well it's a townhouse with a huge master suite, so I guess that's something they've got in common but it's nowhere near as nice and I've only got three rooms furnished, so there's that too."

She reached across and grabbed his leg, rubbing her hand up and down his thigh. "There'll be four rooms furnished after this weekend and we'll get to the rest. You've got a lot more to worry about right now than interior decorating. How's the writ shaping up? I'm surprised they let you get away from the office this afternoon with that looming large."

Warmth grew in Jake's chest as he processed her use of 'we'. That's all he ever asked for, is for her to think of a future together with him. He blinked twice, fighting the stinging in his eyes. Washington traffic was no time to get emotional. "Oh, I've got plenty to keep me busy at home this weekend, trust me. But Rock and Wagner is very different from DCH. I've already heard it from Richard several times about how late I'm staying at the office."

"Must be nice," she said, shaking her head. "I was on the airphone half the way here and I think the first-class cabin thinks I had a malfunctioning vibrator in my pocket with the amount of buzzing once I switched it out of airplane mode."

He laughed, shaking his head. It had been a while since he'd seen her so relaxed and happy. "Well, if all that stimulation has you feeling a certain need, I'm sure we can find the time before we go out to dinner," he offered, turning quickly to give her a wink before turning his attention back on the road.

Placing her hand over his heart, she leaned across the console and whispered into his ear. "It's not the phone or any vibration that's got me feeling a certain need. It's only got to do with a certain sexy lawyer driving a sexy black SUV that's got me feeling needy."

They spent Saturday morning into the early afternoon searching for a dining room set they both could agree on. It would have taken them less time, but Jake had discovered the cost of one that Alexis was ready to buy and nearly had a stroke. He struggled to spend money, figured he always would, and couldn't let her spend more than he would ever even consider, even if they both knew she could more than afford it. With a dining room set finally chosen that they both agreed on and Jake didn't feel was better suited for Buckingham Palace, they returned home and settled into the living room in front of the fire.

The sun had long since set and they worked side by side, legs intertwined, when the silence was interrupted by her stomach growling with a sound that suspiciously resembled a bear warning an intruder that they were too close to her cubs. She snort laughed so hard there were bubbles coming from her nose and Jake had guffawed so long that tears were streaming down his face. Wiping them from his eyes with the pads of his thumbs, he pulled himself together enough to ask if that was her way of telling him it was time for dinner.

Cheeks red from embarrassment, she could only manage a nod. He disappeared into the kitchen, emerging ten minutes later with a loaf of warm Italian bread and some dipping oil. "Dinner will be ready in about fifteen minutes. I hope the bread will keep the beast in check until it is." Laughing, she swatted at him with a sofa pillow, narrowly missing the glass of chardonnay he was trying to hand her. "Hey," he shouted. "I will not tolerate any alcohol abuse in this house."

With a mischievous grin, she spun around, raising her ass as high as she could. "I'm sorry, daddy. Do I deserve a spanking?"

Groaning, he sat the glass of wine on the end table and gave her right butt cheek a healthy swat.

"Ow," she squealed. "That hurt." She moved to rub where he struck her, but his hand was there first, rubbing in gentle circles until the sting shifted into hot pleasure. "Mm," she cooed. "That feels nice."

Leaning forward to kiss the back of her neck, he whispered. "I promised to make it feel even nicer after dinner."

Jake dropped her off at Dulles on Sunday evening for her trip back to Denver. They agreed that with the amount of work they each had on their plates that it would be okay if they didn't get together next weekend. It would give her freedom to stay in Denver if she felt the need without feeling guilty, and Jake was concerned that if he got stuck in New York because of a winter storm, it could jeopardize his meeting deadlines for his case. But they promised each other a phone call each day and not to slip back into all work mode.

Monday, February 24

Jake, 4:00PM: Dining room set arrived. Looks great. Need something for the walls now.

Alexis 5:15 PM: Send pics. We can go to TriBeCa on Saturday and solve that if you're still planning on driving up.

Jake, 5:18 PM: Pics sent. Sound like fun. Mama C's for dinner?

Alexis, 7:52 PM: Sorry sucked into meeting. Looks good. I have good taste lol. Tasting the veal parm already.

Thursday, February 27
Alexis 5:12 PM: Change of plans. Could we maybe check out the River North art district on Saturday instead?
Jake 5:14 PM: Where's that?
Alexis 5:15 PM: Denver
Jake 5:16 PM: I see.
Jake 5:21 PM: I'll try to get a flight.
Alexis 5:32 PM: UR the best. TTYL

Monday, March 2
Alexis 9:15 AM: I just wanted to say I love you. Thanks for being so understanding this weekend. I know it's not what we had planned.
Jake 9:18 AM: At least we were in the same bed. Love you too.
Alexis 10:45 AM: I'll come to you this weekend. It's only fair.
Jake: 10:46 AM: Okay. Have a good day.

Friday, March 6
Alexis 6:48 AM: Just landed in Newark. Any chance you could come up? Exhausted and don't feel like getting on another plane in less than 12 hours.
Jake 6:52 AM: Not even going to ask why you're in Newark. I'll drive up but doubt I can leave early so might not get there til midnight.
Alexis 12:53 PM: Okay. Thanks.

When Jake turned the corner onto Alexis' street, he realized it was the first time he'd done it and not been embarrassed by what he was driving. As if the gods of conspicuous consumption were shining down on him, he found a spot right next to hers. It was like they were telling him he was finally worth enough to park on this street. That wasn't entirely true. His annual income was not in the seven-figure range, but he'd take the parking spot just the same.

He was greeted at the door with a hug and a kiss, which instantly washed away the funk he had from being on the road for the better part of five hours. "Wow. That's quite the welcome. What did I do to deserve to be greeted at the door?" he said once she broke the embrace, and he sat down his messenger bag on the floor.

"I think that's the least you deserve, but I'll save the best reward for later," she said with a grin and a sparkle in her eyes that was full of a promise Jake was more than eager to fulfill. "I've changed plans for us the last two weeks and I really appreciate you not getting upset."

Wrapping her back into his arms and looking her in the eye, "who says I'm not upset?" He assumed the smile on his face made it clear that he was just teasing.

"I don't know," she cooed, trailing her hand down his chest and below his belt. "He seems rather excited to see me." Her hand stroked the length of his cock, which was pressed tight against his slacks. "Not upset at all."

A deep, throaty laugh escaped him. "Well, he's a traitor because we had a sound plan worked out on the drive up here about how I would guilt you into a weekend full of sexual favors to make up for changing plans two weekends in a row."

"Mm, I don't think you have to use guilt to talk me into that." She slipped out of his embrace with a last squeeze down below and walked toward the living room. "But unfortunately, it will just have to be tomorrow because I have to fly back early on Sunday."

There was no controlling the heavy sigh that seeped from deep inside his chest. "I thought you said you had all your accounts under control and your new team was up to speed on everything."

Sinking down on the couch, she looked up at him from under her long lashes and patted the cushion next to her. "It was. It is." She leaned back further and crossed her arms over her chest as he sat down next to her. It struck him that she looked like she was preparing to protect herself from his reaction to what she was about to say. "That's kind of why I had to fly back here this morning. Dewey called a meeting of all the group managers in the Denver office and Andre."

"Oh?" his brow arching high as he settled back and threw his arm over the back of the sofa. The relaxed posture was a juxtaposition to the tension clear in his jaw.

Exhaling a long slow breath, she continued, "Andre has been named the new VP in charge of the San Francisco office and interim head in Denver, too. They fired two of the group managers and asked me to cover, supervising their units until they find a permanent replacement for both the VP and managers' slots."

"You've only had your own pod for what, four weeks? That's seems like an awful load to put on your shoulders." Her brows narrowed, and she tightened her arms around herself, so he quickly added. "It's not that I don't think for a second you can do it. They're just making it hard on you."

Relaxing slightly, she placed her hand on his thigh. "I know. You're right. I feel a lot of pressure on me, but it's what I've always wanted. But it also means I'm going to have to find a place out there. I thought the meeting today was to say that they were going to shut the office and bring my group back here to New York, but this means it stays open and they're not going to pay for a hotel room for me forever."

Pushing himself off the sofa, he paced toward the foyer before turning back. Her eyes followed him, but she sat quietly, waiting for what he would say. He stopped in front of the fireplace, leaning on the mantle. After a long silence, he spoke into the dormant hearth. "So now we split time between Denver and DC instead of here."

She slipped off the sofa and walked up behind him, wrapping her arms around his waist and kissing his shoulder before pressing her face against her back. "I know it isn't ideal, but we knew I'd be reassigned somewhere else." She tightened her grip on his waist, "at least it's not San Francisco."

"Mm, a real blessing, that," he said, pulling out of her hug and walking toward the kitchen. "I could use a drink."

"Are you hungry? I could warm something up. I think there's leftover lasagna in the fridge."

"No, thanks." He knew she was trying to redirect the conversation to more neutral ground. He didn't want a fight, either. He just needed time to process. "I grabbed a gourmet dinner from one of the rest areas on the Jersey Turnpike."

"God. That's awful. I'm sorry."

"No need to be sorry. A greasy, mushy, lukewarm burger is a treat I won't often be having with the new arrangements," he forced out a chuckle. Pouring two fingers of scotch into a rocks glass, he tossed it back in one gulp before pouring a second. Crossing to the refrigerator, he added ice to his glass before turning to go back toward the living room. He stopped, looking down at the glass in his hand, and shook his head.

In two long strides, he was at the sink and emptied the glass before putting it in the dishwasher. Running his hand through his hair with enough force that it stung, he looked up to see Alexis standing at the counter, eyeing his every move. "It's what my dad used to do." Her blank expression reminding him she was not capable of reading his mind. "Drink away his frustrations." He looked down at the floor and drummed his knuckles against the counter, as if to mark time with his thoughts. Shaking his head, he looked up at her again, "let's go to bed. We've both had a long day. And I think I might like to just hold on to you and go to sleep."

She crossed to him and tipped up on her toes, placing a kiss on his creased forehead. "I think I might like that too."

Thursday, March 12
Alexis, 10:42 PM: I know you're going to hate me, but would you be willing to come here this weekend? Promise it's the last time. I need to find a place and haven't even started with how crazy things have been this week.
Jake, 10:49 PM: Just checked, flights are off the charts. I'll see you next weekend.

Friday, March 13
Alexis, 8:04 AM: Okay. Miss you.
Jake, 8:05 AM: Miss you too.

Last night's call with Alexis was still on Jake's mind as he took his place at the conference table for the weekly Wednesday morning staff meeting. In the space of just over a month, they had slipped from talking every night to maybe one night a week, and then on the weekends they didn't get together. The call last night lasted less than five minutes. He couldn't help but think that they should be able to talk at least twice that long just about the work they were doing, but she shared very little about her challenges in Denver, except to complain about lack of support and the incompetence of most of the team. He wanted to be her biggest cheerleader, but it was hard to cheer for a game you didn't know much about.

It was halfway through the meeting when he realized he hadn't been paying the least bit of attention to what was being said. He needed to take a lesson from Alexis and focus more on his job than on his relationship. It was only his boss, Richard, being called out of the meeting that had him snapping back to what was happening in the room he was in. It was fortunate that he was paying attention again because Richard was signaling to him through the window to join him in the hall. Quietly, he pushed away from the table and made his way out of the meeting.

His brows pinched together in concern as he shut the door behind him. Had Richard noticed he was daydreaming in the meeting and going to call him on the carpet for his inattention? It would be a bit of a high school move, he thought, but they were paying him handsomely for his work, and the least he could do was show up and participate.

Richard's stern expression had him even more concerned. Richard was the kind of boss he always respected and always wanted. No nonsense, and to the point, but in a way that made you feel they viewed you as an equal in a team effort, not as some sort of lackey who didn't have the aptitude to figure things out on your own. The intensity in Richard's eyes had him concerned he might have made a mistake that was going to result in jail time. He only hoped it wasn't him.

"Jake, you need to know that you are facing a steep hill and have a very short time to climb it."

Confusion filled Jake's mind as he tried to study Richard's expression and figure out what the hell the man was talking about. He was never this obtuse. What the fuck are you talking about, pushed against his lips but while Richard's face remained stoic, there was a strange twitching at the corners of his mouth that had Jake concerned that man might be about ready to explode with rage. He opted for a more neutral, "I'm sorry?"

"Just got off the phone with District Attorney Young…"

Fuck, fuckety, fuck, fuck. The Court refused to hear the case, and he's calling for my head on a platter.

"… they're going to hear the case."

"I'm sorry. I really thought we had an airtight argument." Jake was about to continue when Richard's words finally seeped through and computed. His jaw slacked, and he sank back against the wall.

The twitching at the corners of Richard's mouth morphed into the smile that had been threatening to break through all along. "Beckett v. The State of Illinois will be heard on Wednesday, April 22nd at ten AM. They didn't do you any favors. Get your team together and get to work. You only have a month to finalize what you're going to say."

"I won't be saying a damn thing, but I get your point."

The laugh that bellowed out of Richard could easily be heard in the conference room and likely ten floors below on the sidewalk. Jake knew this because he could see every eye on the other side of the glass walls of the conference room staring out into the hall in their direction. When Richard contained his mirth, he patted Jake on the shoulder. "Oh, you'll be talking quite a lot, I think. Ed wanted me to relay to you that not only will you be with him for the oral arguments, but you will also have the lead."

"Richard, I ah …," he stammered, trying to force out words with a tongue that suddenly felt swollen and dry.

"Take a deep breath, Jake, and get ahold of yourself. John wouldn't have suggested I put you on this case if he didn't have full confidence in you and, for the record, I don't have a single doubt, either. You're Ed's lawyer. It's your job. Now let's get back to that meeting. It appears some priorities might have shifted a bit."

He walked out of the meeting an hour later with half the lawyers on staff reporting to him for the next month. A little over two months ago, he was stuck in the middle of petty office politics and a month from now, he would argue a case before the Supreme Court that could sway one of the single most divisive political issues in the nation. *How is this my life?*

Closing his office door behind him, he knew he had to share this news with Alexis. He'd like to be able to go home to her tonight and celebrate, but he would settle for the sound of her voice on the other end of the phone. He dropped into his chair and pulled his phone out of his jacket pocket. Two rings and then voice mail. She must be in a meeting. Text message then,

Jake: Big, big news! Call me as soon as you can. XOXO.

Her reply came more quickly than he expected if she was in a meeting.

Alexis: Busy, busy. Will do.

He let out a long, slow breath and sank back into his chair. It didn't seem to him like she was in a meeting, just absorbed in a project. Sure, he understood that, but couldn't she tell this was not just a hi I love you sort of thing? Not a please pick up my suits from the dry cleaners on the way home along with a gallon of milk. He didn't have any doubt about her commitment to him, but it was evolving into just what he feared would happen between them in a long-distance relationship. Distance and a disconnect. They'd have to have a talk soon, or he knew he would lose patience.

A call from John Rock congratulating him on the success did a bit to turn his mood around and distract him from ruminating on the exchange with Alexis.

His frustration with her reply had faded. He went to dinner with a couple of associates from the office to talk about the case, which helped him stop perseverating that it had been over six hours and she still hadn't called or texted.

Frustration turned to anger and hurt by eleven-thirty when he pulled out his phone to call her again. He felt he had given her more than ample time to reply. Twelve hours, she couldn't find time to call in the space of twelve hours. Yes, this was exactly what he had envisioned happening when he said long distance would be too much of a challenge for them. He put the phone down. He didn't want to have an argument with her. He knew he was mad and might say something they'd both regret later.

His phone rang at five past twelve. He was almost asleep, and it startled him awake. "I am so sorry, honey. It's just been an awful day. This office is a total shit show, and nobody is doing anything except me." She continued complaining about how disorganized things were and how this one and that were, letting the most basic things slip through the cracks. It was a story he'd heard many times and while he was sympathetic to her plight, his half-asleep state and already high frustration level didn't really serve either of them well.

"I'm sorry to cut you off Alexis, but you really couldn't find five minutes to call me before now? I asked you to call before noon. I asked that you call as soon as you can, I had something big I wanted to share. Frankly, it seems like you just didn't care."

"I'm sorry. I just told you I had a hellacious day. Yes, this was like the first time I could focus enough on what you had to say." Neither of them at this point were using the most loving of tones.

"I'm sorry you had a bad day and I realize you are under a ton of stress with very little in the way of support. I just think on the rare occasion that I reach out to you in the middle of the day to call me as soon as you can, you might pick up on the fact it's an unusual circumstance and call back before over twelve hours have passed. While it's not an emergency, it was important to me. That's all I'm saying."

"I said I'm sorry, Jake."

"Sometimes sorry isn't enough."

"Please, let's not do this now." He could hear a deep inhale and a slow exhale on the other end of the phone before she asked in a much calmer voice. "Please tell me your news."

He matched her calming breath. "My news is that my first petition is being taken up by the court and I've been asked to be part of the team for the oral arguments."

"Wow, really?! That's fantastic. Everyone must be excited."

"They are."

"Do you have a date for the hearing yet?"

"April 22, one of the last sessions for oral arguments."

"That's only a month! How on earth are you going to be ready?"

"At this point, all there is to do is to respond to the opposition briefs. The case has been made and we'll answer the questions the Justices ask. There will be a lot of prep meetings, but we'll be fine."

"I know you'll be fine. You're going to be perfect."

While he appreciated her excitement for him, he was upset she hadn't seemed to acknowledge his point. She honestly felt she couldn't find the five minutes for him. He just didn't see how that was possible. He was too tired to argue, so he just moved on. "Thanks. Are you still going to come here this weekend?" He knew what the pause on the other end meant. "Please tell me we're not going to lose another weekend."

"Honey, I don't know. I'll call tomorrow night when I've had a chance to see what they are doing. I wasn't very impressed with what they were showing us at the meeting this morning. Honestly, it's fifty-fifty. I'm sorry."

"Okay," he wasn't trying very hard to hide his frustration "well I was already half asleep when you called, and you have a long day tomorrow. Call me with an update tomorrow night if you want."

"Are you angry with me?"

"Alexis, I'm just tired. I want to go to bed." Again, not his most convincing performance.

"Fine, good night. I love you."

"Love you too."

"Bye."

He dropped the phone back onto the nightstand, then rolled over and fluffed the pillow with more energy than was truly necessary. Maybe he'd be in a better frame of mind tomorrow.

Chapter 36

Alexis

lexis was settled comfortably into United flight 1299, laptop in front of her, coffee in hand as she edited presentation slides, cross-referencing information with the stack of papers she had on the seat beside her. She'd worked her way across most of the country. It didn't happen often, but she was lucky enough to have the row to herself.

She wasn't fully focused on her work. She had spurts, twenty or thirty minutes, when she could push Jake from her mind and be productive, but then she'd be back to mulling over their conversation last night. He sounded upset, sounded hurt, and she just couldn't fully understand it. Sure, he had asked her to call, but she did when she felt she could give him attention. If she'd answered when he called in the afternoon, she wouldn't have fully been there for him, distracted by the shit storm that was her everyday work life.

A FaceTime call notification came through on her laptop and Tiana popped up on her caller ID. She was already distracted, so she answered. Maybe Tiana could ease her mind, she thought. "Hey there, T. How's it going?" She smiled as her friend's face filled her screen.

"You're on a plane?"

"How'd you guess?" she laughed, rolling her eyes. "That's my life these days, always on the go."

"When do you land in New York? Maybe we can grab a bite to eat."

"Actually, on my way out to Denver, sorry."

"Oh," Tiana sighed, her smile dimming. "When will you be back? I've met a new man, and I was hoping maybe you and Jake could join us for dinner Saturday night. We haven't gotten together in forever and I'd really like your opinion of him."

Alexis laughed. Tiana always asked her opinion about the guys she dated but never listened to her advice. "That sounds nice, but if I make it back this weekend, I'll be going to Washington to give Jake some undivided attention. He's in a mood."

"What's got him in a mood?" Alexis could hear the accusation in Tiana's tone. She knew her friend always had her back, but wasn't shy at calling her out when she thought she deserved it. She just wasn't in a place to accept that sort of sisterly love at the moment.

"Oh, stuff, I guess." She didn't want to get into it, but knew she had to give her friend something or she'd be facing the inquisition. "We don't get much time together. I've got so much to do for work that plans get canceled. He's usually pretty understanding, but like yesterday he called before I'd even finished my morning coffee, and I was just frazzled; I didn't want to give him half my attention or feel like I had to cut him off short and get back to work, so I just sent it through to voice mail. Then he texted telling me to call when I could. He thought I should have called him back sooner."

"When did you call him?"

"I guess it was like midnight. He was half asleep, so a little cranky. He'll be fine."

"You waited until midnight to call him back?" The volume of Tiana's screech had her wincing, and she felt the other passengers' eyes boring into the side of her head. For a moment she regretted not putting her ear buds in to take the call, but then her ears would probably be bleeding now if she had.

"Yes, it's when I finally cleared my head enough."

"What did he need you for, Alexis?"

She arched her brow, but it had a zero impact on her friend, who sounded more like a mother deeply disturbed by a daughter who was the class slut. "He found out a case he was working on was going to be heard by the Supreme Court and he was going to be there for oral arguments."

"That sounds like a pretty big deal. I mean, it's not my thing, but surely that doesn't happen very much."

"It is a big thing." *Especially for Jake,* her conscience reminded her. "The Court maybe hears a hundred fifty cases a year. They get thousands of petitions. He did an amazing job getting the case heard. I am so proud of him. I knew he could do it. It's why I wanted him to take the job in the first place."

"So, he basically wins his way into the world series, and you didn't have the time to let him tell you. Seems to me he would have taken half your attention to deliver his news. Honestly, Alexis, I'd have been upset too. I'd have been hurt."

Alexis chewed her lip and sighed. "The distance isn't easy for either of us, Tiana. We love each other. There's no doubt about that, but I always feel like I'm pulled in two different directions. I have to trust Jake will always be there because my job won't be. It's like they keep piling more responsibility on my plate and waiting for me to fail. There is no way I am going to let that happen. NO WAY, I'm giving my father the opportunity to say I told you so."

Before Tiana got a chance to reply, they announced they were making their descent into Denver and all electronics needed to be shut down. "Sorry, I've got to go. We're getting ready to land."

"Okay, we'll talk later." Tiana's tone communicating she wasn't going to forget to finish this conversation. "Just don't take Jake for granted. Love you like a sister."

"Love you too, bye." Alexis switched off her laptop and began pulling her papers together. Getting ready to hit the ground running. She hoped she could head home tomorrow afternoon. She didn't want to let Jake down and she wanted to see him every bit as much as he wanted to see her.

What Alexis found when she walked into the Denver office was not what she hoped for at all. She was on the phone to Andre and already making the decision that she needed to be there more than just twenty-four hours if things were going to come out as they needed to. Jake would understand. She knew he would. They were a team and right now; she needed to be in Denver. They'd have next weekend.

She dreaded the call she made, but she had no other choice. Her job had to come first.

"What's Andre think about this mess?" She heard the 'and why isn't he doing anything about it' insinuation in Jake's question, or at least she thought she did because she felt the same way. She also heard the 'he's the one that should do something about it' but they both knew it was no use saying it because it wasn't going to happen.

"Oh, he's upset, that's for sure, but he's dumped this in my lap and is expecting me to sort it all out."

"Is he staying the weekend, too?"

Again, Alexis was certain of the unsaid, 'he damn well better be,' so she winced and held her breath before she admitted, "he's not even here. It's only me, and it's been that way for the last month. I ask him for help. He gives it a cursory look, says a couple of obvious things that a freshman business major could do in their sleep, and sends it back to my court. It's pretty much all my baby, and at this point it would be easier if I just did everything myself. I guess that's what I'm doing, anyway."

Jake was either standing in a wind tunnel or was thoroughly exasperated based on the force of the breath he let out. "I'm sorry you're stuck in a crappy situation. I hate to say it, but you've got to start thinking if this is all worth it to you. Is whatever reward that they're going to throw your way really going to be enough given what it's doing to your health and our relationship?"

She was used to him questioning the sanity of her dedication to DCH. She heard it from everyone else that meant anything to her as well: Carole, Tiana, her grandfather. What she wasn't ready for was the connection to their relationship, and that had her heart pounding faster in her chest. "What do you mean, what it's doing to our relationship?"

"I mean, are you happy? Is being together once every three or four weeks for a day and a half enough, especially when we don't even talk over twenty minutes a day on days when we do talk? That's what I mean. I'm not happy. I think I've given a lot and I'm doing my best to be supportive, but not only are we missing the day-to-day things that help people bond, we're not even sharing the big moments. Yesterday was a big moment for me. You chose not to be there for me." He groaned on an exhale and his voice quieted. "I'm sorry. Maybe we can get some time next weekend. I hope so anyway."

"I'm sorry Jake. I really do miss you. I'm doing the best I know how to. I guess I should go. I promise we'll have next weekend. Promise."

"Okay. I love you too. Good luck."

"Thanks." She pressed the end button and set the phone on her desk. Leaning forward, she held her head in her hands, rubbing her pounding temple with the tips of her fingers. If she'd just held on and remained the Ice Princess, none of this would be a problem. If Trevor had just kept his dick in his pants and lived up to his end of the bargain, none of this would be a problem. But this was a problem because she loved Jake and he had a problem. And that meant she had a problem beyond the lack of professionalism and ineptitude that infected most of the people on the other side of her office door. *If I can just solve the problem on the other side of that door, then I can finally spend some time with Jake and neither of us will have a problem anymore.*

She opened up her laptop and started typing. If her weekend was ruined, then so was everyone's who worked for her. There would be a staff meeting tomorrow morning and if they chose to miss it, then they chose to resign. She'd have to check with HR to see if she could actually fire anyone, but details could always be worked out. The Ice Princess might be powerless when it came to Jake, but she could still conjure her up professionally and the bitch better be ready because she was due for a virtuoso performance.

Chapter 37

Jake

Jake had known all along that a long-distance relationship was tough and, with Alexis being who Alexis was, it would be even tougher with her. The call they just finished was not the first time he had been angry with himself for taking the Washington job, despite how well he was doing and how much he loved going to the office. Once again, he rolled over in his mind whether he really could or should be the one that was always, well, a vast majority of the time, making the concessions. He just wanted, no, needed, to be Alexis' priority sometimes. In that moment, he could not think of a single instance when she had chosen him over work. Twenty months to go on the contract. In that moment, he wouldn't have bet on his relationship lasting another twenty days.

Alexis followed through on her promise of being there the next weekend. She insisted on coming to DC given his upcoming oral arguments. Not only was she there for the weekend, but showed up mid-day on Friday. This gave Jake some cause for hope. She even called the afternoon of the oral arguments to find out how he felt they went. He began to believe that they would last twenty days and maybe even the full twenty months.

After his day in Court however, things returned to distance and excuses. Jake knew she felt pressure and while he knew she imposed a lot on herself, he was also keenly aware of the toxic, work is God culture of DCH. He wished with all his heart she could break away and find a healthier environment. She was talented and passionate about so many causes. There must be a hundred opportunities in DC where she could not only succeed, but thrive.

May came and went with only one weekend together before spending Memorial Day at her grandfather's home in the Hamptons. Carole and Brian were there, and Jake was grateful for that as Alexis spent most of the holiday weekend on her phone or laptop. Carole physically forced her to surrender the laptop on the beach Sunday afternoon holding a pail of seawater over her head, threatening to pour it on the laptop if Alexis didn't put it back in her tote. It was the only four hours of full attention Alexis gave anyone the entire weekend.

Carole and Brian did their best to compensate for Alexis' lack of attention to Jake. And encouraged him to hang in there. They both truly believed that Jake was the best thing that had ever happened to Alexis and voiced it regularly. It eased the outward awkwardness for Jake, but did little to change the gnawing want he had inside. He was back to being second on her priority list, and a distant second at that. Jake drove back to DC as soon as they made it to the brownstone late Monday afternoon. Alexis had tried to get him to stay at least a while, have a bite to eat and perhaps a quickie to last them the week but Jake wasn't hungry and perhaps for the first time in their relationship had no interest in having any kind of sex with Alexis, quick or not.

His drive back to DC was a slow one through holiday traffic, which gave him far too much time to think. He was getting close to his limit with the ups and downs, the incredible intimacy followed by the interminable distance that was what defined being in love with, and loved by, Alexis Chambers. He didn't know it was possible to be so heartsick and still be in a relationship. He loved her. She loved him. Somehow it just didn't seem like it was enough to sustain their relationship. Any relationship.

The first two weeks of June affirmed his belief that their long-distance relationship was truly doomed. His spirits sank lower, and he felt it was going to affect the quality of his work if he kept being distracted by it. They had plans to be back on Long Island for the Fourth of July and if something hadn't changed by then, he would have to end it. This time, he knew it would have to be a complete break. He wanted it to succeed, but he'd done as much as he could, no more pleading, no more forgotten promises. She knew what his modest expectations were and, other than in brief spurts, she had chosen not to value them.

Anxiety around Jake's office was increasing. The session for the Court was nearing its annual summer recess, meaning all decisions would be handed down and they would hear only emergency petitions. Jake would discover whether Ed Young and he were successful in their arguments. This Justice or that had requested additional briefs, but no more information was forthcoming. That was common for the Court and the consensus among the legal scholars and those that watched the Court on such things was that they would likely lose 5-4 in a court dominated by conservative thought. He didn't want to lose, but figured he would be content with that. It was status quo and that would be a good get for one's first time arguing before the Court. It might even be okay losing perhaps one of the liberal judges, but a five to four loss would be good, very good. He'd have done his job well.

The second week of June, Alexis called late on the Friday afternoon to once again break the news that she would be in Denver over the weekend. She promised it would be the last. There was a presentation on Monday and after that, they would put those accounts to bed until November at least, with any luck until after the first of the year. Jake thought to himself, when have they ever had luck with finding time together? They ended the call with promises of conversation on Saturday, "A nice long one," Alexis said. Again, Jake had his doubts and thought about what alternative plans to make for the Fourth.

Mindlessly, he threw work for the weekend into his messenger bag, his thoughts still racing about his personal life, when Richard appeared at his doorway. "Let's stop for a drink. I've had a long week and you look like you could use one yourself."

Happy for the opportunity not to be alone with his thoughts, Jake agreed. They walked a few blocks to a bar that they had been to on several occasions when someone was moving on after an internship or some other such celebratory occasion. It was an interesting place with an English pub sort of vibe, dark but not dreary and this time of night it was wall to wall with lawyers and the rest of the political upper middle class that worked in DC but lived on the other side of the Potomac, the one's that didn't bat an eye at the twenty-dollar drinks they were selling.

They spent a while with shop talk and speculating on when the Court would rule on Jake's case before Richard addressed what Jake was feeling like was the white elephant in the room. "I'm a little surprised you came out tonight. Didn't you say Alexis was coming in this weekend?"

He pushed his hand back through his hair before looking over at his boss. "Plans changed."

Richard patted him on the back and gave him a sympathetic smile. "I'm sorry, man. That seems to happen a lot with you two."

"It does," he said flatly after taking a long sip of his scotch. "She's trying to work her way up the food chain and doing a great job of it. The problem is that she's not quite high enough to refuse to get stuck working crazy hours. I'm beginning to think she never will, as long as she stays with DCH."

Richard took a slow, measured sip of his drink before leaning back and meeting Jake's eyes. "Does she like what she's doing?"

"That's the thing. She really doesn't. When we get a chance to talk, she spends half the time complaining about the people she works with either being incompetent or back stabbers just out for themselves and then the rest of the time complaining because she's never practicing law but doing the job of an MBA. Her life would be so much easier if she'd gone to Harvard Business School instead of Yale Law."

"So why does she do it? It's not like she couldn't join you here. There're more lawyers than politicians in this city."

"True, but I think she feels like she needs to succeed in business, not law, in order to satisfy this obsession she has, to prove her father wrong." He shrugged his shoulders, taking another drink. "She's a great lawyer, passionate about causes, despite that, that's not enough for her, it's…" wiping his hand over his face and rubbing his five o'clock shadow, "it's complicated."

A grin pulled at the corner of Richard's mouth, and he waved his hand, "sorry man. I'm not laughing at you. It's just that every time I hear someone say, 'it's complicated' all I can think about these days is…"

"Harry Potter," they both said in unison. Jake smiled and felt a little lighter.

"Well, I feel like I'm about as desirable as Griphook to her these days," Jake mused, shaking his head.

A silky voice interrupted their conversation. "Don't tell me a handsome guy like you is a Potter fan, too. What more could a girl ask for?" Jake turned to find a tall redhead stepping up next to him. "I didn't mean to eavesdrop," she continued, batting long lashes, "but you already had my attention. I'm Kate," she smiled, stretching out her hand.

It took Jake a beat to register what was happening, but eventually offered his hand. "Jake, and this is Richard."

As Richard nodded, a brunette slid next to Kate and handed her a drink. "I'm Amanda."

Jake cocked a brow at the latest arrival. "You don't have to introduce yourself, Amanda. We work in the same office." He remembered her and had been avoiding her from his first day at the firm.

"Good to see you, Ms. Grass," Richard added, though from his tone, it wasn't clear if he truly was pleased to see her. *Perhaps Richard feels that Amanda Grass is a sexual harassment suit waiting to happen too,* Jake thought.

"Wow. Cool. You guys all know each other. Let's all go grab a table together," Kate suggested in a way that made Jake think she must have been on a pep squad at some point because no one was that cheery naturally.

"Thanks, but I need to get home to my partner and kids," Richard said, sliding down off his stool. "Buy the ladies a drink, Jake, and use the corporate card. Amanda's an employee, so we can write it off under team building expenses." He patted Jake on the shoulder and gave him a wink before heading out the door.

He didn't want to be rude and follow Richard, but he certainly didn't want to be the focus of attention for these two women, either. It wasn't that they weren't attractive. They were more than attractive. And over the next fifteen minutes, they made it quite clear that they were more than willing, together or individually, gentleman's choice, so to speak. But regardless of how dour he felt the prospects for Alexis and him were, he wasn't going to allow that part of his caveman brain to win out.

They were certainly persistent, but eventually he convinced them he was not interested in taking them home, regardless of the absence of strings. He said his goodbyes, made a quick pit stop, and headed straight for the door before they could spot him and give him one more opportunity to change his mind.

He walked out of the bar and headed back to the office to get his briefcase. The humidity fell over him like a wet blanket. He had half expected to find them waiting for him on the sidewalk and was more than relieved to find that was not the case. No unmarried man alive would have faulted him for taking them up on the offer. No man except him.

He wanted a drink. He never drank alone, and he never drank too much, but tonight he would make an exception. He needed to be numb. He needed not to think. Not to think about Alexis and how he would never be important enough to her. Not to think about how close he had come to selfishly taking comfort from a woman who meant nothing to him. Not to think about how empty the future looked.

Jake pulled into his driveway, walked up the front steps, and shut the front door behind him, fully intending not to emerge again until Monday morning. July Fourth was just a few weeks away. He poured a full glass and sat down in his recliner. Fired off a quick text to Richard, thanking him for hanging him out to dry and informing him that his application for wingman had been rejected. Mindlessly, he scrolled through the cable guide, clicking through without hardly reading the options.

Unconsciously, he chose a show. He honestly didn't care what was on. It was noise, something to potentially distract him from the dialog in his head. He was on to his second glass when his phone rang. Richard. Jake found that odd because he never received a work call off hours, especially on a Friday night late. He answered and hoped he didn't sound as buzzed as he was feeling.

"Hi Jake, I apologize for hanging you out to dry. At the moment, it looked like you might be enjoying the attention."

"If things were different, I probably would have enjoyed it. Alexis and I might not be perfect, but I will not flush it away. Somehow, I don't think you called to quiz me on Ms. Grass and her friend."

"No, I didn't, just a bonus," he chuckled. "I thought you might like to know that I got the heads up the Court will announce their decision on Monday."

"Wow, okay. Thanks. It's going to make for a long weekend, but I appreciate the heads up."

"Not a problem, man. Forgive me, Jake, it's your business, not mine, but don't drink yourself into a stupor tonight. Find someone to talk to that you trust." Jake could hear a heavy sigh through the phone. "I'm not trying to interfere in your personal life, but you're an exceptionally talented lawyer. I don't want to see that talent dimmed by the darkness you seem to hold inside you lately."

"Thank you. I appreciate that. I have had a couple of drinks, but this is the first bottle that's been in my house since I moved here four months ago. I'm fine. Just a bump in the road and all will be good tomorrow."

"Okay, good. See you on Monday. Big day man, big day."

"Thanks, bye."

Jake took a long look at the half glass of scotch in his hand. He would not allow this to drive him to where his father was. Not Alexis. Not anything. This was the first but also the last time he was ever going to drink alone. He downed the glass in one burning gulp, shivered and turned off the TV. Tomorrow was another day and tomorrow he'd consider everything with a fresh mind. A sober mind.

Monday morning came and Jake was far calmer than he expected to be. In his heart, he knew that there was nothing he could do at this point. All that could be done was done, weeks ago. He held to his five to four loss prediction; he could accept six to three, a more pessimistic voice chimed in at the back of his head.

At five passed ten a call came in, John Rock conferenced in from New York, Ed Young was on speaker from Springfield, Richard sat behind his desk, Jake was on the couch across from Richard, and leaned forward as the voice spoke on the other end. "Seven to two." Jake let out a sigh and slumped, looking down at the floor. He didn't think losing would bother him so much. He was so absorbed in his thoughts he almost missed the rest of the sentence. "We did it, gentlemen. We flipped three conservative Justices. AG Young, Richard, Jake, congratulations. Job well done." Jake couldn't believe his ears. There were cheers all around, except from Jake. He was too stunned to speak.

Ed Young was the first to speak as the excitement subsided. "We need to give all the credit to Jake. I gave him the guidelines, he put it all together. Forty-five of the forty-nine pages were his. Every retort was his. Jake, thank you. I'll be in DC Friday and dinner for the entire team at The Old Ebbitt is on the great State of Illinois. Please bring your wives. Fuck." Ed cleared his throat, "I apologize, Richard, partners," he corrected. "This is great, so important. We've done some good and lasting work here. Look forward to seeing you all Friday."

Jake sank back onto the couch. He scrubbed his hands over his face before raking them back through his hair, exhaling loudly. Richard smiled, shaking his head with a chuckle before meeting Jake's stare. "You thought you lost, didn't you?"

Jake smiled and nodded. "It's a conservative court. I figured if we held to five to four against, we'd leave the door open for another challenge in a few years if the outlook changed. Busted my ass with the best legal arguments I could think of, but still, that doesn't always matter as much as it should."

"You really don't have any idea how bright of a lawyer you are, do you? I've worked for John Rock for nearly twenty-five years. I have never seen him jump on someone as quickly as he jumped on you. He brings people along slowly, so they don't get themselves into the weeds and get pulled under. He has given you responsibilities that make me flinch and I've seen a crap ton young man, you're a damn savant. Now enough fluffing you up. Go call Alexis, get her ass on a plane and if she won't come, then I'd look up Ms. Grass. A man deserves to celebrate a victory like this. Not my business, I know, but you need to let off some steam. Go play some golf, do something. You have fifteen minutes to shift your calendar and then I don't want to see your face in this building until Thursday. Am I being clear enough for you?"

Jake smiled and exhaled once more. "Give me a half hour and I'll be out, promise. I won't even bring a single sheet of paper home with me."

"Fair enough." Jake got up and headed out the door. "Seriously Jake.

Superior job, congratulations."

"Thank you." And he closed the door behind him. He walked back to his office with a lightness in his step that hadn't been there for months, maybe not since right after he and Alexis first got together. He closed the door of his office behind him and dialed Alexis.

Alexis answered on the first ring. "Congratulations baby! I am so very, very proud of you! You must be over the moon. How are you going to celebrate today?"

Jake smiled a broad smile. It felt so good to him, she already knew. "How did you know? I wanted to tell you."

"Oh, when you told me you thought they were going to announce this morning, I made a couple of calls. I have a source or two."

"Thank you. That means so much to me. You just don't know. Richard kicked me out of the building until Thursday. I have a half hour, twenty-five minutes now," he amended, "to move my schedule and get out." He laughed, "First time I've ever been kicked out for good performance."

"Enjoy it, you deserve it. I'd tell you to fly to Denver, but you'd be alone here, too. I really am sorry about that."

"It's okay, but you have to find a way to be here in DC for dinner Friday night. Ed Young will be in town and John Rock is coming as well. It's important to me Lex, please put stuff on the back burner and let's have an enjoyable weekend."

"Oh." She paused, thinking for a moment. He could hear the hesitation in her voice. "Of course, honey. I promise. I'll fly in Thursday night if there's a way, no later than noon Friday. Hell or high water, I won't let you down."

"Thank you. Can't wait to see you! Have a good day. I've got twenty minutes now to clear three days. Bye."

"Love you, bye."

As soon as Jake hung up the phone, his door burst open with a flood of co-workers clapping and shouting congratulations. He accepted them graciously and then asked them politely to leave so he could clear his schedule and leave as he'd been ordered to do. They all laughed and went about their business. As they left. Amanda weaved her way in. "I just wanted to apologize for Friday. I stepped way over the line. I didn't mean to make you feel uncomfortable."

"Amanda, there's no need to apologize, really. You're a beautiful woman and I'm more than flattered. It's done. We're good, right?"

"We're very good, thank you. I'll clear your calendar. Go enjoy your time off."

"Thank you. It's unnecessary." He waved her off and moved back behind his desk, picking up his phone.

"I know, but I want to." She sighed and met his eyes. "Let me do this for you."

He met her gaze and saw a friend staring back at him, not someone who wanted anything more than to help. He took in a deep breath and let it slowly out. "Okay, thank you. See you Thursday."

"Great." She smiled a warm, friendly smile. "Have fun." She picked his phone up off his desk to hand it to him. "Wait a second." She opened his contacts and typed in her name and number, then sent herself a text. "If you need anything over the next couple of days, just send me a text or call. I'll let you know if there are any issues with your schedule." He knew he couldn't hide the concern he was feeling inside, but she continued to smile at him like it didn't concern her a bit. "Don't worry. I'll be totally professional."

He took his phone from her hand, fully intending to delete the number as soon as he was out of her sight. "Thanks." And he walked out of his office, leaving her behind.

He spent the afternoon walking the National Mall and then perusing the exhibits at the American History Museum before heading home and making dinner. He made a note that he'd have to go to the store tomorrow and step up his spices game. A man cannot live by Italian mixed seasoning and garlic powder alone, he thought.

He remembered Alexis had said she had a presentation today, part of her justifying missing another weekend with promises of things being easier. Nothing big scheduled in Denver until late fall. He hoped she was right. He knew she wasn't lying to him, but he knew enough about DCH that there was always another fire somewhere, which meant she was probably lying to herself. He fired off a quick text; It still thrilled him she had not only answered his call immediately, but cared enough to find out on her own.

Jake: Thanks again for this morning, still smiling at your thoughtfulness. How did your presentation go?

He hit send and turned on the TV. A few minutes later, she replied.

Alexis: It was a total fucking abortion. I danced around and kept the client. Andre and Dewey are in flight now. They're firing the team, maybe me too, but told me to plan on a strategy and regroup planning meeting all day tomorrow, probably Wednesday too. Sorry I'm complaining to you again. I think it's time to start looking around. We can make some plans this weekend. Miss you, babe, really looking forward to celebrating with you Friday night.

Jake: So sorry honey, you can always complain to me. All for you making a change, you know that ;-) Looking forward to this weekend too!

He knew she would be distracted, so he wasn't going to force a string of texts on her. A smile filled his face. Hearing her finally consider making a change was big, in his mind, even bigger than winning a case in the Supreme Court. He had no delusions about her pulling the trigger yet, but this was certainly a step in the right direction. He climbed the stairs to his room and drifted off to sleep.

Jake tried to relax over the next couple of days, went to the driving range, rode his bike to the Mall, and toured a couple more of the Smithsonian museums, tried to read a book that had been on his nightstand for a year. The fact was he missed Alexis; he missed her easy company; he missed both of them lost in their own work but somehow touching toes under the covers, unconsciously connecting. He hated this long-distance crap. She'd only rented a one-bedroom apartment in Denver, saying she didn't want any semblance of roots. She might not be rooted, but she was there, and it didn't seem all that temporary to him.

They had a brief conversation on Tuesday when she had a break in a meeting with Andre and Hamilton Dewey. The anxiety she was feeling was clear in her voice as she explained they were mapping out the future of the Denver office she had been, for all intents and purposes, managing for the past two months. She had sounded much more confident when they talked Wednesday, when she explained she was going to have a large role in hiring and configuring the new business groups they were putting into place to compliment the team she was already leading. He couldn't help the pride he felt for her at all she had accomplished, even though he knew that the increased responsibility would mean an even greater strain on their already fragile relationship.

She assured him at the end of both conversations that she would be there for Friday's big celebration. Jake was grateful that she wasn't standing in front of him because he was sure he wouldn't have been able to hide the fact that he had his doubts. So much so that he stooped to reminding her it was very important to him and his career. "It won't be a good visual if I'm the only one stag at the table, Lex. I don't want to be that guy, but I need you to put me first this time. I need you here for me. I'm sorry to put it that way, but I do."

She let out a long slow breath, not in exasperation but in understanding. "I know, honey, I know. And I certainly owe you at least that. God, I don't know how many times I did it for Trevor and he never came close to deserving it. I'll be the perfect trophy wife for you Friday night," she promised. "I've had a lot of practice."

Shortly after noon on Thursday, she called him at the office. His gut told him it wasn't going to be good news, but he forced himself to believe she was just calling to tell him what time to pick her up at the airport. She said she was trying to get here tonight when they first talked about it. "Hey babe. How goes the rumble in Denver?"

"Hi, how's your day going?" Her voice was shaky and lacked its usual confidence. A knot tightened in his stomach.

"It's going fine. The time off was nice, but I'm paying for it now. What's wrong?"

"Nothing's wrong," he could hear the breath she released. She was a terrible liar for a lawyer. "I've been promoted."

"Congratulations and you thought you were getting the axe Monday night. What's your new position?"

Her hesitation was a dead giveaway that it was something he would not be happy about. "I've been named associate vice president and general manager for the Denver office. Dewey said I've been doing the job for the last two months anyway and if I'd been given the authority instead of just the responsibility, they would have been in a better position now. Andre no longer has anything to do with this office. It's all mine. I can hardly believe it. I'm like one step away from managing partner." He could hear the pride and confidence in her voice by the time she finished telling him.

Denver, Jake thought, *fuck, fuck, fuck.* "I don't suppose you told them you need to review their offer sheet first?" He was trying to hide the frustration in his voice, but likely wasn't too successful. This all but assured that she would be in Denver for years. The knot was tightening in his stomach and mixed with the guilt washing over him for not being more supportive and happier for her. And he was truly happy for her, but he was already mourning what he knew would be the death sentence for their relationship.

"Jake, you know it doesn't work that way here. You hesitate for a second with DCH and you're out on your ass."

"Surely, Dewey at least allowed you to review your new contract before he forced you to give him an answer."

"I haven't seen a contract yet," she huffed. "I've been so caught up in making plans and, honestly, so damn excited about making it this far, this fast. I'd forgotten to ask about it."

"Jesus, Lex." He ran his hands through his hair, giving it a pull in frustration he was glad she couldn't see. "I'm a little surprised you're this enthusiastic about the move. Just a couple of days ago you said you wanted to make a change, get back to being a lawyer…," he stopped himself mid-sentence, swallowing the thickness in his throat. "I am happy for you. You've certainly made the sacrifices and worked hard enough for it. We can add that to the list of celebrations for tomorrow night. We'll figure it out." It was a force, but he was trying to not totally rain on her parade. She had worked more than hard enough to earn it.

There was a long silence on the other end of the line. "That's kind of the problem." he could hear the strain in her voice.

"What's the problem?" he asked, already knowing the answer.

"Dewey is staying through the weekend. His plan is for us to complete the ninety-day plan and make the announcement of my promotion, and present the plan on Monday morning. He's scheduled meetings all weekend. The new group managers that will report to me will be here Saturday morning. I can't come, Jake. I know I promised, and I know how important it is to you, I really do. I can't tell him no. This is my career."

"Alexis…" he took a deep breath, trying to compose himself. He desperately wanted to scream at the top of his lungs. "I have been as understanding as I possibly can. I've tried to support you and not stand in your way even if I think you killing yourself for a company that will fire you for simply keeping family commitments." He paused. Laying it all out on the table over the phone didn't feel right to him, but she gave him no choice.

"I know Jake. I really am sorry."

"I am very sorry. I hate having a conversation like this on the phone. We had a deal, Lex. I'd try the long-distance relationship thing, and you'd do your best to make sure we were together most weekends. This will be the third weekend in a row that we haven't been together, and you spent four waking hours with me on Memorial Day weekend. I saw ten times more of your sister and brother-in-law than I did of you. They're great people and I like them a lot, but I love you."

"We spent one weekend in four together before that. I give in and I do my best to be understanding and not guilt trip you. I honestly don't have a problem coming in second to your career most of the time, but I can't do it all the time, Alexis. I can't do it this time. Not. This. Time." He sounded cold and detached, even to himself. "This dinner is more than just appearances for office politics. Yes, you're my 'trophy wife' and I need you to be by my side for appearance's sake. It would be one thing if I was single, but everyone knows I'm in a relationship. I've been here almost six months and no one, no one has met you. I've reached the end of what I can handle. I'm sorry. We had a deal; we'd talk before you accepted a new position. Not after. Not, 'I can't because I'd be out on my ass'. I know the fucking contract that you signed because you asked me to look it over in case you missed something. You have the right to refuse a transfer or a promotion. They can't fire you for that, and if they did, you could sue them blind. They know that and they know you know that."

"They've backed doored you through this whole transition. Takeover this pod temporarily. Now it's yours, but you can bring it back to New York. Oh, we're keeping the Denver office. Help us manage it until we name someone. Oh, look, you're the one we named, but we're not going to give you a formal offer upfront. We'll let you do all the work and then screw you out of every nickel we can in the process. Please, Alexis, look at this through the same critical lens you would if you were your lawyer." He looked down at his aching hand, only then realizing that he had balled it into a fist and had been banging it on his desk with each point he had tried to make to her.

He dropped his forehead to his desk, looking down at his feet. "I'm sorry."

"Don't be honey. I know you're just trying to look out for me."

He pinched the corners of his eyes, trying to hold back the stinging emotion threatening to pour out. "I am, but I also have to start looking out for me. I asked you for one thing, one thing in six fucking months, most of it in exile from each other. I'm sorry Lex, I am, but if…"

"Don't, Jake. Please don't," she interrupted, her voice trembling.

"I'm done. I'm done loving a woman that I never see. I never thought I'd be this guy, delivering ultimatums, but it's my last gasp at saving us. You need to be here before I leave for work tomorrow morning or we're done. It's your choice. You can walk up to Dewey and let him know you have a commitment and you'll be happy to hit the ground running Monday. I need to be your top priority this time. This one time. If you can't do it for me. For us. Then I'm just not that important to you. We're not important to you. I know you love me, but you need to value me, too. You can call me tonight if you want and let me know what you've decided to do."

"Jake, please don't do this. I do value you. Why do I have to be there tomorrow morning? Maybe I could try to get there just in time for dinner?"

"I'm sorry, but not this time, Alexis. If I give in to that, there's just too big of a chance that something will happen, and you won't show at all. I'll look like a fool in front of my boss, the founding partner that hired me, and the client that could be an important connection for me down the road. And their partners, poor old Jake, there would be a fucking string of set-ups, a nice eligible lawyer bachelor. No fucking way. I'll hire a god damned escort first."

"Jake Douglas you would not!"

He had no intention of hiring an escort, but he was in no frame of mind to admit it to her. "God damn it, Alexis, I mean it. Find a way to make this happen or I'm out. I gave it another chance because I love you more than it's healthy to, but I'm tired of being hurt and lonely and then feeling guilty about feeling hurt and lonely." He let out a humorless laugh. "Look at it this way, now you can paint me as an asshole that gave you ultimatums. You had no choice but to leave my arrogant, misogynistic ass. Goodbye, Alexis. I have work I have to do. Believe it or not, I love you very much."

Chapter 38

Alexis

Alexis croaked goodbye into a dead receiver. She swung around in her chair to look out the window of her new corner office. Instead, she saw her reflection. She wasn't sure she knew the woman staring back at her.

A half hour later, Dewey walked into her office, startling her back into reality. "I'm sorry to have surprised you, Miss Chambers. We should probably get to work."

She started to get up and follow him into the conference room across the hall, but stopped. "Mr. Dewey, we haven't yet discussed my new compensation package and other expectations for this position."

He scowled at her, meeting her gaze with a glare that might have cowered a lesser person. She was not a lesser person and the Ice Princess was just as effective up the chain as down. There was a moment of silence as he cupped his chin in his hand. He let out a breath that sounded more like a pig grunting, "We can make time for that later, I suppose. Right now, I want to get these details ironed out."

"As do I, but I don't believe it would be very good business if I did not have a full understanding of what the expectations are and what my compensation will be before I begin a new role with this company."

She knew Hamilton Dewey was not used to being challenged. He did not like being challenged. And he did not expect to be challenged by an employee. And she was certain that the fact that she was a female would make it even more unpalatable for him. It was clear she was right by the deepening scarlet hue of his jowled face, and the narrowness of his gaze. Alexis braced herself for the verbal onslaught she was certain was to follow. She was more than surprised by his response. "Very well. If you excuse me, I will pull the information together and have a formal offer letter for you in an hour. Is that acceptable?" It came out of his mouth in a snarl, but he hadn't fired her on the spot or refused her outright, so she called that a win, albeit temporary. She still had her job and at least for the moment she could still meet Jake's demands, so she had the love of her life. But she had the sinking feeling by the end of the day she would have to give up one or both and right now she didn't know for sure which one she was going to choose.

"Thank you, yes," she replied, bringing herself back to the present. "I have a quick call to make, and then I will wait in the conference room. There is a lot to accomplish here." Dewey nodded and walked out the door. She rolled her eyes as he left the door wide open, paying no attention to her comment about making a call. She got up, closed the door and pulled out her cell, dialing Carole.

"Hey sissy. This is a pleasant surprise. You never call me in the middle of the day."

"I know, but I need a friendly voice right now."

"I would think your first call would be to Jake. Was his line busy?" She laughed, teasing her big sister.

"Oh, I talked to Jake already, but you're not my second choice. He's the reason I need to hear a friendly one."

"Aw sissy, what's wrong?"

The compassion she heard in her sister's voice suddenly had had her fighting back tears. "I'm pretty sure we're done for good this time." Tears leaked out the corners of her eyes when she spoke the words, she'd been too afraid to even think.

"What do you mean, pretty sure, isn't that something that should be clear?"

"Well yes and no," and Alexis told Carole the entire story. She knew her sister would see right through her, so she didn't try to gloss over her part in it, and added that she'd just given an ultimatum to Dewey to make a formal offer.

Carole paused after Alexis finished. "I can see where you feel you're stuck between the devil and the deep blue sea. What is it you really want, Allie? What is it that is going to make you truly happy? This Dewey guy sounds like he's a total tool. Is it smart to hitch your wagon to a guy like that? When's the last time you smiled at work, felt like you had a good day? Do you still love Jake, or do you feel like he's asking too much of you?"

"Christ Carole, you should be the lawyer. I feel like I'm being cross-examined as a hostile witness."

"I'm sorry. I think those are questions you need answers to, and fast."

"No, you're right, thank you. I need to answer those questions."

"What about Jake? Do you love him?"

"Oh God, Carole. Yes. I do." She played with the pen on her desk, clicking it, watching the tip appear and disappear. "I could never ask for a better man. He has been so supportive of me. Never once stood in my way until today. And it's not like he's standing in my way now. He didn't tell me not to take the job, even though I know he hates the idea of me being in Denver long term. I don't really deserve him. He certainly doesn't deserve the shit way I've treated him. He's totally right. I have taken him for granted and never once put him first. You know I suck at relationships, Carole. I always have, I probably always will. I should probably just let him go so he can find a nice girl that will always put him first. Let him have that picket fence and 2.5 kids he claims he doesn't care about."

"Alexis, that is such a total load of bullshit I want to puke. I've seen it in his eyes. He loves you like more than I've ever seen anyone love anyone. It's a fucking Hallmark movie of the week. I'm jealous as hell. Brian has never looked at me like that. Don't get me wrong we are crazy in love and he's an amazing husband, a good man, but Jake totally adores you. That's why he lets you get away with being a total shithead."

"Gee thanks Carole, that's a real pick me up."

"Any time." She laughed, easing the tension in Alexis' chest. "By the way, I've seen the same look in your eyes. You need to make your own decision. You know me though, I'm all heart and not much brain. If it was me, I would be out the door and on my way to Jake before that sack of shit Dewey came back. He couldn't be bothered giving you a formal offer with the promotion. I bet he thought he could get away without giving you more money. I know," she sighed with resignation, "that's just too impulsive for you to do."

"Yes, a little." She gave an ironic sort of laugh. "Thanks Carole. Believe it or not, this helped. I still don't know what I'm going to do, but at least now I'm thinking straight, not buzzing around in circles."

"Love yah sissy, please call me later and let me know what you decided."

"I will, love you, too. Bye." And Alexis hung up and walked across the hall to the conference room. She was very curious to see what Dewey would come back with.

Chapter 39

Jake

Where the hell is the Masterson file I asked for?" Jake bellowed before slamming his office door so hard two pictures fell from his office wall. "Fuck," he grunted, walking over to pick them up from the floor.

There was a soft knock on his door moments later. "Come in," he barked, rising and placing the fallen pictures on a credenza.

A paralegal poked her head in the door with a questioning brow. "I have the Masterson file, Mr. Douglas."

Jake let out a long breath. The uncertainty in her eyes and the hesitation in her voice gnawed at him. He was never "mistered" in the office. The wounded, angry bear routine he was currently displaying was spilling onto everyone around him in the office. At some point, he was going to have to apologize to them, but for now, the best he was willing to do was acknowledge the error of his ways to the woman presently in his office. "I'm sorry Erin. Could you just leave it on my desk, please? I need to finish cleaning up the mess I made."

"Of course," she smiled, hurrying to his desk to put down the file, eying him like he was a wild bear that might attack her if she let her guard down. She quietly turned and scampered toward the door. "Is there anything else, Mr. Douglas?"

"No. Thank you, Erin." He smiled at her, though he knew it must have been closer to a sneer before she closed the door behind her and left him alone with his thoughts. And his temper. Walking over, he picked up the file, and couldn't remember why he had wanted it in the first place. He might not be the drunk his father was, but he'd certainly inherited the asshole gene.

He slogged through the rest of the afternoon, looking at his phone frequently to see if there was anything from Alexis. He hated what he had done, but didn't feel like he had any choice. He ached, realizing that it was probably over. For the first time, he was feeling like it all had been a waste of time. He had refused to believe she was telling him the truth when she said career was her top priority when her actions confirmed her every word. Maybe he just had too high of an opinion of himself that he could change her mind.

It was after five, and the office was emptying. If he wanted to, he could have left. He had more than caught up on what had piled up on his desk over the two and a half days he was out, but the truth was he just didn't want to go home and sit alone in front of the TV. He knew he'd just keep playing the same loop over and over in his head, regretting doing what he knew had to be done.

Pulling his things together, he walked out of the office and out to the parking garage. Taking a left, instead of his usual right to head home to Arlington, he drove around the mall and monuments, losing track of time and heading in no particular direction. Finding a spot directly in front of the Supreme Court, he parked and got out of his car, staring up at its impressive façade. It had been an incredible honor to argue a case inside that building in front of men and women who had navigated their way to the pinnacle of their profession. Of his profession. He wondered what sacrifices they had made along the way to make it to the top. Were there woman and men in their lives that they had left behind in order to pursue their goals? There was no question the men and women in their lives had made sacrifices, most of them anyway. There were one or two that frequently made headlines for dabbling in political waters that called their spouse's integrity into question. Were there arguments over the dinner tables at night about PR gaffs that would have to be fixed? Ultimatums made like he had done this morning with Alexis, and did they regret doing or not doing what they did to get to where they were?

He didn't want to sit on that bench. Not that he'd refuse an opportunity, but it wasn't his end goal. What he wanted was to make a difference, just like he'd done for the state of Illinois defending the constitutionality of a law the guaranteed the privacy of everyone, regardless of age, or sex, or marital status to keep, whatever they wanted to, private. No one could be forced to share their medical or mental health records, not to parents, not to employers, not even to the government, not without their permission. That was good work. That's what he wanted to do and while he had a tremendous opportunity to do more of the same for Rock and Wagner, he could certainly find something worthwhile to do in Denver if it meant keeping Alexis. The trouble was, it couldn't be a zero-sum game.

He couldn't be the only one trying to adapt so that they could stay together. With a heavy sigh, he got back in his car. The clock on the dashboard read 11:35. He'd been staring at that damn building for over three hours.

He was disappointed but not surprised to find his driveway empty when he pulled onto his street. With no missed calls and no texts saying she was on her way, he accepted there would be no last-minute stay for the end of his relationship. He'd be going alone to the dinner tomorrow night and likely many more in the future because he was done with relationships. His first love had chosen his father over him, and his true love had chosen a job. He wasn't perfect, but he thought he was at least worth something. Apparently, he was wrong.

Chapter 40

Carole

Brian elbowed Carole in the ribs. She stirred, and he nudged her a second time. Her tone was less than understanding. "Hey if you're looking for a fourth time tonight, you're very much missing the mark in your approach to getting laid."

"Your phone." He grunted, also still in a semi-state of sleep.

"What?"

"Answer your damn phone, Carole. It's been ringing for the last five minutes, sleeping beauty."

Carole rolled over, trying to clear enough of the sleep from her eyes to focus on her caller id. Four calls in a row from Alexis. She took a deep breath and was about to press call when call number five came in. "Hey just because it's eleven in Denver doesn't mean I'm still up. What's the matter, sissy?"

"I'm not in Denver, I'm home."

"You're home? What are you doing home? If you're not in Denver, shouldn't you be in Washington with Jake?"

"I'm home because I quit."

"You what?! I thought you were supposed to get that offer sheet for your promotion. Isn't that what you said?" She sat up fully. Brian rolled over and put a pillow over his head.

"Oh, he came back with an offer sheet. It was a fucking insult, a third of what other general managers make with the excuse that he was giving me a big break, even though I still had a lot to do to deserve that kind of money. I can't even begin to say what he meant by a lot to do. Let's just say he and dad have a history and he planned on using me to get revenge on our father. He more or less told me he'd moved me up because he knew dad would hate that, but now the stakes had to be higher."

"You're fucking kidding me," Carole squeaked, her voice near the pitch of dog whistles.

"I'm too fucking mad to be joking," her voice was low and quiet. Carole knew her sister well enough that when she got that quiet, things were going to be bad for someone. "You were right. Jake was right. They were just going to keep jerking me around, always moving the carrot. You know what, sis… I didn't go to business school. I went to law school and I'm not practicing law, certainly not the kind I want to be practicing. I'll find another job. Shit, I'll live off the trust fund and work pro bono if I have to, as long as I'm doing something worth a shit."

"Good for you. It's about damn time you finally saw the light. But why aren't you with Jake? Did you call him and tell him you'd be there?"

"I haven't called Jake. I couldn't. It's too late."

"Why couldn't you do it? I'm sure he doesn't care what time you call him, especially if he knew you still were going to be there for him."

"Not too late that way. He doesn't love me anymore, you didn't hear him Carole, he was mad, cold even. I didn't call because I can't hear I told you so, not yet. I know I deserve it. I've been such a fucking fool, sis."

It was a good thing Alexis wasn't standing in front of her at that moment because the urge to wrap her hands around her sister's neck and choke her until she came to her senses was overwhelming. "Well then, don't double down on the foolishness. Fucking swallow your pride and call him. He loves you more than life, a love like that never goes away. Do you hear me, Alexis? It. Never. Goes. Away. He's not going to tell you I told you so. He might be mad, but he's mad because he hurts. You hurt him. He's been so unselfish, and you have taken advantage of that. He's not just given inches, he's given you miles, and you took continents. Call him. Save this while you still can."

"I can't Carole, I've ruined it. I don't think I could see him and not be able to just lose myself in his arms. As shitty as this day has been, I don't have the strength to fight another battle."

"Sissy, you will regret this the rest of your life if you don't find the strength to fight for him. It's not too late yet, but you are really pushing it to the limit. If you leave him hanging tomorrow night, you might win him back, but it will never be the same, and when he realizes you could have been there on time, well, you just might not get him back, period. It's time to swallow that ocean sized pride of yours and ask for the forgiveness you need. He'll give it to you. Call him now and get on the first flight in the morning. If I were you, I'd sleep at the airport just in case."

"Thanks Carole, I'll talk to you tomorrow. I wish it was as easy as you think. Maybe we can have dinner. Love you. Bye."

"Love you too, sissy" She hung up the phone and snuggled into Brian. He rolled over and gave her a kiss, grabbing her ass and pulling her into him.

"You're a good sister. She doesn't know how lucky she is to have you." He kissed her again with a deeper meaning. "So, if I did want to for the fourth time tonight, what exactly should I do?" he asked, wiggling his eyebrows.

She giggled, rolled slightly to her back and spread her legs, "Oh, I think you know exactly what you have to do."

Brian scooted down under the covers without another word.

Chapter 41

Jake

Jake winced at the sun streaming through his window, shutting his eyes tight and then slowly opening them as his sleep fogged brain adjusted to the brightness. Reaching out a flailing arm, he groped for his phone on the nightstand, coming up empty, but knocking his wallet, watch and glass of water to the floor. By the amount of daylight already flooding through the curtains, he would guess that it must be somewhere around six-thirty, which meant he had overslept. He must have left his phone downstairs, which explained the lack of an alarm and mentally added an alarm clock and blackout curtains to his ever-growing household item shopping list. Though in his semi-awake state, not having his phone handy to add the items to the list meant he would probably forget them until the next time this happened.

With a groan, he pushed himself out of bed and trudged down the stairs. Rolling his head side to side as he descended the stairs, he felt the satisfying pop of his neck cracking, but the fog remained. He'd gotten a good night's sleep but still felt exhausted needing coffee more than most mornings. Padding barefoot through his foyer, he found his phone sitting on the hall table, dead. Grabbing it, he walked into his kitchen and plugged it into charge as he started the coffee to brew.

He crossed through his dining room, taking in the furniture Alexis had purchased. They still hadn't used it, and the thought crossed his mind that they likely never would. Pushing the concern that he'd have to get rid of that reminder of her, he made his way into the living room and clicked on the TV for the morning news. He'd give the phone a few minutes to charge and check to see if there was a voice mail from Alexis. She'd chosen work so many times he doubted this time would be any different and that doubt deepened his sense of exhaustion. He would always love her. A love like this didn't just go away, but he'd have to let her go. If she was coming, she would have been here by now.

He trudged back into the kitchen, checking the cabinets for something resembling breakfast food and coming up empty. It was time for him to stop waiting for Alexis and begin planting roots for a life on his own. He couldn't keep grabbing pastries from the coffee shop. For the first time in his life, he could afford it, but his waistline was suffering the consequences, and that was not okay. Grabbing a mug from the counter, he pulled the pot from the still churning coffee maker. It would be damn strong but would provide the shock to his system to get him moving forward and into the office.

Halfway through the pour, his doorbell rang, followed by an urgent pounding, startling him and causing him to pour half of it on his hand instead of into the cup. "Fuck," he groaned, putting the mug down on the counter and shaking off the scalding liquid. Before he could find a towel to clean up the mess, the pounding resumed. "Coming," he bellowed, "keep your fucking pants on," he grumbled as he walked to the door. For a moment he thought maybe Alexis had come after all, but knew she wouldn't be pounding on his front door so vigorously.

Rounding the corner, he could make out a dark silhouette that was decidedly male, dashing any hopes he had of her arrival. He opened the door to find a police officer, three suitcases, two garment bags, and a canvas tote on his front stoop. He blinked twice and looked again, wondering if maybe he had lost his mind, but the scene remained the same. "What can I do for you office…," he mumbled before his peripheral vision picked up a second officer approaching a familiar Audi parked in his driveway.

Even through the tinted windows he could see Alexis, head tilted awkwardly to the side, her long, flaxen hair, tangled and half covering her face, mouth open and, knowing her as he did, he could imagine the drool leaking down to her chin. His only thought was that she never looked more beautiful, but what in the name of God was she doing sleeping in her car in his driveway at six-thirty in the morning?

"Is everything okay? Is that someone you know?" The officer asked, pulling back Jake's attention. The cop sounded nearly as confused as he felt.

Jake processed the question a little more slowly than he likely should have. "Um, ah, yes. Everything's fine… that's my girlfriend."

"Did you have some kind of argument?"

"No, well yes, I guess why?" he stammered, still uncertain of what was happening. God, I need some coffee.

The expression on the cop's face told Jake he'd wished he hadn't stopped to check on the situation and had just continued toward his own morning coffee. "Did you kick her out, and she's refusing to go or something?" the officer asked, looking at the yard sale on Jake's front stoop.

Jake couldn't grasp why most of her closet was packed and sitting there on his front porch. He felt he should give some sort of answer. "Oh. No. I think they're supposed to be coming in, not going out, but well… I just woke up and maybe I didn't hear her knocking?"

At that, the cop gave him a smile. "Okay, well, should we stick around in case you need protection?"

Jake managed a smile. "No. I think I'm good. She can't be too mad; I didn't know she was coming." His focus was now on officer number two who was about to wake the sleeping Alexis, Jake was not sure how this was going to play out but, temporarily forgetting what was likely to be an awkward conversation to come, he was more than curious to see how Alexis reacted to being startled awake by the Alexandria police.

"Ma'am?" was the only thing officer number two said before a screaming Alexis sprang to life.

"Oh, my god! What…? Where the hell…?" Alexis yelled, franticly trying to pull her hair out of her eyes and sit up. "Oh, God. I must have dozed off." She sputtered out as she arrived at semi-consciousness.

"Are you alright? Is there a problem here?" the officer calmly asked her.

Alexis rubbed her eyes with the heel of her hands, and Jake watched as she tried to surreptitiously wipe the drool from the corner of her mouth before answering the bemused officer. "Oh, well yes. It's fine. I must have… I guess he didn't hear me knocking. This is turning into a bit more of a surprise than I planned, I guess."

The officer smiled and looked at his partner standing in front of Jake. With a nod, he tipped the brim of his hat toward Alexis. "That's good. We'll leave you to sort this all out." He turned back toward his waiting patrol car. "Have a good day." The second officer said before getting in and driving away; leaving Jake and Alexis to stare at each other from fifty feet apart.

Alexis pulled herself from the car and tentatively walked up the cement path towards Jake's door. The dark circles under her puffy eyes made her look like she hadn't had a decent night's sleep in a month. The deep vee between her eyes and the creases on her forehead broadcast an uncertainty that Jake hadn't seen on her before.

"Hi." Jake said, not being able to fully process what was happening. Had he really given up hope to the extent that this seemed so impossible?

"Hi." She forced a tentative smile to her face, climbing the three steps up the landing.

"Come inside. I'm not going to bite you."

"Well, that's a relief. Do you think maybe I could have a kiss though?" the tone of her voice gave away the uncertainty she felt in his answer. "Or have I fucked things up so badly that I can't have a second chance?" Tears leaked out the corners of her eyes.

He moved the luggage into the foyer and lifted her chin, pressing his lips softly against hers. Her lips parted on a sigh and, taking advantage of the opening, he swept his tongue across hers, relishing the sweetness that was uniquely hers, mixed with the saltiness of falling tears. Her shoulders softened as she looped her arms around his neck, snaking her fingers through his tousled hair.

"I love you, Alexis. I will always love you. You might have cut it a little close, but you are here. I can taste you," he said, smiling and wiping her tears from her face. "You really could have called me and let me know. I would have left the door unlocked at least." He ran his hand through his hair, which did nothing to tame the uncontrolled bedhead. Shaking his head and smiling at her, "you didn't have to go all the way to New York to get something to wear tonight. If you didn't have anything with you, DC has some nice stores, I'm told."

She stood in front of him and shrugged her slumped shoulders. Her lips parted like she was about to speak, but then pursed together to form a weak smile.

"God Lex, you look like you've been through a war. Why on earth would you drive five hours in the middle of the night?"

"Because I couldn't risk losing you. I tried to call you last night, well really this morning, and it went straight to voicemail. Four times I called. I knew I hurt you. I knew you were serious about this being it. I almost gave up. I sat on the bed and cried myself into oblivion. I couldn't fly and chance not getting here before you left for work. Somehow, I found something left inside me, threw as much of what I owned into the car as I could and drove. I drove as fast as I could. I got here about five-thirty. Then I sat in your driveway for fifteen minutes before I got the courage to knock on the door. Then you didn't answer, and I thought maybe you were ignoring me, hoping I would just go away. I figured you'd have to say something to me if I was just sitting there when you left for work, but seems like I just passed out. Do you know why I brought all my bags up with me?"

Jake shook his head and shrugged. "You couldn't decide what to wear tonight?"

"Because I thought maybe it would make it harder to send me a way." Tears streamed down her face, and she took a deep breath, attempting to quiet her trembling lower lip. "God, Jake, I am so, so sorry. I have been such a selfish little bitch. I don't deserve you, not at all." She brought her palms up to cover her face as she lowered her chin.

"Shh, babe," he whispered, pulling her into his arms and kissing the top of her head. Stepping back, he tipped her chin up with his finger so he could look her in the eyes. "Let me get you some coffee while you go into the living room and sit down before you fall down."

As he rounded the corner into the living room carrying the mugs of steaming coffee, he found her curled into the corner of the sofa, forehead resting on her knees which were pulled up tight in front of her. Her toes were curled over the edge of the cushion like she was trying to hold on to it to keep herself from spinning away. "Here you go babe," he said, handing her the mug before sinking down next to her and pulling her feet into his lap. "You're here now and that's all that really matters to me, but do you want to tell me about what's on your mind?"

The words spilled out of her mouth in one solid stream. "You were right Jake; you can tell me you told me so. I deserve it, but I'm so scared I've ruined it all between us. I know my promises don't count for much, I've given you so many empty words that I meant when I said them but didn't have the conviction to follow through because I was chasing my plans, a stupid plan that didn't mean anything. It was just to build myself up, prove my father wrong. It was a lie. I believed it because I was the one that was telling it," she gasped, taking a long overdue breath.

"I'm never going to say I told you so. I'm not that guy." He smiled, pressing his thumb into the ball of her foot and she moaned her appreciation. "God, Alexis, I would even consider moving to Denver for you, but I need you to show me I will come first. At least sometimes."

Her eyes widened at his words before she covered her face with her hands again, shoulders shaking with muted sobs.

"You being here right now is an excellent step in that direction," he added as she cried again. Hoping the change of subject would help, he asked, "what happen with your promotion? I'm assuming that you told Dewey he'd have to wait until Monday for you to start, otherwise you wouldn't be here." Her eyes went glassy and lower lip trembled again, so he quickly tried to change the subject. "I've got to ask; did you really empty your closet and bring it with you just because you thought it would be harder for me to send you away?"

She wiped the unshed tears from her eyes and managed a weak smile. "No, I only thought of that when I got here. I brought it all because, if you'll have me, I'm here to stay. No more long-distance bullshit."

"What about the promotion?" Jake didn't want to press her, but he was lost at what all this meant.

"There is no promotion. I quit."

"You quit?"

Alexis nodded and took a deep breath. She gave him the rundown of the confrontation she had with Dewey, demanding an offer sheet, and having it come up well short of what she expected. "When I confronted him with the inadequacy of the offer, he told me I'd get nowhere at DCH unless I made it worth his while. He said if I wanted to get back at my father by advancing in the corporate world, then I had to let him sleep with me so he could get back at my father."

"What the actual fuck! I'm going to fucking kill him."

Alexis leaned forward and squeezed his knee. "Easy does it Jake. Not that I don't appreciate you going all alpha wolf to defend me, but it's not necessary."

"The hell it's not."

"Jake, listen, please, and let me finish." He inhaled deeply and let out a slow breath, leaning back on the sofa. His shoulders were still tight, but he nodded and let her continue. "I recorded the entire conversation. Colorado is a one-party consent state, so he can't have the recording tossed. He wouldn't tell me what he had against my father, but as soon as I was on the plane home, I called my grandfather. Dewey tried to date my mother, but according to Papa, she always refused him. He guesses that somehow in Dewey's warped version of history, my father stole my mother from him."

"Nobody in your family ever mentioned this when you went to apply there?"

"I told no one until after I got the job and then, at least according to my grandfather, it wasn't important enough to mention. He said he had completely forgotten about it until I asked yesterday." Jake shook his head as she continued, "anyway, the real issue here is that if you want me, I'm here to stay. It's my turn to be unemployed and work at Starbucks, if that's what it takes. Somehow, I think I can find a job as a lawyer somewhere in this city. I hear there are few law firms here." For the first time today, she smiled genuinely.

"Are you sure? New York is your home. Your sister is there, your mother and grandfather are there, you won't miss that connection?"

"Jacob Douglas, my home is with you. From the moment you walked into my office that night, giving me cheap wine, and a shoulder I didn't know I needed to cry on, my home has been with you. You have proven to me time and time again how important I am in your life and sacrificed so much, risked so much for me. You didn't care what it could cost you. You fell on your sword for me when I didn't deserve it. My home is with you and always will be."

Jake leaned in and kissed her, pulling her onto his lap. He nuzzled into her neck and breathed her in, her wonderful scent and feeling the warmth that radiated from deep inside of her.

"Are you really okay with me just walking through the door and forcing myself into your home? You've made a life for yourself here. You've been successful without me. Wouldn't you rather have a trophy wife that wasn't so tarnished, one that was just there for you every time you wanted?"

"Alexis, you are the only trophy I've ever dreamed of, because of your head and your heart, not just because you look good on my arm. I value you. I love you because of all of you. Your good points and the not so good and I'm totally fine with you not being at my beck and call. You wouldn't be you if you were. All I'm asking, all I ever want, is for you to make our relationship a priority. That we decide based on what's best for both of us, and know that sometimes the other person comes first, not a total abandonment of self, but a combination of two. Is that something you're willing to commit to?"

She took a deep breath and met his gaze. "I am totally committed to you, Jacob Douglas; from today forward I will be yours and yours alone. My career will never be more important than you because there will always be another job but there will never be another you. If you ever decide to propose to me my answer is yes but don't you dare do it a minute before you're sure you want too, for once in my life I will wait patiently for what I want and not push and cajole my way into it. If you want me, I'm here to stay. If you'd rather ease back into this, then I will head back to New York, and we can figure out how to best move forward. All you have to do is tell me what you want, and I will do my best. You have my total commitment to making this happen. All I ask is that you tell me soon because I am so terrible at waiting and not knowing."

Jake smiled, ran his fingers through her long blonde hair before cupping the back of her neck and pulling her into a kiss. Leaning back and looking into her uncertain, eager eyes, he brushed his thumb softly over her cheek.

"What I want is what I've always wanted, for us to be a team, to be together. For us to be comfortable that our decisions about everything benefit us both. Of course, I want you here, Alexis Chambers. I want you with me every day for the rest of my life. I don't need to wait a second longer to ask you to be my wife. Maybe it's not as romantic as me on one knee with a ring in hand, but it couldn't be any more from my heart. Alexis Chambers, will you marry me?"

Their eyes locked and hers were the deepest blue he'd ever seen them. In in the depth of her eyss he could see all the love she held for him. And for the first time, not a trace of fear or doubt lurking beneath the surface. She knuckled away a tear and swallowed. "Yes, Jacob Douglas, a hundred times yes." Their lips crashed together in a salty, passionate mess of surrender.

When they finally came up for air, Jake realized the time and felt completely torn what to do next. Alexis recognized the confusion on his face. "What's wrong?"

"Well, I need to be out the door in five minutes." The corner of his mouth tipped in a mischievous smile. "And as I'm the only one here that has a job, I should probably get a move on before I get fired. I wouldn't want us to start our lives together, unemployed and homeless."

She snorted a very unladylike laugh and punched him playfully on the shoulder. "Then I suggest you get a move on, sir."

"But I would very much like to take you to bed right now and doubt I'll be much good at work today if I don't. I'll be way too distracted." He cocked his brow, gauging her reaction.

Looking up at him and batting her lashes, she purred, "I am more than exhausted. I am going to go to bed so I can at least look close to human tonight for your dinner party." She pushed herself off his lap and walked toward the stairs. Turning back and leveling a seductive glance in his direction she added, "if you should fall on top of me while getting ready for work well, I don't believe I would have the strength to fight you off and you could do with me as your heart, or should I say the very stiff cock I see poking out in your shorts, desires." Giggling like a schoolgirl, she sprinted up the stairs.

Jake walked into the kitchen, topped off his coffee mug, and followed her up the stairs. By the time he reached the bedroom, she was already naked under the covers, pretending to be asleep.

Alexis

He crawled up on the bed and kneeled beside her, looking down at her. She opened one eye and was fighting back laughter. He leaned down and gently kissed her lips. "I wasn't thinking before. You've had a very long night, and a longer day before it. I should let you get your rest."

She let out a laugh. "If you're not naked with your cock inside me in the next five seconds, I'll make you wait a week." A threat she knew she'd never follow through with, but apparently, he wasn't about to take the chance. He jerked his sweatshirt over his head and flung it to the floor, and rolled to his back to pull off his shorts in nearly the same motion. He slid under the covers and slid down between her legs. She took him under the arms and guided him back up to kiss him. "Please, just you inside me this morning. I need that closeness now. Is that okay?"

He kissed her long and deep. She spread her legs wide, and he moved between them. She reached down and stroked his cock; he was already hard and ready. She pulled him toward her and rubbed the tip along her slick folds; she was ready too. Guiding his swollen head, she notched it against her entrance. She ached inside at the need she felt for him.

Jake arched his back, and she raised her hips to meet his thrust as he slowly slid inside. Her pussy closed around his steely shaft. A low moan rumbled out of his mouth as her walls gripped tightly around him. She could tell from the look in his eyes that it wouldn't take long for him to come. Slowly, they moved in unison as he slid in and out, his pelvic bone meeting hers in blissful pressure.

He stared intently into her eyes, and she returned the gaze. Her hands on his hips urging him inside of her with a gentle rhythmic push and pull. "Don't worry about me this morning, my love," she whispered. "All I want is to feel you inside of me. I want to wake up later and know that we were together this morning, and it wasn't all a dream. Can you do that for me?"

"If that's what you want."

"I want it and I need it more than air."

He leaned down and kissed her neck. She struggled to control her breathing as he increased his speed. She raised her legs and locked her ankles behind him, her fingernails raking up and down his back. "Yes, Jake, yes, that's it, that's it, let me feel you inside me, I want it harder, I need it," she mewled. She knew he loved it when she talked like that and even more so because he knew it was true, not some idle scripted porn crap, but a genuine desire for him.

As hard as she tried to maintain contact with his gaze, it became more difficult with each time his cock filled her completely. She could feel her vision narrowing in and when his hand cupped her breast, fingers twisting her peaked nipple with the perfect mix of pain and pleasure, she came apart, feeling like her body was shattering into a million tiny electric sparks. One magnificent firework, whistling and shimmering in the dark sky and lighting up the entire world. It was only as her body slowly melded back together and floated slowly back to earth that she could feel the beautiful pulse of him emptying himself inside her. The warmth of his release helping to ground her and glue her back together.

What she felt when he released inside her was something she couldn't describe. She just felt complete. And for the first time in her life, she thought that one day this man, this beautiful, wonderful, loving man, would do just that and they would create a life together. The tears that spilled down her face were the visual evidence of the overwhelming mix of emotions escaping from inside her. Fear, joy, love all these, and so much more; and she felt his release, its pulsing warmth throughout her body. "I love you, Jake," she purred. "I love you so damn much."

Chapter 42

Jake

The file Jake had been reading hit his desk with a thud as he breathed out a heavy sigh. He was having just as much trouble focusing today as he had yesterday; the difference being that today he hadn't bitten off anyone's head and he was humming to himself. Looking at his watch, he realized that he'd spent nearly an hour and only gotten two pages deep in a case he needed to review with his team Monday morning. This will have to come home with me this weekend, he thought. As he picked it up off his desk to stuff it into his briefcase, there was a knock on his office door.

"It's open," he called out as Richard's head appeared from behind the opening door.

Jake looked up to see a smile spread across his boss's face as he entered his office. "So, it's true then?" the lilt in Richard's voice suggested that Jake was in for some razzing.

"What's true?" he replied, knowing there was no point in not playing along.

"That the miserable bastard that has been living in your body for the past two days went back to whatever planet he was from, and we have our old Jake back."

He laughed and shook his head. "Keep this up and I bet I can find him."

"Uh, uh, uh," he sing-songed, "we don't need our paralegals and admin assistants hiding under their desks, bad for both morale and productivity. So, what exactly has happened, to shine this ray of sunshine up your bloomers, the little woman finally condescended to pay you a visit?"

"Ah, you know me too well," Jake laughed. "As a matter of fact, she has, and will be my plus one for this evening's dinner with our new favorite client."

Richard sank into the chair in front of his desk with a sigh. "Thank fuck. I was really worried about you, Jake. Seriously. I'll have to have Lance pull her aside tonight and find out what we need to bribe her with to get her to be around a little more." He wiggled his eyebrows at Jake, which Jake found just a little unnerving, but then that's probably why Richard had done it. "Wife talk, you know," he added, laughing at his own joke.

Jake pinched the bridge of his nose. "I doubt Lance would appreciate being called your wife."

Richard waved his hand dismissively. "Nonsense. He's the under in our marriage and that's just the way he likes it."

"Regardless, it won't be necessary."

Richard sat up straighter and leaned forward. "You're not going to break your contract and follow her to Denver, are you?" all amusement gone from his voice.

Looking closely at Richard's expression, he could see the worry in it and decided not to string him along. The man was dangerously out of shape and with the stress their jobs put on them regularly, Jake didn't want to be the one thing that put him over the edge and gave him a stroke. "I signed a contract and I have no intention of breaking it. You're stuck with my grumpy ass for the next eighteen months, at the very least."

"Okay, then why don't you want my Lancy to convince her to spend some more time with you? Don't tell me that this dinner is a farewell affair. There's no way you'd be smiling about that. I was reasonably certain that's what had you all growly ass bear."

"Jesus, Richard," Jake laughed, "what's got you all up in Yenta mode?"

"I'm not in Yenta mode. I care about my employees and you, sir, have been hanging on by not much more than your sheer natural brilliance." Jake opened his mouth to argue but Richard held up his hand and continued, "you put together one of the most insightful and ingenious arguments I have ever seen, and your head was only half in it. I'm not going to lie, Jake; I had my concerns, but Rock told me to keep my powder dry and let you work your way through your stuff. Damn, if the old bastard wasn't right, again. Frankly, I can see how much that woman means to you and with her by your side there's no doubt in my mind with a couple more years of seasoning you'll be ready to step in and take over as managing partner when I retire."

"You're not going to be ready to retire for a good fifteen years, Richard, and you know it." Jake smiled and rocked back in his chair. He was never comfortable hearing praise, and he wondered if it was because he'd so often heard nothing but criticism from his father. Regardless, managing partner was a goal that, even if he was to set it, would be many years down the road. Something to see in his fifties, not before he'd even passed thirty-five. "Don't go jerking me around, Richard. There is a host of folks ahead of me for something like that. I am nothing special and that win for Young was as much luck as it was skill. I bet Agnew and Rossi were deep in their cups when they sided with the liberal judges."

Richard leaned further forward and waited to speak until Jake looked him directly in the eyes. His pursed lips tilted up in an ironic smile. "You don't have any idea just how good you are, do you? Huh," he laughed in disbelief, "here I thought you were slow-playing your hand, suckering everyone in with your kind humility, but that's really who you are, isn't it? These last couple of days really were because you were overly stressed and nothing more. I'll be damned."

"What?" Jake asked. "Honestly, Richard, this is just a little awkward."

"I'm sorry Jake. I'm not telling you this to make you feel uncomfortable. I really came in here to make sure you were doing okay. I'm glad Alexis made it for tonight. I'm glad she's here for you. You deserve it." He pushed himself up out of the chair. "Don't push yourself Jake. All that paper will be here Monday morning. I'm taking the rest of the afternoon off. If I've got to spend my Friday night talking shop, then by God I'm going to enjoy my Friday afternoon and you should, too."

"Thanks, Richard. Maybe I will. I've got a couple of errands to run before dinner."

"I'll see you later, Jake," and before Jake could respond, the door closed behind him.

He shuffled through the files on his desk and put a couple more into his briefcase before firing off a text to Alexis. She'd likely still be sleeping, so he wasn't expecting a reply.

Jake: Just had a thought… is it okay to introduce you at dinner tonight as my fiancé?

Her reply was almost instantaneous.

Alexis: Not without a ring, my darling … lol
Jake: Okay, we'll be at the jewelry store at nine tomorrow morning before you change your mind.
Alexis: Never going to change my mind, but you're on your own with the ring. I want it to be from your heart.

Jake: It would be if you picked it out on your own–you're really not going to help me?
Alexis: Only to tell you my ring size is 7 and I don't want some gaudy honking big ring; just something you think I would like. Sorry, maybe I'm old-fashioned in this, but that's me… just an old-fashioned girl.
Alexis: who is oozing with this beautiful man's cum. Fuck Jake, you've been saving up lmao
Jake: That's the old-fashioned kind of girl I love, even if she's no damn help to me.
Alexis: Oh, I think I can help with certain things ;-)
Jake: Fair point. I'll be home by six. Get some sleep.

He looked at the clock on his wall, and it was five past three. Pressing the intercom button, he told his assistant he was leaving for the day, grabbed his briefcase, and headed out the door.

Without a conscious thought, he headed out the main entrance and onto sixteenth street, walking toward Lafayette Square, took a right up L street to a jewelry store, for reasons that escaped him, he knew was there.

He entered the store with a purpose in his step but more than confusion in his mind. Part of him said that he needed to take his time, not rush, remember what she said, it was his way of showing his love to her. Not something to just take the best that was available just to get it done. Make sure it was perfect. Then there was the other half of his brain telling him to put a damn ring on it before she came to her senses. A cigar band would do if it came down to it. An attractive woman in her late thirties or early forties greeted him when he walked through the door, interrupting the entertaining debate raging in his now addled brain. She was pleasant and somewhat motherly in her manner; she looked like she could give him honest advice, which, of course, was likely the reason they hired her.

Unable to pull off the 'just looking' gambit, Jake opted for laying all the cards out on the table. He was nowhere other than she was a size seven and it needed to be around a carat, elegant but nowhere close to flashy. She showed him a variety of cuts and tried to educate him on the benefits of each one. She told him about the four C's or maybe it was the six C's, could have been the fifty C's. His head was already buzzing with too much information and a strong desire to close his eyes and point when he saw it. It was the one, and he knew it beyond a shadow of any doubt. I'll take that one. 'Mom' smiled and pulled it out of the case. It was a carat and a quarter oval diamond surrounded by deep blue sapphires with a simple platinum band. He could already see it on her finger, and he didn't even ask the price. He pulled out his Amex platinum and placed it on the counter. "Let's get this done. I need to get home before we're late for dinner."

Chapter 43

Jake

Jake and Alexis walked up to the arched entrance to The Old Ebbitt shortly after seven. He hesitated for a moment out front, letting out a slow breath and straightening his jacket. Alexis looked up at him and smiled. Pushing herself up on her toes, she kissed his cheek. "What's got you so edgy tonight? This is a celebration, not a presentation," she said with a laugh.

His eyes met hers and noticed the slight flush of her cheeks. It almost seemed to him like she was glowing. With a shrug of his shoulders, he returned her chaste kiss on the cheek. "It just feels different tonight."

"Different?"

He nodded, "like we're going in here tonight as one and not two." With a laugh, he shook his head. "I know it sounds crazy. It's hard to explain, but for the first time in my life, I feel like I'm complete. Nothing to prove and nothing to make an excuse for."

Alexis stepped in front of him and cupped his face, ghosting her thumbs over the strong edges of his cheekbones. "It doesn't sound crazy at all. We might not know where we're going or where we're going to end up, but we know now that no matter what, we'll be there together. It's like tonight is the start of our journey together."

Jake pulled her close, smiling into her hair, and he kissed her on the top of the head. *More than you know, my dear,* he thought as he turned her and walked through the large brass and glass revolving door into the historic restaurant.

They walked past the white tablecloth covered tables to a long table in the corner. Jake took in his surroundings and felt a sense of accomplishment. He was sitting in a place that had hosted countless Presidents and statesmen in its nearly hundred-seventy-year history and it didn't escape him he could be dining with a future President tonight. Even before they met, he knew that Ed Young was an up-and-coming politician. What a kick it would be to sit in his living room bouncing his son or daughter on his knee and pointing to the TV and telling his child that he once worked on a case with the man speaking from behind the presidential podium. He chuckled to himself, picturing Alexis coming to his defense when their child didn't believe him.

Their child, they hadn't talked about when or even if she wanted to start a family. There was time for that talk, and he only needed her, so whether or not they had children, he was fine with it being entirely up to her. All he knew was that she had said yes to spending the rest of her life with him, and he was going to put a ring on it and seal the deal just as soon as he could.

Jake snapped himself out of his head in time to introduce Alexis to Ed Young and his wife Anne, along with Richard and his husband Lance, who were already seated at the long table hidden away in as close to a private area as was available in the restaurant. Alexis looked stunning in a sapphire blue cocktail dress that matched her eyes. Haltered modestly in the front but a completely open to the small of her back, the hem of the A-line skirt fell just above the knee. She would have looked perfectly at home among Hollywood's A-list. Her long blonde hair was styled over her shoulder in waves that had Jake thinking of how damned sexy it was going to look spread out beneath her when he had her in bed later.

They had barely settled into their seats when John Rock and his wife Joan arrived. John gave Alexis a hug and a kiss on the cheek. She blushed as he reminded her of the little girl she was when he first met her at her grandfather's home and how proud her Papa was of her at the woman she'd become. Jake was glad that this wasn't entirely a table full of strangers for her to face.

Dinner had been comfortable, with an easy ebb and flow of conversation. He couldn't help but marvel at how perfectly Alexis fit in this environment. How her elegance and intelligence put everyone at ease. She was so much more than an accessory. He couldn't imagine a scenario where he would even want her to take second place to his aspirations. If anything, he would stand back and allow her the spotlight.

While they were waiting for dessert to arrive, John looked over at Jake and smiled, then looked at Alexis. "I'm so happy you could join us tonight. The last I heard, DCH was trying to lock you in a cage somewhere in Colorado."

Alexis laughed and glanced at Jake out of the corner of her eyes. He could tell she was on to what John had up his sleeve. "Well, they tried, but I decided I had a good reason to escape."

"Well, I hope you plan to escape often. I hear Jake is insufferable to deal with at the office when you're away for extended periods. When do you have to head back?"

The twinkle in John's eyes let Jake know he was definitely up to something, and her gentle squeeze of his leg let him know she was onto it, too. "Honestly, John, I've decided to leave DCH and stay here in Washington."

"Really?" he replied with only a halfhearted attempt at showing surprise. "Where are you going to? There are certainly plenty of options here for someone as talented and experienced as you."

"I'm not sure yet, to be honest. It was rather a split-second decision to leave, and I think I'm going to take my time," she looked toward Jake and laced her fingers through his beneath the table before turning back to face John, "discuss things with Jake and decide what's going to work best for us."

John sat back in his chair with a broad smile. "I'm thrilled for you. And I know your grandfather will be, too."

"Thank you," she smiled. "I hope he will be happy for me, for us."

John nodded and took a sip of his coffee. "I'd offer you a job myself, but I'm sure you want to forge your own way. You're very much like your grandfather, you know?"

She smiled and looked down at the table, twisting the spoon she had just stirred her coffee with. "I've always thought I was more like my father." For the first time tonight, Jake saw her shoulders droop and voice grow soft with reticence.

John laughed and shook his head. "Alexis, I may not know you well, but I've heard much about you through your grandfather through the years. You may have your father's stubborn determination, but you are smarter and have more integrity in your little finger than he has in his entire body. Forgive me for saying it, but your father is a selfish, bitter man and only growing worse by the year. He would never in a million years have achieved what you did with the Woman's Legal Assistance Foundation. Not only did that take skill, but empathy for those less fortunate."

"I knew I recognized your name from somewhere," Anne interrupted excitedly. "I've been racking my brain all evening trying to place you. There were such wonderful things I heard about your work there. Why did you ever leave and go into industry?"

Alexis let out a humorless laugh. "I'm embarrassed to even try to explain. All I can say is that I wouldn't make the same choice today." She turned and looked at Jake for a moment before leaning in and placing a soft kiss on his cheek. "Though if I hadn't made that mistake, I never would have met Jake, so I guess it turned out okay in the end."

The conversation was interrupted by dessert being served, which led to much conversation about who had chosen the best sweet treat. As plates were pushed aside and groans of gluttony echoed around the table, Ed cleared his throat and stared across at Jake. "Forgive my bluntness, but I've been trying to find a place to subtly slide this question into the conversation all night, but nobody has cooperated and given me an opening." He leaned back in his seat and steepled his fingers under his chin. "The first time we met you were quite open with the fact that fighting for those that don't have a voice in the legal system, like your mother, was the reason you became a lawyer, but you've never even hinted at what your long-term goals are. I'm used to everyone I meet letting me know what I can do for them whenever I take the next step up the political ladder, but you've never even hinted at it. And no offence to John and Richard, but you don't strike me as the guy whose ambition is to make partner and run a law office for the rest of your professional life."

"Are you asking me what I want to be when I grow up, Ed?" Jake laughed and took a sip of his coffee, obvious in his direct avoidance of the question.

Ed smiled. Jake noticed the side-eye Ed's wife was giving him. Apparently, putting people on the spot with awkward questions wasn't unusual for him. Ed continued, ignoring his wife's disapproving glance. "I suppose that's one way to put it, but I believe you're doing important grown-up work now. You're something special Jake, I know it, Richard and John know it. I can tell by the way Alexis looks at you, she knows it, too. I'm not sure that you do, though, which is why I'd like you to think about what your next step up the ladder is and what it leads to?"

The weight of everyone's stare fell solidly on Jake, and he felt the heat rise on his face. He didn't shy from the spotlight, but he felt unusually uncomfortable at the moment. Alexis ran her hand up and down his thigh in a silent show of support. He appreciated the gesture, but that kind of touch from her was more arousing than comforting, and he shifted in his seat.

"It's interesting that you should ask me that Ed. Alexis and I were talking about the future just this morning," he spared a glance in her direction and arched his brow. He put his hand in his pocket, feeling the small velvet box. Alexis stilled her hand on his leg, squeezing his knee firmly enough that her nails dug in, clearly communicating to him they had an agreement, he wouldn't say anything about their engagement without giving her a ring, but he couldn't formally propose right now. These people were the most important in his life and had come to be his closest friends in such a short time, but Alexis didn't really know anyone but John. It should be special for both of them, not just him.

"I know it's sacrilege to say in this city, but I can't picture myself running for political office. I can honestly say, and not because of the company," he paused, looking at Richard then John, "that I don't have any intention of making a change for a long time. I feel I am making a difference here, especially if we continue to have opportunities like the one you gave us, Ed. Helping you win that case and solidify the precedent of privacy rights, that's what helps people like my mother." He sighed and ran his hand through his hair. He shared a look with Alexis, and the pride in her gaze made his chest tighten. Making her proud was his only goal for the rest of his life. He knew he should give Ed an answer, and he had a dream, one he doubted he'd ever realize but a dream none the less. "Someday it might be nice to be on the bench. When I clerked for judge Mitchell at the second district court of appeals, that made an impact too. While the politicians make laws, our founding fathers saw fit to give the judicial branch power to interpret those laws. I'd like to be the type of judge Mitchell is; one that reads the law and applies it based on contemporary standards and morals."

Nodding, Ed smiled. "I like the way you think, Jake. You'd make an excellent judge." Taking a drink of his coffee before continuing, "I have to say I'm surprised, though."

"Why is that?" Jake asked, arching a single brow.

"I never pictured you as a conservative like Caroline Mitchell. You certainly argued a very liberal case before the bench and won decisively."

Jake let out a deep, hearty laugh. "Oh, lord, Ed, I'm anything but conservative. I was the token liberal on her team of clerks. Maybe once in the two years I clerked for her, I might have changed her mind. She liked to have one clerk that specialized in arguing against her, so she was certain of her positions. Quite impressive really, wanting to make sure she wasn't living in a partisan echo chamber."

"It is impressive. I don't agree with the woman on much of anything," Ed frowned and shook his head, "but it's likely that she'll be the next nominee to the Court if the Republicans have a shot at nominating. We could do a hell of a lot worse." He looked across the table at Jake for a long moment before the corner of his lips ticked up in half a smirk. "We just have to get you on the path to be there to be a counterbalance to her someday."

An inelegant snort escaped from Jake as he choked on his coffee. Wiping his watering eyes with his napkin, he laughed, "and we can check the pigs for wings while we're at it."

Alexis

Everyone laughed along with Jake at his self-deprecation, but Alexis caught the look on John Rock's face and realized that Ed wasn't the only one who thought Jake had more potential than he gave himself credit for. She squeezed his hand, feeling like she agreed with Ed and John about the man she loved.

Alexis chuckled at the thought of how typically Washington their party was, lawyers and politicians, but how atypical the man she was sitting next to was. Jake was probably the smartest person at their table and yet he did everything but try to dominate the conversation. She watched him as he sat back and took it all in, rarely calling any attention to himself. Jake had made sure she wasn't left out and was made to feel a part of their group. His hand was always touching her somewhere, as if he was trying to make sure she was still there, or perhaps letting her know he knew she was.

The conversation ebbed, and she smiled when she noticed John quietly slip the waiter his credit card to cover the dinner. Ed protested it was his celebration to pay for, but one didn't argue with John Rock and expect to win even if you were a man that had a damn good chance at residing at 1600 Pennsylvania Avenue someday.

They made their way out of the restaurant, pausing outside on the sidewalk to say their goodbyes. Alexis hugged John like the old family friend that he was and stepped back to wait for Jake to finish a conversation with Richard and Ed. She smiled at the way he interacted with the men, thinking that it might be the first time she'd ever seen him in a professional role that she wasn't somehow threatened by and felt foolish for all the time she wasted not enjoying the view. Feeling a hand on her shoulder, she turned to find Anne Young standing next to her.

"Jake's a good man." She smiled, lowering her voice so only Alexis could hear. "Ed likes him and, more importantly, trusts him, and that's saying something for a man like my husband. He doesn't trust easily."

"He is a good man, and the most trustworthy man I think I've ever met. Fortunately for me, a patient one, too."

Anne's smile widened and her eyes told Alexis she knew exactly what she was talking about. "I know you told us you weren't certain what you were going to do now that you've decided to join Jake in DC."

Alexis laughed and shrugged her shoulders. "It's all rather sudden. I want to take my time and decide what I really want to do."

Anne nodded. "I think that's a smart thing to do. Please let me know if you decide you'd like to get back to championing woman's issues. My college roommate has just accepted a position in the Cabinet. I can't tell you who or what position, because it hasn't been announced, but she is planning on putting together a special task force and I think you'd be a wonderful addition to her staff. You're young, smart, and based on what you achieved with the WLAF, more than experienced in just the issues she would like to tackle on a national level. Just let me know if you're ever interested in something like that."

Alexis combed her fingers through her hair and pursed her lips. The idea of getting back into the ring to fight for causes she felt passionate about seemed like too much to hope for after more than a year in the consulting cesspool. "I can't promise anything because from now on Jake and I decide things together," she smiled, meeting Anne's eyes, "but give her my number. It's something I'd truly like to hear about."

"Perfect. Thank you so much." Jake sidled up next to Alexis and put his arm around her waist. "It was such a pleasure meeting you both. I hope we'll see much more of each other in the future."

"I do too." Alexis gave her a hug and then turned to Jake and walked toward their car.

Chapter 44

Alexis

Jake pulled out of his parking spot and turned onto 14th street toward the National Mall. Turning left onto Constitution Avenue, he headed toward the Capitol Building. Alexis leaned over and gave him a kiss on the cheek.

"What was that for?" he asked, smiling in her direction.

"Just because I love you." She settled back into the comfortable leather seat and rolled down her window, enjoying the refreshing breeze of an uncommonly cool early summer evening absent the city's usual high humidity. "It might not be New York, but Washington is a beautiful city."

Jake turned onto First street and parked behind the Capital. This late on a Friday, it wasn't too hard to find a spot.

"Why are you parking?" she asked. "I thought we were heading straight home to make up for lost time." She wanted to spend the entire weekend in bed with him for no other reason than to show him just how much she loved him. She had been fairly certain he was thinking the same thing until he didn't immediately pull back out of the parking spot.

"Oh, I thought maybe we could take a little walk to burn off some of the cheesecake we gorged ourselves on."

Alexis leaned over and kissed him again, running her fingers down his chest and teasing the buckle on his belt. "I can think of other things to burn off some calories."

Jake chuckled and kissed her forehead. "There's nothing to say we can't do both," he mused as he stepped out of the car.

Alexis dropped her jaw in surprise, but followed him out of the car. If he wasn't smiling so broadly, she might have felt rejected. He took her hand, and they walked in silence together, taking in the majestic sight of the U. S. Capitol building.

Stopping across the street from the Supreme Court, Alexis nudged his shoulder. "Did you ever think that someday you would stand before the Justices and plead a case? It's still hard for me to believe you did that. Not only that, but you won." She squeezed his arm and pulled him closer, his nearness warming her to her very core.

He looked down at her and smiled before leading her across the street and up the steps. "I was there and I'm still not sure it was real sometimes." Halfway up the stairs, he stopped and turned to face her. "When you told me this morning that you would marry me, it was the happiest moment of my life. Better than hearing that what I'd done behind those walls," he nodded up in the building's direction, "had been successful, better than anything I've ever experienced. The only thing that will ever be better is the day I stand in front of you and say, I do and make it official, or maybe if we're lucky enough to have children one day."

"Would you like that? Do you want to have a family with me?"

"Do you?"

She raised her hand to his face and traced her thumb across his cheek. "I never thought I'd be the motherly type. I was so caught up in making my way up the corporate ladder. But I've been thinking a lot since the day I met you and while I know I'm not ready yet, I would like us to have a family someday. I love you Jake and I know without a doubt you'd be the father that mine never was."

Alexis looked up into Jake's brown eyes, and they were darker than she'd ever seen them. His gaze sent shivers down her spine, and the warmth that pooled at her core had her panties soaked through. She would let him take her right here on the steps of the Supreme Court if it wouldn't get them arrested and disbarred. But she was more than done with this walk and ready to get him home and into bed. She might not be ready for kids, but she was happy to practice making them. She took his hand and tugged him toward the sidewalk, but he didn't budge an inch. In fact, he pulled her back toward him.

She protested, but he gently placed a finger on her lips and spoke. "Since the first night in your office, I think I knew you were the one for me. And not long after that, I thought of how I'd ask you to marry me. I don't think I dreamed you'd ever say yes. And I know the way I asked you this morning was never what I'd imagined, but you said yes and that's all that really matters. But as you pointed out, it's not official until I give you a ring, and making it official is something that can't come soon enough."

"Jake, I …" she stopped mid-sentence as he dropped to his knee.

"I thought about doing this at dinner, but then it didn't seem right. It should be just you and me, and somewhere that means something. Two lawyers on the steps in front of the highest court in the land seems fitting to me. It also seems fitting because we have a supreme kind of love that not everyone gets to experience." He reached into his pants pock and wrestled out the small velvet box.

"Jake," she gasped, bringing her hands up, hiding her gaping mouth.

"Alexis Chambers, would you do me the great honor of being my wife?"

Tears flowed down her face as she gawked at the oval cut diamond surrounded by deep blue sapphires with a simple platinum band. "Yes," she croaked, her throat thick with emotion. She cleared her throat and said it again. "Yes, Jake Douglas, there is nothing, nothing I want to do more."

Chapter 45

Alexis

They were crawling into bed when Alexis exclaimed, "Oh my god, Carole!"

Jake was taken completely by surprise. "What's wrong with Carole?"

"Nothing, I just haven't told her yet. She's going to be so pissed if she's not the first to know and that I've waited hours to tell her. God, she's still probably on pins and needles, wondering if you took me back."

"You really thought I'd turn you away."

"I know you well enough to realize that you don't make idle threats, well I've never heard you threaten anyone, but you say what you mean and mean what you say. I don't think if I had not been on your doorstep this morning you would have taken me back. I don't. But honestly, maybe that was the shock I needed to come to my senses, to realize that I would be throwing away the best thing that's ever happened to me. This sounds so cheesy, but nothing means anything to me anymore if I can't share it with you. It's you that taught me that, my brilliant, beautiful, sexy man." She kissed him deeply.

She made Jake kiss her while she took a selfie, holding the ring in front of her face. It took more tries to get the picture right than Jake could count. He didn't mind, the kissing more than making up for it. When she finally had one that met her approval, she attached it to a text that simply said:

Alexis: I said yes!

"I give her less than a minute to call," she laughed. "Last time it was to tell me I was being stupid; she was so right. This time, I suspect she will be more than happy."

He spooned in behind her as she looked to the phone for Carole's response and fondled her, vaguely familiar to what had happened less than an hour earlier at the top of the stairs. She pressed back into him, "I think you like feeling my tits."

"Please tell me you're not just coming to this conclusion now."

She laughed, "Oh no, I came to that conclusion within the first twenty-four hours we were together. I'm just confirming my thoughts."

"Well then, okay, there is absolutely nothing about you I'm not wild about, mind or body."

She didn't have a chance to reply when the phone buzzed, notifying her that Carole was there on FaceTime. "Hey there, sis. What took you so long?"

"OH MY GOD ALLIE," Carole squealed loud enough to distort the sound from the phone to talking through a kazoo mode. "I am so happy for you, so thrilled for both of you!" she added, more in control and fanning her tear-streaked face with her hand like she was drying her nails. "Look at you both lying there in bed, just so perfect. Start with when you got there. I want all the deets."

Alexis gave Carole the full rundown of the day's events. They laughed and cried a little and were having a lovely sisterly chat. The longer they talked, the more Alexis wedged herself into Jake's body so that they were fully spooning by the end of the conversation.

He rolled onto his back and put his hand on her thigh. They lay there quietly for a moment, both staring at the ceiling. She rolled toward him and began gently stoking his chest, running her fingers through his chest hair. "I was wondering…"

"Mm?" was all he managed in a way of response.

"Would you be terribly upset if we didn't have as long of an engagement as I did before?"

Jake laughed. "In all honesty, I want nothing to do with an engagement anywhere close to as long as you had before. I realize it takes time to put it all together, but a year should be enough, don't you think? I want us together for the rest of our lives and the wedding doesn't change that one way or the other, but if we're getting married, then let's get married, you know what I mean?"

Alexis smiled and gave him a kiss on the cheek. "Oh, my beautiful man… you know very well that you are the only man I have ever wanted to marry and when I want something, I don't wait long. How does the Fourth of July sound, at my grandfather's?"

Jake leaned in and kissed her lips. "It sounds perfect and just over a year to make all your plans will be enough time?"

"Oh babe, I don't want a big wedding, just our families and a few friends and I'm not talking about a year. I'm talking about three weeks."

Chapter 46

Jake

It was a beautiful summer day with not a cloud in the sky. And hotter than hell. The only relief came from the occasional breeze off the Atlantic Ocean, the 'front yard' of George Johnson's home in East Hampton. There were other people on the shore, but nowhere near the throngs on the public beaches on the Fourth of July. In the distance to the east, there was no mistaking the sea of people crowded cheek by jowl on the sand, spilling into the water for relief from the heat. In front of George's home, there were only the tranquil sounds of crashing waves, the squawk of the gulls and some hushed conversation from family and friends patiently waiting for the main event to begin.

Jake looked up beyond the bluff in front of the house. The large white tent set up on the tennis court was completely blocked by the enormous 'cottage'. He gave a side glance toward the neighboring property, the residents going about their holiday weekend festivities. Smoke rising from the outdoor kitchen on their patio. He was glad that the wind was in the other direction. If he caught the scent of food, he was sure his stomach would growl loudly. He had managed to down only a bagel for breakfast and skipped lunch entirely. His stomach was in knots. He couldn't be more certain about the choice he was making, but the chance that Alexis would come to her senses and run from the altar was a constant buzz in the back of his brain.

A gasp passed his lips as he spied her come over the top of the dunes. His brother's firm hand gripping his shoulder with an affectionate squeeze, grounding him in the moment. His Adam's apple bobbed as he swallowed down the overwhelming emotion. He felt his throat close, and his vision grew cloudy as he fought back tears of pure joy.

She wore a simple white linen dress, scoop-necked just enough to reveal the crease of her cleavage, high enough to raise only the most prudish of eyebrows. Wisps of baby's breath in her golden hair, barefoot, with a bouquet of summer wildflowers, daisies, snapdragons, yellow, red, and white roses, tiger lilies among others he did not know, colorful, beautiful but paled by the comparison to the woman who was holding them. Smiling broadly as she walked down the weathered wood of the boardwalk that served as the aisle. Her father nodded courteously to him as he gave him Alexis' hand and he sat next to her mother. It was more of a welcome to the family than he had expected from Greg.

Jake's brother stood beside him to his right and Carole to the left of Alexis. It was a small group, just family, and a handful of friends that sat in folding chairs on the beach, arranged so casually they could have been easily taken for one of the hundreds of family gatherings along the Long Island shore, but this was a special gathering. Perspiration beaded on Jake's lip and his shirt clung to his back, damp with sweat as the July sun beat down on him. *Perhaps a suit and tie were not the best choice*, he thought. Alexis had tried to convince him to go with shorts and a polo, but beach wedding or not, he just wouldn't have felt right without a tie at his own wedding.

It was a simple and sweet ceremony. They had written their own vows, which caused her father no end of distress, distress above and beyond what he felt for not only the match his daughter had made but the lack of pews and altar at her chosen venue. Jake's father could not remain sober enough to come. His sister, crying, as she told him she had no choice but to leave him behind at the hotel.

For Jake, it was his sister, brother-in-law and their two children; his brother, sister-in-law and their four kids in tow. He had asked Rob to come, but he had declined. They hadn't spoken much since Jake had passed on Rob's offer to join him in his new venture. Rob's business had taken off, but Jake didn't regret his decision for a moment. He was exactly where he was supposed to be in his career and he was where he was supposed to be, standing next to Alexis, about to become her husband.

Alexis had her mother and father, Carole and Brian, Tiana, two friends from college and their significant others, John and Joan Rock, and George, who had been more than gracious in providing the venue on only three weeks' notice. He was the only one to ask if this was a shotgun wedding, but that was only to see the horror on his granddaughter's face. Jake had thought the old man might pee himself in laughter at her reaction to the insinuation that she was with child. He learned that there was a bit of a 'devil' that lived under the old man's crusty, conservative façade.

It was over before he knew it and when the minister pronounced them husband and wife, he thought he had missed something. Somehow, when he had pictured this moment in his mind, it would have lasted much longer. When he and Alexis kissed, he felt her slip something into his jacket pocket. As their lips parted and he pulled back from the kiss, he could see the mischief in her eyes. His wife seemed to have developed a thing for going commando, especially once she found out about him knowing she was free and easy got his motor running. And, damn her, it did. Biting his bottom lip, he stifled the laugh that wanted to escape. Yes, this was a very casual affair.

Despite the size of the gathering, George had insisted on all the normal trappings that came with a wedding in the Hamptons, including a dance floor and a catered meal. Both he and Alexis had argued for burgers, hot dogs, and a keg, and only the last was a concession given for the 'after party' on the beach and fireworks.

They had their own table but were only there long enough to eat and hear the toast from his brother, the best man. Alexis' father stayed only long enough to have the father, daughter dance and made his excuses. Alexis was glad that he came at all and didn't make a scene as he had at Christmas. Her mother stayed and Alexis suspected they were still in separate rooms. Jake's sister stood in for the mother - son dance and it was then that he felt his only regret for the day. His mother would have dearly loved Alexis, and Alexis would have been equally fond of his mother. He didn't really believe in heaven but figured if there was one, she would smile down on him today, likely with a tear of joy in her eye. His sister seemed to read his mind and kissed him on the cheek, "she's here in our hearts and happy as a clam."

Jake's nieces and nephews disappeared more quickly than Alexis's father. They were undoubtedly in George's pool, safely under the gaze of the hired babysitters, His brother and sister having some free time with their spouses for a welcome change. Brian sat down next to Jake and put his hand on his shoulder. "I'd welcome you to the family, but I honestly think you were in on Christmas Day. This just made it official."

Jake reached over and shook his hand. "Thank you, Brian. It really means a lot to me." Brian waved him off with a don't mention it sort of gesture and Carole walked up between them and stuffed something in Brian's hand. He laughed and shook his head, stuffing what he had been given in his pocket.

Jake gave him a quizzical look. Brian smiled and pulled out a bit of fabric from his pocket, which were obviously panties. "Seems your bride informed mine she was flying free again today and sisterly competition kicked in. Guess we both win." They both laughed and toasted each other. "I don't know what you did to our Alexis, but she's a different person since you came into her life. She was always so serious, so businesslike. Now, she's that, but happy and free. It's like you woke something up deep inside her. God bless you man, you're good for her as I'm sure she is good for you."

"She is very good for me, Brian; you have no idea. I didn't believe in love anymore when I met her. I figured if I ever got married, it would just be cold and distant, like pretty much any marriage I have ever seen. It's kind of scary being this vulnerable, you know. I wouldn't change it for the world, though, not a chance."

They continued their conversation for a bit when George came over to join them. "So how are my favorite grandsons doing?" Jake and Brian acknowledged him, and he continued. "Thought I should let you both know of some changes I made in my will. Best to hear it from the source, don't you think?" he continued, obviously a rhetorical question. "For a long time now, since my Ester passed, all my holdings would pass down to your mother-in-law, but we've been talking a lot since Christmas and things are not very good between her and Greg. Frankly, I'm not sure I can trust him not to make life very hard for her if he has the chance, but that's not your concern," he said, absentmindedly waving his hand. "I just want you both to be aware so you can support her and your wives when the time comes."

George paused for a moment, his gaze distant, before returning his attention to Brian and Jake. "Anyway," he continued with a heavy sigh, "the point of this little chat is to let you know Carole will inherit this property and Alexis will get the brownstone. The four of you will receive a lucrative trust."

"Jake, John tells me there's a good chance if you continue with Rock and Wagner that you'll be needing a place in New York, so it will be good to know the two of you have it waiting when you need it. Brian, of course you and Carole already have your rooms here. I would like it if you would feel comfortable in treating this place as your own from now on. I'm likely to spend more time in Florida going forward and would hate to see this place vacant too much of the time, so talk it over with Carole, would you?" Both men gave him a nod in acknowledgement.

"I'm telling you this because I trust you both as men of integrity and in the off chance that something ever happens, I would like your word, as gentlemen, that you will respect their inheritance and not try to worm it in to some divorce settlement."

Jake spoke first, and without hesitation, though Brian supported him fully. "Mr. Johnson, I have no intention of ever leaving her, I said for better or worse and I meant it but if she gets smart and runs for the hills you absolutely have my assurance, I will never try to take something I didn't earn or have claim to. I grew up with nothing and I don't believe I'm owed a thing beyond what I earn."

"Good. I hate to soil this grand occasion with this kind of talk, but, well, we might not have a chance to talk again before the shit hits the fan. Lois is beyond furious with Greg for leaving today. Just thought you fellows should be prepared. Your wives might be upset soon with what's going on with their parents."

Brian interrupted, "What about Lois? Won't she be upset to have these places go straight to her daughters?"

"Not at all. She and I have discussed this. She'll likely keep the house she's in and there's more than enough to sustain her in the trust she already has. If the courts go bat shit and give the house to Greg, well then," he stopped shaking his head. He let out a long breath as though just talking had exhausted him. "she'll still be just fine. I'm not planning on going anywhere soon, but I'm nearly ninety. I can't stop time. I just needed to make sure that Greg couldn't get his mitts on a thing. Both of you are ten times more trustworthy than him. Anyway, I've brought down the mood on what is a joyous day for you, Jake, so let's get a fresh glass of single malt and tip it back. I think John has something he'd like to speak with you and Alexis about before he leaves."

"Okay, I'll grab Alexis away from her college friends for a minute and meet you there. And thank you for your confidence, sir."

George nodded and dragged Brian off to the bar while Jake went to collect his wife.

Alexis and Jake arrived at the Rock's table just as George came along, server in tow, with fresh drinks for everyone. Joan, ever the social one, complemented Alexis on pulling together such a lovely wedding in such a brief span of time and said if she ever left the law, she should become a wedding planner. Alexis was gracious, but clear that it was something she would never consider. John laughed and told Alexis that he had something she may find more appropriate.

He pulled a letter from his jacket pocket and handed it to her. "This is a copy of a letter of introduction that I've taken the liberty of sending on your behalf. I understand that you have a keen interest in woman's equality issues." Alexis nodded enthusiastically. "Good. Edith Lopez, the new

Secretary of Health and Human Services, is an old associate of mine. I also believe she has a connection with Anne Young because when I mentioned your name, you were already on her radar. We were speaking the other day and she will launch a new program in the fall geared toward women and pay equity. She needs a legal team, and I thought of you immediately. If you haven't found anything yet, call her when you get back from your honeymoon. I think you just might like what she's got in mind for you. It's worth looking into, anyway."

"Thank you so much," she leaned in and kissed his cheek. "It's very kind of you to think of me." The blush that rose on Alexis' face showed her genuine appreciation for the gesture.

"Don't mention it. Glad to help and let's be honest, it helps me out by keeping one of my star lawyers happy because his wife will be working in the same city and home at night for dinner." They all had a good laugh.

Teddy and Ron, his oldest son, appeared at this point thoroughly covered in sand. Ron, thirteen but looking older, was more than excited as he announced it was nearly dark and time to head to the beach for the special wedding present they had for Jake and Alexis. Teddy stopped in New Hampshire on his way down from Maine to buy fireworks. Jake, sharing his brother's proclivity for pyrotechnics, had sent him money to 'get some of the good stuff' to fire off on the beach after the ceremony. Never one for doing things half-heartedly, Teddy more than doubled his brother's investment and came with more explosives than luggage for the weekend. Ron was a chip off the ole block and loved the chance to do something so much fun, and yes, illegal, with his father.

The group all headed down to the beach and settled in for the show. It was quite a show, over fifteen minutes of constant fireworks. Causing oohs and aahs from everyone, even cheers from the neighbors next door who had joined them on the beach for the celebration. As the grand finale crackled and exploded away, Jake turned to Alexis and kissed her, igniting an entirely different kind of fireworks. It was a perfect ending to a perfect day. The best day of their life and the first day of the rest of their life together.

Epilog: Twenty years later

Alexis

The house was strangely familiar, two doors down from the home where they had started their married life together. It seemed like both yesterday and eons ago. The house was still in move-in mode, with boxes everywhere and far more chaos than Alexis could fully accept. She yelled up from the bottom of the stairs, "Ellen, George let's go, we're already late!"

The reedy voice of eleven-year-old Ellen rang down from the upper floors in a panic. "I can't get my bow to stay straight, mom, and Georgie is being mean!"

Jake stepped in, using his best deep dad means business voice. "Both of you get down here now. Ellen, mom can fix you bow on the way there."

This pronouncement was followed by the sound of two pairs of feet running down the stairs. Both Douglas children arriving out of breath and looking not as put together as either of their parents wished for or expected. Jake spoke again, "Georgie, you're fourteen and for as many times as I've shown you, you ought to be able to tie a tie!"

"God dad, what's the big deal?"

"You know very well what the big deal is," Alexis chimed in a motherly tone that even after fourteen years felt foreign in her throat.

"But we've been to the White House plenty of times before."

"George, seriously, come here." And Jake straitened his son's tie and pushed down the cowlick for the umpteenth time.

Meanwhile, Alexis fussed with Ellen's hair bow and set it straight in her hair. They were both the spitting image of their parents. George dark and handsome growing into a solid man like his father and Ellen, the same golden locks, and bright blue eyes full of wonder and the sparkle that led you to believe there was much more going on inside than the angelic outer appearance would lead you to believe.

Jake and Alexis had aged very well. Alexis still every bit the beauty she was on her wedding day twenty years ago, just a hint of crow's feet at the corners of her eyes which she fussed constantly about, but Jake insisted he found incredibly sexy and never missed an opportunity to tell her.

Jake reached that point in life where he was referred to as distinguished rather than handsome. He still had a full head of hair, but it was now salt and pepper, saltier every day if you asked him, but he was still Alexis's beautiful man. She lovingly gave his tie a quick straitening and a kiss on the cheek, wiping the hint of lipstick away, the way mothers seem always to do. The four of them, as put together as they would likely get, opened the door, and walked down the stairs to the waiting limo in front.

A man in a dark suit with an earpiece held the door for them as they piled into the car. He secured the door and then hopped into the waiting Suburban behind, speaking into his sleeve. The car sped away from the house. Jake forced a nervous smile and Alexis put a hand on his knee and gave it a squeeze.

George surveyed the inside of the vehicle they were in, with a wonder that he rarely expressed in front of her anymore, now that he was a mature fourteen. Ellen sat and smiled, looking back and forth between her and Jake. "You guys look really important."

"We do?" Alexis laughed. Her daughter had the same lack of filter that her sister Carole had.

Alexis wore a dark blue skirt and jacket, a white blouse underneath, pressed just so, with a red, white, and blue scarf around her neck. Jake had on a black suit and white shirt, a red and blue tie. "Is uncle Teddy going to be there to watch the fireworks with us? He love's fireworks."

Jake smiled, thinking back to the fireworks twenty years ago. "No sweetheart, not this time, but we'll make sure he's with us next year, okay?"

"Okay Daddy, maybe he'll see them on TV."

"I would imagine he will. He might even glimpse his favorite niece on TV too, you never know."

"There will be TV cameras there?"

"Yes honey, the President will be there, and there are always TV cameras where he is."

They continued the ride in relative quiet, both Jake and Alexis lost in their own thoughts. They came back to the present as the car slowed and rolled through the White House gates and came to a gentle stop. Almost immediately, the door opened, and two members of the President's senior staff greeted them.

"I'll get the kids settled and meet you in there." Alexis said, as one of the staffers whisked her away.

Jake

Jake watched as aides led Alexis and the children toward where the ceremony was going to be held. Affection filled his chest, taking in the easy way she adapted to her surroundings, not phased a bit by the opulence of the White House. She might just as well have been taking her children out for a day at the local shopping mall. He loved her more now than the day they were married, twenty years ago today. And every bit as in awe of the fact that she loved him too.

The Deputy Chief of Staff shook Jake's hand and led him off in another direction. Jake took a deep breath as he stood in the outer office to the office with the curved walls. His usual confidence seemed to escape him for the moment but, he hoped and prayed it would return to him soon.

"President Young is ready for you now." He walked through the door and into the Oval Office. There was something about that room that made confident, accomplished people turn into stuttering fools. He had been here dozens of times, most recently six weeks ago. He thought he was there for a casual visit with an old friend and his wife's former boss. At most, a friend that wanted to pick his brain on this issue or that, as they had done so many times in the past. It turned out that day, Ed Young had something else entirely on his mind.

"Mr. President." Jake greeted him formally.

"Jake, it is so good to see you again. You're looking well. Where's Alexis?" he asked, looking around Jake's still formidable frame.

"She went to get the kids settled. I imagine she'll be in shortly."

"Jake, you know Chief Justice Mitchell."

"I do, Madam Chief Justice." Jake nodded and shook her hand.

"Please," the President motioned toward a chair, "sit down and relax. We still have some time before things get going. We haven't just talked about things in forever. Though I guess that comes with both of our jobs. Get to the point and move onto the next meeting. We have no time for niceties.”

Jake laughed, “That is true I suppose, but I imagine it's much truer for you than for me.”

“Alexis mentioned to me last week that it's been twenty years since we first met. Lord, it doesn't seem like that long ago, does it?” The President turned to Chief Justice Mitchell. “I first met Jake when he had only been in DC for about fifteen minutes and working on a case, I wanted The Court to hear. It was his work that got us heard and mostly his work that got us the win. I knew then he was going to be something to reckon with in the years to come.”

“I got the same impression when he clerked for me, Mr. President. I didn't agree with his personal views, but I never could poke a hole in his legal arguments. Frustrating as hell for someone like me to have to agree with a liberal like the two of you,” she laughed. “Ten years on the circuit with some dicey cases and not one overturned. I have to say, Judge Douglas, I've tried more than once to find a reason to overturn your liberal opinions and haven't been able to yet.”

“Thank you, Madam Chief Justice. I'm flattered.” Before he could continue, Alexis strode with purpose into the room. God, Jake thought, she can light up a room, even the Oval Office.

“Mr. President, so good to see you again.”

He walked over to her and gave her a kiss on the cheek. “Madam Secretary, the pleasure is all mine. I miss having your honest critique flying across my desk.”

“Oh, I'm not so sure about that sir and it's just Alexis now,” she laughed, a slight blush deepening the color of her already rosy cheeks.

“I am. I could use your voice here. Don't get me wrong I have a ton of bright hard-working staff but too many of them are scared to speak truth, or debate with power. You were always honest and direct and if it meant stepping on some toes, even mine, you would do it. I'd put you back in charge of Health and Human Services in a heartbeat if it didn't cause so damn many ethical problems.”

“Yes, sir. It wouldn't be against the law, but there would be plenty who would claim it was, and that would not be an insignificant political headache for you. Honestly, I don't miss the long hours. I'm content guest lecturing at Georgetown.”

“I would be too, some days.” The President said with a wistful smile. As if to put a period on the social aspect of the proceedings, a knock came on the door as the President finished speaking. “I believe that is our cue.

Alexis, Jake, Madam Chief Justice, this way, please." President Young motioned toward one of the large French doors that opened to the portico outside.

The three exited out the door, followed by the President and an aide. They walked along the portico and onto a dais with a podium and several dignitaries already seated, including the Vice President and Speaker of the House. Other aides directed them to their seats next to their children, who were already in place. The Chief Justice took her seat on the opposite side of the podium.

They had barely touched the seat when Ruffles and Flourishes sounded, causing them all to stand, followed by the well known announcement, *Ladies and gentlemen, the President of the United States.*

President Young stepped up to the podium and surveyed the crowd of over three hundred assembled neatly in rows before him in the Rose Garden. "Madam Chief Justice, Mr. Vice President, Madam Speaker," and looking toward Jake and Alexis, "Honored guests. Today is a special day for America and a special day for me. I first had the privilege of meeting Jacob Douglas shortly after his arrival here in Washington. He was a young lawyer, not too long out of law school who, frankly, I did not expect to play a major role in a case I was preparing to bring before the Supreme Court. I quickly found that not only would he be playing a larger role on the legal team that was assembled to support me, but he would turn out to be the brilliant legal mind behind our success. I had the honor, while a Senator from Illinois, of voting to confirm his nomination to the U.S. Second Circuit Court of Appeals, where he has served honorably for the past ten years. And as he has pointed out to me on more than one occasion, he had never had a decision overturned." The President turned and smiled at them as the crowd enjoyed a laugh.

"I have had the pleasure of knowing his wife, Alexis, for nearly as long. I have seen her growth and commitment to public service as a three-term member of the U.S. House of Representative from New York and honored to have her as my Secretary of Health and Human Services during the first two years of my administration. They are formidable in their accomplishments, but even more formidable as role models, for their ability to exemplify how to have a loving, thriving family and a successful, meaningful career. I am truly grateful to count them as friends."

"It is, therefore, with great pride and pleasure that I present to you the newly confirmed Associate Justice of the Supreme Court of the United States of America, Jacob Leonard Douglas. Madam Chief Justice, will you administer the oath of office?"

The crowd rose in applause. Alexis' eyes filled with tears of joy as she kissed him and hugged him. She whispered in his ear, and she placed her panties in his jacket pocket. "I am so very proud of you; those are to remind you that you will always be my beautiful man."

It had been a wonderful ride. As with any marriage, it had its ups and downs, but their love, commitment, and respect for each other were constant. He shook the President's hand and stepped toward the podium with Alexis holding the bible as he stood to take his oath. Alexis smiled and looked up at him, eyes sparkling with so many emotions. Jake felt the bump of fabric in his jacket pocket and smiled. The newest Associate Justice would have fun in chambers when he got home tonight.

Acknowledgements

There are so many people without whom this book would not have become a reality. First and foremost, my family, who have tolerated my moods and relative absence for the past few months while I pulled this book together and figured out all this new stuff that I never dreamed was part of being an independently published author.

Thanks to the wonderful community of authors, I have met both online and in person over the past two years of this journey. From aspiring newbies, like myself, to best-selling champs, you have all been so gracious and giving of time and honest advice.

To my outstanding beta readers, especially Lisa, Louise, Laura, Rachel, Chrissie, and especially Samantha, who all pointed out the hard truths when I needed it, but also encouraged me when I needed that too. Is it wrong for me to say that no one has ever said anything nicer to me than "you made me cry?"

For the understanding and patience of my cover designer who took my vague ideas and made them a reality and, for your patience, when I got a little picky, thank you. And to my vastly underpaid editor, thank you for making me look good!

Thank you. Thank you. Thank you. I could have never done this without all of you, and I am eternally grateful.

A Message From the Author

Dear Reader,

Thank you so much for reading my book. I hope you enjoyed it. I know all too well how precious time is; and that you took some of yours to read my words is an honor.

For as long as I can remember, I have loved writing stories, even as a kid. Through the years, I have written love songs, love poems, soliloquies to love lost and the first few thousand words of dozens and dozens of romance novels (notice a theme?). But I never once thought about becoming a professional writer.

Fast forward to a few years ago when I was working on my masters in marriage and family therapy. A professor suggested to my class that we journal as a way of working through emotions we might experience working with folks struggling with their mental health. I balked. Not this kid. Journaling is not my thing. The idea of sitting down once a day and penning out a dear diary entry was a big fat nope. Instead, I took whatever emotions were floating around my addled brain and wrote short stories.

Late one evening, while working second shift at a residential facility for kids with emotional challenges, I shared one of my stories with a coworker. "You should publish this," was her comment and when she wouldn't let up once I repeatedly try to laugh it off as nonsense, I went home that night and gave it some serious consideration.

So, that's nice and all, you're thinking, but how did A Supreme Kind of Love come about? Well, a few weeks later, I was experiencing a bit of writer's block and asked her what I should write about. Her response was, "I don't know, something about an office maybe?" Then she added, "Christmas is coming and I love Christmas stories. That would be nice, too." I decided to do both and just like that, Supreme Love was born.

It was supposed to be just a short steamy story, but The Office Christmas Party, the original title of ASKOL, didn't stop. Or, more accurately,

I couldn't get Jake and Alexis to shut up. Their story was supposed to be pretty much chapters 5 and 6 and a lot spicier, but Alexis wasn't that kind of girl and Jake turned out to be more than just a handsome face.

Six weeks later, the first draft of what you just read was complete. It's been a year and a half and a ton of edits, but I hope you'll agree it was worth it. It was important for me to tell Alexis' story because it's one that so many women face today. The false choice between career and healthy relationships, accepting society's definition of success instead of defining it for oneself. Jake's journey is important too, as you can only truly support someone else if you know how to stand up for yourself. They both get to learn that "love is not love until love's vulnerable."

Again, thank you so much for reading. If you want to read more from me, please go to my website, https://brynbyrnes.com and sign up for my mailing list. I have a couple of projects underway at the moment but haven't decided which will be next. If you're on my mailing list, you'll be the first to know. I will tell you it will either be about a quirky Colorado mountain town or a coastal Maine village where the locals are cantankerous, and the damn summer people? Well, they're the damn summer people. You can also follow me on Facebook, Instagram, and as soon as I can figure it out TikTok… technology is not my friend.

God bless,
Bryn XOXO

About the Author

Bryn Byrnes

Bryn began writing, not to be a professional writer, but to work through all the complex emotions felt during the 9 to 5 work as a mental health counselor. Who'd have guessed that it would come out as romcom and steamy contemporary romance?

Fortunate to travel the world, Bryn's roots lie along New England's rocky coast where they can frequently be found walking their writing partner, Beau, a three-year-old golden retriever. Inspiration for Bryn's stories comes from watching and listening to all the fascinating people encountered along the way.

When not chained to the keyboard, Bryn is active on Facebook and Instagram. We'd love to hear from you there or contact us directly through their website https://brynbyrnes.com/

www.ingramcontent.com/pod-product-compliance
Lightning Source LLC
Chambersburg PA
CBHW071157100726
47908CB00002B/416